THE HEALING OF CROSSROADS

NICK O'DONOHOE

D1559728

ACE BOOKS, NEW YORK

This book is an Ace original edition
and has never been previously published.

THE HEALING OF CROSSROADS

An Ace Book / published by arrangement with
the author

PRINTING HISTORY
Ace edition / December 1996

The Putnam Berkley World Wide Web site address is
http://www.berkley.com/berkley
Make sure to check out *PB Plug*, the science fiction/fantasy newsletter,
at http://www.pbplug.com

ISBN: 0-441-00391-5

ACE®
Ace Books are published by The Berkley Publishing Group,
200 Madison Avenue, New York, NY 10016.
ACE and the "A" design are trademarks
belonging to Charter Communications, Inc.

PRINTED IN THE UNITED STATES OF AMERICA

10 9 8 7 6 5 4 3 2 1

Ace Books by Nick O'Donohoe

THE MAGIC AND THE HEALING
UNDER THE HEALING SIGN
THE HEALING OF CROSSROADS

ACKNOWLEDGMENTS

My cryptozoology research for this book had two major sources. The first was **Mythical and Fabulous Creatures: A Source Book and Research Guide**, edited by Malcolm South. The other was **Alien Animals** by Janet and Colin Bond. I used other sources as well, but learned from these two and enjoyed them thoroughly.

Thanks to Cindy Capra and to Laura Grant for information on cesareans. Additional information came from **Recovering from a Cesarean Section** by Manuel Alvarez and Karyn L. Feiden. Any mistakes from any of these sources are my own.

Thanks also to Jerry Siegel and Joe Shuster, for giving us an American legend to put in with Beowulf, King Arthur, and Roland.

I owe a major debt of thanks to my agent, Don Maass, and my editor, Ginjer Buchanan, for their advice and patience.

Thanks and love to my parents for a cruise and a trip to the Costa Rican rain forest; I never thought I'd visit a beautiful alien world myself.

The disease-related crises BJ Vaughn faces are also faced by real people who need real resources. For information, consult the Huntington's Disease Society of America, 140 West 22nd Street, 6th floor, New York, NY 10011-2420.

The Huntington's Disease Society of America was not consulted in the research for this book and is in no way answerable for its contents. I am.

Many thanks to the people who have written to me and e-mailed me about the Crossroads novels; there is nothing like hearing from a reader. My e-mail address is Nicholasod@AOL.COM.

Lastly, this book is gratefully and lovingly dedicated to my wife, Lynn Anne Evans, North America's finest consulting fantasy veterinarian.

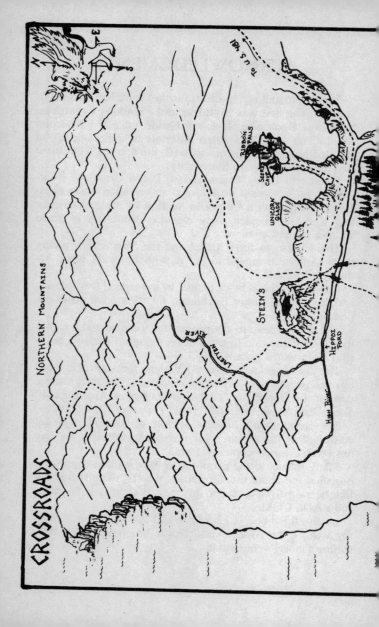

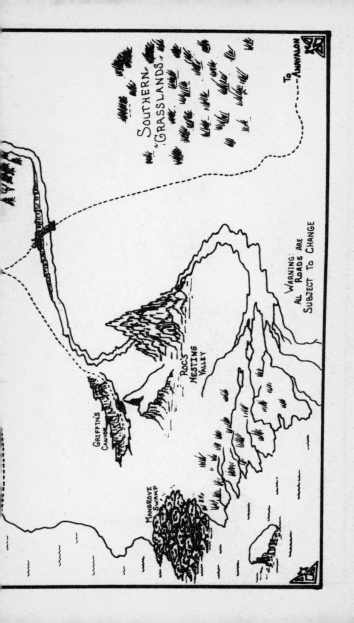

SOUTHERN GRASSLANDS

TO ANWALON

WARNING: ALL ROADS ARE SUBJECT TO CHANGE

ROCS NESTING VALLEY

GRIFFIN'S CANYON

MANGROVE SWAMP

THE
HEALING OF
CROSSROADS

O·N·E

FRIEDA WALKED DOWN the concrete-block hall mechanically, smiling at people when she was supposed to, looking active and intelligent when she passed faculty, trying not to make any eye contact at all. The blocks were painted dark burgundy to shoulder height, then an off-white which suggested fading and age in a building that was two years old. On the wall, aesthetically pleasing silver frames held commercial renderings of skinless cattle, longitudinally eviscerated sheep, flayed and dissected pigs spread open, complete with text boxes and arrows to organs. The drawings all had prominent logos from pharmaceutical companies. Not one of the animals had a shred of personality or pain left to it.

She turned a corner in the tunnel, and she was in the faculty wing and the hospital. The front lobby, finally complete, had plush furniture and an Astroturf rug that absorbed and disguised all known types of urine. Bronze letters on the glass wall in front of her announced, "WESTERN VIRGINIA COLLEGE OF VETERINARY MEDICINE."

She opened the door and passed through the glass wall unflinchingly.

The next stretch was harder: she smiled at classmates, made small talk, expressed interest in their work. That last part wasn't so bad; all of them had cases like her own and, for now at least, all cases seemed new and different. She

1

stopped and spoke, listened and clucked sympathetically, turned a corner, and ended up in the wing of faculty offices.

"Hey, Frieda." She turned at the voice. "You should look up; I thought I'd run into you."

She jerked her head up quickly, her hands fluttering over her clothes quickly. She was wearing jeans and a peasant blouse. She was aware that the blouse made her look fat, and normally she didn't care. After all, didn't the jeans also make her look fat?

Just now, she wished she could suck in not just her stomach but her thighs and her upper arms and just about her entire life. "Hi, Matt." She was acutely aware that she sounded quavery and trivial. "How are you?"

Matt Lutz looked like a young James Bond, all straight flawless hair and clean flawless teeth. His clothes always looked ironed and they almost never got dirty, even during ambulatory rotations. He had on a lab coat, unstained and unwrinkled.

"I just came from surgery." He looked like he'd just come from eight hours' rest.

"How did it go? Is the patient okay?" She said hastily, "Not that it wouldn't be—I mean, your skills are good—" She trailed off, not wanting to sound as though she were judging him.

"I can't say how my skills are." He smiled. "That's for the sheep to decide. It had swallowed baling wire. I pulled a three-inch piece out of the rumen."

Frieda wasn't uncertain about Matt's skills; they were excellent. In less guarded moments, Matt himself acknowledged that, and he never accepted anything less than excellence in himself or in others. Nothing ever seemed new to him.

"Did you check the reticulum for more?"

"Of course I did."

Of course he had. "Okay. Sure. I just thought—" She floundered. "I mean, it's the likeliest stomach to stop wire, you know? I mean, it's the first stop, and we're always supposed to keep checking after finding the first problem, just in case—" She hated how she sounded, and she hated backing off on an important question.

He nodded patiently, unoffended. Matt was what Frieda's father, the son of a tool and die worker from Hibbing, Minnesota, called "Die stamp confident." In a crisis when there was no backing off and no second chance, he never hesitated. During the four years of vet school, Matt had never hesitated in an answer, or backed off even in an unusual situation.

Frieda envied him with a passion that bordered on lust.

All the same, she caught a look in his eye that she had never seen, on him anyway. "You look upset. Are you okay?"

He looked confused for a quarter of a second, then flashed the assured smile that dazzled vet school freshmen. "I'm a little confused, that's all. Nothing I can't handle." He strode down the hall, leaving the impression of a coat flying behind him even in summer.

She walked to the fourth door in the hall.

The door in front of her had a name plate: DOCTOR SUGAR DOBBS. It also had a cartoon of a blushing cow slapping a man wearing a palpation sleeve. A sign below it said, KNOCK EVEN IF IT'S OPEN. The door was half-open, as it almost always was.

Frieda had seen it closed once, this morning. When it opened, a classmate, Cody Sayers, had come out, flashed his usual friendly smile, and limped off looking worried. Frieda had no idea what the occasion had been, but knew it was important; Cody never looked worried.

She looked one more time at the note: "Stop by my office this afternoon, around two o'clock." She checked her watch again, pocketed the note, resisted the temptation to take it out again, and raised her arm, taking a deep breath before knocking.

From inside, a dry voice said, "Most folks enter without knocking or reading, either one. The rest read and knock right away. It's gotta be Frieda Christoff out there."

Frieda shut her eyes and pulled her hand down, clenching her fist for a second. The voice said, "You can come in, Frieda."

Frieda looked at him and, because he was grinning amusedly at her, quickly looked away to the bookcase. It had the usual texts. Below them were rows of three-inch-thick black, orange, and green three-ring binders labeled by subject: ABNORMAL REPRO, BOVINE/SURGICAL, OVINE/SURGICAL, EQUINE/SURGICAL. They went on for shelves.

Nearer to hand, battered stacks of the *American Veterinary Medicine Association Journal* lay next to equally well-thumbed copies of *American Rifleman*.

On the wall beyond the desk was a Greenpeace poster of a blue whale, a sticker for the National Rifle Association in its lower right corner.

On the desk was a silver triptych frame. The frame on the left held a photo of Half Dome at Yosemite and, in the foreground, a tall, muscular woman with long dark hair and amused eyes. The one on the right held a newspaper photo of a man clutching a rope around the neck and shoulders of a Brahma bull as it sunfished out of the chute. The man's hat slumped over his eyes; the common opinion was that the man was Sugar Dobbs. Between the two photos was a recent snapshot of a baby, nearly newborn, lying between two Tingley boots and wearing the most ridiculously small cowboy hat conceivable, his T-shirt emblazoned "SHANE."

Leaning back in a chair at his desk, looking completely relaxed, was Doctor Sugar Dobbs.

He was wearing a faded T-shirt from the Nevada Ropers and Riders. His long-sleeved oxford cloth shirt for teaching hung on a hook opposite the door. Above it hung a string tie. Some days he wore it for teaching, others he didn't; Frieda had never found a pattern. He was staring amusedly into her eyes.

Frieda glanced away. The wall directly above the desk was littered with Post-its. One was a to-do list:

- Clean bedroll.
- Check truck suspension.
- Buy extra plugs, alternator.
- Fill gas can, water can.
- Rinse canteen.

- Check and double-check first-aid kit.
- Buy ammo.

Below it she noticed a gap where the concrete blocks showed through; there was a blank space for two or three notes. Below them, a curled Post-it said, "Talk to Frieda."

She stood beside the door, waiting.

Sugar grinned, shaking his head. "I'm sorry, Frieda. You're a good student, but every time I see you near that cartoon, I think of you freshman year—" He subsided into chuckles. Frieda winced.

It had been the first large-animal assignment of freshman year. During the same rotation, they had pulled on sleeves and stuck their hands in cardboard boxes painted with cow designs, feeling in the dark to pull out frozen dead calf fetuses in a pretense at assisting an awkward birth.

On the day they first worked with the real thing, the class ahead of them had a cameraman waiting, capturing the expression on each freshman's face—panic, disgust, embarrassment—as he or she stuck the sleeve up the rectum of Mrs. Grundy or one of the other demo cows and felt downward desperately, usually confusedly, to try to palpate the cervix. Because of the large number of students, Mrs. Grundy and the others were in the middle of the barn, well away from the stalls.

If the trials had been alphabetical instead of by lot, Frieda would have stood a better chance. As it was, Frieda was the fifth and last, and Mrs. Grundy was getting seriously irked.

Frieda tugged on the sleeve, stood on tiptoe, and tentatively stretched into the cow's rectum, sliding her arm in all the way to the armpit.

Mrs. Grundy, by now offended beyond belief and with even bovine patience exhausted, clenched her buttocks and strode dignifiedly away, dragging the stunned Frieda.

She could have struggled free, but chose not to. She stayed in and stumbled along until two people got the cow under control. She blushed furiously while the entire class laughed at her, and she was grateful that her hair had come loose from the tie-back and drifted down to cover her face.

*   *   *

Frieda muttered to herself.

"What's that?"

"I felt the ovaries, too. I stayed until I felt them." She had been astonished, in the midst of all that laughter and humiliation, suddenly to feel and identify a living organ.

Sugar nodded. "I remember." He spun his chair around and nudged the door with his foot. "I'd rather say this with the door shut. Can you be comfortable with that?"

Not likely. "Sure." She went over to the student chair, a battered wooden affair with one loose leg. She set her backpack down on it and stood behind the chair, hands clutching the back.

From his desk he pulled a folder with a blue tab, leafing through it purposefully. Frieda realized uncomfortably that the first word on it was her last name.

"Okay," he said. "Frieda Jean Christoff. Home, Auberon, Wisconsin. Straight A's in high school. Straight A's undergrad. Straight A's first three years of vet school." He looked up. "That right?"

She nodded miserably. It had only been a matter of time . . .

"Doing all right in large animal, too," he said—to her complete surprise.

Sugar reached across the gap and said, "This is a visual test. Tell me anything you can from this photo. This is your patient."

Frieda grabbed it, looked at it quickly, nearly dropped it, and held it tight. Sugar waited, then said, "You know, a surgeon has to be confident. Now look at it again and tell me what you know for sure."

Finally he said, "Tell me something, anyway."

It was a meadow somewhere in the Appalachians, far up a mountainside, half of it clear-cut and turned to pasture. To either side of the meadow were stands of timber in full leaf. Behind the meadow, near the top of the mountain, the rich green darkened to pine. The meadow grass was tall, but still green; Frieda still couldn't get over the lushness down here. The background was dotted with forty or fifty large, blurry white shapes.

In the foreground, Sugar stood to the left, a young woman with short dark hair and wearing coveralls stood to the right, and a beautiful young woman with dark eyes and rich curly hair was between them. She had her arm around a small white horse with—

Frieda blinked and looked again. The goat beard and spiral white horn were still on the horse.

She handed it back. "Is it a digitized photograph, or is it a dressed-up horse?"

He pulled his hand away, refusing to take it. "Look closer. Don't ever stop looking just 'cause you think you've found one thing wrong; lots of patients have more than one thing wrong. Why would this be a patient?"

Frieda took it back reluctantly. And stared. And saw the shadow under the horse's bulging sides. "It's pregnant."

"You sure? A minute ago you didn't even think it was real."

Frieda was too intrigued by the picture to be flustered. "It can be pregnant and unreal at the same time, right?"

Sugar Dobbs's laugh startled her. "That's pretty near dead on—'pregnant and unreal.' "

Frieda looked intently at the picture, saying nothing. Finally Doctor Dobbs said dryly, "If you can do an o.b. diagnosis from that picture, you better be teaching me."

"I wasn't even looking at the"—she caught herself—"at the patient." She pointed toward the bottom of the curly-haired woman's loose-fitting overalls, where a pair of ankles, apparently in wool socks, disappeared into the grass. "Isn't there something funny about the angles in the client's legs?"

Sugar took the picture back hastily. "You aren't someone who focuses on folks' handicaps, are you? 'Cause you'll be working side by side with—"

"Cody?" She was pleased and a little surprised. "He's not handicapped."

He blinked, started to say something, changed his mind. "Anyhow, get used to seeing strange things. You'll see a lot this summer; this isn't the end of the interesting cases. In the first place, it's an ambulatory rotation." He tapped the photo in her hand for emphasis. "Real ambulatory. Now tell me more about the photo."

She looked up with defensive innocence. "Isn't the woman on the right the one who did the goat surgery, on the videotape we saw?"

He regarded her solemnly. "Is it?"

Of course it was. Frieda was kicking herself. "I think—" She bit her tongue. Sugar hated "I think." "I'm sure it is."

"Good eye. I'm glad you know faces. Anything else?" He was amused.

Frieda stared at the picture, unwilling to state the obvious. "The younger woman, with the curly hair? The wind's blown her hair over; there's a white spot—"

Sugar said hastily, "I want to hear about the animal, Frieda. That's why you're gonna be a vet, to talk about animals."

Frieda disagreed silently. She wanted to be with animals, not talk about them. "Just a minute . . ." She said finally, "Well, she may need assistance foaling, if that's the word."

" 'She' who?"

And that was the question she would never answer. Not on a picture like this, not to someone who could laugh at her and, if he wanted, destroy her whole career. . . . She wondered if he understood that; to her, every day when she got up, her whole career hung in the balance on a single mistake.

She said finally, "It could be a fake."

"Why would it be?" She ignored the question. "Okay, how could it be?"

"I thought I said"—she knew she had—"digitized, changed pixel by pixel."

Sugar frowned. "That stuff makes me nervous. Anyway, why would I do that?"

Frieda shrugged. "For a joke." Inside she thought angrily, *To hurt me. Can't you understand that?*

Sugar threw up his hands. "Okay. I can't prove anything. It might be real, it might be pregnant." He leaned forward. "If it is, it might could foal this next Monday night. Could you pretend to help, just in case?"

Frieda said carefully, "If I did, what would I do?"

"*If* you did," Sugar stressed dryly, "you might be the primary presenter on the case. First presenter on it at all, in fact." He corrected himself. "First presenter on foaling, second presenter on the subject species."

From his briefcase he pulled a thick manila folder. "Here's some of the previous research on the patient species." He grinned at her, daring her to say anything more specific. The word "unicorn" hung in the air between them, like some terrible taboo.

Frieda took the packet dazedly. This was getting awfully elaborate for a joke.

The notes, a report from a student rotation, had been badly typed on a mechanical typewriter with a misaligned "K" and a strong need for cleaning. Sugar Dobbs was notoriously resistant to computers.

But normal rotation records were computerized these days; either vet students handed in diskettes or work-study students typed them in. Sugar hadn't wanted anyone to see this report.

Frieda braced herself and looked back in his eyes. "Do you want me not to talk about this to other students?"

"Well, did you plan on it?"

Once he asked, the answer was obvious. Frieda had no close friends, and she couldn't imagine discussing these things with a stranger.

She ducked again, focusing on the notes. Included with them were photocopied pages from a book which, judging by the typeface, was fairly old. A title was scribbled across it: *Lao's Guide to the Unbiological Species.*

After a few seconds, she looked up. Sugar was staring at her amusedly, waiting for her to look at him. She dropped her eyes hastily, letting her hair swing over her face again.

She muttered, still cautiously, "I don't know much about the patient species."

Sugar snorted. "Nobody knows a whole lot about 'the patient species.' "

At least she knew from the notes that a presentation had been done before. "How did the first student manage to research . . . the topic?"

He chuckled. "Do you know, the first student never bothered to ask, just slogged through the library and made a presentation. Never guessed that I only knew half of what she found." He handed Frieda a photocopy, stapled at the upper left-hand corner. It was thick enough that the back page was in danger of falling off.

She read the copied title page: *Lao's Guide to the Unbiological Species*.

"Lao can be flaky, but he's the best authority we have. In print, at least."

She scanned the text, focusing on a single line: "The animal, more discerning than the primate, recognizes the nice distinction between virginity and innocence. Beyond that quality, a sympathetic affinity for the injuries of innocence . . ."

She flipped back to the first page hastily. "Where did this come from?"

He grinned. "If you have questions, ask Mrs. Agnes Sobell, at the reference desk. Main library."

"Not the veterinary library?"

He shrugged. "It wasn't planned with this kind of thing in mind. 'Course, it wouldn't hurt if you were up on horses and goats. One other thing: you'll be presenting in front of the client. I should mention that the client is kind of sharp about medicine, too."

That was the last straw. It had been hard enough the first time she had made a mistake presenting. "Doctor Dobbs, are you sure I'm the right person for this?"

He leaned forward. "Get it straight. The client needs doctors, and fast. One reason I asked you to go on this is that I think you're one of the very best we've got. The extra work might not hurt you, but I figure you and the other ones I asked can get up to speed fastest of anybody." He added carelessly, "You've got two days to be ready."

Two days! "I'll do my best." She tried not to stammer. "Doctor Dobbs, what else will be on this rotation?"

"Know what? All the other students working on this rotation were so blown out by their own cases, they never thought to ask what else they'd do."

She took it as a rebuke. "I was just wondering about the schedule. Is it a summer block?" Most of the other students hated going to school through the summer, and missed their homes. Frieda never complained about it.

"It spills beyond the summer," he admitted. "Might could, anyway."

"My senior year is already fairly full." After all, she was taking his Large Animal rotation now; he must know. "Will it interfere with the other work?"

"Not hardly. The rest of the school won't even notice it, in fact. It's kind of a covert schedule." He grinned. "What's the best way to hide a course rotation, if you want to keep it private?"

It was an odd question, but she took it seriously; with Sugar's questions you had to. "Give it the same name as another rotation." He shook his head. "Make it take the wrong number of weeks." He frowned and barely nodded. "Or break it up."

"You got it. Rotation will be irregular, intermittent, through the last year. I'll handle schedule problems." He scratched his head. "That business of giving it the same name, I'll have to try that. Good one. Anyway: the nature of the rotation—there are four of you, this one is different, on and off for many weeks through senior year; the last one was too much of a rush and there wasn't one last year, for"—he winced—"political reasons."

He didn't say whose politics, and Frieda didn't ask.

"And it's not as if any of you need the credit, but it'll be listed out there just the same. One thing: it may interfere with interview schedules. Have you set up your plans from here?"

She shook her head. "I planned that for the spring, when I was sure—" That she would graduate at all. "Well, more sure what I want to do." At present she had two plans of action: go live at home without practicing, or find an agri-business where she gave shots all day and, if she was lucky, never faced a single crisis. Or if she woke up one day and the entire operation was wiped out, her fault, she'd go live at home without practicing.

She was cautiously open to a third option.

Sugar looked annoyed, and she had no idea why. "Well, if you need help deciding, come talk." He slapped his leg.

"In the meantime, do your homework. One more thing—
be ready to manage a team, not just the folks on the rotation."

"A team?" Puzzled, she looked again at the photo. "I
wouldn't want to crowd the patient—"

"And you'd better not. But you'll be mostly in charge of
three other students, an undergrad volunteer, a farm worker,
and some . . . other folks." He leaned forward. "We're not
talking about just one patient. There are dozens of them, all
bound to deliver the same night."

Frieda stared at the white spots in the background again,
her heart suddenly too full to let her be afraid. Dozens of
them?

Then she came to. Of course there weren't.

Sugar sighed loudly. "All right, say it. I could swear on
a stack of Bibles that I'm not fooling you, if that would
help. Would it? What's it gonna take?"

She finally burst out, "How can I believe in this?"

"Don't you want to?"

Part of her thought, *More than anything.* She realized
belatedly that she'd clenched her fist again. All she said was
"It's hard to believe anything this unusual."

"It gets harder." He leaned forward. "Before it's done
we'll camp in strange worlds, we'll eat strange meals, we'll
interrupt everything you've done to do something you never
dreamed of. Can you take that without complaining?" He
grinned. "Sure you can. You never complain about anything."

He meant it as a compliment, but her mind automatically
brought up a rebuke from her past: *Good old Frieda. You
could spit in her drink, and she'd thank you before throwing
it out.* She ducked still farther, pulling the book bag close
to her, saying nothing.

Sugar, watching her, grunted, "Well, I guess you won't
complain about working with the others."

Frieda looked forward to working with Cody. He was
almost continually happy. Frieda wondered what that felt
like. "Who are the others?"

"Valerie White."

She quit smiling. Valerie was what news stories called a

groundbreaker, the first black student at the vet school. Virginia, for all its changes in the last thirty years, was still like that.

Valerie had about six times the edge Frieda did, and her edge showed constantly. Frieda also found that hard because her hometown was nearly all white; she tiptoed constantly around Valerie, afraid she would do or say the wrong thing. Frieda suspected that Valerie had complete contempt for her.

"Who else?"

"The other one is Matt Lutz."

"Oh." The one person she prayed would never, ever, catch her looking like a fool.

"If you're through dancing with excitement, I probably ought to get back to work."

She was out the door when Sugar said flatly, "Frieda."

She turned in the door and stopped.

"You're supposed to say something like, 'It's my dream.' "

Frieda briefly, vividly remembered last night's dream: a completely shaved kitten, Frieda's stitches skeined across it like something from a quilting bee, pawing her leg and mewing plaintively as the stitches unraveled and it sagged apart. "Sorry, I'm sorry," she said helplessly.

Sugar looked at her, his eyes blank and noncommittal. "We had kind of a problem a few years ago, a student trying to break into the drug supply."

Frieda tried to look interested, wondering what this had to do with her.

"Turned out she wanted drugs so she could commit suicide painlessly. We keep a better watch now, not that we weren't careful then."

"The schedule here's pretty hard. We try to find out what stress is gonna do to students. That's part of being a doctor. We worry, once in a while, about suicide in juniors and seniors. I guess you can see that now."

Ah. "It never occurred to me," Frieda said firmly.

As she closed the door, she thought mechanically, *It will never occur to me. I will never die by accident, and I will never commit suicide, and in spite of everything I want, I will always, always feel this way.*

She sealed it off, as she always did, and went to the library.

T·W·O

BJ SHOVED ASIDE the cup of tea she didn't need and walked to the rest room, which she did. Probably she could have used a mirror at the funeral parlor to check herself; somehow she couldn't picture her mother doing it, so she wouldn't either. It was BJ's first funeral as the family representative.

The fluorescent light made even her weather-darkened skin seem pale; she was fit, but the indoor lighting made her look anemic. Out of habit she checked herself for signs of illness, then shook her head quickly and straightened her jacket, tucked her blouse, and brushed futilely at her hair, which nowadays showed the influence of too many strange winds. "Mention the beach, if anyone asks," she muttered to herself. It was important to look nondescript and normal.

Looking right today was important. BJ remembered all the times when she'd seen her mother, standing at a mirror in the hall below the stairs, give a final tug to her hem and a final firm pull at the sleeves of a jacket that was darker and stiffer than anything BJ's mother wore on any other day of the year. "Where are you going?" BJ would ask.

Her mother would say firmly, "I'm going to a social occasion." She'd stare at her own face, far too long. "To represent the family." This was her mother, who had never done a thing firmly but had always done it with laughter

and enthusiasm, as though every occasion would be her last
time.

BJ's mother was over fifteen months dead, the most recent family funeral. It was BJ's turn to represent the family.

The directions to the funeral parlor were clear, but even
if they hadn't been, BJ could have found the funeral parlor
easily. She parked, walked briskly, if a little awkwardly in
dress shoes, across the lot, and nodded politely to the greeter
at the door, a man in his twenties with superb sincerity.
"Salem family?" he said with sympathy but no grief.

"No. Chesterton—I mean, yes, thank you." BJ pictured
her mother doing this, over and over, never saying a word
to her or Peter. She moved to the book and signed her name:
BJ VAUGHAN. She hesitated momentarily, and wrote
"Post Office Box 795, Kendrick, VA."

The funeral parlor was well decorated, Victorian in keeping with a universal feeling associating earlier eras with de-
corum and death. It was tastefully ornamented with carpet
as bland as sherbet and as tough as asphalt. BJ clasped the
tiny black clutch purse she had bought an hour earlier and
nodded from side to side whenever she thought someone
might have been trying to recognize her.

The woman in the casket was emaciated and alien, beyond the undertaker's art to make her sympathetic and human. BJ looked closely at the face, trying to decide what
she saw there.

BJ's training was with animal medicine, but even in humans, she could still see telltale signs: muscles relaxed
where they should have been receiving nerve impulses,
poses which, for the undertaker, were natural but which for
the body no longer were. Aunt Kathryn had died ill.

BJ said a mumbled prayer, part of which was heartfelt
thanks that, now, she herself would never finish like this.

"Hello?" A broad gray-haired woman in a black, rough-
textured skirt and jacket strode up to within six inches of
BJ and stopped, disturbingly close. "You're Laurel's child,
aren't you?" She clasped both of BJ's hands, hard. "I remember you. Thank you so for coming. Not a good funeral,
is it?" she added vaguely. "If it were a good funeral, every-

one would bring a casserole." She finished—a concession—"Elizabeth Chesterton Blount."

"My mother's Aunt Betty." BJ squeezed the hands back.
"I'm pleased to meet you. My mother often spoke of you."

"She did?" Betty looked disarmed and grateful at the
revelation.

BJ would never have had the malice to say "And she
thought you were a stiff." "She remembered you from her
childhood. And from"—she glanced around—"other occasions."

"We're not much of a group for get-togethers. Nice that
we get together at all, I suppose." She looked around the
room. "You look enough like poor Laurel that I knew you.
And I remember you from when she . . . well."

BJ nodded. "I probably met you at her funeral; I met so
many people that day." She thought. "And I think I met
you once at Grandpa's."

But mentioning Grandpa was a mistake; Betty backed off,
murmuring politely, and sought out more discreet relatives.

BJ was glad. She looked around the room at the older
relatives who chatted with each other, at the parents who
introduced their children. Except that most of the conver-
sations seemed as though they were between mere acquain-
tances, it looked like any other family.

"Excuse me. BJ?"

She turned, startled, and stared into a navy blue sport coat
of thick-weave poly-cotton mix. She had to look up four
inches to make eye contact.

He wasn't more than twenty, sandy-haired and light-eyed,
pudgy and earnest. "I've heard about you. You're in medicine."

BJ winced. The people in her family who said "in medicine" were usually out of their depth, sweeping ineffectu-
ally at crises solved by tests but guessed at from the first,
commonly by family histories. "I'm a veterinarian."

"Right." He stuck out a hand. "I'm Andy Chesterton.
We're first cousins."

"BJ Vaughan—I'm sorry; you knew that." She tried to
think back. "Your father would have been my Uncle Wyatt." She had an uncomfortable memory that Uncle Wyatt

was dead, one of the ones nobody liked talking about.

He shrugged, and in a normal gathering only BJ would have known how much that shrug cost. "My father died of a fire in his bed. Smoking, maybe. Nobody knows how it started. Everyone has a fair guess as to why he didn't stop it."

"I'm sorry about your aunt—"

"Sure. Your aunt too." He shook her hand without seeming to notice.

She said, "Were you close?"

He frowned. "Nobody in this family is close. Listen, can we go to the hall and talk? I'm sorry to be so blunt." He seemed terrified. "It's important."

BJ said, "In that case, there's a coffee shop not far from here."

"Look, if you'd rather not talk I understand."

She shook her head. "I've spent a lifetime of relatives dodging me." She was only twenty-eight, but the gap of experience between herself and Andy was astonishing and a little disturbing.

She ordered tea and diluted it with milk. He ordered coffee, black, but spoiled the effect by having it with pecan pie. He huddled in a corner of the booth and waited.

"Andy, I'm disoriented. Who are your brothers and sisters?"

He shook his head. "I'm an only child."

"So there's just your mother—"

"And she's clueless." He sipped hard at the coffee, winced, and ate a huge forkful of the pecan pie, the gooey syrup between pecans leaving long, curved strings to the plate. "I want you to take a look at something. It's going to look crazy at first, but I swear it's not coincidence."

He pulled a much-folded, neatly printed sheet of paper from his pocket. "This is our family tree." He spread it out, using the napkin holder and the salt and pepper shakers to hold it flat. The chart covered four generations. Birth dates and death dates included known causes of death, where there was one, and ugly black question marks where there weren't. Fascinated, BJ found her grandfather, her mother (with a question mark), and Kathryn Chesterton Salem. She touched her own and her brother Peter's names.

Andy coughed. "Look, I don't mean to scare you."

"Why should it scare me?" But she already knew, and she was already trying to think of a way to explain.

He pulled out a second sheet, this a table of names in columns. "This is a list of dates of funerals in the family, and the ages of the people who died, in columns by family." He tapped the first sheet. "You can see where the early deaths fit on the family tree."

BJ was impressed. Why hadn't she ever thought of doing this?

"I did the Dysarts, the Blounts, the Vaughans, and the Chestertons. In all branches of the family, way too many of the young funerals—well, middle-aged funerals—are on the Chesterton side." He stared defensively at her. "That's your mother's side."

"Yes, I know." She braced herself and said gently, "My mother committed suicide."

"Um. My father probably did, too." He chewed his lip, then said finally, "I'm real sorry, BJ, but that's why I need to ask you: did your mother know something? Is there something wrong with our family?"

When BJ said nothing, he said, "Please. I know we've just met; I know it's crazy and awkward. Did your mother tell you something? Dad never told me anything. Wouldn't tell me."

She was silent for a long time, and stared at him. He was ruthlessly tan, the image of men in cologne commercials. The muscles in his shoulders showed that he worked out, but they were still layered over with baby fat. His eyes were troubled, but still clear and, to BJ, very innocent.

In her mind, she saw her mother's note again: "*BJ, this is the hardest letter a mother could write. It is even harder for me, knowing that someday you may face the same choice. . . .*" For the first time, she understood her mother's crisis and ceased to resent never being told about the family while her mother was alive.

She waved a hand. "I'm not trying to dodge you. This is hard." She sipped her tea, trying to prepare, then gave up.

It was cruel to make him wait, and she'd never be ready for this. "All right. There's a disease, called Huntington's disease, or Huntington's chorea; do you know what it is?"

He shook his head. His knuckles, on the Formica table, were white.

"It's degenerative, and it's always fatal. It's an autosomal disease—" He looked blank, and she finished, "It's genetic, and it's dominant. Half the people in our family get it—unless both of their parents had it, in which case the odds go even higher. It's neurological."

He said in a tight, shaking voice, "What's it like?"

BJ waved her hands, struggling to find words. It was not lost on her that she was waving her hands; there had been a brief period of her life when she had been careful to hold them still. "It's a little like multiple sclerosis, and a little like schizophrenia. You can't control your muscles the way other people do, and you go through mood swings, excitement and depression. In the early stages, lots of times it's misdiagnosed as schizophrenia or as bipolar personality unless you give your family history."

He automatically put a bite of pie in his mouth, but looked like he might be sick. "What do you mean about controlling muscles? What's it like?"

"Like clumsiness. Like fluttering. You drop things, and your balance is off—listen: talk to an M.D. about that part; otherwise you'll be afraid you've got it every time you drop something or break things." She tried to smile. "We're also a human family. We're normally clumsy."

"Normally clumsy." He considered. "That describes me." He licked his lips. "Is it always—" He swallowed before saying "fatal." "Does it always follow the same course?"

BJ remembered her mother, and her mother's side of the family. "Always. Once it starts, between thirty-five and fifty-five usually, it progresses steadily." She did not bother saying that there was another, earlier form, called juvenile chorea. If Andy was as intensely curious as BJ had been, he'd know soon enough.

His breathing came quick and shallow. "Is there a cure?"

Now BJ felt wretchedly selfish. "Not yet. They're exploring a chemical treatment; it slows down the decay of the brain cells. Nothing else, really."

"Okay." But he stared down at the Formica, and it clearly was not okay. In the neighboring booth, two high school girls argued about someone named Trent and whether he was still a virgin. It was a silly, pointless conversation, lively and sweet and a little alien to Andy and BJ.

He said finally, "So what can I do?"

BJ didn't comment on the emergence of "I." "You can have yourself tested. It's not that expensive, and once it's over, you know." She added frankly, "Knowing is harder than not knowing. I know it doesn't seem so from your side of the fence, but it's so."

"You've been tested?" He put his hand to his mouth, like he could force the question back in; it was too late. The motion spilled his coffee; it slopped over the chart, a dark stain over half the family.

BJ blotted at it with a napkin. "I've considered it." BJ did not add that she definitely had Huntington's chorea, and would not add that it was now irrelevant to her. "You think it's a relief knowing. Then you remember the rest of your family."

He closed his eyes, considering. "Sure. I see that." And BJ could see that he did, a little. Andy hugged himself, although the coffee shop wasn't cold. He said faintly, "Thanks."

BJ was stunned. "For what? I found out two years ago, and my whole world fell apart. I'm so sorry to tell you."

Andy rubbed his forehead tiredly, thumb and fingers moving on opposite sides of his face, looking like an old man sorting out a marital quarrel. "It's a lot better than half-guessing and not knowing." BJ could picture him doing the same gesture at fifty, if he had the chance. "The weird thing about this is how ordinary it all feels, even talking about it. Can you imagine something this weird when you're back at your life in the real world?"

BJ smiled at him. "I don't really work in the real world."

He flashed a smile at her, assuming it was a joke.

Andy insisted on paying for BJ's tea. They walked to the

funeral home parking lot together. "Are you going to the
cemetery?"

He shuddered, and BJ understood why her mother had
kept them away from funerals. "Gotta go." Then he spun,
looking directly down into her eyes. "Aren't you afraid?
Don't you look at the calendar, count the years, scared that
it's going to happen to you?"

BJ wondered what his reaction would be if she said, "It
already has." Instead she said, "Didn't I hear that you'll be
going to Western Vee University?" It was hardly coincidence. Some families went to U.Va., some to Western Vee.

"In physics. That's right; you went there, didn't you? To
vet school, too. What have you done since you graduated?"

She shrugged. "I'm in private practice now."

Their good-byes were awkward; they had talked on a
level to which courtesy barely applied. "Have a safe trip
home," she said.

"Actually, I'm not going home." He grinned faintly.
"I'm meeting friends at a beach house on the Outer Banks,
gonna spend a week." He fumbled in his sport coat pockets.
"Once I'm on the Outer Banks it's easy—I've got directions
here somewhere—"

BJ said absently, "South 95 to 295 bypass around Rich-
mond, 95 to 460, the Petersburg diagonal, 64 bypass around
Norfolk, 17 south through the Dismal Swamp, east on 158
before Elizabeth City."

Andy stared blankly at her. "You sure?"

BJ, staring inside herself, could name every culvert, every
rare and unexpected southern frost boil, every roadside decay where contractors had skimped on materials. "Fairly
sure."

"Okay." He stepped forward and hugged her. "Thanks
for telling me the truth."

That decided her. "Andy? When you get back to Western
Vee, leave a note in my post office box." She scribbled her
address for him. "There's a physics professor I want you to
meet."

"Sure." He got into his car and she turned away.

The graveside funeral was brief. The weather was beautiful, warm with a light breeze, and a cardinal was singing

nearby—defending territory, BJ remembered. These days she was more alive to nature than she had ever been.

The preacher offered a short prayer, then read from Proverbs: "If thou faint in the day of adversity, thy strength is small." He meant it as praise for Kathryn Salem.

BJ, however, thought of her own mother and winced. A quick glance around the graveside gave her the impression that others felt similar guilt. Kathryn Salem's two daughters, in their late thirties, were oblivious. One of them had a boy, maybe ten years old, with her.

The casket was lowered, and the mourners left quickly, filing past it.

Someone, an older relative from western Virginia, sang a song fragment at graveside:

> Oh, can't you feel it brother,
> And don't you want to go,
> And leave this world of trial,
> And trouble here below?

BJ took that as her cue. Without more than nodding to the relatives, she walked back to her car, actually a rental.

Kendrick, Virginia, was three and a half hours to the west by highway. There was no time to drive there.

Sighing, BJ pulled her shoes off and took her hiking boots from the passenger seat. She took her backpack from the car and began walking. At the first alley she turned right. The brick walls of the alley faded to sandy brown and became stone facing, then rough stone, then a canyon wall.

In forty steps she emerged between dunes onto a sandy path, in sea grass. Behind her, Arlington was nowhere to be seen.

Less than a minute later, she had turned twice on the stray paths. There were no seabirds, and the tang of salt was long gone from the air. Clay-colored buttes rose to her right. The wind rippled through a field of clover, ahead and to her right. A hawklike bird call, lone and echoing, rang off the rocks. She smiled and took a side trail to her left.

The trail rose quickly, changing from sandy soil to black, to rocky with moss. The moss became dotted with circles of lichens; the soil was covered with pine needles. A low cloud cover hung overhead.

In five minutes of walking, BJ had not seen a gum wrapper, a beer can, or a Styrofoam burger container.

The sun burst through as she rounded a corner nearly two thousand feet above the sea.

A rainbow arced above the empty green valley ahead, framing a hundred-foot waterfall. BJ all but wept. Who would have thought that she'd see all this beauty on her way from a funeral?

The bend in the road masked a shift from dirt to stone; to either side the ditch fell away. She walked across an ageless stone bridge, high over a winding canyon. Ospreys, or something like them, hovered below her, scanning the mist-shrouded rapids for fish. One of them dove suddenly, all but disappearing in the depths. BJ felt oddly nostalgic for large, winged predators.

The other side of the crevasse gave way to round, green hills. Fog hid the hilltops, but BJ could tell that they weren't that much higher than her vision indicated.

Every few steps the texture of the roadway under her changed, as though it were a patchwork of other roads: paving stone, cobblestone, and now dirt. The road rose slowly, and she appeared now to be walking a narrow ridge with deep valleys on either side.

A bulky quadruped the size of a cow, with an oddly protruding jaw and even more oddly protruding lips, bellowed on her left and fled downward into the mist. As though she had heard a foghorn, BJ moved toward the center of the road.

The hills to either side melted into soft, round protrusions, as old as the Appalachians. The mist parted briefly, and a valley opened almost at BJ's feet. BJ took the first trail down, dropping into the mist immediately.

As she came out of it, the trail passed an overlook, with a splendid view of Kendrick and of the Western Vee University campus. The town was less than five miles away.

BJ turned off the trail and onto a gravel road, turning up a driveway almost immediately. At the end of the driveway was a typical farmhouse, with white siding and a wrap-around front porch. The tar shingles had moss on them; the porch floorboards were chipped and needed repainting. It could have been anywhere in the Virginia hills, an ordinary old house with new or old owners of no particular oddity.

The screen door swung wide, and a huge beak stuck out, followed by a fierce face, an eagle's but far larger, with piercing, golden eyes. An eagle's talons, impossibly large, caught the door on the backswing; a lion's body except for the wings leapt onto the porch.

The face cocked to one side, staring. Its beak opened, and a sharp, clear voice spoke. "Lovely outfit. Queen and huntress, chaste and fair? Ah—sorry, wrong goddess."

BJ said with relief, "It's so good to see you." Life felt suddenly normal again.

T·H·R·E·E

AFTERWARD BJ WOULD think, with fondness and sharp regret, how much like a lazy Sunday afternoon it was, all sunshine, friends and family. It reminded her of sitting with her mother, the *Washington Post* trashed over the living room, the two of them shaking their heads over Peter's latest disastrous girlfriend and arguing good-naturedly and almost indifferently about the news.

The Griffin bent his head in a bow, his claw extended. BJ was pleased to see that he was balancing well and that his wings, which had suffered several fractures since she had known him, seemed to be healing well. "Hello, my dear. How very good to see you."

He sounded like someone's highly educated grandfather, and he looked like something a legendary hero would fight. "That's not true." BJ corrected her thoughts angrily. "He looks absolutely beautiful."

She fumbled in her backpack, suddenly shy. "I brought you something."

"For me? Delightful. Does it panic, repent, and bleed?"

A strong, deep female voice inside her said, "Ignore him; he's in one of those moods."

"I never ignore him." And BJ knew that Laurie never did, either. "It's a book." She held it out lamely, realizing that of course he could see it was a book. Why did talking to the Griffin always make her feel like rewriting her own speech?

He took it in a claw eagerly and turned it over. "*Alice in Wonderland.* It seems to me you mentioned this book to me once."

"I got you a first-edition facsimile, well, the first edition with the Tenniel illustrations." She had been very pleased when she found it; she thought he would care about things like that. "It should be called *Alice's Adventures Underground.* And here's the sequel." She passed him *Through the Looking-Glass, and What Alice Found There*. I hope you like them."

"I shall, of course." He had the first book pinned to the porch floorboards, and was peering with interest at the illustrations. "Is this a fantasy, or the story of a real world somewhere?"

"It's a fantasy"—BJ, hesitating, glanced at Laurie's amused face behind the screen—"as far as I know. Could I come in?"

He swept the books up in one talon and tossed them over his back. They sailed in a graceful arc and landed between his folded wings, which flexed protectively over them. "By all means." He reared back, looking like something on a family crest, and held the screen door open with one foreleg while he gestured with the other. "Please come in." He called inside, "We seem to be feeding a female migrant worker."

She didn't get inside; instead, the handsomest man she had ever known all but leapt out. "BJ." He walked with a cane, the product of injuries from a recent fight, and his smile when he saw BJ was so beautiful that it hurt. "How very wonderful to see you." He made a low bow and kissed her hand, then laughed and swung her close to him like a dancer, kissing her lightly on the lips. "Please don't be offended."

"I'm not." She held him as well, feeling clumsy and for once not minding. "How are you healing?"

"Badly." His hair, smooth and brushed straight back, sparkled in the sunlight. His skin shone almost as brightly, bronze and perfect in the midafternoon sun. Estevan Protera looked like any woman's ideal Latin lover. "I came here so that Ms. Kleinman could offer any expertise. She seems remarkably good at healing the infirm."

"It's my bedside manner," came the voice through the screen door. The Griffin and Protera turned automatically; Protera, turning back to BJ, smiled and shrugged as though embarrassed.

BJ fingered his dress. "This is new."

He nodded, adjusting the hem slightly. "A wonderful purchase; mail order, and it fits better than tailor-made. Please, come off the porch; I'm not completely comfortable out here." He looked as relaxed as a panther in the bough of a tree.

The Griffin said, "Now that I have my full presence on the porch, one would think anything was acceptable."

"One would, wouldn't one?" Protera offered an arm to BJ. "Please come in."

The living room was a weird blend of western Virginia parlor and Middle Eastern seraglio. The sofa was vintage, a horsehair sofa with wooden arms; it was long enough and sturdy enough to accommodate the Griffin.

The wall held black-and-white photos: a forestry crew from 1912, a panorama of the New River, a blurry and improbable shot of an elephant in a rail yard, being hanged by the neck from the chains of a rail yard crane. Next to them were huge color reproductions: several theatrical Romans taking a vow over swords, and what looked like a lion hunt.

"The one on the left is Jacques-Louis David, *The Oath of the Horatii*. Honor over life. The lion hunt on the right is Delacroix. Observe the musculature." BJ already had, and had concluded that the artist had sketched real lions close up. "These are reproductions." The Griffin stared at them, brooding. "The originals are in the Louvre and the Chicago Art Institute, respectively. I wanted them, but Ms. Kleinman convinced me that would attract too much attention."

While his back was turned, BJ glanced into his bedroom. It was simple and spartan, a king-sized futon on a bare floor, a bed tray with a single tea cup on it, floor-to-ceiling books. BJ was amused to see, lying by the bed, two sets of knit burgundy slippers, or one set of four. Either the slippers had stretched out, or they were perfectly shaped to fit talons and paws.

He turned back around. "I hope you appreciate the computer," he said with obvious pride. "There have been some improvements since you were last here."

It was a wonder. The monitor hung on an arm bolted to the wall over the couch; it was clamped to the arm table so that it could be tilted without falling off. The keyboard, curved in the middle for ergonomics, hung from brackets on the wall; a scimitar with a parallel curve hung just above it. Below the couch, a sleek-looking and probably state-of-the-art modem lay against a telephone jack. The main body of the computer, with its drives and boards, stood just under a cherry coffee table holding a lacquer bowl full of black stones and deep blue irises.

"Are you on the Internet?" BJ, who had spent much of the past year and a half away from television, let alone computers, barely knew the term.

"Occasionally."

"Inevitably." Laurie stepped into the room, and quite nearly dominated it. Laurie Kleinman was overweight, and her long, straight brown hair seemed an anachronism from her artsy days in the English Department, before she became a veterinary anesthetist. In the past she would have retreated in a cloud of menthol cigarette smoke from her own strong opinions, knowing she might be overheard. Now she seemed imperially assured, the Griffin moving to her side as naturally as he once had to the side of a king.

The Griffin noticed the open bedroom door for the first time and moved swiftly into the bedroom. "Have you seen my reference section?" Apparently casually he bumped the bed, dropping the coverlet down and hiding the slippers. "Let me show you one of my favorites. This is from a bestiary of sorts."

He leapt up at the bookcase and, with a single talon, flipped a book out and caught it, opening it in one smooth motion, flipping through it with his claws as he cocked a single eye at it. "Here it is. Professor South's source book and research guide to mythical and fabulous creatures."

He held the book in careful balance and read aloud solemnly. "Mind you, this is the griffin: . . . 'The creature is belligerent, rapacious, and vigilant. When entrusted with guardianship, it is protective and, occasionally, even gentle; as an avenger, it is relentless in the pursuit of evildoers." He nodded, satisfied. "A marvelously accurate book."

"I'll say," Laurie snorted. "He can't talk about griffins without drowning in polysyllables."

"May I?" BJ took the book and skimmed up and down. "This is interesting. 'Made into a drinking cup, a griffin's claw was said to change color when it came into contact with poison.' "

"An exaggeration certainly, but a great species attracts great myths."

Protera arched an eyebrow amusedly.

BJ read on. "An early German medical manual even prescribed putting a live griffin on a woman's breast as a means of curing infertility."

Laurie snickered. "That ought to do it."

The Griffin snapped his beak several times in embarrassment and annoyance. BJ glanced at Protera; to her surprise she found him looking thoughtful rather than amused. "I think that the German writer was a good observer, but a bad interpreter. As for the griffin and poisons"—he waved an immaculately manicured hand—"Perhaps, if the writer was in a place where he saw griffins, he was likelier to see accelerated or easy healing."

That stopped them all, especially the Griffin. "Good God, Doctor, you think he visited—"

"I think," Protera said firmly, "that he was not in Germany. I think that he may have been in some country where fecundity is the norm, and that he met a griffin there." He tapped his cane on the floor lightly. "I also think there is a meal to be eaten."

Laurie posed like a bored waitress. "Welcome to Kleinman's and Griffin's. Smoking or non-smoking?"

"It doesn't matter, does it, my dear?" Protera said. "No one smokes here."

Laurie beamed. Quitting was her greatest achievement. "Why don't you sit at the head?"

BJ said on the way into the dining room, "It smells wonderful, Laurie."

"Sure does," she agreed, and dropped an easy hand on the Griffin's back. "Actually, he did the cooking."

The Griffin flexed one of his forelegs, which BJ had seen claw divots in paving stone. "I slice, dice, pare, and I suspect I could puree."

From nowhere, Protera produced a bottle of sauvignon blanc. "Don't forget: you corkscrew." He tossed the bottle.

The Griffin, rearing back within two feet of the ceiling, caught it with only the slightest swirling of the contents. A second later there was a loud *pop,* and he waved the cork at the end of a talon. They all offered their glasses hurriedly.

There was no question that the Griffin would offer the toast. He held a glass high, and it barely jostled in his talon. "To Crossroads."

They raised their glasses and toasted. "Crossroads."

They sipped, each thinking of a place they had all risked their lives for, but knew to varying degrees. Laurie had visited it only in crisis, Protera had lived and researched there for less than a year, and BJ had founded its first veterinary practice. The Griffin was its bravest and greatest defender.

Protera set his glass down. "The wine is from the Maule Valley. In Chile." For just a moment, his accent sounded stronger, and he seemed wistful. "Strange, how the farther away from home you are, the easier it is to associate things with home."

BJ said nothing, still thinking about Crossroads. She had associated too much with home today, and felt better away from it.

"And the stew?" the Griffin said gently. "Does that remind you of home as well, Estevan?"

Protera tasted it. "Excellent. I must say, if I had cooked it, the spicing would be quite different; I have a fondness for saffron, cumin, and coriander."

Laurie said before the Griffin could say anything, "Don't start."

BJ said only, "The stew is wonderful." It was, too: onions, red peppers, tomatoes and carrots in a thick gravy created by a garlic-rubbed meat. "What's the main ingredient?"

"Venison." BJ looked sharply at him; he coughed. "I needed the exercise, and really, the herd hereabouts needs thinning. Surely you don't object—"

"Of course not." And it was true, she told herself defensively; the deer in western Virginia had no natural predators except for a very few mountain lions whose existence was sometimes disputed. She took another bite of the meat and told herself, again defensively, how good it was.

After a few minutes she was enjoying it again, completely distracted by the conversation. Laurie, the Griffin, and Protera discussed and disagreed constantly, shifting topics as easily as they passed side dishes. The discussion ranged from the latest pictures from the Hubble telescope and what they implied for the age of the universe—

—to depiction of the transient moment in the paintings of Watteau and Fragonard, and whether the momentary flirtation of an eighteenth-century woman in a garden swing was changed one whit by the age of the universe—

—to garden herbs and aromatherapy as having any validity beyond stress relief, and subsequently whether or not stress relief had broader implications for cancer and AIDS patients—

—to, as a second wine bottle emptied, relativism and fundamental ethics, whether or not there was an underlying universal ethic which transcended all the worlds they knew. (Affirmative: A. Griffin; Negative: E. Protera; Judge and Referee: L. Kleinman.)

BJ, alternately fascinated, amused, and appalled, talked very little; she felt like the only child at a table of grownups, and wondered how old she would be before the feeling went away.

Eventually the conversation meandered into a debate on artificial intelligence and the Turing test, and died there. The Griffin turned to BJ. "It's wonderful that you returned. You walked here, didn't you?"

"Yes." BJ added carefully, "I rented a car in Washington. To get back here, I hiked a little, but mostly I could walk."

Laurie, dabbing bread in the stew, snorted. "Listen to the two of you, tiptoeing around words. Right now, a Scrabble game would end in an air strike."

But the Griffin was watching BJ. "You walked. I take it the walking surface was easy throughout?"

"Most of the way, yes. It was wide enough for a car or a horse-drawn wagon. The surface wasn't consistent. Sometimes it was cobblestone, sometimes dirt or clay—" She frowned. "It may have been oyster shells for a while—"

The Griffin looked at her admiringly. "Brilliant. All roads pass through several worlds."

BJ stared into the trees, brooding. "Which means that each road has several chances of touching on invaders."

He barely hesitated. "And many times the chance of losing them. Only thinking species will follow the roads well, and only those who read maps."

"That's the trade-off." BJ had agonized over it; any species fleeing over the road from one world to the next might never find its way to safety. "It's very hard to reach Crossroads now."

He thumped his talon on the table; the plates bounced up and back. "You can't protect Crossroads and leave it always exposed."

"Crossroads is no help to anyone," BJ reminded, "unless it's exposed. I might not be alive"—she should have said *would not be alive*—"if it hadn't been for Crossroads, and for the maps."

"*The Book of Strangeways.*" Protera frowned and stared into his wineglass. "A book of maps to let one walk between worlds. That was a gift beyond all the gods . . . I am sorry that all the copies we know of were destroyed." He added quickly, to BJ, "Though I trust your judgment in that matter."

BJ said, "There's a new *Book of Strangeways.*"

In a perverse way, she was proud of the silent stares she received. It took a lot to silence everyone at this table.

"Excuse me." She ran to the living room, returned with her backpack, and pulled out several marbled books with glued and sewn binding, the edges of the pages showing the roughness of paper with rich rag content. BJ had searched through many craft and book fairs before finding a book-binder good enough; after questioning BJ, the bookbinder had taken extreme amounts of time on each book. BJ handed the top book to the Griffin first, as was right.

He laid it flat on the table so the others might see it, and turned the pages carefully. "Wonderful cartography. Did you use a fountain pen?"

"Kind of. I mean, yes, but it takes ink cartridges." She was proud of how the maps looked. Her mother had kept a garden diary, and had sketched constantly in it; BJ was careful to duplicate the delicacy as well as the care and detail.

He flipped through the pages, following twisted lines across rivers, up and down mountains, and through tortuous canyons. "And you have created all of these roads?"

BJ thought of her walk back to Kendrick from Washington. "And others, but I erase them as I go." She reached into the backpack. "And I bought five more identical blank books"—she slammed them down on the table and flipped the top one open—"and as soon as I have the time, I swear I'll sketch the new roads in . . ."

Her voice died away.

Laurie, looking over her shoulder, said only, "Nice penmanship." The Griffin, stretching, flipped one toward Laurie, who slapped it between her palms like a tense softball player; two more to Protera, who without seeming to move caught one in each hand. They paged through the books, holding up elegantly sketched maps to each other without comment.

BJ broke the silence. "It's nothing I'm doing. I don't know how this is happening."

"Ignorant goddess," chided the Griffin.

"I wish you wouldn't call me that."

"You must get used to it." He tilted his beak down and peered over it, his way of frowning. "It is a recognition of your skill: the road-maker, the maker and keeper of Strangeways. Successor to the Stepfather God, who brought so many species to Crossroads, and who chose you. Being called Goddess is like learning to be called by your last name, or being called Doctor." The Griffin carefully speared the meat with a fork and dexterously dropped it in his beak.

BJ changed the subject. "Couldn't you eat more efficiently with your—without the fork?"

"Of course. And you could eat faster by putting your face in the plate. Efficiency is hardly the point of table manners."

"Or of anything else." Protera sipped from his wineglass. "I used to think it characterized physics; the past decade or so, I'm not so sure. BJ, may I offer you more stew?"

She accepted gladly. "Thanks. I'm sorry I didn't ask earlier—"

"She'd have had to interrupt," Laurie commented.

"—but how is your leg?"

"It is mending, thank you. I should be pleased; for the first time in my life I have a body part which can predict rain and snow. It slows me down very little." He added almost unwillingly, "I expected it to heal more quickly."

"I know a place where you'd heal faster," BJ said, and bit her lip, waiting. The Griffin would heal faster there, too.

Laurie left the table and stared out the front window. The Griffin appeared to take no notice.

Protera said smoothly, "I appreciate the invitation, but I have teaching obligations here." He glanced slyly at the Griffin. "As does my colleague."

BJ was nonplused. She tried to picture the Griffin in one of the gray stone buildings on campus, pointing to the chalkboard and tapping on the desk for emphasis as he skewered (verbally) some unlucky student. Actually, her best undergraduate teachers had been a little like him. "You're teaching?"

"Not yet." But he sounded self-satisfied, the way he often had after scoring a well-hit point off an intelligent adversary. The Griffin coughed. "While the demands on Professor Protera are nearly constant, on the other hand, my distinguished career allows me to emerge from retirement whenever—"

"Oh, no." But she was laughing. "You're retired faculty?" Of course. He would never be less than senior faculty. "How did you do it?—My God, did you break into the university records?"

"Of course not." He genuinely looked offended. "That would have been detected immediately. There are constant safeguards against such an intrusion."

"Besides," Protera broke in, "it would not have helped. As it happens, a few weeks ago there was a small fire in the computer room, after five o'clock on a Friday. All administrative and registrar's records were destroyed."

"All?" BJ, who was nervous around computers, had once seen a graduate student whose computer hard drive crashed containing the only copy of a Master's thesis. "My transcript is in that computer."

"Thankfully, there were backups." Protera would not look at her. "Stored off-site, moments before, ready for reloading after the weekend."

After a moment, BJ got it. "So you tampered with the backups—"

Protera bowed. "And when they were reloaded, all lost material was restored. Shortly thereafter, mail began arriving to the Kendrick post office box of Professor Emeritus A. Griffin."

"You two did this all alone?"

Protera looked shocked. "We could never. Harriet Winterthur, from Mathematics, did much of the programming; I merely wrote a few lines of code and"—he gestured at the Griffin—"my friend here outlined the strategy."

BJ wheeled toward him. "This Doctor Winterthur—" She had a vague recollection of the name, on an article about Crossroads and instability. "She knows about you?"

"Dear Harriet." He tilted his beak down, into what looked like a smile. "Fascinating, when she talks about her field."

Laurie said, "If I didn't trust your honor, I'd damn well kill her."

"Show some proportion. We e-mail each other, and she has some suspicion of what I am."

"She is a friend of mine," Protera broke in. "We both study Crossroads, and we share a fondness for Peru, though hers is as a tourist." He smiled wryly and tugged self-consciously at the shoulders of his dress. "I believe she has a crush on me."

Laurie started to snicker, but covered it with a cough. "Understandable." Protera nodded, smiling. Being in love with a griffin, BJ reflected, must be broadening.

At the end of the meal, BJ pushed her plate aside, sighing. "I certainly wish Melina could have come."

Laurie shook her head. "We invited her, but she won't come away from her work. Not now. She even sleeps in the fields, with her flock. Her serenity," Laurie corrected herself, and no one argued. "Serenity" was the appropriate word.

"Why?" But BJ already suspected the answer, and caught her breath.

The Griffin moved forward, speaking with unusual emphasis. "*They are finally ready to give birth.*"

BJ didn't need to ask who he meant. Part of her suddenly longed to bounce up and down like a child, too excited and happy to sit still or stay quiet. "They can't be. They were due in the fall."

"They mated early last time," the Griffin said crisply. "If you recall, Crossroads has been a trifle disrupted."

BJ blinked. Even for the Griffin, that was a remarkably terse way to describe invasion, the death of a presiding demigod and of a king, and the evacuation of an entire world.

The Griffin went on. "It seems that all this activity threw their cycle off."

"How soon will it happen?"

"Melina says it will be the night after tomorrow. The first summer full moon."

BJ swallowed. "I should help."

The Griffin pointed a single claw at her. "You must help. We will require more help as well. I wish Stefan were already trained—"

Laurie frowned. "He was a shepherd. If Melina can help, he can help."

"Then he must, as well." The Griffin tapped on the hardwood floor, thinking. BJ noted with amusement that the dining room floor was pocked with thousands of pinpoint indentations. "All right. What else can we do?" He was looking at BJ.

"I could call some friends who have graduated," she said

slowly, "but none of them could get here in time, even if I—well, even with my help."

She waited for someone else to make a suggestion. No one did. Finally she said, "I'll go see Doctor Dobbs"—it was still hard to call him Sugar—"and see if he can help."

"Excellent choice."

She added, "Why am I in charge?"

"Because you're a doctor, to animals and to those who are part and mostly animal. Because you'll know what to do. Finally, because Crossroads has no king, and you are its only leader."

The Griffin's eyes seemed to stare a long distance away, and Laurie quietly put her hand on his back. The king of Crossroads had been the Griffin's closest friend.

BJ broke the silence. "But you're its leader. You're—" She stopped.

"The Inspector General? Yes. And the inestimable Professor Protera knows it now, as do far too many beings. I work best when I work alone and unrecognized. I am no leader." He looked to say more, but cut off suddenly.

"I'll speak to Sugar Dobbs. He won't be shocked; you and Laurie have—" BJ stopped in midsentence. "He already has a student veterinary rotation planned for now. That's why you approved him."

The Griffin chuckled, a muted rumble like a lion's roar. "You're still difficult to deceive."

BJ set her wineglass down, annoyed. "The one thing I find really hard about this," she said, "is that everything done concerning Crossroads has one or two covert agendas attached."

The Griffin stared calmly at her. "The longer you live there, and the more you care for it, the likelier you will be to behave the same."

BJ shook her head vigorously, her dark hair twisting from side to side. "Never." But she couldn't stay upset. "Anyway, it's good that we'll have help. I can't wait for the foaling. The kidlings." She laughed at herself. "Whatever."

Even Laurie looked excited, and the Griffin's neck feathers rippled once. Estevan Protera, for no reason BJ could imagine, looked troubled.

He shook his head and smiled around the table. "That was a wonderful meal; still, we must not let the day get away from us." He rapped sharply on the table for emphasis. "And so to war."

The Griffin nodded tensely. "Hunters feed, but war hungers."

Laurie scowled. "Leaving me the dishes, no doubt. Bums."

"War, madam, is not refined."

"Big news." She turned to BJ. "Give me a hand, will you? After all, he did cook."

Protera said diffidently, "I would gladly—"

"Forget it. You'll need your strength." Laurie stood and said brusquely, "C'mon, BJ." Housework clearly annoyed her.

BJ hastily carried dishes to the kitchen, where Laurie, scowling furiously, scrubbed at plates until the muscles in her forearms stood out. BJ asked, "What's going on?"

"Standing ritual after dinner. You'll see."

Midway through the dishes, BJ said diffidently, "You know, I only knew you as an anesthetist. I never thought of you as domestic."

"I never did, either." She added frankly, "I never expected he was, either, but thank God."

BJ checked over her shoulder. The Griffin was talking through the bedroom door to Protera, who was changing clothes. "How is he? I haven't had time to examine him."

"He's healing," Laurie said, then admitted grudgingly, "Slowly, though. The bones are fine, but the muscles—"

"Oh." BJ blinked and stopped washing for a moment. "That's why he hunts deer, isn't it?"

"It's working, too."

"Slowly."

Laurie said nothing.

BJ asked, "Will all the damage heal if he stays in Virginia?" Laurie said nothing. Finally BJ finished, "He should go back to Crossroads."

"Of course he should," Laurie agreed. She scowled at the dishes, not acknowledging anything else.

She spun around, stacking plates on the kitchen table hard

enough to chip them. "And he won't, as long as he thinks
I need him more than your damned Crossroads does."

She stormed outside, the back door slamming behind her.
BJ swept the china chips into the trash basket, wondering
why she was being surreptitious.

Protera returned to the kitchen, dressed in a fencing plas-
tron, loose cotton pants, and a mesh mask. Incongruously,
he was still leaning on his cane. His injured leg was encased
in a plastic splint. "Shall we go outside?"

He stumbled on leaving the porch. Laurie grabbed his arm
quickly; he steadied himself. "Thank you." Despite his
limp, he moved easily to a place in the side yard, between
two pine trees. "I'm quite ready." He leaned on his cane,
completely motionless except for the warm breeze ruffling
his hair.

Laurie threw him a sword; the blade glistened oddly. He
caught it with his free hand.

"Plastic-coated." He saluted again with it, and the blade
glistened in the sunlight. "I trust his control more than my
own."

"Noted and appreciated." The Griffin braced to leap,
then paused and turned his head toward BJ. "One day, you
will need more of this training." He cocked an eye at her,
and for a moment she felt oddly like prey. "Tell me the
truth, which of us would you rather have teach you to
fight?"

"Doctor Protera," she said immediately; she needed a
human trainer. She added hastily, for the Griffin's feelings,
"Because I hope never to fight a griffin."

The Griffin nodded. "Sensible. However, you would
learn more from me."

Protera raised an eyebrow. "Are you quite sure, sir?"

"Quite sure, but it bears confirming." He saluted briskly
with a talon, the motion a blur. BJ shivered involuntarily; it
made the same swish as the steel sword.

"Well, then." Protera raised his guard, shifting it slightly
from center to protect his splinted leg.

The Griffin crouched, his tail lashing with a softer swish
than the whir of talons. Protera, cane at the ready in his
back hand, spun the sword with a relaxed, loose grip, never

out of balance, always ready to parry and counterattack.

The Griffin sprang, his lion's hind legs carrying him the eight feet to Protera in less than a second. Protera rolled to his left, his wrist constantly twisting to keep his suddenly upright sword between himself and the Griffin. He rose to one knee as the Griffin landed, three-legged; the sword whipped forward at the point where eagle feathers and lion fur met on the Griffin's breast.

The Griffin's massive left talons tapped out faster than BJ could see and slapped at the blade. It bounced sideways, but spun under his foreleg as Protera disengaged and, incredibly, lunged one-legged inside the Griffin's forelegs, catching himself on the cane to complete the lunge.

The Griffin, grunting, shifted balance quickly and parried with his other talons. Protera, dangerously overbalanced, parried frantically as he hopped backward on his good leg. Before the Griffin could charge, Protera spun the cane in a surprise move and rapped him on the beak. The Griffin, blinking, backed out of range.

The Griffin sprang again, and Protera braced for a charge, like a matador waiting to give the death blow to a bull. Laurie made a sick sound in her throat.

There was a whoosh of air as the Griffin's great wings unfolded; his body rose suddenly as they caught the afternoon breeze. He sailed easily over Protera's head, out of reach, and tucked his wings as quickly as he had opened them.

Protera, unable to turn around fast enough, dropped frantically to the earth as talons whipped through the air where he had been. He spun on his cane like some parody of a trapeze artist, and pushed off one-handed, beating back a talon as it slammed down at him. Suddenly he was upright, stabbing at the exposed foreleg as it retracted; the Griffin retreated hastily. Protera followed, remorselessly thrusting at the Griffin's head and chest. The great talons barely caught the sword in time, with no counterattack possible.

The Griffin reared back, his entire scarred chest exposed. Protera, having braced for his thrust to be beaten back, stumbled. The great talons slammed together, closing on his sword; he barely slid the blade free for his retreat.

The Griffin sprang again, and BJ thought helplessly, "He's done that before." Protera was the best swordsman she had ever known, but she couldn't stand the thought of the Griffin losing.

Protera ducked, rolled to the left, and spun on his cane again to turn around and face the Griffin. This time his guard, and the push-off from the cane, were perfect.

But he was facing empty lawn and the line of hedges.

At the firm tap on his shoulder, he dropped his sword, smiling and shaking his head. "How did you do it?"

"You expected me to spring or to fly behind you. I dropped and spun as you did, and rolled back to my original position." He flexed his wings, shaking the grass clippings and dust out of them. "Instead of trying to get behind you, I convinced you to turn your back on me—not, by the way, a wise move."

"Excellent." Protera bowed, cane at the ready as he retrieved the sword. "And a great deal of exertion. Do you mind if we rest a moment?"

The Griffin answered calmly. "Take your time, Doctor. We will begin again the moment you're ready." But his beak remained open, and his tawny sides were heaving.

Laurie had gone inside. BJ met her on the steps; she was carrying a pitcher of water, a glass, and a large crystal bowl for the Griffin to use. BJ said quietly, "The fighting is therapy, isn't it?"

Laurie snorted. "I hope so. He thinks it's combat preparation." Her forehead creased with worry lines. "It began over a month ago. When they started, the matches were short, and Protera won every time. He never complained, but I think it was hard on him." She watched the Griffin's heaving sides and added quietly, "If you can convince him to go back inside Crossroads, I'll go along with it."

Before BJ could say anything, Laurie strode forward, a small steel-tined brush in her hand. "Time to get the grass out."

The Griffin said reproachfully, "My dear, I prefer not to groom before guests."

"They're nearly family. Besides, you'd rather be filthy in front of them? You're too heraldic to stay this dirty." She swept the brush down him in smooth strokes, plucking clippings and twigs from his back and sides. Finally she knelt to do his belly, so he wouldn't have to lie on his back; she left her other arm across him in an embrace. The Griffin, his dignity forgotten for a moment, swung his great head back and stroked her hair with his beak. Protera and BJ watched silently.

Laurie stood up when she was done. "Estevan, what about you? Okay, not the brush; can I get you a towel or—" She stopped as he shook his head embarrassedly. Incredibly, Protera was still spotless.

She glanced down at the dust trails and the clawed divots which ran through grass, tree roots, and stone alike. "You two are hard on a lawn."

The Griffin raised a feathered eyebrow. "Lawns are an attribute of civilization, not the entire point of it."

"And anyway, you have such fun doing this."

"Work should be pleasure—for when you are older, even your pleasure will be work." He shook himself, ruffling his feathers and letting them settle. "Professor Protera, are you ready for another match?"

BJ checked her watch and sighed. "I'm really sorry to leave, but I need to retrieve my car and drive back here to Stefan's."

"I imagine you do," Laurie said dryly. "I guess your pleasure isn't work yet."

BJ tried to frame a tart reply, found herself blushing, and said only, "Thanks for the nice meal."

The Griffin and Protera bowed, then turned to combat. Laurie smirked and nodded, ignoring the resumption of the duel.

BJ, sighing, returned up the path. Because she was embarrassed, she walked the three hundred-odd miles to Washington in less than twenty minutes.

F·O·U·R

FRIEDA WAS TRUDGING across the lobby of the main vet school building when someone tapped her on the shoulder. She glanced up and Cody, smiling but apprehensive, pointed back outside.

Matt, well in front of him, had continued walking at his usual breakneck pace. Cody looked at him and chuckled. "No way can I keep up with that."

"Who can?" Valerie said behind him. "Show-off. Come on, Frieda." She passed Frieda a note in Sugar's usual scrawl, with a sketched map under it. The note said simply, "I'll meet you on-site. Choose a good map reader. Frieda, hope you don't mind presenting in front of the client."

Frieda closed her eyes and hoped fervently there would not be a crowd.

BJ could tell by the sunset just how beautiful the night would be. The mountains of Virginia had perfect weather in summer: warm and usually sunny days with deep blue skies and haze on the horizon, cool clear nights with soft breezes and thousands of stars. BJ was looking forward to staying outside most of the night.

Still, she was glad she had a thick jacket in her field gear. Mountain air cooled rapidly, and as she turned onto the road to Laurie and the Griffin's farm, she shivered as the sun fell behind the mountaintop ahead of her. Stefan put an arm around her. "Put on your jacket, love my own."

She smiled at him and, tipping back the fedora she had given him, scratched his head, rubbing between the horns under his curly hair. He was wearing a thin shirt and summer slacks. BJ envied him his woolly body, though she teased him about it.

Once he had startled her by laughing and saying, "But how you love my woolly legs tight against your smooth ones!" She had blushed and quit teasing back.

Laurie was waiting on the step, rolling a pencil between her fingers rapidly. From time to time she raised it, stared at it, dropped her hand again. She was missing smoking. "About damn time, BJ."

"I had an errand."

Stefan smiled happily at Laurie, who smirked at BJ. "I'll just bet you did."

BJ chose not to respond. "Is the Griffin coming?"

"And leave home tonight? Try to drag him away." She jerked her head toward the house. "Come in a sec."

They entered, Stefan leaping surefootedly up the steps despite the padded sneakers over his hooves.

There was a single light over the Griffin's computer, illuminating dozens of reference works and flight magazines open around them. He cocked his head in greeting, but kept an eye on the screen. "Sorry I can't join you. It's mission night."

"Mission night?"

"May sixteenth, 1943, to be more precise. " His speech, always formal, sounded stilted, and he had a British accent.

Laurie sighed. "Too many war movies. If only I'd broken the VCR in time." She gestured at the joystick beside the keyboard. He's an on-line pilot, with a simulator program."

"Actually, I lead an RAF squadron. If you'll excuse me, the lads are waiting." His talons flicked forward and back in a blur; he spoke crisply and clearly as he typed. "Good evening, men. I've just driven back from London, where I spoke to Sir Arthur Harris, called to Downing Street for the occasion. Sir Arthur and I reviewed the revised roster for tonight's foray and then the casualty figures for the month.

I'm not ashamed to say we both found our eyes moist as we went over the names, hallowed forever in the RAF, of men no longer on the roster. Let us never forget them."

He shook his head and typed more. "Enough of that. Tonight's mission, in the Ruhr, involves the Mohne Dam—a primary source of hydroelectric power for the Germans, and the *Wehrmacht* depends on it more than even the German High Command knows. Still, they are aware enough that it will be well defended: flak and *Luftwaffe* both.

"I'm afraid Jerry will be waiting for us tonight, and I don't need to tell you that Britain, and Europe as well, possibly the entire free world, are depending on what we do tonight. Because of the gravity of the mission, I will be flying a Spitfire tonight alongside you. That is all. Good luck and good hunting."

Messages blinked in one by one: "Thank you, sir." "Will do, sir." "We'll do you proud."

The Griffin leaned over the keyboard and joystick, punching keys and muttering. Laurie said, "Some of the geeks out there would die for him—in simulations or out in the real world. Can you believe it?"

But her eyes were shining, and BJ could believe it.

Laurie drove her own pickup to the site. She had packed blankets, a stretcher, and, BJ noticed uneasily, a portable anesthesia machine for field surgery. She also had a powerful camp flashlight. BJ and Stefan followed her; he was bouncing up and down on the seat like a child, too excited to stay still. "Thank you for letting me come. I will help the best I can. Oh, love!" He kissed her suddenly. "I know you have done this so many times, but for me it is the first."

"I haven't done it that many times. A few foalings, some lambings—"

"Oh, lambings." He said seriously, "You know I have done those, BJ. I was a shepherd when we met." He added solemnly, "I was a lamb once myself."

"Then tonight should be easy." She put a hand on his shoulder, partly to hold him on the car seat. "Unicorns are just bigger ungulates."

He laughed at her, and she laughed back, showing her own excitement for the first time. "I know: not really. Unicorns are unicorns."

They turned off onto a pair of tire ruts with a hump of grass between them. The headlights showed the seed-laden grass stems springing up behind Laurie's pickup, and the swirl of dust from the tires. BJ was too busy holding the car steady to look around.

Then Laurie's brake lights went on, and she pulled into the grass beside the road. It was closer cropped than the road had been; this was grazing land. BJ pulled off beside her.

The moon, rising orange-red over the valley behind them, shone on a clear-cut field between two stands of trees which gave way to pine farther up the mountain.

BJ looked down, entranced. The town of Kendrick was barely eight or ten miles behind them. She could clearly see the stadium lights at the university.

The thud of hoofbeats behind her was disorienting; she looked around, startled. Sugar, entering the field, stared down from the back of Skywalker. "How y'all doing?"

BJ smiled. "For a second there, I was expecting someone else."

Sugar grinned, patting the mare's sides. "Easy, Walker." Skywalker, whom a client had signed over to the school to treat or destroy, was nominally the vet school's, actually Sugar's. He claimed he rode her because she needed the exercise. He dismounted easily, reins in one hand, and tied Walker to the aerial of Laurie's truck. "Any sign of my new crop of doctors?"

Laurie pointed. "If that's not them, we've got a lot of explaining to do."

But they didn't yet, BJ realized, glancing around uneasily. There were no patients to be seen.

She watched the vet school truck bouncing down the gravel road, and an odd nostalgia gripped her. Nothing would make her wish for the vicious overwork and misery of vet school, yet it had brought her here.

The twin line of headlights cut across the field as the vet school truck arrived. The students leapt out and looked around, a little wildly, not thinking yet to unload the cabinets at the side and back.

Frieda, sliding from the passenger side of the front seat, was overwhelmingly grateful that she had read the map right, and that Matt had listened. It had felt good to function as a team already; she prayed that she would do as well in the night ahead.

BJ waited for Sugar to speak and, when he didn't, stepped forward. "I'm glad you could come. My name is BJ Vaughan. I'm—" She caught herself before saying she was the doctor. "I'm one of the clients."

Frieda recognized BJ from the photo, and from the goat surgery video.

"I am the client, too!" They all turned as a dark-haired figure leapt down the hill. "I am so sorry, BJ, for being late, but they walk slowly now and you know they will take no path—"

"It's good to see you, Melina." BJ swore she wouldn't grin the way Sugar did, behind her, but Melina's enthusiasm was funny.

Frieda, watching fascinated, tried unsuccessfully to pin down Melina's accent. She looked remarkably like the sister of the dark-haired young man in the flashy hat. Melina was the younger woman from the photograph, BJ the other woman. Where were—? She swallowed, wondering if it was still all a joke.

Melina embraced BJ, Stefan, and Laurie in turn, then stopped herself in time and nodded awkwardly to Sugar. "It is very good to see you."

Sugar nodded to her. "How you doing, Melina?"

"Fine." She fingered the Coptic cross at her breast, a gift from a former student of Sugar's. Despite her not being a student, Sugar seemed to make her shy. Frieda could sympathize.

Behind them, the moon grew whiter as it climbed. As their eyes adjusted to the light, each stem of grass was visible, if not defined, waving in its own shadows.

From the vet school truck, Sugar brought out a Coleman lantern and hung it on a tree, lighting it with a match struck off his zipper. The light, too brilliant to look at, cast harsh shadows that contrasted with the moon.

Cody and Matt were struggling to unload pads which Sugar had placed in the truck earlier. Frieda wondered if he hadn't done it by himself. Matt looked toward the lantern. "If there are complications tonight, we'll be fumbling in shadows. Why should we do this after dark?"

"Because babies come when babies come," Sugar drawled. "Ask your mom. It's just your turn to be inconvenienced, instead of inconvenient."

Matt resumed unpacking, but said firmly, "Then we should have induced by daylight." Sugar gave him a look, which he missed. Frieda wondered if Matt wasn't right, but said nothing.

Cody straightened up, brushing grass seed off his coveralls. "That's the last of it, I think. Valerie?"

She was peering in the back of the truck. "There's stuff we might need later." She sounded unhappy, disapproving. Frieda glanced in the cabinet at the back of the truck: Gigli wire for sawing fetuses apart, chains for pulling them in difficult births, syringes and a bottle of T-61 for euthanizing patients. "I guess that's all," she agreed faintly, and looked around. There was nothing but the green and pearl of grass in moonlight, already a little dewy from the night. "Where are the, the—patients?"

"First meet the client," Sugar said. "BJ Vaughan, meet Cody Sayers."

He grinned, a little shyly, and limped forward to shake hands. BJ caught herself stepping forward to meet him, and waited.

"Valerie White."

Valerie nodded absently, still looking around for the patients.

"Matthew Lutz."

"Pleased to meet you." Matt had a pleasant voice and a firm handshake. The empty hillside didn't seem to trouble him at all.

"Last, today's presenter, Frieda Christoff."

"Hi." She caught herself longing to ask hundreds of questions and cut off. "I'll do the presentation in a minute."

"In front of me?" BJ glanced at Sugar, who looked innocently back. "I appreciate it. I presented on unicorns once, when I was a student."

So now it was out in the open. "Doctor Dobbs told me. Well, he didn't say it was you, but I guessed." She stopped.

"Good guess," BJ said, realizing she sounded like Sugar. "And this is Stefan." He was standing earnestly behind them, dying to be introduced. "Stefan is an undergraduate observer from Western Vee, and in a pre-vet program, but he has field experience with unicorns."

She heard Stefan chuckle and she told herself resolutely that she would not blush even in the dark. Over a year ago the two of them had watched these unicorns mate. "He's looking forward to hearing you, too," she finished lamely.

Frieda said nothing. BJ waited, at first sympathetic, then nervous for her.

Still Frieda said nothing. Sugar prompted, "Better start. They'll be coming down soon."

BJ said, "Excuse me, Frieda."

The student looked up, frightened, and locked eyes with BJ—which was all BJ wanted. "Don't you need notes?"

"I wasn't sure I could use them, so I memorized. They're in the truck, though," she said earnestly and quickly, "so I can get them if you need to see them."

BJ shook her head. "Maybe Doctor Dobbs needs to see them. Did you find a lot about the species?"

"Not too much," Frieda said. She exhaled, somehow relieved by the interest BJ was showing. It was nice of her to care. "There was some material in *Lao's Guide* . . ."

Soon she was speaking easily, swept away by the material. The other students listened, frankly amazed: Cody and Valerie delighted, Matt thoughtful. She finished with additional material from the Western Vee University Library, then paused. "That's about all of the medical history, and there isn't much natural history unless you count Pliny and Ctesias." She paused again. "So I decided to."

Sugar said neutrally, "So you decided to trust fanciful sources."

"Oh, no. I decided to read them. I mean . . ." She floundered. "I didn't think there were unicorns, and they did.

And they were right and I was wrong, so I decided to see what else they might be right about.''

"Fair enough." He glanced at his watch, then at the moon. "They'll be here any minute. Oughta be here now . . . want to say something sensible about unicorn foals?"

"Not really." Frieda hoped, in the dim light, that she couldn't be seen blushing. "The obvious parallels are horses and goats. Probably they'll be single births, with occasionally twinning, born headfirst, capable of standing shortly after birth. Some may be born with the amniotic sacs still on them. Once they're freed, they should nurse right away. I'll bet the mother foals standing up." She looked anxiously at BJ. "Do you have any reason to think there will be complications tonight?"

BJ started to say "No," then remembered Protera's dubious expression. "I don't know. They're not supposed to deliver now; the gestation time is off.''

"Are they always born at night?"

Sugar frowned at the question; BJ pointed to the full moon. "I think that governs it. It governs their mating." She looked momentarily confused. "Well, a full moon does govern their mating."

Frieda looked up quickly. Sugar, back in the shadows, grinned. So did Stefan.

Before Frieda could ask any questions, Melina said happily, "Finally." The entire group by the lantern stared up the hill into the darkness.

They stepped slowly downhill, as pale and luminous as the moon: full white bodies and slimmer bodies near them, white horns flashing brighter than any moonlight should make them. They broke stride continuously, avoiding any rhythm and any path. The onlookers stood frozen; before they knew it, the flock (the *serenity*, Frieda reminded herself) was moving among them, nosing curiously at those who had come to help them. They stopped before the tire ruts, none of them putting a hoof on the track.

Sugar shook his head violently in momentary disbelief; BJ smiled as Skywalker, behind him, shook her head in the same motion.

BJ listened to Frieda relate information which was now

familiar without being mundane; she remembered with a quick ache how odd it had felt to present a medical rotation on an animal which was not supposed to exist.

A male unicorn stepped toward BJ, nodding his head forward. Improbably, there was a thick gold band in the middle of his horn. BJ, smiling but cautious, touched the horn. Frieda envied her confidence.

The horn, dry and smooth, felt free of cracking or colloidal fragments. If it hadn't grown back together, at least the mend had held. BJ stepped back. "Did you find out anything about birthing—"

She stared around. Frieda was gone.

Then a curly-haired brunette human head, all bright eyes and flashing smile, popped up practically in the middle of the serenity. Frieda, feeling a mare's bulging belly, called delightedly, "Twins. This one's having twins."

"Really?" BJ, suddenly cold inside, stepped over quickly and felt the unicorn's belly. "You're right. I would have expected—"

"What?" Frieda tensed. "Is something wrong?"

"Not exactly," BJ said. "But she should have delivered by now." She swallowed, remembering feeling that same belly nearly ten months before. "Long ago."

Frieda touched the mare's sides, sensitive as a blind woman reading a surface for the first time. "Maybe their twins take twice as long?"

BJ looked blankly at her, finally nodding. "We just don't know, do we?" Sugar frowned. He didn't like admitting to students that doctors just didn't know.

"Or maybe different unicorn species have different gestation periods."

It was the first gaffe Frieda had made; BJ hated to correct it in front of Sugar. She said gently, "As far as I know, there's only the one species."

Frieda coughed and looked tense and unhappy, then masked it over with concern. "Actually, you know, maybe that's not true?" Her voice rose, making questions out of statements, in case there was an argument. "Because, in China, there was the enlightened unicorn, the Ki-Lin? And in India and Persia, there was a unicorn with a brown face and blue eyes?''

BJ said as agreeably as possible, ''This is the only unicorn species I've had any evidence for.''

Frieda nodded quickly and ducked her head, letting her tangled hair drift over her eyes again. One of the male unicorns glided up to her, facing her. He bobbed his head, tapping her softly with the horn. Frieda looked up into the calm eyes in time to see the face turn brown and the eyes turn blue.

She exploded in happy laughter and unhesitatingly threw her arms around his neck.

The others were staring at the unicorn; BJ was watching Frieda. Sugar said out of the side of his mouth, ''Did you know they could do that?''

''No clue,'' BJ said. She was still watching Frieda and thinking, ''And I didn't know she could do that.'' The mousy, beaten-down girl was gone, and Frieda was suddenly wild and beautiful. ''Happy,'' BJ thought. ''I'm seeing her happy.''

Frieda pulled her arms back and ducked her head again. ''I'd better get started.'' The male unicorn nodded once, its face whitening again, and it drifted behind her, staying as close as though it were a guard.

Frieda avoided looking at anyone as she gave the orders.

''Matt, would you move through the herd—''

''The serenity,'' BJ and Melina said in unison.

''Thanks,'' she said, trying to mean it. ''Would you move through the serenity and check for potentially difficult births?''

''Glad to.'' He stepped forward, unconfused and unafraid, as calmly as though he were in a corral full of ponies.

''Thanks,'' Frieda said with relief. ''Valerie?''

''Yeah.'' Valerie had been looking at Matt with something like loathing.

''You go in the other direction. Either of you shout for Cody or I—or me, if you find any problems.''

''How will I know a problem?'' Valerie said frankly, then saw Sugar wince. ''Right. If I can't handle it, I'll call you.''

She strode off; short though she was, her determination gave her a stride nearly as long as Matt's.

For the next few minutes, the students seemed disorganized, moving from mare to mare and doing exams. BJ understood the disorganization; they were gaining knowledge, learning enough so that they could use their experience where it was needed most. She understood something Sugar had already forgotten: the painful self-consciousness the students had, realizing how little they had experienced and how much they needed to know.

Melina knelt by a unicorn. The right leg of her sweat pants rode up, exposing a woolly leg which bent backward at a strange angle. One of her shoes had fallen off; her sweat sock, held on with rubber bands, had a hole in the toe and her hoof showed through.

Frieda, passing by, stopped dead and stared. Glancing around quickly, she shrugged out of her sweater and dropped it over Melina's feet. "You must be cold."

Melina looked up quickly, confused, and tucked the sweater quickly over her feet. "Thank you."

Frieda knelt beside her without comment. BJ, watching, thought in a sudden rush, "I like you."

The male whose face had changed color nudged Frieda, gently but firmly. She pushed back at it, more gently. "I need to work."

He cocked his head and caught her in the fork of his nose and horn, forcing her away from the female.

"You can't do this," she said desperately. "I need to work."

"Turn around," BJ said suddenly. "Go where he wants."

Frieda looked over her shoulder at Sugar for confirmation. He said, "Your call."

Frieda said to the unicorn, "If you're sure." She added, "Valerie, could you please watch the one I'm leaving behind? I'd feel awful if . . ."

"Got it." Valerie stepped around the male, eyeing its hind legs narrowly, and crouched by the female. "Vulva's dilating, but no sign of a birth yet. Maybe the males are birth coaches."

"Keep watching," Frieda said, and, seeing Valerie's sudden flash at the order, added, "and thanks. I feel better." She turned around, walking slowly and carefully like a woman on a tightrope as the unicorn guided her this way and that through the grass. BJ followed.

They stopped before a female who stared at them as quietly as the others had, but who was showing more whites to the eyes. Her ears twitched periodically in spasms. Frieda touched the female's nose, running her hand along the flanks until she reached the hindquarters.

BJ watched, intrigued. The woman with her hands on the unicorn was neither the miserable neurotic hiding behind her hair nor the beautiful laughing woman embracing a male unicorn, but someone new and intent.

The vulva was not dry, and there were no signs of strain. Birth seemed easy for them.

Frieda reached to touch the vulva. There was a sudden contraction, and two tiny hooves slid out, touching her fingers as though reaching for them.

Frieda gasped, then called out, "I'm seeing front legs." She grabbed them, rotating her palms slightly and testing her grip on the slippery surface. "I'm going to pull gently," she emphasized the last word, "only exerting force if the foal—"

"The kidling."

"—Only if the kidling stops." She added firmly, not a trace of a question in her voice, "If you feel much resistance when you are pulling, call out immediately and ask for assistance."

"Yes'm," Cody said solemnly. He was only half joking; a male unicorn was driving him, more slowly than BJ had been driven, toward a female.

Matt said calmly, "I did all right in Equine Repro." He was striding from female to female, checking quickly for difficult births. "This will be like that."

"Not exactly?" Frieda was turning the kidling's legs, rotating the body on its axis. "Because the unicorn mare is so much smaller than a horse mare? And I think maybe the kidling is a little big?"

BJ knelt quickly. "What's sticking?"

Frieda slid her hand along the legs. "The head," she said

wonderingly. "How can the head stick—oh, please no. They aren't born with horns, are they?"

"I don't know." BJ steadied Frieda as she overbalanced. "I doubt it. Check the head. Feel up the neck, see if the head is bent back—"

"There it is," Frieda said with relief. "There's the chin"—carefully she reached farther in—"and there's the forehead, and there's no horn, not even a bump. That's an awfully big head," she said dubiously, "and it's bent back like it's rearing back inside her."

BJ said flatly, "Retropulse, tug on the jaw and pull the head down."

Frieda, looked at her, nodded quickly, and began pushing in on the head even as she said, "Doctor Dobbs?"

"Do it." He was on his way over, actually pushing unicorns aside.

He arrived too late; the retropulse was successful. Frieda tugged down as BJ had suggested, and the head came free. The moist kidling dove out, smoothly and easily, into Frieda's arms. She fell into the dust, holding the head aloft in one hand like a fallen fielder holding a caught fly ball. "BJ!"

BJ grabbed the kidling, feeling its moist sides. Between them they flipped the kidling up and down, clearing its airway. Fluid dropped from its nostrils; BJ knocked heads with Frieda, this time hard enough to see stars, as she dropped and breathed into the kidling's mouth and nose.

When she pulled back, they both stared. Between and just below the line of the kidling's ears, a small disk shone. BJ, marveling, put a hand above it; it disappeared in the shadow. She glanced over her shoulder at the full moon.

The tiny hooves flailed as the kidling coughed and struggled. BJ snatched it out of Frieda's arms and pulled it upright, letting it gasp its way to life. She walked it—him—to his mother's teats, relishing the weak but obviously vital trembling of his legs.

Together they watched him nurse. "Unicorn milk," BJ thought, remembering the book at Laurie's home in Virginia. She wondered what properties medieval writers would say it had; she realized, watching the kidling nurse, that it didn't matter.

She turned back to Frieda. "We did it."

Frieda looked at her bleakly. "No, you did it. I can't alone." She dashed into the serenity, as much in need of them as they were of her.

BJ felt a hard ridge at her back as a unicorn horn nudged her toward the next birth. "I'm ready," she said to the male, and walked.

She barely arrived in time. The birth itself was easy, a quick dive from darkness into light for the kidling. BJ, kneeling under the kidling, staggered as it dropped but held it out of the dirt. She looked up for the light disk on the forehead and saw that it was there, but fainter than the other had been; maybe the moon was under a cloud. She steadied her legs, then buckled her knees as she lowered it to the ground, waiting for it to balance on its own trembling legs as a colt would.

Its legs buckled with her own, and she realized that it wasn't breathing.

She fell back, holding it in her arms, and said sharply, "Sugar!"

He caught the kidling, letting her fall to the ground; a small rock stung one of her shoulder blades. She was up in seconds, stuffing her fingers in its mouth and wiping them from side to side to clear blockage. Sugar nudged her and she removed her fingers; the whole operation took three seconds.

Grunting he heaved on the kidling, and flipped it in his arms. Veins stood out in his biceps as he cradled the kidling's head in his right arm and dropped it suddenly, then caught it and pulled it up, snapped it down again and caught it, repeated it. A little fluid came from the kidling's nostrils and mouth. BJ wiped the nostrils quickly, nearly bumping heads with Sugar as he gulped air and ducked down to blow it into the nostrils. Did it again. Did it a third time, and waited.

The silver disk on the kidling's forehead faded out completely. BJ knew, without looking up, that the moon was still full and bright above them. The tiny forehead fell into shadow as Sugar tried again.

She leaned forward and blew into its nostrils when Sugar quit. After six or seven times, he pulled the kidling's head back. "No go." He added firmly, as though she were a student, "There's a lot of others being born tonight."

Without a word, BJ rose from her knees to move to another unicorn. From the corner of her eye she saw Sugar, more gently than she would have thought possible, laying the dead kidling on its side next to the mother.

Across the serenity, Valerie shouted, "Birth coming here." And then, "Oh my dear Lord."

BJ ran over. A bubble was extruding from the unicorn's vulva. "Amniotic sac, that's all. That happens in horses. Will you be okay here?"

Melina, breathless, sprang to her side. "I'll help." Valerie opened her mouth in annoyance, shutting it as Melina continued, "What should I do, Doctor?"

BJ stepped back, meeting a diligent male unicorn halfway, and accepted being herded to another birth.

For a while things were normal—if unicorn births without complications could be considered normal. Kidlings presented themselves, front hooves first in a diving position, and dropped freely out. After clearing the mucus from the kidlings' nostrils, the students lifted the kidlings upright and set them to nursing. Tiny circlets of moonlight shone intermittently across the serenity, and BJ grew to hope that the one stillbirth was an anomaly.

"Doctor Dobbs!" Valerie shouted, with a volume that snapped every head, human and unicorn, toward her. She corrected herself. "That's wrong. Frieda?"

She ran over. Sugar, clearly by effort of will, was holding back.

BJ didn't have to; she was right behind Frieda. Valerie pointed. "Hoof."

Frieda looked sick. "Rear hoof."

BJ dropped down. "Retropulse."

Valerie reached in, felt around, and grunted, "No room."

"It's because of the twins," Matt said. "The presentation is terrible." Compared to the others, he sounded verbose.

Suddenly Sugar was there. "Get the blankets from the truck, and the surgical pack. In back there's some lidocaine.

'Scuse me, Valerie.'' He dropped to his knees, barely giving her time to move back. "Sorry, Frieda; I'm taking over. You assist.''

"Fine.'' She added quickly, "Matt, could you bring the lantern over? Also all the Betadine scrub in the truck, and gloves. BJ, Melina, could you tell me everything you know about cesareans and unicorns?''

After a moment's silence, Sugar said, "They just did. Good call about the lantern and the other stuff.''

"I'm sorry,'' she said quickly. "I know you just took the case over, but I thought—''

"You're right. I said, 'good call.' '' Frieda shut up.

Seconds later, the unicorn was on the ground, sprawled sideways. Her belly was her highest point, the twins presumably one above the other. Frieda, following Sugar Dobbs's silent pointing, poured a line of Betadine solution down the belly. It stained the white hair brown, a parody of the male's brown face earlier. The female unicorn watched calmly, big-eyed, whites of the eyes barely showing.

Sugar nodded to her; respect and unicorns seemed to go together. "I'm gonna inject you with lidocaine. It'll numb the spot where I'm cutting.'' Matt raised an eyebrow as Sugar injected a little, pulled out, and did another, a series of injections for a line block. The unicorn barely twitched; compared to Sugar she was completely at peace. Sugar slapped gloves on and picked up a scalpel.

He grunted, "Something's on the back of my neck. Brush it off.''

Frieda, steeling herself, pulled the unicorn horn away from his cervical vertebrae and waved a warning index finger at the unblinking male. He swung the horn toward her. After a second, she nodded and turned back around, careful to keep her contaminated right glove away from the female's abdomen. The horn tickled on her neck.

The incision was easy and quick, a vertical line down the unicorn's flesh. There was something obscene in seeing that white purity, first stained with the scrub, then spotted with blood as Sugar pulled the scalpel toward himself.

After the initial incision, Sugar took several more cuts to get through the muscle tissue and the surprisingly pearly fat, finally exposing the smooth wall of the uterus. The students and even BJ braced themselves for the final cut. Sugar unhesitatingly slid the scalpel into and across the uterine wall, catching an almost equine nose as it popped through as though curious about the world outside.

He reached in two-handed and lifted out a body, smeared with placenta and with the blood of the incision, and handed it to Cody. "Got it?"

"Got it." He was braced like a weight lifter, his hips slightly canted to compensate for his short leg. "Hi, little fella. Val? I need help." He swung the body up and down, following BJ's instructions. Stefan, who had been about to help, backed off. Valerie nearly clunked her teeth on it as she dove in to breathe into its nostrils; after it snorted and coughed she stood, wiping her mouth, but grinning.

"That's one," Cody said as with Valerie's help he flipped it upright, and looked blankly around. "Wait. How will it nurse—"

He was bowled over as a female came forward, nuzzling the unsteady kidling and walking over it until her teats were over the kidling's eager mouth.

"Man down," Valerie said.

"Can't help." Sugar was up to his elbows in the female unicorn, pulling the second kidling. "We're kinda busy."

Frieda, reaching forward, was nudged aside. She turned, expecting a unicorn, as Matt knelt by the body. "Ready, Doctor Dobbs?"

"I guess." He handed off the body, glanced at its muzzle, and said sharply, "Clear the lungs now. BJ, close for me." He added, "Talk it through."

"Right." From the surgical pack she took up a curved needle in the hemostat, focusing on the patient instead of on how short a time ago she had been a student. "You already know that it's number one suture. The uterus—okay, I'm going to invert."

"Cushing-Connell sutures," Matt murmured.

BJ went on as though she hadn't heard. "You know it from lab; roll the edges of the incision into the organ. That way you're almost guaranteed a good seal on the organ." She was suturing as she talked, her fingers moving sure and fast. Part of her remembered, a little over two years before, how her trembling hands were always on the verge of dropping things. "Have you done bellies or bladders?"

"Sure," Valerie said, but even her edge was daunted. At first they had been looking at BJ with that polite distance that students reserve for clients, the teacher being the only really important human on-site. Now they seemed to accept BJ as some sort of adjunct faculty.

"Right; you're in senior year. With hollow viscera, you always invert. Inverting patterns aren't usually cruciates—" She talked on, surprised at how much she knew what she was doing. "Another set of sutures in the fascia, just to bring the subcutaneous layer back together. After the sub-Q, final layer in the skin."

"How do you avoid too much tension on the incision?" Cody said.

Frieda said absently, "Suit the tension to the tissue," astonishing herself.

BJ said, "Right. You'll get a feel for it." She was on the surface now, sewing off the skin. "And I'll admit I'm guessing, but for unicorns in this world I'd administer an antibiotic orally, probably tetracycline or another broad-band, and I'd request a follow-up for the kidling—" She looked over her shoulder and all but stopped. Sugar's and Matt's empty looks, and the lack of sound behind them, told her more than she wanted to know.

BJ continued mechanically, "And for failed births, I'd monitor the mother and possibly the father for other signs: depression, failure to eat. An authority I knew said, 'They are very spiritual animals.' " She faltered for a moment, and suddenly felt Stefan's slender hand on her shoulder. "If she looks like she can make it, let her go with her own kind when they leave."

Cody said, "How did you get so good at surgery so fast?"

"I did way too much of it," BJ said. "A good practice in a good place doesn't do as much surgery as I did."

Valerie nodded sagely. "Sure. Like a doctor in a war zone."

BJ looked up in surprise. "Something like that." She finished closing without explaining anything more, and walked away in silence.

The rest of the night had all the mechanical numbness of the evening after a car accident or a plane crash. BJ knelt repeatedly behind a unicorn, pulling a struggling or an inert kidling. Very little anyone did either helped a birth or hurt it. Very few of the mothers had a bad presentation or a difficult birth. Nearly a third of the kidlings were stillborn.

Stefan moved from figure to figure in the herd, touching them, petting them, offering comfort. He seemed able to ignore the stillborn forms and see only the living who needed him. From time to time he looked wistfully at the vet students and their work; each time he shook his head and turned back to his own work.

The gray of morning found the students, staff, and volunteers moving one by one toward the van as the unicorns no longer needed them. The workers' sweatshirts and jackets had blood on them, and their knees were mudstained from hours of kneeling. After a few minutes' silence, everyone realized that the birthing night was over.

Laurie's face was an expressionless mask. Stefan wept, quietly and unceasingly. Melina nudged her head under his arm, almost like an animal; the two of them flowed together like brother and sister, grieving openly.

Sugar scratched his head and, standing next to BJ, said quietly, "Bad night."

"Oh, yes."

"Any reason you know that I don't?"

She shook her head, her arms pulled tightly against her chest. "None."

But she remembered Protera's unvoiced doubts, and resolved to talk to him.

The moon, swollen and unnatural, was low in the west. In front of them, the serenity began moving.

Two unicorns each, a male and a female, approached each stillborn kid side by side. They gently shoved horns under the bodies and raised them, lifting each small corpse momentarily to the stars. When a body rolled midway down the horns, the unicorns carrying it lowered their heads until their horns were parallel with the ground. They bore the body to the blanket where the female lay recovering from surgery. Gradually the unicorns circled her, and the circle closed tightly around the pile of small bodies which they had laid beside her. This once, they all faced away from the outside.

BJ remembered what she had been taught and had learned: unicorns cherish and try to heal innocence and grief. It made sense, she told herself; they came together to heal their own grief.

Sugar said, almost against his will, "We need one for a necropsy."

BJ pictured taking one of those perfect tiny bodies, incising it, removing the organs. She remembered, as a student, hearing a junior reprimanded for calling a necropsy "lab meat."

Matt said easily, "Any one will do, right?" He stepped forward, reaching toward an unguarded kidling inert in the grass.

A female unicorn strode forward as Matt stretched out his arms. Without any hurry, her horn tip sliced across his jacket, then back again higher up, then once more in an effortless zigzag. The fabric drifted down in a long tatter. Matt, gaping, stared down at the ruins of his denim jacket. "What was that about?"

"About?" Valerie, tugging him backward, fingered the denim. "It was about an inch from making *you* lab meat."

Matt said stubbornly, "But what was it for?"

"A real good warning," Cody said. He joined Valerie, putting a hand on Matt's shoulders. Matt tried to shake them off, found that he couldn't, pulled back with them in a daze.

Sugar said, as much to the unicorns as to the students, "Look, I know it's awful, but we've got to do it. We have to know why it happened. A necropsy could tell us a lot."

BJ nodded, licking her lips. She couldn't be sure that the unicorns wouldn't kill her, but it had to be done—and if it was dangerous, she felt she had to try before Melina and Stefan, grieving and reckless, put themselves in harm's way. She tried to catch their eye as she stepped forward—

—And nearly stumbled when Frieda stepped in front of her. She moved into the serenity, saying wretchedly, "Sorry,

sorry, sorry . . .'' The unicorns moved aside, one by one, until she all but disappeared in the middle of the bodies. BJ strained forward, wishing that Frieda wasn't so short.

When Frieda emerged she was staggering, bearing a kidling in a fireman's carry and trying to look dignified. Matt strode forward, pushing against the unicorns; Valerie, snorting almost angrily, followed, shoving on the unyielding bodies. In the end it was Cody, pressing forward gently, who reached her first and helped with the burden. Even when he had it, Frieda would not let go.

She took it to BJ and not Sugar. BJ was startled until she remembered that she was the client. As Frieda knelt, BJ knelt and took it off her shoulders, quietly grateful for Cody's earnest support for both of them. "How did you get it?"

"That one let me." She pointed through the serenity to the unicorn on the blanket. Beside her, another female was nursing a wobbly legged kid.

"The one who had twins." BJ looked bleakly across at the ranks of unicorns. "One lived, one died. Well."

As Melina detached from Stefan, Laurie said gently to her, "You should stay with us tonight, honey."

Melina, bereft, shook her head. She turned and hugged BJ so tightly that BJ could hardly breathe and, not thinking, licked BJ's nose. BJ, pretending not to be startled, kissed Melina's nose and held her.

The unicorns were moving. The pile of tiny corpses was lifted up and separated into bundles, seeming to float across their mothers' backs. The unicorns moved, double-file, up the valley. Melina followed them. Only the mare healing from the cesarean remained, and a single stallion stayed with her. As they watched, she struggled up slowly.

"Is she safe to go with them?" Frieda asked. The mare's horn, and the horn of the stallion beside her, swung toward Frieda.

Valerie said, "You want to tell her she ain't?"

Cody smiled tiredly. Matt, fingering the ruins of his jacket absently, said nothing. After a moment, Frieda went up to the blanket, murmured a few soothing words, and finally, unable to help herself, leaned against the unicorn and

stroked her side silently. The male watched her, horn at the
ready. BJ noticed uneasily that Sugar, hand in his jacket
pocket, was watching the male narrowly. After a moment
Frieda kissed the mare's nose, patted the sleeping kidling
body awkwardly, and withdrew to where the students were.

They huddled beside the truck, close to the only familiar
thing in the field. Unused to the silence of a Virginia night,
they were assuming their voices wouldn't carry. Upset as
BJ was, she noticed that Sugar, a few yards away, was listening.

Cody said emptily, "What went wrong?"

Frieda shook her head, fighting back tears. "I don't think
we know."

"It shouldn't be that hard to find out." Matt was staring
at the grieving unicorns, seemingly unperturbed.

Valerie said, "You shouldn't have laughed like that, early
on."

Frieda was startled. "Why not?" She pictured being
blamed, out of some sort of sacrilege, for all this death.

Valerie shook her head, uncertain what to say. "You
oughta worry about looking ridiculous in front of the client."

Sugar said sharply, "She oughta worry about the patient." Valerie shut up.

The sky was turning gray. BJ turned to address the
others. "Thank you for your help. Those of you who
volunteered—" She swallowed. "I wish it had gone better."

"Those of you who are students—" She turned and
looked at them, and nearly faltered. Valerie, moist-eyed and
grimly angry, had her hands balled into fists. Matt was confused, almost frightened. Cody, his smile finally gone,
looked lost and alone. Frieda, head down, stood apart from
everyone.

BJ finished, "All I can say is, patients die. I've had a lot
of them die. I think you did fine tonight. Ask Doctor Dobbs
if you did anything wrong. Believe me, if you did, he'll tell
you." She smiled a little, hoping to get an echo back. She
did from Valerie and Cody; Matt disregarded her and Frieda
was inconsolable. "Get used to it if you can." She looked
around the field. "To be honest, I never have."

She turned to Sugar. "Do you have a bill?"

Sugar fumbled in his pockets, confused for once. "Shoot, that's right. I didn't even think to bring one."

"That's all right." She had gone to the bank earlier, to the savings account she had used for her veterinary practice. "I made an estimate today." She counted out the bills, then handed him the sheet. "I assume it's the same cost, no matter what."

Sugar, at a loss, pocketed the money and signed "PAID IN FULL" on the estimate.

"Bill me separately for the necropsy. Tell me the moment you have results. I'll be in touch if I need anything else." BJ struggled to find something more reassuring to say, finally giving up. "You'd better go home and get some sleep."

Matt pulled the truck keys from his pocket. At the jingle, like sheep following the bellwether, the students fell in line and slouched to the truck. In three minutes they were gone. Laurie nodded and walked uphill; without a word, Sugar mounted up and rode Skywalker down.

BJ stayed upright until the last of them left, then collapsed into Stefan's arms in great, racking sobs. She was still crying when the moon, bloodred again, set and was gone.

F·I·V·E

IT WAS THREE days later. Deep inside the Jefferson National Forest, several miles from Kendrick, Stefan was driving down a formerly paved road which was now crumbling into separate patches of asphalt. Above her, birds sang: cardinals, robins, and the always amazing mockingbird. The morning breeze was still blowing, but the cloudless sky and summer sun promised that today would bake.

BJ, yawning, pointed to a yellow blaze on a tree by the roadside. "That's it." Stefan pulled BJ's rental car off beside it and leapt energetically out, sprinting over to open the passenger door. His beloved fedora fell off; he bent to catch it, exposing his horns.

The passenger, a woman in her fifties, stepped out without noticing, or pretended not to notice, the horns. Probably she really hadn't noticed, BJ reflected; mathematics professors were often odd, and Harriet Winterthur hardly looked normal.

Her tangled gray hair hung past her shoulders in no particular style. Wisps of it curled up with the humidity. She wore a long, tattered brown sweater, unbuttoned as her only concession to the Virginia heat; one sweater button was missing. The sweater pockets, and the pocket of the blouse inside, blossomed with scraps of paper and stray pens. It seemed to be a process as magical as Crossroads itself; BJ discovered on the short ride from Kendrick that, although she had sat next to Harriet for only ten minutes, all BJ's pens and pencils were gone.

Now Harriet fluttered her hands over her pockets, checking for missing information, and nodded. "Thank you, Stefan." She pulled a remarkably old army surplus knapsack from under the seat and set it down after checking the web straps and closing meticulously.

Stefan ran back to the other side of the car; a drive at dawn and little sleep in two nights didn't seem to bother him. BJ had already gotten out and removed her own knapsack. She put the hat back on him. "You've got to be better with this."

He grinned. "BJ my love, there is no one but us here to see." He took the hat off again, set it on the roof of the car, and kissed BJ. She kissed back, realizing again how long it would be until she saw him, and the on-the-lips kiss evolved into an embrace the most eccentric math professor could not have ignored.

When upward of a minute later they pulled apart, gasping, BJ glanced at the edge of the road. Harriet was studiously frowning at some wild columbine, as though it had done something wrong. BJ tossed the hat in the air, Stefan leapt and caught it, and jumped back into the car. "I need to return your rental car and then go to the library. Care for yourself, my BJ; I care for you so much." And although she was likely to see him in a week or two, he had tears in his eyes. He added courteously, "Good luck, Doctor Winterthur." She nodded without looking up. The car spun gravel and was gone; BJ sighed and hoped he wouldn't have an accident.

When the dust settled, Harriet walked onto the road. "He seems very nice." She smiled at BJ and added with unsettling vagueness, "I almost called him a nice young man, but I was afraid that would insult him."

"Stefan likes compliments." She hoped she didn't look tousled and that she wasn't blushing. BJ was wishing she had checked herself in the side mirror before he drove off; Stefan was an amazing kisser. Thank God he had a normal human tongue and not a ruminant's. Thank God also for his other human attributes, and she thanked God, not for the first time, for birth control.

Harriet said, "I thought your colleague would join us."

"He said he'd be here."

She blinked at BJ. Harriet Winterthur had dark-rimmed bifocals, with thick gray eyebrows over them; it made her look melancholy and severe at the same time. "Do you think he will be late?"

BJ shook her head. "He's usually punctual, Doctor Winterthur." She looked around, troubled. "I'm amazed."

"Oh, no, my dear." The Griffin emerged from the wild rhododendrons on the opposite side of the road. He brushed stray twigs from his hide with a talon. "You are surprised. I'm amazed."

It was almost certainly a quote, but it applied to Harriet as well, who dropped her hands to her sides and dropped her jaw. "Oh, my." She peered at him for a while, then caught herself. "I don't mean to be rude; you're quite impressive."

"Thank you," he said gravely. "As are your credentials, Doctor Winterthur. And your e-mail."

BJ said tightly, "How long have you been there?"

"Actually, my stalking skills are still excellent. I arrived an hour ago and scouted for strangers." He added with mocking blandness, "I waited to appear until your ride left."

"You didn't need to," BJ said. "It was Stefan."

"I gathered." BJ blushed. "If we are all quite ready, perhaps we can begin." He gestured to the trail. BJ took the lead, the Griffin the rear.

For the first twenty yards they were on the Appalachian Trail, blazes marking their path as they descended. "Trail" seemed a misnomer; at this point it was wide enough to drive a truck on. BJ paused at a fork in the trail and pointed to another gravel road. "Left here."

They moved left along a small ravine, which was dry this time of year. The rhododendrons gave way to scrub cedar between larger trees.

"Left again." The trail led them over a large wooden bridge, much like an abandoned railway bridge, with moss growing on the beams. BJ offered a hand to Harriet, but let it drop when the older woman, holding the worn railing lightly, kept pace with BJ easily.

At the other bank, BJ pointed to a muddy but still passable road. "Left again."

Harriet followed, but coughed. When she had done it a third time, BJ said, "Is something wrong, Doctor?"

"I wanted your attention. Aren't we simply going back the way we came now? Won't we cross over the road we drove in on?"

The Griffin said softly, "Look ahead, Doctor."

She did. The morning sun on the mesa colored the bare rock in wild shades. Something like saguaro grew near its base; the cactus branches were overgrown with Spanish moss or its cousin.

She sat down and wiped her glasses. "There is a great deal of difference," she said shakily, "between understanding something as a model and seeing it in reality."

"Are you all right?" BJ asked.

Harriet, smiling to herself, answered dreamily. "When I was young, and leaving home for the first time to go to school, I walked into town to catch the bus. I had no money for breakfast." Her voice slipped from its normal cadences into a New England twang, practically a Maine Down-Easter accent. "And I thought, dear God but I'm hungry. So I walked a far ways out of town, and there were wild onions growing in the ditch. So they were breakfast. I wasn't popular on the bus or in my first day at school, but I was full." She looked at them. "I'm hungry now. I think it's what I feel when I'm going somewhere strange."

The Griffin said, "At the end of today's walk, you'll have one of the best lunches imaginable. You will also be perfectly safe the entire way, if I have anything to say about it."

Harriet glanced at the Griffin's scars, but only said, "Thank you." BJ handed her an apple from her knapsack; Harriet munched it thoughtfully, staring at the switchbacks in the road ahead.

Before long they turned right, descending what was now a pine-covered woods. Strange birds called in fluting melodies from the trees. The Griffin said, "Now I'm hungry."

The road, a stone slab surface, dropped steadily until it met a huge, roaring stream with eight- and ten-foot waterfalls split by boulders. The road crossed a bridge made of a single stone slab.

The Griffin raised a tufted eyebrow at BJ. "Sentiment?"

BJ said defensively, "I think it's beautiful. It's how I first came into Crossroads."

Harriet said suddenly, "You're doing this, aren't you? Making the road, not simply choosing it."

"Not making." BJ found herself moving her hands, trying to explain. "I shape a road, but all the road surfaces and the turns are already there. Even the worlds we go through are already there. Does that make sense?"

"Of course it does," she answered briskly. "As I said in my first study of Crossroads, it involves reality tectonics. Worlds touch, and you step between them at a point of contact. The intersection would be like a coastline, fractal and theoretically infinite no matter how short it is."

"Infinite?" The Griffin cocked his head. "Short and yet infinite, because fractal? Doctor, perhaps you'll be disappointed in Crossroads; it may not be odd enough for you."

Her smile was more relaxed. The Griffin, BJ reflected, had a strong way with women.

They turned left at the bridge. The road, familiar to BJ and somewhat so to the Griffin, wound around a cliff as the ravine narrowed; they walked in cool shadows. Harriet Winterthur clutched her sweater close.

They turned a corner and burst into sunlight, halfway up the cliff above Laetyen River. At this point the river was broad, the current swift. In the distance, they saw mountains to rival the Rockies.

Finally Harriet said huskily, "I've worked so much from reports and from field data. I never dreamed—" She broke off. "Such a loss."

BJ remembered that Harriet Winterthur's essay on Crossroads, kept in the Western Vee library, was about chaos theory and the inevitable fall of Crossroads.

She touched the older woman's arm. "We still have a

long ways to walk. There's lots more to see."

Harriet nodded.

The bluff rolled down into hills as they walked. BJ had to remind herself not to hurry. For her, this stretch of road was like a long lane home.

Harriet Winterthur strode forward determinedly, her slightly clunky but extremely sensible flats keeping pace with BJ. She kept to the side of the road, as though she expected a truck to roll through any minute.

As a result, she was badly startled when a small grayish-brown body, the long tail striped like a raccoon's, leapt up at the edge of the grass and dove. "Good God, what was that?"

The Griffin rumbled, "A fast-moving, inconsiderate snack."

"I named them dumboes." BJ was pleased to show him something new in Crossroads. "They came in on one of the first roads I made after—" She caught herself. "After I learned how to make roads." The Griffin eyed her narrowly. She continued, "That was a baby, I think. They usually travel in bunches."

" 'Bunches?' "

"Herds, coveys, flocks, packs. Nobody's made a word for it yet." BJ scanned the grassland sloping down between them and the river. "Watch this."

She leapt to the side of the road, clapping her hands.

The grass parted in front of her as thirty furry bodies sprang up, their neatly rolled ears snapping out and flat just as their strong rear legs brought them to the top of a ten-foot arc. They banked to the left in unison, catching the breeze and sailing forward a full thirty feet before landing.

The Griffin sniffed. "Damned hard to catch, if you ask me."

BJ pointed. "Look!"

The landing of the first pack had startled a second set, who soared off in unison, twenty of them silhouetted above the horizon briefly, legs and bodies stiff and straight behind them.

"I've never seen that before."

The Griffin soared forward and leapt, none too quickly,

into the tall grass. BJ was silently embarrassed at how slow he was.

The dumboes leapt back up, never even close to him, and glided slowly and surely upwind toward BJ. Halfway there they startled the first pack, which rose quickly and dropped rapidly in the breeze.

The grass rustled close by her. A talon shot up and snatched the lead dumbo. The others quickly veered off. The talon withdrew into the grass; there was a squeak and a crunch.

The Griffin emerged, wiping his beak. "Professor Protera is right; the bank shots are truly more satisfying."

"Wouldn't it have been more sporting to fly straight after them?"

The Griffin said patronizingly, "My dear, it's called 'hunting,' not 'work.' By the way, did you notice how many of them are very young?"

BJ hadn't. She looked around in the grass, much of which was cut off and stubbly. "I can't see them now. . . . I wonder if they're what's been eating the grass here."

"If they are, I volunteer to help thin the herd; they're quite delicious."

Harriet frowned. BJ had already noticed that when Harriet Winterthur thought, she frowned, as though ideas were usually unpleasant. "Don't you know, you're just making a faster breed of dumbo."

The Griffin cocked his head. "Natural selection?"

"Yes, controlling behavior. They fly by rule: if you sense something disturbing, fly. If another dumbo flies, follow him. If the place you land isn't safe, fly again."

The Griffin remarked, "It sounds like the behavior currently emptying America's cities."

"I hope you don't think humans are smarter than dumboes in that regard," she said impatiently. "But my point is, you catch only the ones who fly back to their point of origin. The farther away from that direction they fly, the safer they are. In a very few generations, they'll be harder to catch."

"Then I or my species will discover a new trick."

Harriet said with gloomy satisfaction, "If you all don't starve first."

BJ was glad this was not a long cross-country trip.

It was made still shorter as they turned a corner, midway on the bluffs over Laetyen River, high above the broad waters. BJ stared blankly at the battered rear of the truck for a full ten seconds before realizing it was hers.

On the steering wheel was a note: "It's gassed up, and I've started it every week or so. The keys are in the ignition—Fiona."

"Excuse me," Harriet said, reading unashamedly over BJ's shoulder. "Is that from Fiona Bannon? Is she here?"

"Oh, yes." BJ frowned at the note.

"Imagine that. She found a way. She asked me to be her advisor, but I refused. Her project was too broad, had no rigor, and was unlikely to obtain results."

"She obtained some," BJ said.

The Griffin regarded BJ with amusement. "Which do you find more annoying—that she doesn't do what you expect, or that for once you've met someone as smart as you?"

BJ shook her head. "She's very smart. It's just"—she struggled for justification, knowing that both of the Griffin's statements were accurate—"I wish I were sure what Fiona would do next."

"That's easy enough." He hid his beak behind a talon, smiling into it. "She'll look to see if she's astonished and annoyed you."

Which was true, BJ reflected. The truck started on the first turn of the key; they drove off, leaving a small steamy cloud from the moisture in the tailpipe.

The drive made BJ nostalgic. In all of her time in Crossroads, here was the one road which had remained constant: the winding stretch down from the bluffs, across valleys and finally into the rounded hills before the plain dominated by a multiple-road crossing and a single, stone-ringed hill topped by a building and two ponds.

There was a lane through the hill. Once inside it, they could see the familiar ring of earth and stone, and the mill-race running from the upper pond to the inn.

No one came out to greet them. BJ opened the outer door cautiously, freezing when she heard a sudden click.

From the darkness came a rustle, then a ponderously careful voice, stress bringing back to it just a trace of a Polish accent. "Welcome to the rebuilt Stein's. We will make every effort to serve you as in the past, and only ask that you follow the same rules as in the past:

"It is not polite to ridicule another's race, world, species, or unique body parts—"

BJ heard Stein's voice plod through the familiar rules: no cursing, talking species only, gambling permitted but no cheating, recreational fighting only. When BJ had first come here, a disreputable and venal parrot had recited those rules.

The perch was still there; tied to it was a boom box. A rod-and-lever arrangement, connected by a string to the outer door, had pushed the PLAY button down.

Stein finished, "And now the hard part. On this box is a button marked with a square, to stop the tape, and another with double arrows pointing right, to rewind. Please press the square, then the double arrows, so that the next patron may hear this message. Thank you."

BJ reached her hand out, smiling as she heard a more normal voice say in the distance, "Is that all, Fiona? Because I swear, I'd rather hang this thing on the spit than talk into it again—"

She stopped the tape and rewound it. A voice from beyond the short hall said formally, "Thanks for doing that. Please, come in."

"You still don't show yourself to strange guests?" the Griffin said calmly. "My, how uncivil."

"You want better manners, maybe you should help me get a better class of guests. More of them, anyway."

If they had been invaders, slits in the hallway wall would have opened, and weapons would have come through. Instead, the inner door opened.

BJ all but ran forward and hugged him. Stein, as always, did not appear to have a weapon; he wrapped both arms around her briefly, then stepped back. "Let me look at you," he said, but he was looking at Harriet Winterthur.

The Griffin made quick introductions. "Doctor Winterthur, this is Stein, the proprietor here. The young woman peering mistrustfully from beside the fireplace is Fiona Bannon—"

"We've met," Fiona said sharply, but came forward. "Glad you found the truck. Did BJ tell you that I learned to work magic here?"

"I had no idea."

Fiona smirked. "I've discovered a little more order in a supposedly chaotic universe."

"Don't say that so fliply, Fiona. I've devoted this part of my life to chaos. Chaos is formulaic. I suspect that magic is mostly chaotic."

BJ said, "Actually, I'll bet that magic is formulaic. It's life that's chaotic. My life, anyway."

Fiona said stubbornly, "It's not an organized body of knowledge—yet. But I did learn some formulas." She corrected herself. "Formulae."

Harriet looked at her closely for the first time. "I learned the formulae when I was very young," Harriet said softly. "In any number of fairy tales. When magic is formulaic, its equations balance; there is no learning without a cost. Did you learn that?"

Fiona turned away. The left side of her face had healed quickly in Crossroads, but it had scarred. "Eventually." She went back to the fireplace and checked the cauldrons simmering there.

BJ was reminded of the dinner the previous Sunday. This meal, however, was more businesslike, even without talk of business; they ate quickly and didn't linger over food. Possibly this was because Stein and Fiona paced the courses, and were accustomed to innkeeping.

With a flourish, Stein set a spring-cooled bottle of chardonnay in front of Harriet Winterthur. "Since it's your first visit, why not?" The Griffin, with a quick look at the size of the bottle, requested water "since it was a work day." BJ drank chilled goat's milk, sweet and whole and practically a meal in itself.

The salad, a simple mix of tomato and lettuce with a wine and oil dressing, included green onions. Harriet Winterthur smiled to the Griffin and BJ; Stein looked curious, but didn't ask. The honey bread was as good as BJ remembered, steaming from the oven. She bit into it and looked in surprise at Stein.

"Like the dill? Fiona thought of that." He sighed. "Every time I let someone into this place, they tell me they know more about cooking than I do."

Fiona grinned, bringing in a stack of wooden bowls. She was limping less than BJ had expected; Crossroads' healing powers had done her well.

The soup course was a milk chowder, made from freshwater clams. BJ had been braced for a gritty texture, but it tasted clean and wonderful. "You rinse the clams for a couple hours. They clean the mud out of themselves." He frowned. "I wish we could get saltwater fish again. We need more trade." He looked sideways at BJ. "No roads, no trade."

The main course came from the cauldrons too: a vegetable and mutton stew with a thick, salty gravy. Stein cut them each a half of a small, circular, thick-crusted bread loaf and ladled a serving of stew into the halves. BJ couldn't remember having loved stew so well. She lifted her spoon and looked curiously at a tiny, potato-shaped orange vegetable.

Stein caught her. "Never seen it before? They grow here, if you know where to look."

He beamed. "Fiona has a garden. I asked her to work it for me, while she was here. We need more trade; we need the garden until then."

Fiona said, "It was nothing. Nothing but backbreaking." She shrugged, but you could see she was proud. "The onions did well, and the potatoes, I never expected so much of them. Those potato-shaped things that taste like carrots? You can't keep them from growing. I'll walk you through it later, if you want. You wouldn't believe the weeds, though: thistles, dandelion, downlander—that's a parachute seed like milkweed, but takes over a garden like you wouldn't believe." She kneaded her side automatically. "Why can't I find anything magical that works against weeds?"

Harriet frowned, but said nothing.

* * *

At the end of the meal, Stein looked around. "So. You want to talk about what's bothering you? You didn't just come all the way here for the best meal around."

"We need to bring species back, any of them that are birthing, more quickly than we thought," BJ began, but Harriet interrupted.

"We have a larger problem," she said.

The Griffin looked indignant. Stein shushed him with a slight hand wave and said, "Let the professor speak." Fiona grinned wickedly.

"Thank you." Harriet smiled at Stein, then frowned and went on. "There is a new animal here, the dumbo—"

"Those things." Stein shook his head in disgust. "They're shy for the first week or so, now, I don't know, they're all over. Cute, but a pest."

"A few are cute, yes. More are a pest. Many more are a crisis." She leaned forward. "Let's assume, for the moment, that about sixty percent of the female dumboes were pregnant when you imported them." She looked around the inn earnestly. "After all, you know that quite a few were born, and if they're cyclical at all, they get pregnant synchronously."

BJ thought this was pretty loose for a species they knew nothing about. "Let's say fifty percent."

Fiona broke in. "Coin-toss probabilities? Sure, why not?" She took a pencil and paper from her pocket and scribbled quickly. "Why didn't I bring a solar calculator in with me? We'll need it before we're done."

BJ said, "Can't you do it in your head?"

Fiona frowned, "Not and be certain. Anyway. Okay, that means one-quarter of the two hundred animals you brought in reproduced—fifty of them. And how large are the litters? BJ?"

She had knelt, wondering, and held a new litter in the grass. The newborns, as pink and blind as other marsupials, struggled in her palm, each barely the size of a teaspoon. "Eight to a litter."

"And do dumbos have eight nipples?"

BJ shook her head. "Doesn't apply. They're marsupials with no nipples; they leak milk, like the other monotremes do, and the youngsters in the pouch do their best."

" 'Their best,' " Harriet Winterthur repeated hollowly. "Tell me: in a world where they have an adequate food supply for the mothers, no predators, and no congenital defects or viral illnesses at all, what is the mortality rate for newborns?"

BJ was stunned. She hadn't thought in those terms.

Finally she said, "Fairly low."

Fiona held her pencil in place. "I'd like a figure."

BJ, irritated, said, "Well, you won't get one. If you need something to guess with, say that it's twenty-five percent." A chilled part of her brain was admitting that was probably excessive.

"Okay. Leaving six alive from the births. Which means"—Fiona struggled with the pencil briefly, crossing out numbers as she added and multiplied—"there are three hundred new dumboes, for a total of more or less five hundred. In one month, they've increased by two and a half times." She set the pencil down. "And we're not sure that they only have one litter a year."

Math was one of the few subjects BJ had found a struggle. "So, if they have two litters a year—"

"—And the same number get pregnant, and the same number survive, that's—hang on, I hate pencils—that's seven hundred and fifty newborns, and twelve hundred fifty total dumboes." Fiona licked the pencil end and circled the total. "In one year. These are fake figures, but you get the point."

Harriet said, "We need a predator. We need it quickly."

BJ swung toward Stein, who nodded unhappily. "Young lady, we will need to find the most hostile species comfortable in Crossroads and invite them to their new home." He added, "You don't like bringing in a predator, do you?"

"I didn't agree to this so that I could kill animals."

"Strange," the Griffin murmured. "I agreed to my job because someone ought to kill them."

Harriet said, "They must have had predators in their world."

"A terrible one. A pack hunter, faster than a fox, all sharp teeth and grasping front paws. The moment after I opened the road, the dumboes flew onto it to get away." BJ had stepped into the road and shouted to prevent the predator from following.

"Could you bring that predator in?"

BJ said dubiously, "I don't think it would follow me. Anyway, it seems awfully savage."

The Griffin regarded a talon nonchalantly. "Good predators are."

"And highly evolved animals usually have predators. Most of the dumboes' features evolved to help them escape." Harriet ticked them off on her fingers. "Concealment in the grass. Flight. An instinctive flight behavior, based on sensing a potential predator. Probably enhanced senses to alert them to the presence of a predator."

Fiona asked, "Do you think they have electroreceptors?"

"What?"

"The platypus does. The spiny anteater does. It's how some marsupials sense prey. I'd love to find out if they did." Fiona looked wistful. "If I could find a way to give them electric shocks—"

"You'd do it, wouldn't you?" BJ said. There was an awkward silence.

"Back to the problem at hand," Harriet said. "Didn't Crossroads ever have an efficient predator?" She stressed "efficient" and looked at the Griffin over her glasses. He bristled, but said nothing.

"We had the Great—think of them as rocs," Stein explained, looking thoughtful. "They're the most efficient predator I've ever seen, believe me, but only for large animals. Anyway, they're gone."

"There are some foxes, I think," BJ said. But they aren't pack hunters, and I bet they'd have trouble with dumboes." She was having a lot of trouble with Harriet Winterthur's view of the world.

"Then we genuinely need an outside predator." She sighed. "That's too bad. Planning a species is nearly futile; nature relies on chaos. Even humans, viewed as a species, are chaotic."

BJ said hopefully, in a last-ditch defense, "But everything

humans do is for order.'' She waved an arm vaguely. ''Look at alphabetical order.''

''Alphabetical order,'' Harriet said firmly, ''was random at first.''

Which wasn't directly to the point, but thereafter BJ gave up on objecting.

Stein said, ''What would the ideal predator be like, Doctor?''

''Predators should be unintelligent and should react by pattern. They can hunt as individuals, but they should react predictably as a species. A single individual is simply not a measurable predator.''

''Doctor,'' the Griffin said dryly, ''I'm hurt.''

Harriet met his gaze, but finally dropped hers. ''Granted, some individuals are exceptional.''

''What you need,'' Fiona said determinedly, ''is a cryptozoologist.''

The term hung in the air. Finally the Griffin said, ''Forgive me, but that sounds like an embarrassing misuse of Greek and Latin.''

''A cryptozoologist studies unrecognized species, largely by report, and tries to determine their existence.''

Stein said finally, ''And this is a field of science?''

Fiona frowned. ''It doesn't depend on the actual existence of the thing studied.''

''I understand completely.'' The Griffin studied his talons. ''I myself am a cryptopacifist.''

Fiona stood, wavering slightly. ''Face it. You're all being cryptoecologists.'' She walked to the door of her room and turned around. ''Sorry to excuse myself. I have to nap, these days. Good-night.'' She grinned suddenly. ''Okay, good kryptonite.''

When her door closed, BJ said quietly, ''The garden was a bright idea.''

Stein shrugged. ''She needed the sunlight, and she needed quiet work that made her feel better. All right, so I also could use the vegetables.''

Harriet said wonderingly, ''What in God's name happened to her?''

''Quite a bit,'' Stein said. ''I wish you'd been her advisor;

she went looking for another one, and found her. Listen, professor, I'm confused; what made you so sure the dumboes were the greatest threat to Crossroads?''

If she noticed how she was turned away from asking about Fiona, she didn't show it. ''There was a mathematical paper,'' she began carefully, ''by a man named Yorke. It was entitled 'Period Three Implies Chaos,' and it can be applied to what happens when a species population reaches a certain level.''

''And what was that?''

''It becomes predictably unpredictable.'' Harriet looked at their faces and said sharply, ''I know that chaos sounds unpredictable to you, but it makes a great deal of sense to people who study it. Remember that chaos is predictable without being precise; even if a mathematician can no longer predict what will happen after a certain point, he will be able to tell you at what point it became unpredictable.'' She added frankly, ''And in real-life terms, we all get either religious or scared about those points.''

Stein tapped his fingertips together. ''One of the things we didn't talk about in front of Fiona. If you open the roads to find predators, won't they be open to invaders?'' He looked around at them. ''Face facts; there aren't enough of us to defend our table, let alone the country.''

BJ shook her head. ''The roads are even crookeder this time, harder to follow. Someone would have to let an army in.''

Stein closed his eyes. ''Oh, good. That's never happened.''

''Excuse me.'' Harriet Winterthur addressed only Stein. ''I'm afraid I don't know what you're talking about. Has Crossroads ever been invaded?''

BJ, startled, opened her mouth. Stein spoke first. ''Actually, Doctor, it gets invaded a lot. There were two big ones. The first was the *milites*—the Romans. They ran the country until they marched out.''

''By accident?''

Stein raised an eyebrow. ''They had an accident, yes. Later, a woman named Morgan built an army and came in, four times.'' Stein added bitterly, ''We didn't stop her.''

"Couldn't," the Griffin corrected almost gently. "Everything that could be done to stop her was done."

"Couldn't, didn't, does it matter? The first time, when she didn't have the book, she used wolves to get in."

Harriet blinked. "Trained wolves?"

Stein sighed. "I wish I could just say yes. It's so much easier than saying 'werewolves.' "

"The Wyr," BJ broke in. "First she addicted them to morphine—it was easy; they had no idea what she was doing to them. Then she forced them to track their way into Crossroads and to fight for her."

Harriet surprised BJ by scowling and turning red. "And I suppose she kept them at a bare maintenance level of morphine, to control them." She shivered. "Poor things! Still, I shouldn't wonder they were nasty."

"The Wyr might not be so bad—"

BJ, annoyed, said, "They aren't. I know the Wyr better than any of you. I've fought with them, I've healed them—I've kept one as a pet. Well, a friend."

"A child," the Griffin said quietly. "I grieve to remind you."

BJ, her eyes shut tight, remembered a wolf cub guarding her jealously, and remembered putting a badly wounded wolf cub to death. "Thanks. I grieve to be reminded." She took a shuddering breath. "And the Wyr are not predators. They're probably too human—bad word. They're too sentient to serve as a predator to thin a species. Still, I could ask Gredya for advice."

"Gredya?" Harriet was sitting with her mouth slightly open, absorbing too much information at once.

"One of the Wyr. She did fight for Morgan, but she became my friend later." She added, with a sudden chill, "And she's not in Crossroads, and she's pregnant."

"Ah. Is that a problem?"

"It was for the unicorns. We don't know why." The necropsy on the unicorn kidling had revealed nothing. Sugar sent frozen tissue samples by Federal Express to Doctor Lucille Boudreau, a Duke researcher in human medicine who occasionally worked at Western Vee and who had become involved with Crossroads. She sent back some very inter-

esting but otherwise useless pictures produced by an elec-
tron microscope and a note regretting that they had no way
of taking similar pictures inside Crossroads. She also volunteered to return to Western Vee.

"But aren't unicorns a blend of horse and goat?" Harriet
tapped her fingertips together, as Stein was doing. BJ carefully avoided smiling. "I suspect that birth crises will be
restricted to those animals who are chimerae."

The Griffin winced; BJ avoided eye contact with him.
Stein, with visible effort, did not react.

Harriet, assuming they had misunderstood her, added, "A
blend of two species in one body." She added as a polite
afterthought to the Griffin, "Like yourself. Other species, of
course, would have no trouble."

The Griffin said, "If you're very, very sure of that, I'm
happy to put any species at risk you like. So long as you
explain it to them later."

BJ said only, to the Griffin, "Remind me. We should talk
later."

Harriet frowned. "But how many species have left Crossroads?"

They gaped at her. "All of them we could coax out,"
Stein said finally. "The Wyr, the unicorns, the Hippoi—
they're centaurs—and The Ones Who Die, those are half-
deer, half-human."

She shook her head. "I can't imagine that."

BJ smiled. "Obviously you never taught at USF. A couple of them are alumni."

The Griffin clicked his beak several times, genuinely
alarmed. "This is urgent."

Stein looked down at the Griffin's talons, which were
tapping on and denting the wood floor. "Don't do that."
The Griffin stopped immediately. "All right, here's what
we'll do. BJ, a lot of this falls on you; like I said, I don't
know animals."

BJ nodded. "I'm also the only one who can make
Strangeways."

Stein looked sharply at Harriet, who smiled back, unsurprised. She said to BJ, "Can't you just walk out and get
these other species?"

"It's not that simple." BJ suddenly realized how hard it was to explain building Strangeways and knowing worlds. "Like you said, I can find the meeting points of worlds. I won't know who's in that world, unless I've been there before."

"So what's the problem?" Stein leaned forward. "You can make roads to every world there is, and you know where they—ah."

BJ finished, "When those species left, I went with some of them on the roads to other worlds, not all of them. I'll have to search for some."

Stein said heavily, "And there's no map."

"All the old Strangeways were destroyed, and anyway we destroyed all the old copies of *The Book of Strangeways*."

"Believe me," Stein said to Harriet, "it was necessary. It was a brilliant idea, at the time." He didn't mention that it was BJ's idea. "So: first you'll figure out which animals you know to get, then you'll try to remember the old roads they left on, then you'll work on the animals and worlds you're not sure about."

The Griffin said suddenly, "One of the Wyr." They turned to him. "It's been months, but they can scent their way from world to world if there's a used road."

Stein looked thoughtful. "There may not be much scent clinging to any world, but maybe it would work. BJ, would your friend Gredya help, if you got her back here first?"

"She might."

"That's where you start, then."

BJ said thoughtfully, "If I can, I'll do it by gestation period—shortest first." She turned to the Griffin. "Afterward we'll need the vet rotation to come in."

He snorted. "They'll feel like obstetricians and pediatricians."

"I hope they don't feel like teratologists; I don't know how many freaks and birth defects there'll be."

The others were quiet for a moment.

Suddenly Stein shifted back from command to being an innkeeper. "Enough tough decisions, eh? Now, Professor, we have to find a room where you can stay. Not so hard in an empty inn.''

She looked around. ''A lovely inn. I seldom take the time for a place like this . . . How nice to have the excuse.''

''We'll have to make sure your stay is pleasant, then.'' He bowed again, deftly picking up her bag before she could. ''Let's go look for your room—one with cross-ventilation, I think.''

BJ stood. ''I need to go home to my cottage. I'll leave the truck for you, Doctor, in case you need it.''

She looked genuinely alarmed. ''Dear God, I haven't driven a clutch vehicle in years.''

''Fiona can help you.'' BJ looked out one of the small windows of the inn and smiled. ''At least there won't be much traffic.''

The Griffin discreetly left with her. ''I need the exercise.'' BJ was glad of the company, and knew that he was doing it to see that her cottage was safe. At his insistence she slung her knapsack around his neck. They walked down the road together, and BJ felt as though he were carrying her books home from school.

He turned his head to watch her. ''What do you think of Harriet Winterthur?''

BJ considered. ''Very smart. Educated. She seems a little wistful.''

''I thought so too. I worry about misreading people.''

BJ said, ''You didn't misread Stein.''

The Griffin stopped in his tracks. ''Oh, dear. Was I so obvious?''

''It was obvious that Stein liked her. I don't think either of them realizes that you had a second motive in bringing her into Crossroads.''

''Ah.'' He resumed walking. ''Stein is a valued friend; I'd rather not offend him.''

''You couldn't.'' BJ added casually, ''I hope you'll be around to walk her home when she leaves. I may be traveling.''

''I hadn't thought of that yet. I suppose I'd better stay a few days—I don't believe it. You've become subtle too.''

''Not subtle enough,'' she said frankly, ''and I'm not doing it for your romantic life.'' Quite the opposite, she thought. ''I want you to heal faster.''

The Griffin sighed. ''If I stay for a few days, then return for a few and so forth, will that satisfy you?''

''If it's the best I can do.'' BJ was betting that the Griffin would quickly resume his duties in Crossroads, and that they would keep him here. She tried not to think of Laurie.

''Very well. But give me a copy of *The Book of Strangeways* for the Western Vee library. Also, you should begin processing your notes to *Lao's Guide*, so that if something happens to you, someone else may use them.''

It wasn't a cheery thought, but BJ could see its merit. ''By the way, what can we do about the chimerae?''

The Griffin looked away from her. ''Nothing. I don't know where they went, and my species—the males of my species, those who look like me—left with them. They flew; there was no road. If they haven't the sense to return for birth, there is nothing to be done.'' He added bleakly, ''And they are due immediately, if they have not already birthed.''

''Did they always give birth here before?'' BJ's stomach was plummeting. ''And I helped drive them away. Griffin, I'm so sorry.''

The Griffin said sharply, ''You did it to save Crossroads, and it worked. I would have done the same.'' He slumped, for once looking tired. ''I can't even follow to find them. Disreputable as chimerae are, it would have been nice to have a child . . .''

They walked in silence the rest of the way to BJ's cottage, where the Griffin bowed and left. BJ saw him spread his wings carefully and glide slowly downhill in noiseless flight.

BJ opened her unlocked cottage door. The bed was the same. The exam section, with its stainless steel table and its small but precious portable X-ray machine was the same. She would need to start up the generator and see if it was in shape.

Her bookcase was the same, her pantry the same. She smiled at the claw marks on the pantry door, three feet off the ground; she would miss Daphni. She stepped outside and hung her bedding on a frame near the springhouse, to air out.

"I have a medical emergency," a sharp voice said behind her.

BJ spun around. For a second she thought the Griffin had returned, then realized that this was a silver griffin, larger and older. They had met before, not amicably.

She was still wearing her backpack; in it she had a weapon, a catchlet. She had used it in swordplay before. Against a griffin she might last all of fifteen seconds with it.

She managed to say, "Are you hurt?"

"The emergency," the Silver said brusquely, "involves obstetrics. Please put together the supplies you might need."

"How long do I have to plan?"

He gestured with a single sharp claw toward the cottage door. "Go. Now."

BJ ran in, considering her options. The Silver was at the only door, and could chase her down if she tried to escape out a back window. Griffins were by nature ruthless, even her friend; a failed escape would be fatal.

BJ grabbed some cloth, some Betadine, some bandages, a surgical pack, and a spare thermometer. She also packed her much-thumbed copy of *Lao's Guide*, as well as her own notes. She couldn't think of anything else that wasn't already in the backpack, and she had very little time.

She ran out the door. "I'm ready." She slipped the backpack on her shoulders, looking around.

The folding wings whistled overhead; she felt talons grip her shoulders before she understood. Before she could struggle, the cottage was shrinking below her.

S·I·X

"TRY TO KEEP still," the Silver said brusquely, or was he gasping? "This is a long flight, and it will be difficult."

"I could ride between your wings."

"I think not." He rose into the air suddenly on a gust of wind, tossing her body up and catching her firmly by the rib cage. BJ gasped. In the pain she barely noticed as their speed increased.

When she could talk again, she said reproachfully, "Tomorrow I'll be bruised."

"I think not," the Silver repeated, and BJ froze.

The landscape below her shrank until she saw Stein's and her cottage, the Laetyen River, and Ribbon Falls at once. She shut her watering eyes as the breeze around her grew suddenly cold, and the Silver grunted as the wind shifted. When she reopened her eyes, she looked down quickly; Crossroads was gone.

She watched the ragged landscape crawl below her. There was a pair of potholes each a quarter mile across, carved by some gigantic river current. A tiny trickle spilled into a mile-long circular spill pool from some monstrous waterfall. The Silver dove toward it; as they approached, BJ realized that the "trickle" was hundreds of feet high.

The plain above the falls was gouged into immense channels, canyons, and crevasses, as though a planner had laid out the course of the world's greatest river and then lost interest before adding the water. BJ thought how much Estevan Protera would enjoy this view, and wished bitterly and selfishly that it had been he instead.

They flew well up the channel; the setting sun reddened the channel walls and flashed silver ahead off the tiny remains of a lake. The hills to all sides bore ripple marks, high above where BJ and the Silver flew, testimony to earlier water levels. They banked to one side of a gravel island over three hundred feet high; the fading sunset turned the western end to violet and left the upstream eastern end in shadow. They were low enough that they no longer saw the lake. Instead they saw, half-torn and melted, a glacier wall. They reached it and flew alongside; BJ saw slowly melting chunks, easily the size of a two-story house, fallen from the wall above them.

"In winter," the Silver intoned, "the flowing ice forms a natural dam across the valley, and the river backs up behind it beyond the horizon, in a bowl valley nearly as broad as Crossroads itself.

"Every spring, the runoff from the mountains adds to the pressure on the ice, which gradually weakens. Finally the water melts a tiny channel through the dam. In hours, the channel is larger, then the size of a river, then the size of a river in flood. And suddenly the ice is gone, and the entire lake drains from here to the western coast in a matter of three days. Below us it carves out the Scarlands, the largest river bed on any world I have ever known."

"And above it," he said bitterly and hopelessly, "in the former impoundment lake, a former island that no one but a fool would have deemed permanently safe, is a mere mountain again, undefended from the approach of small prey."

The moon, earth's moon and no longer full, had risen ahead of them. They flew lower, and BJ saw the fresh scars and gashes in the stone hills to either side. Above them were ripple marks; an entire lake had stood here only a few months before.

The Silver was headed for a lone hill in the center of the valley. Firelight gleamed from its multiple peaks. From time to time the light was blocked by moving figures, tiny and frantic. They dashed around a pile of twigs.

Perspective snapped in; the hill was a mountain, many of the twigs logs. The tiny figures were griffins and chimerae.

The nest was broad and clumsy, a rookery for deranged rooks. Twigs mingled with trees, thatch, and mud. It covered most of the mountaintop.

Scattered through it were honking, excited chimerae; surrounding them were concerned griffins.

The promontories of the island had huge bonfires on them, the billows of smoke making a haze of the moon. With their talons, the griffins threw branches and logs on, flapping their wings to fan the fires. Sparks trailed backward from the fires like comet tails, and the flames leapt seven and eight feet in the air, throwing light below.

When the Silver settled in place, a chorus of loud squeals rose as rats scattered in every direction. BJ stepped forward, rubbing her shoulders, and looked quickly at her footing. The twigs were slippery—

The twigs were crawling. There were foot-long millipedes, speedy leeches, huge bounding fleas, and ticks. Some of the ticks, gorged and slow, were the size of golf balls.

BJ said dazedly, "Will these be live births or eggs?"

The Silver gestured in disgust at the broad nest. As BJ's eyes adjusted to the flickering light, she swallowed and nearly choked.

The griffins circled the wood, apparently unwilling to step on it until it was vital. Ahead of them were chimerae, waving their wings excitedly and poking at huge eggs, larger than ostrich eggs, half-buried in the nest. The air smelled of damp and rotting wood. The tree limbs were stained with liquids and unidentified solids. BJ squinted, uneasily aware that some of the solids were crawling.

She turned to the Silver. "There may be complications."

He said coldly, "I would never have come for you if there weren't."

He was panting excessively, his chest heaving and his beak open. BJ realized that he had flown to the nest, back to Crossroads, and back to the nest in one day. "Are you all right? Do you need help?"

He turned away from her. "I didn't bring you for me. Help our young."

The air was filled with noise: confused honking from the chimerae, a babble of conversation from the griffins—

And something else. BJ strained to hear it: a muffled, inarticulate cry coming from somewhere near her.

She peered ahead, squinting through the moonlight and the firelight. One of the eggs was rocking back and forth.

She stepped carefully to it, watching her footing on the branches. A sudden drop between the logs might mean a twisted ankle or worse. She knelt and listened at the first shell. She picked it up in her hands, dusting off the stray feathers, fur, and muck. Finally, appalled, she called out to the watching griffins:

"The shells are too thick. The young can't break out."

She rapped sharply on the shell with her penlight. Several of the griffins gasped; a Gold said in absolute outrage, "Well, then," and flew forward, talons spread. BJ ignored him.

Before the Gold had settled in, BJ was peeling back pieces of shell, pushing on a tough, remarkably plastic and resistant membrane attached. Suddenly the membrane tore and a small beak appeared.

BJ ripped the rest of the shell away frantically. "Something similar happened in my world," she said, peeling fragments. "Well, the reverse, really. The bald eagles were unable to reproduce. It was a by-product of DDT in their food; their shells were too thin. Something has happened here; they're too thick."

Like a magician finishing a trick, she plunged her hand into the egg and pulled out a damp, gasping, confused griffin chick. Its wings were downy and useless, its fur fluffy and protective. Its eyes were shut tight, and it squalled with terror and hunger.

BJ set the chick on its hindquarters and watched, appalled, as the smeared twigs and sticks beneath it seemed to come alive. The parasites, alerted by the motion, scurried to the spot.

Something with a millipede body and pincer head skittered up the chick's leg, coiled in a tight spiral around its own head while holding on with its legs on one side, and began burying its head. The griffin chick squeaked.

BJ, grimacing, uncoiled the struggling millipede and pulled its head free. Hardened as veterinarians get, she felt queasy touching it and angry about the red weal in the chick's side. She squished the millipede's head against a log; she had no compunctions about killing it.

She lifted the chick up and held it; warm-blooded infants want other warm bodies. There was no place to set it—

A desperate voice behind her said, "Is he all right?"

Of course it was a "he"; the voice was the Gold, nearly grazing her shoulder as he lunged forward and looked the chick over intently.

The griffin chick suddenly coughed. BJ wiped the albumen from his fur and feathers. She turned to pass it to the Gold. "Take him. Keep him off the ground. Can you put him between your wings till you find a clean place?"

"Of course." The Gold rocked back on his hind legs and took the chick tenderly, raising him until they were almost beak to beak. "Your name is—" The Gold glanced quickly at BJ and, turning his head nearly all the way around, lowered his voice, whispering directly in the chick's ear hole. He stroked its head with one of his talons, sharp spurs carefully averted.

"Over here," a voice said sharply. "And be quick."

BJ stood, looking at the Bronze who had spoken and at the rocking egg beside him. In a semicircle around her, griffins stared intently, every movement of their beaks and eyes filled with urgency. Beyond them, the chimerae belched flame, flapped wings, called hopefully to her.

BJ cleared her throat. "I want your attention."

The griffins swung attentively to her, and even some of the chimerae turned interestedly.

She swallowed and said firmly, "I hope you saw that. Tap the shell open; when the young emerge, pat their backs firmly and carefully to expel fluid, and clear the beak and the air passageway—" She looked at the razor-sharp, steel-hard talons around her and added, "carefully and gently.

That should be enough.'' She turned back to the nest.

She lifted a motionless egg and said brightly to the nearest chimera, ''Hello. Hi, honey. How are you? Come on, speak.''

The chimera obligingly belched noxious gas and flame. BJ, turning the egg in front of it, braced herself and cracked the egg in half against a log.

The griffins gasped. BJ, sure of herself but half-afraid to look, stirred the egg contents; there was no chick, no embryo.

''Get the chimerae to belch and candle the eggs in front of the flame. If you see a viable infant inside, break the top of the egg with your beak. Be certain to puncture the sac inside the egg.''

One of the chimerae honked happily. BJ, eyes stinging with the sulfur, waited for the noise to die down and went on. ''If the chick doesn't breathe at first, put your ear to his chest and listen for a heartbeat; feel for breathing motion. If you can, breathe into his lungs to start them—frankly, I'm not sure how you can create a seal with beaks; try engulfing the entire head in your beaks. If that doesn't work, call me over before giving up. I have syringes with me; I'll resuscitate them or give them a shot of Dopram.'' She looked at the semicircle of grim faces. ''Bring the stillbirths to me; I'll try everything I can think of.''

Several of the births were easy, and one of the stillbirths actually lived. A Copper ran up, the tiny body clutched in its beak without breaking the skin. BJ had the chick cradled in one arm almost before the Copper let go, feeling for breathing as she pulled out a syringe with her free hand and pulled the needle cap off in her teeth. She jabbed the chick, waiting to see if the stimulant did any good, staring nearly as intently as the griffin in front of her.

When the chick thrashed and squawked, she actually laughed, rubbing its downy head before handing off the chick to its father. She walked on to her sixth egg of the night, head high, confident.

BJ was stunned when she tapped the shell open after hearing scratching and saw a kitten head emerge, one paw preceding it onto the shell edge.

She rolled a sheet of paper into a tight tube, wedged the infant chimera's mouth open with a twig, and blew down the airway.

A noxious belch rolled back. BJ turned her head, eyes watering, and passed the now-struggling chimera to its mother. She noted, without surprise, that the kitten was male.

The next egg was barely open when she realized she was too late. Sometimes now she knew by looking at a patient whether it was going to live or not; it was the intuition that went with training. She cleared his airway, forced air into him, gave him a shot of Dopram, waited. When she poked him, his reflexes were slow; his chest barely moved.

"His haw is too far down," someone murmured. BJ had heard the term in Virginia; she looked at the eyes, carefully lifting the lowered third eyelid. The chick's eyes didn't focus, but she could not be sure that was abnormal. She touched the lid; it didn't blink.

She brought the stethoscope up then, but she knew. The body stiffened in her arms before she stopped listening.

She turned, holding the tiny body. It was only an illusion, but it seemed to weigh more, as though its spirit had lifted it until now.

She passed it to the waiting griffin and saw that it was the Silver. "I'm very sorry."

"As am I." He took the body tenderly; it seemed to rise out of her hands. "Thank you," he said in a husky, deeply sad voice. "I will hold him in love's own rough hands and bear him someplace gentler."

He moved awkwardly for once, shuffling two-legged with his burden in his talons.

BJ followed, hating herself but needing to ask. "What will happen to the baby chimerae from here?" She immediately wished she had said "infants."

"The chimerae kittens will be raised by their mothers, who will quickly transform into a second set of fathers." Arrogance crept into his voice. "The griffins are ours." He regarded his burden. "Even this little one." His arrogance faded. "Why does he seem worth more to me, dead, than those others do alive?"

"Love does that," BJ said.

*   *   *

After twenty births, two-thirds of which were alive, BJ walked tentatively to the Silver, one of the griffins who weren't busy with offspring. The other childless griffins were feeding the fires and checking on their dead sons; the Silver gave sharp, quiet orders and otherwise stayed by his son's body. BJ said, "I need to ask a question."

"I don't expect impertinent questions."

BJ answered sharply, "This one's pertinent. Are all these hatchlings supposed to be male?"

After a short pause, the Silver said tiredly, "You're right, it's pertinent. Yes they are. The chimerae shift sex when they come into season." He glared. "Would you care to make any comments about this?"

BJ was tired, too. "I would." She gestured at the nest. "I've seen two cases of undescended testicles on griffin chicks, a few cases of testicles missing entirely on chimera kittens, and a range of deformities on both. On earth it's sometimes associated with estrogen exposure in the environment; nobody knows too much about it yet. Here—" She stared around at the desolate landscape. "It could be from mineral runoff, could be from the change in environment. Could be anything. I have no idea whether or not it's curable."

"Is that all?" the Silver said, his voice nearly a whisper.

"No. I tapped under the talons—" She mimed it with the pen light. "Baby birds lock their feet onto branches; it's a survival instinct. Some of the griffins and chimerae have it, some don't. I have no idea how important that is."

She watched the Silver settle back on itself in pained silence and felt suddenly ashamed of herself. This was not how you spoke to clients, no matter how annoying they were. "I'm sorry."

"Not yet you aren't," the Silver said, turning away. His talons raked tracks in the bare rock. "Not by half."

BJ stared after him, stiffening. She had at least assumed she would be killed quickly.

A chimera honked at her frantically, singeing its whiskers still more. BJ carefully picked her way across the logs and

mud, trying not to listen as small animals scurried away.
The chimera looked at her hopefully and rolled on its back,
exposing a matted belly for scratching.

BJ sighed. "Fran." She sympathized with the Griffin
deeply; knowing a chimera was an embarrassment—and this
one was the Griffin's mate, at least for reproduction.

In the tumult she almost missed it: a muffled tapping,
somewhere under Fran. "Move, Fran." She shoved. "Come
on, honey. Please."

The tapping sounded weak. In desperation BJ broke off
a stick and poked Fran with the sharp end. Squeaking in-
dignantly, thrashing its scorpion tail, Fran rolled away. A
monstrous, engorged tick dropped off Fran and rolled into
the nest material.

Beside it lay an egg, forced down until it was all but
buried in the nest.

BJ knelt, grateful she was wearing blue jeans, and dug
frantically until she had exposed the egg. She lifted it out,
listening. The tapping had stopped.

She rapped on the shell with her stick, then stabbed it
until she had made a hole big enough for her fingers. Peeling
the shell fragments, which stuck to the inner lining, she con-
verted it into a bowl.

A small golden, downy head, eyes shut tight, lolled back
in the egg. It didn't move at all. She placed her stethoscope
on the chick's chest; the heartbeat was faint but discernible.

She wedged a stick in its beak and rolled a fresh paper
tube, blowing down the griffin chick's mouth. She picked it
up with her thumbs across its diaphragm, squeezed out air
and blew in again. Fran, peering over her shoulder, made a
small worried noise.

Something tickled the back of her neck. She brushed it
back and felt Fran's scorpion tail, poised over her spine.
"He needs the help," BJ said, and stayed in place, trying
not to think about the time she had seen that tail spear a
bird flat into the ground.

After three tries at resuscitation, she reached into her pack
and pulled out a syringe and the bottle of Dopram. She
pulled the needle cap off with her teeth, jabbing the needle
through the rubber top the second she could. She flipped the

griffin chick over, looking for and quickly finding its feline umbilicus. It was attached, improbably, to the avian yolk; BJ wondered briefly what platypus eggs were like. There was no time to guess at dosage; she injected a few milliliters and waited, biting her lip. She shared the anxiety of the griffins as she thought, *please, God, not this one, don't let me have to break the Griffin's heart . . .*

The dosage or the respiratory assistance or the moment itself was right—maybe all three. The chick coughed suddenly, then gasped repeatedly, waving downy wings. It turned shut, blind eyes toward her, and let out a long, wailing cry of hunger and loneliness.

She picked him up. "I'll see that you're fed. You are—" She realized that she wasn't sure who he was. If a name was secret and important, she had no right to give it to him. "You are the son of Asturiel," she whispered, and on impulse kissed his damp forehead above his beak.

His eyes, deep and golden, flickered open for a long, impossible moment, and she felt that he was intensely aware of everything she had said and everything she had done.

Then they closed, and he was nothing but a cross between a baby eagle and a lion cub. BJ set him down, trying to think what to do.

A childless griffin, the Bronze she had spoken to earlier, passed close enough to touch. BJ said quickly, "Can you care for this one? His father's not here, and I need to—"

The Bronze glared over his shoulder and said abruptly, "I will not carry him, if I cannot carry my own." His back empty, he flew into the night, leaving the Griffin's chick blinking on the nest. BJ snatched him up quickly before any parasites scrambled onto him.

She dumped the syringes out, hastily stuffing them into the front flap. The bottle of Dopram she pocketed. She hoisted the griffin chick high, stuffed him into the backpack and walked forward into the nest.

The eggs were done, and the chimerae and griffins had gone to their parents or had been taken to be buried. The chimera kittens were already nursing, not caring at all about the filth and pestilence around them.

BJ, sagging with her backpack in her lap, brushed gigantic ticks off herself, too tired to be disgusted. She stood, wavering with exhaustion and climbed the boulders at the edge of the nest until she was above the twigs and logs. The parasites circled the rock below her and returned to the nest. The griffin chick in her backpack slept without opening its eyes.

A row of cairns, well-formed and neatly aligned, marked the graves of those chicks who had failed to survive the night. A similar but less tidy row, erected by the griffins, marked where the chimerae had buried and abandoned those kittens who had died.

Now BJ watched as, one by one, the griffins rose, their progeny tucked protectively between their wings. The chimerae honked forlornly, then forgot, surrounded by their own mewing kittens. The kittens, as happily unkempt as their mothers, nestled into the twigs and fell loudly to sleep. Snoring filled the air.

A Gold, his chick asleep between his wings, walked up to BJ. "I believe your work here is done."

BJ stared around the nest. The chimerae were nestling down with their young. The bonfires were down to embers; the shadows barely moved on the twigs. BJ's skin felt crawly; more than anything she wanted a bath. "Aren't you going to clean this?"

"Why bother? They'll leave it in a week or so, now that the eggs are hatched. Within a day, the nest would be vile again anyway. After that, they'll nurse the kittens, who are remarkably resistant to parasites and filth. A month will see them weaned." A tick dropped from one of the limbs onto him; he dislodged it and flapped his wings with involuntary disgust. "In a few months, the mothers will be male again."

He turned away. "I don't intend to discuss it." He flew off.

That left BJ alone with the sleeping chimerae. As she watched, one of them belched contentedly, a foot of flame streaming against the nest. BJ turned away—

And was face-to-face with the Silver. "You have been witness to the single most shameful part of our lives."

"I know." She had known from the first what would happen to her when the birthing was done. There could be no acceptable promise of silence, and she refused to plead. "Please see that this chick is returned to the Griffin—to the one known as Asturiel." It was no breach of trust; she knew that the Silver, senior to the others, was aware of the Griffin's name. "Tell him—"

The Silver broke in coldly, "That is not possible."

"Then I'll return him myself." She was tired and emotionally ragged, but too angry to weep in front of the griffins. "I'll find a way. If you kill me, take him to his father; if you don't kill me, I'll do it myself. Don't leave him to die, and don't leave him with someone else like—like a cuckoo." Part of her realized it was foolish to insult a griffin, but part of her had realized, long earlier, that she was going to be killed.

"You have presented me with a quandary," the Silver said, his voice tight. "Be still while I think."

BJ stood caressing the griffin chick, patting his fur smooth. "If I die here," she thought bleakly, "I'm not only hurting Stefan and the Griffin and my other friends. I am failing an entire world." She felt like a small child clutching a stuffed toy for comfort.

After a long silence, the voice of the Silver sounded far away, detached. "Hold onto him very tightly. Do not thank me, do not speak to me while we are in flight, and do not mention this place and what you saw here—ever, ever again."

BJ automatically opened her mouth to thank him, shut it, nodded. Seconds later they were airborne. The moon drifted behind a cloud; BJ, clutching the sleeping chick against her chest, hung in silent darkness.

S·E·V·E·N

THE PHONE CALL woke Frieda up.

She looked around her apartment in confusion. For a vet student's apartment, it was extremely neat; Frieda cleaned whenever she had a chance. She had as an undergraduate as well, driving her roommate crazy. The compact discs were sorted, the computer under a dust cover, the windows washed, the woodwork spotless.

She stumbled around, searching for the phone. How, in a place this tidy, could she be missing it?

On the third ring she picked it up, behind the stack of books (Ctesias, Pliny, the photocopy of Lao, a medieval bestiary and several books of Greek and British mythology). "Hello."

"Conference," Valerie said crisply. "New River, at the Tube Camp. Bring lunch."

"Conference?" She remembered where she was, the lengthy study session the previous night and, finally, two nights ago, carrying a dead unicorn kidling. "Right."

"Wow, are you sleepy. Thought I was bad." Valerie added, still in her usual blunt tone, "Want a ride?"

"If you don't mind."

"Wouldn't have asked if I'd minded. Get some sleep. Be ready at eleven." And she hung up. Dimly Frieda recalled someone telling her that Valerie hated talking on the phone.

It was eight-thirty. Frieda set the alarm for ten, went back to bed, got up and put the offending books on her bookshelf, and went back to bed.

Valerie honked once. Frieda, waiting by the door with a Playmate cooler and a backpack, ran out. Valerie was rolling again before she shut the door. "Thanks for being ready."

"Thanks for the ride." Frieda, with a cup of tea in her, was still tired but much more clearheaded. "Who wanted the conference?" But she knew.

"Matt. He did some checking into school records." She looked sideways. "He says we've got a problem."

That was all she said. Frieda relaxed against the seat, hugging the cooler and enjoying the drive out of Kendrick. The air was warm already, but a breeze rippled through the greenery on Brushy Mountain as they sped down a two-lane blacktop into the hills to the west.

The New River was misnamed; it was one of the oldest rivers in America. It looped through the eroded Appalachians, often placid, dropping intermittently into rapids, paralleling a nearly abandoned railway into West Virginia and coal country. To Frieda, staring down at it as they plummeted from the blacktop onto a gravel road that dropped them to the level of the railroad grade, it was completely foreign, nothing like the woods and farm fields of Wisconsin. It was nearly as foreign as a unicorn.

Tube Camp had been a summer Bible camp. A man named Leroy Farrow had bought it, recognizing the potential in a riverfront canoe and inner-tube rental smack between Western Vee and Radford University. He ran a shuttle bus from below the falls back up to the camp; students and others shot the falls and rode back to do it again.

Out of respect for the previous owners, he had leaned a hand-painted sign against a decaying hitching rail: PLEASE DO NOT DRINK BEER WINE OR LIQUOR IN THE CAMPSITE. Out of courtesy—Frieda thought Wisconsin students were kinder, but these were the most courteous people she'd ever known—students kept their coolers shut and their bottles and cans unopened until they were out on the river.

From the tube rack by the river, Matt and Cody waved to them. Matt was in solid blue swim trunks and, Frieda noted without surprise, had a washboard stomach and incredible pecs. Cody, beside him, had beach sunglasses, a rumpled tank top and outrageous purple and green Jams that seemed to hang to his knees. Cody's arms were superbly muscled, but one shoulder dropped an inch; he was in thong sandals. Without his built-up shoe, Frieda could clearly see how short his right leg was.

Valerie said, "We're not late. You were early."

Matt said, "Glad you could make it."

Cody said, "Frieda, will that cooler hold some more lunch?"

They rented five inner tubes: four tractor-size, for people, and a small one with a rope for the cooler. They put in at a dock—plywood tied to two more inner tubes—and drifted downstream.

The New River was wide and flat here, but the current was fairly fast; the tree branches trailing down into the water were all tugged sideways. Frieda lay back in her tube, looking upstream at the hills and, more than half a mile up, a small rapids.

The tube spun around slowly, and she faced downstream. They had gone a quarter mile, and she heard something ahead, soft and indistinct, around the bend of the river.

Valerie paddled close to her. Valerie looked spectacular in a bathing suit, all curves and muscles. Frieda had always felt in shape, but at the moment she was steeped in envy. It was like tubing with an Amazon.

"Been to the Tube Camp before?" Valerie asked.

"No. I've heard of it. It's near McCoy Falls, isn't it? How big are the falls, and where are they?"

The sound ahead was getting louder, like white noise or static. Valerie grinned. "Oh, they're big enough."

They floated toward the bend, and the trees to either side no longer muffled the rumble of waters ahead. "I'd suggest," Valerie said, "hauling ass toward the left channel, where the rapids are."

Frieda stared in disbelief. The rapids were filled with rocks, separated by chutes of white water with standing waves. To the right there was only a straight line in the water, nothing more threatening.

She was about to object when she realized that the line was an artificial horizon line, the top of a falls. She dropped both arms in the water and paddled frantically toward the left.

Cody joined her, looking remarkably relaxed in his shades and Jams. "If you can't swim," he said solemnly, "I'd like to take the cooler."

Frieda, still paddling, framed a reply as the current took her away.

The gaps between the rocks, when she got to them, turned out to be nearly eight feet wide. She shot down a flume of water sideways, backward, and, briefly, facing forward; the tube nearly bounced out of the water on a standing wave at the bottom. After that, gasping, she drifted into a quiet pool, circling in an eddy. The cooler bumped gently against her.

Cody followed her down, whooping, then Valerie, with a yell that echoed off the surrounding hills and rocks. Matt shot down with perfect poise, stretching one hand out to steady himself and smiling as he saw Frieda and Valerie. "Are you all right?"

"Yes, thanks," Frieda said, and Valerie said, "Why wouldn't we be?"

Cody, back-paddling, struggled to get into the pool and relaxed as the eddy took him to a calm area. "Here, Bathsheba, we will make our home." He nearly overbalanced as he grabbed the edge of a broad rock. "Nice table, huh? Lunch is served."

Frieda and Valerie joined him, crawling out onto the rock as clumsily as the first amphibians probably made landfall. They emptied the cooler, hardly noticing as Matt bumped against the rock and slid onto it effortlessly. After the past year in vet school, they fell into silent team mode surprisingly well, setting up and distributing a meal.

Matt said, to start things, "Not our usual setting, is it?"

Valerie said, "Too much nature." She said it disapprovingly, as though cities were natural and country perverse.

"That's what makes it nice." Frieda looked around. "Just look at the falls." More students were plunging down them, surging past them to another set of rocks. "And I'll bet that there are tons of animals all around us, if we knew where to look."

"Heck of a snake right over there," Cody said solemnly.

Valerie huddled into herself. "What kind? Where?"

"You don't like snakes?" Cody was enjoying this hugely. "How you gonna work with exotics?"

"I work with you, don't I? What the hell kind of snake is it, and where?" She was standing up now, almost on tiptoe.

"Just a water snake," Matt said. "It's over just to the right of Cody." He added carelessly, "Just in front of that huge spider."

Cody spun his head back, gave a remarkably high-pitched scream, and leapt into the water. At the last minute he held his sandwich over his head; he kicked his way quickly to a rock ten feet away and sat back down.

"The snake left," Frieda announced. "You scared it."

"Didn't scare the spider, though." Now Valerie was enjoying herself. "Come on back; I think he wants some of your sandwich."

"Uh-uh. Nope. Not gonna happen." But Cody, calmer, munched on his still-dry sandwich, peering suspiciously at the nearby rocks.

Matt looked at both of them impatiently. "Can we do a little business?" He went on. "We had an unusual experience the other night."

Valerie snorted.

Matt was unperturbed. "From things Sugar Dobbs said when I was in his office, I think this is only the beginning of the strange cases. Is that all of your impressions?"

They each nodded. Frieda, hugging her knees, wondered what could be as unusual as unicorn births.

"And we all know that we're not the first rotation to work with these animals. We know that was BJ Vaughan's class." He looked around at them. "I decided to find about them, so we could tell if this rotation is going to be worthwhile at all."

Frieda started; Valerie stared, wide-eyed in disbelief. After a moment, Cody said, "Any guesses at their class standing before the rotation?"

"Top ten percent of their class," he said, adding simply, "Just like us."

Valerie said, "What did they do after graduating?"

"One's in Africa, doing famine work, so it's hard to tell. One's doing graduate research at Cornell. One's at a regular practice, but I hear she hates it. The other one's BJ." He waved his peach for emphasis. "Only one has a regular vet job, and she doesn't like it."

"You think the course is the reason?" Cody said softly.

"Matt, read the journals. Almost half the vets out there wish they'd done something else. The money's bad, the hours long. You've gotta want it."

Matt ignored him. "Something else. I looked at their transcripts."

Frieda gaped. "Matt, that's illegal."

"Also tough to do," Valerie said, but she didn't sound happy.

"A friend of mine from undergraduate classes here works in the registrar's office." He looked at the others. "I've never asked before. I had a good reason."

"That makes it legal, then." Cody stared neutrally at Matt.

Matt went on doggedly. "I wanted to see how this rotation appears in their transcripts. They each showed one independent study, and all of them but the guy at Cornell got an A. He got a B-plus."

Valerie said, "Shame on him. Who cares, Matt?"

Matt said, "So I started asking around the vet school about taking independent studies. Everybody acted like it could never happen. I checked with the graduate office. They pointed out that, since the course work is the same for all students, there wouldn't be any need for an independent study."

Cody said around his munching, "Is there a point to this?"

"We none of us need this rotation," Matt said flatly. "It's a waste of time, and God knows we don't have any time.

Sugar Dobbs is doing this for some crazy reason of his own. Probably research.''

They sat in silence for a few seconds. Frieda said finally, ''I think he's doing it because the animals need it.'' She felt silly immediately, but nobody said anything sarcastic.

Matt frowned. ''The unicorns needed it. Maybe the next animal needs it. But *we don't*. We need to learn about domesticated animals and livestock, horses and cows, sheep and goats—''

Valerie said with feeling, ''Man, I don't need to know any more about horses.''

Cody, amused, added, ''I can skip pigs.''

Matt ran a hand through his damp but unruffled hair, exasperated. ''Don't you get it? Those skills transfer to other animals, even if the knowledge doesn't. It goes on your transcript, and employers look for it. But you can't go to an employer and say, when he asks about your experience, ''Well, I've worked with unicorns.'' He looked around. ''Imagine trying it.''

He had a point, Frieda reflected. Viewed that way, this rotation would be the most useless work she'd do for vet school.

She thought of what she'd be giving up if she quit the rotation. ''Has he mentioned specific other cases to you?''

Valerie said, daring her to laugh, ''Centaurs and birthing. He had ten pages of handwritten notes, and a postscript by a student named Lee Anne Harrison.''

''Werewolves,'' Cody said, in a mock-horror accent. He dropped it and said simply, ''He told me he may drop that one, though, in favor of livestock or anything else that comes along.''

Matt said quietly, ''I'm to look up everything I can find on dodoes. Can you imagine preparing for rounds on an animal that's extinct?''

''Beats being mythical,'' Valerie said thoughtfully. ''Matt, why are you so bugged?''

''This class is ridiculous,'' he said tightly. ''It's no use at all, and it has no place in the vet school.''

''Is that all?'' Cody said. ''Some of the classes I've taken are that bad now. Shoot, Doctor Lindsay gives coffee enemas to cows, and feeds marijuana to deer before surgery.''

Doctor Cloris Lindsay, a colleague of Sugar's, had a strong interest in alternative and folk medicine. Frieda had seen her give a shot of whiskey to a newborn colt, and beer to a colicky horse. Some of her interests, like acupuncture, had the potential for valid results. Some of her other interests were laughable, so long as her lab tests on ill patients weren't actually cruel. Frieda had privately decided that she would save her notes from Lindsay's Large Animal Toxicology and slowly weed out the conjecture and craziness.

Matt ran his hand through his hair again, and Frieda realized for the first time how stressful it must be, working to stay as good at everything as he was. "I don't have time for this. I can't waste time. I want out.''

"I'm not sure he'll let us drop the course,'' Valerie said slowly. It was possible to drop most veterinary courses; however, every single course in the vet school was mandatory until senior year. Ordinarily, dropping a course delayed graduation. It was hard to know the status of this rotation.

"I know.'' He finished, "I want to get the school to make him stop the rotation.''

Frieda's heart seemed to clench like a fist. She had no idea what lay ahead, but had known from the moment the unicorn had changed its face color and let her hug him that she wanted everything about this rotation. "You can't.''

She caught herself as they all turned toward her. "You can't tell anyone he's making you do surgery on unicorns, right? I mean, you said that yourself.''

Valerie grinned, with some relief. "She's got you, Matt. If you don't like what Sugar is doing, what can you do about it?''

Matt said slowly and deliberately, "I can write a letter of grievance to the dean, complaining that Doctor Dobbs is misusing student time and school funds.''

There wasn't much to say to that. Sugar was still untenured; a charge like that would pretty much kill his chances for a tenured job then and there.

Valerie said slowly, "I'm not up for that.''

Cody said with relief, "Me neither.''

"Frieda?"

She said slowly, "I'm not sure he's done anything wrong."

"If you thought he had, would you sign a letter saying so?"

Cody said, "If you could prove it."

Valerie nodded.

The others were waiting. Finally Frieda said unhappily, "I'd need to be completely sure. And I'd want to confront him first, and hear his defense."

Matt shook his head. "You do things like this by the book, all the way. If he were accusing you of plagiarism"— Frieda cringed—"he'd go through the honor court, not try to shake you down. By the book is best."

Valerie frowned. "You still can't do it. How can you show he misused supplies, if you can't tell them what he used them for? —Oh."

Matt nodded. "Right. Neither could he, so he made something up every time he used supplies. I don't have to prove what he did; I just have to show that he didn't do what he said."

The others looked back at him silently. He finished, "So it's settled, for now. We go on the rotation when he calls, we log our classes and our assessments of them, and we keep track of every expenditure."

Valerie bristled. "Did 'we' say that?"

"No." Matt looked tired for once. "But if I'm going to turn him in, you'll all want to keep your own stories straight."

He didn't elaborate, and he didn't need to; if Matt had sufficient evidence of Sugar's fraudulent requisitions, then if he turned Sugar in, the students who used the supplies might all go up on honors charges—and they could never tell an honors court the real use of the supplies.

Around them other groups of students laughed, screamed, shot the falls. Cody swam back over and joined them, but there wasn't much chat after that. Frieda was glad when they all swam ashore and silently took the shuttle bus back to their cars.

E·I·G·H·T

BJ WOKE FROM nightmarish dreams, fighting to carry a griffin chick through knee-deep mounds of parasites. It was her second night of such dreams. This time, however, she had passed the chick to Bambi, who had smiled at her with a human face, balanced carefully on deer legs, and kissed the downy griffin on the beak.

BJ had said, "Son of Asturiel, I'd like you to meet a very deer friend," broken into hysterical laughter, and woken up.

It hadn't happened that way. The Silver had dropped BJ and the chick in front of her cottage. BJ had locked the chick inside, run to Stein's, and sent a message to the Griffin. He arrived and took the chick, saying next to nothing as BJ gave a list of birth defects to look for and (probably needless) care instructions.

He turned before they flew off and said quietly, "I almost hope that I can never repay you. I could only repay you by giving my life for you." And then he was gone. BJ slept eighteen hours and woke at nightfall, stiff all over and her ribs and shoulders covered with monstrous bruises, to discover that Stein had left a meal for her in the springhouse. She slept again, and had now woken at sunrise, back on her normal schedule.

BJ considered her dream, packed her knapsack, made a cup of tea, and sat at the table thinking.

In college she had a roommate who had meditated, and tried to get BJ to start. BJ hadn't found it of interest, but had been patient. Now she sat at the table, breathing deeply and emptying her mind of distractions and stray thoughts.

It felt as though it took no time at all; what had been a struggle in a noisy dormitory was simple in the quiet of Crossroads—or, she wondered briefly, did this have to do with changes inside her? She pushed that thought aside hurriedly; she hated when anyone called her a goddess, and she didn't want to consider what her new talents meant.

Still . . . as she sat with her mind as empty as she could make it, she reached out, looking for another world. She chose, for the ease of it as well as the urgency, one she had visited once with Fields. She felt as she had when flying with the Silver griffin, moving rapidly over land and crossing between worlds. (One day, she thought distractedly, she would have to ask how easily griffins and chimerae migrated between worlds. The thought made her feel suddenly heavy, dropping out of flight, and she pushed it aside.) She saw grasslands passing under her, then forests and mountains, with twists and sudden changes of climate—

Her eyes flew open, and she smiled. She knew the route she needed to take today, knew it as readily as if it were already sketched. She said aloud, "That didn't take so much time," and looked across at the window, then quickly down.

The sun was well above the horizon, and her tea was cold.

BJ downed it, making a face, and walked out with her knapsack.

The first part of the woods she walked, just above Stein's, was full of birch and ash. The woods below, closer to the river, were oak; above her, on the mountains, were cedar and mountain laurel giving way to pine. She didn't bother sticking to a trail; the undergrowth was light, and she knew exactly where she was going.

Her ears were accustomed to birdcalls and the rustle of underbrush; it took her a moment to place the rhythmic thud which grew louder as she walked forward.

Long before she walked into the clearing she had recognized the noise as human, or at least intelligent. She stopped,

uncomprehending, for a moment thinking she was watching
a swordsman make war on a tree.

He swung two-handed, spinning the blade once each time
over his head as he slashed at the trunk. The notch at the
base grew quickly.

The tree fell. BJ stepped back automatically; he swung,
sword in hand, to face her.

He was blond, with prominent cheekbones and brown
eyes. BJ's first coherent thought was, "Half-Cherokee, half-
Swede. That's what he looks like."

He saw her expression. His mouth quirked, and he said
something in another language.

"I'm sorry," BJ said. "I don't—"

"I was telling you," he said, "that it attacked me first."

Automatically, BJ looked at the fallen birch, then blushed.
"Don't lie."

"Why not?" But he lowered the sword. "It's the one
natural thing in any tongue."

He stuck the sword in a grass hummock, and let go of
the pommel. "My name is Dyvedd." Under BJ's stare he
added, unwillingly, "Dyvedd Oghannon. I'd be allowed to
put Dyvedd second, but I'm a bastard."

She nodded. Illegitimacy wasn't terribly important to her.
"The name's familiar."

His look of hope and awkwardness made her say quickly,
"It's just that I've heard the name Oghannon before, from
a friend's stories. I don't know any Oghannon."

He relaxed, or maybe slumped. "No one does, here.
Where I come from, it's a common name. My mother made
sure I'd know which Oghannon, in case I found him and
could lay birth-claim." He grinned again, without resentment. "As if I could prove a claim. There are many Oghannon; either it's a large family or my father was active."

"How do you know English?"

"Is that what this is?" He smiled and scratched his head,
genuinely delighted to know. "It was one of the languages
in Morgan's camp."

At the name "Morgan," BJ froze. "You were a mercenary."

He shrugged, and in that moment BJ saw him withdrawing, entire planets away. "I fought for food, yes."

"And Morgan led you? Were you a part of the raids?" She said it as casually as she could.

"Not the raid when she took the book she wanted so much. The next raid, to prove it could be done, I was in the second squadron." He rubbed the back of his neck, grinning. "Some squadron—the true killers were up front. We were the next wave, the cleaners, the—" He gestured with his hands, sweeping or scrubbing.

"The mopping up."

"Mopping, yes, that's what she called it." He chuckled. "No wonder I didn't know the word. She had to explain what it was in Anavalerse, as well; I haven't lived in clean places."

"That's the first time you didn't know the English word."

"Morgan taught me to speak it. She wanted to teach me reading." He looked straight ahead and finished casually, "She had lots of plans for me. I was ready to desert when she finally marched us in here, the last time."

BJ had been in that fight, had in fact helped choose the battle site. "I didn't think any of her troops came into Crossroads."

"We didn't, but we made it to the mouth of the canyon just outside it. A few of us spilled into the canyon before your fat friend with the hooves closed the road in front of the troops."

"My fat friend." BJ remembered Fields, a satyr and the most careful, loving guardian any land could have, lying wounded in dust and blood. "Were you the one who killed him?"

He shook his head. "Things were confused; it was my chance. I slung Dancer and climbed up the canyon side, barely looked back." His smile curled cynically. "Does that make me better than the men who did what they were paid to do?"

There was no tactful answer for that. BJ said frankly, "I'm glad you're not the one who killed him."

"Would you put a curse on me? Was that part of your satyr man's god-gift?" When she looked startled, he laughed. "How did you think I got here? I looked at the land around me, and looked at the few of you, and guessed you'd be going somewhere better. I followed you, barely in sight, all the way here.''

"If we had seen you, we'd have killed you."

He shrugged. "I don't think so. You were all tired."

She looked at his sword. "Most people chop wood with an ax.''

"You have one?" He stared around her as though expecting a double-bladed ax to hop out of her knapsack. "I'd love to borrow it."

She said finally, hating to give in to his joke, or, at the moment, to admit lack of a weapon. "Sorry, no ax."

"You have a weapon, though," he said casually. "One of those short swords with the hooked crosspiece, the little one-handed things folk say Crossroads uses in bar fights?''

"A catchlet. Yes." BJ showed it. "And your sword is named . . .''

"Sorry. Should have introduced you: this is Dancer." He spun the blade around itself rapidly and made it take a nod at the end of the spin like a dancing puppet: a blade curtseying.

"It's a pretty name."

"Full name Blood Dancer." He pointed to the sharpened diamond broadening out the midpoint of the blade. "And you've never seen that, have you?" Without warning he flipped the sword end for end and caught it on the palm of his hand at the diamond. He held the hilt out to her, his palms flat against the blade. "Go ahead; try it."

The hilt was warm from his hands, as little as he had held it; she wondered automatically what his resting body temperature was. Dyvedd, apparently unarmed in front of her, was annoyingly confident. She swore to herself, "No matter how much this weighs, I will make it look easy." She swung the blade two-handed, bracing at the end of the swing for a recovery time. The added weight on the blade made her stagger.

He stepped forward, horizontal palm catching up with and arresting the blade. "If you want to do that, step with it." He mimed the motion of the blade, uncannily like someone in the batter's box.

She tried again, imitating him and remembering college softball games. Dyvedd nodded. "Better. You'd be dead, but good swing." He tapped her right ribs where the swing around had exposed her. "A sword like this, don't swing it sideways unless you can spin clear around for the next swing. And that leaves your back exposed." He looked down. "You even got the feet right."

"I've practiced," BJ said. "It's a game back home."

"Nasty sort of home you're from, then."

"I miss it," she said, surprising herself.

"I miss mine, and mine was mostly dust and brawlers." He held a hand out. "Give me your catchlet."

BJ only hesitated a second before passing it over, but his eyes looked amused. He raised the catchlet, pulled his arm back to lunge at her, and said, "Hold Dancer upright, like a shield in front of you. Swing from the elbow; use the bottom of the blade to parry, like it's a catchlet."

He lunged. BJ did as he suggested, and found that Dancer spun on its midpoint, making it easy to parry back and forth. He lunged at different heights; she brought the blade up and down, keeping it vertical.

He stepped back. "Good. Now tilt it forward a little and swing the top to parry; move close on me."

That took more muscle, but it kept the catchlet a reassuring distance away—and Dyvedd was much closer to a cutting blade than she was.

At her last blow, Dyvedd pretended she had knocked the catchlet aside. The condescension of the move irritated her. He stood with his weapon to one side, chest exposed. "Now stab straight forward."

BJ lunged at him, ready to parry, and nearly fell into him as the balance of the blade shifted again.

Moving with incredible speed, he caught the tip of Dancer in the hilt of her catchlet and slid upward, taking the weight of the sword off her hands. "That's the trade-off, isn't it? The longer the blade, the greater the weight. The first time you use a sword like this, it's like lunging with a turtle's ass in your hand—not much bite, no speed, too heavy."

"Where are you from?"

"Here and there." He gestured vaguely behind him.

"There before, here now. Before that—" He paused. "I'd walked into Anavalon. It's not much of a place, just dry clouds and dust, and that's why I served under Morgan there, to get back out and to get rich. Not that it made me rich." His mouth twisted. "And what do you do?"

"I heal animals."

"Magic?" The respect in his voice was clear; so was the flat undertone of defensiveness.

BJ shook her head. "Science." He looked blankly at her, so she amended, "Education. It's a skill, to get the same results twice in a row—"

He chuckled, "Most of the time, it's a miracle."

"Oh, yes," she said feelingly. "Still, it's what I try for. When an animal is hurt, someone brings it to me. I work with it, and make it—" She caught herself. "I help it to heal."

His eyebrows came together over his nose; suddenly he looked older, a cartoon of his grandfather or a tribal leader. BJ was completely unready for his response: "I'm sure you study in some other world. Tell me, do you give animals drugs?"

She hadn't expect that word from him. Then she remembered that he had been in Morgan's camp. She nodded. "I give some as medications, to heal. I give others, like the ones you're thinking of, to patients that need not to feel pain."

Hands back on the pommel, he stepped forward, eyebrows pulled down and together, and BJ was acutely aware of their isolation, as she was of the dewy sword trail in the grass. "Don't we need to feel pain? Do you think it's good to feel nothing at all, even for a short time?"

BJ said steadily, "Sometimes I feel pain for myself. I don't choose pain for others. If animals need help which requires pain, I do what I can to make them feel only a little."

His hand was on the sword. "I knew folk, they could turn into wolves. Maybe they were wolves that turned into people; I couldn't say. Their business, that part. Morgan offered them a drug, and the poor silly things lapped it up like weak dogs."

BJ watched his hand, caressing the hilt and holding back from picking up the sword. "They couldn't help it."

"Of course not." His hand draped around the hilt now, ready to pick and swing. "Didn't know, did they? All they knew was, for the first time in their sorry two-bodied lives, things didn't hurt. And that"—the sword was in his hand now, point rising slowly—"that was the thing made it so damn easy—"

"That depends on who you are, doesn't it?" BJ was glad her voice wasn't shaking. "I had a friend who was addicted, and Morgan did it. Another friend, one of the Wyr, was an addict too. I know the drug. I don't use it, and I don't supply it."

After an awkward silence, she added, "Why are you chopping down trees?"

"Because I'm paid to." He lowered Dancer and jingled the purse strung to his breeches. "When I'm paid to stop, I'll stop."

BJ looked around in confusion. Although Crossroads had coins, a gold sixpiece, most services were barter. "What are you going to do with the money?"

"My purse keeps its mouth shut. I should, too." But he went on. "I'm going to be a farmer."

"Is that what you're doing with the money from Morgan, too?"

He shrugged. "I don't have much of that. I burned the scrip, and until they started paying in scrip, I sent money to my mother; can you imagine?" He sounded carefully amused. "Once a pay period, by any traveler I could find headed that way. And one day a trader came back to the camp with a message: 'Your mother is dead.' Just like that." He looked at her seriously. "Can you imagine that? They could have simply kept the money. It's amazing how people, once in a while for no reason, choose to be good." He tossed Dancer from hand to hand. "Now I just save the money."

"You don't need to buy the land."

"And who are you to say that?" But his eyes were laughing. "Anyway, I need tools. Hoe, rake, plow"—he looked down affectionately at Dancer—"an ax . . ."

BJ said dubiously, "I don't know how much of Cross-roads is good farmland."

"Any land you're allowed to work is good enough." He scratched the soil with the point of Dancer. "You tickle the earth, and it laughs up crops."

"Do you know anything practical about farming?"

"More than you'd think." But he didn't elaborate.

A Meat Person came into the clearing, his pink skin showing clearly through the leaves before his approach. BJ could never imagine how these gentle, nearly harmless people could have hunted before they became herders.

Dyvedd, seeing him, dropped Dancer. "Mohnrr!" he roared, and charged, fingers at the corners of his mouth to pull back his lips and expose his teeth.

Mohnrr laughed, his own lips pulling back involuntarily and exposing his long, needle-sharp fangs. Dyvedd shrank back in mock terror, hands shielding himself and forearms over his face. Mohnrr, laughing harder, held his own hands in front of his mouth to hide his fangs.

Dyvedd stood and put a hand on the little man's shoulders. "So. What did you bring?"

Mohnrr held up a packet of meat, not surprisingly, wrapped in wet leaves. Dyvedd shook his head. "I have lunch, thanks." Mohnrr held up one wedge from a gold sixpiece. "Perfect." Dyvedd dropped it into his purse.

Mohnrr held up a wooden dibble for poking seeds in the earth. As with their other woodwork, it bore the marks of the Meat People's teeth, the best carving tool they would ever have.

Dyvedd turned the dibble over in his hands delightedly. "Thank you." He turned to tuck it in his pack, spinning back around as the Meat Person strained up to tap his shoulder. "Something else?" With shy pride, Mohnrrr held up a wood sculpture: Dyvedd, his hair flying, legs wide and muscles articulated, fearlessly swinging Dancer in combat.

Dyvedd looked it over expressionlessly. "Did you chew this yourself?" He pointed to the runnels and gouges articulating the muscles, and to the multiple bite-marks giving soil texture to the base. Mohnrrr nodded vigorously.

Dyvedd broke into a smile; it seemed an effort to talk.

"It's beautiful. I'll keep it with me till I have somewhere to put it." He fumbled and said, "A place of honor, when I have a home." Mohnrrr smiled, covered his smile with one hand, waved with the other, and left.

Dyvedd waited until he left, then carefully wrapped the sculpture in a shirt from his pack and repacked it.

"Know why they look that way? They eat nothing but meat." He shook his head, laughing. "All those teeth, and I frighten them." He turned back to BJ. "Do you know how much these people cook in pits? All with charred wood, burned—" He waved his hands, searching for the word.

"Charcoal."

"Charcoal, yes, and they need a lot of it. Chopping down trees is hard for them; they're small. So they hire me. Well, why not?" He grinned at BJ. "I hope you're not one of those people who hates anyone that chops down trees."

"An environmentalist?" BJ said blankly.

Dyvedd looked blank back. "A wood witch. Anyway, first I chop the trees, then I'll chop the logs into short lengths—saw them, if anyone ever finds me a saw—then split the lengths." He gestured into the trees. "There's a kiln back there they use for making charcoal."

BJ made a decision. "I'm walking out of Crossroads today. I'll pay you to come along and guard me."

He stared at her. Finally he nodded.

"Don't you want to ask where?"

He shook his head.

"How soon can you leave?"

He wrapped Dancer and put on his knapsack. "I just did." He looked around guiltily at the unstacked wood. "I can finish this tomorrow."

It didn't reassure BJ that he kept his field pack ready.

At the inn, BJ went in first, shut off the boom box (Dyvedd stared at it with interest but no surprise) and said, "I have someone with me." She heard Stein approach the door and stop. Dyvedd waited with her in the entry hall.

Stein came into view around the door, his left hand casually leaning out of view. He looked up and down, pausing

casually when he saw Dancer. BJ said, "This is Dyvedd."
She added carefully, "He'll be escorting me when I go look
for Gredya."

"Nice to meet you. BJ, if you think you need a guard,
I'm sure I can find one—"

"Dyvedd will be fine."

"I can see that," he said, poker-faced. "So, have you
known each other very long?"

Dyvedd, standing as casually as Stein, left his hand on
his sword. "We met this morning."

"He'll be fine," BJ said firmly. She wanted to add "And
I know what I'm doing," but she wasn't entirely sure it was
true.

"Believe me," Dyvedd said, "nothing will happen to her.
If it did, how would I get back? I'd be maggot meals."

"That's true," Stein said tiredly, "but could you phrase
it more nicely in a restaurant? Come on in, get some breakfast." He moved away from the door and waved them in.
Dyvedd frowned, looking Stein over; he didn't seem to have
a weapon.

When Stein set the bread on the table, the plate hadn't
stopped rattling before Dyvedd grabbed a slice. He smeared
butter and honey on it in a blur and downed it. "Farmer's
breakfast," he mumbled. "Been working hard already."

Fiona called from the kitchen. "Stein? Is someone here
already?" She came out and stared at Dyvedd, looking him
up and down well. BJ had been so concerned with the threat
his muscles might pose that she hadn't registered how handsome he was.

Stein said formally, "Fiona, this is Dyvedd; Dyvedd,
Fi—"

Dyvedd, swallowing, said noncommittally, "We've
met."

Fiona gaped at him. "I'd remember."

"In Morgan's camp," he said, avoiding her eyes. "You
were tied up in the corral. Not for long, just one evening—"

Fiona's face drained of color, and her knees buckled.

BJ was at her side, but no faster than Dyvedd was at the
other. "You remember, then." Fiona nodded jerkily, me-

chanically. "Bothered me, too. I'd seen lots. Well."

BJ helped her to a seat. Stein, unobtrusively, was behind Dyvedd, an apron bunched in the old man's arms. Dyvedd stared at the apron for all of a second, then up at Stein's face. He grinned and patted the apron appreciatively, backing away. He poured a stein from the nearest pitcher, sipped it to be sure what it was, gave it to Fiona, and sat by her.

"Fiona?"

The redhead jerked up, her eyes wary.

"I saw you from a distance." He said each word carefully. "Never got close. Not my wish for an evening."

Fiona nodded. "I wouldn't have remembered." She took the stein and sipped, then looked into the distance, her lips moving as she talked to herself.

BJ caught Dyvedd's eye. He nodded and stood. "I'll be going. Here's for the bread—"

"No charge," Stein said in disgust.

There was a sudden, loud snap as a coin hit the table under Dyvedd's palm. "I'm paid as I go and I pay as I go," he said levelly. "Anyone else, I'd be glad to cheat him out of a drink, but I've done no harm here." He stressed the last few words. "The money's yours."

Stein eyed him warily, and BJ was reminded once again of what it was like to cash a check at a rural Virginia grocery store, eyeballed by the night manager. Finally Stein sighed. "Thanks for your patronage. Come again."

Dyvedd grinned at that, the ghost of laughter in his eyes. "I may cheat you next time."

They walked north from the inn, toward a pass in the mountains. Clouds had blown through the pass, and were running in white streams down the ravine to either side. They reassembled into a layer somewhere above BJ and Dyvedd.

Dyvedd looked at the low-hanging clouds with satisfaction. "It's a soft day. No heavy rain."

"How can you be sure?"

"I've lived outside a lot." He pointed to the thin streamers where the clouds dissipated at the edge. "That lot will spit rain, not piss it."

BJ understood the metaphor without liking it much. She liked it still less as they moved into the clouds and the moisture, tiny droplets that hung more than fell, clung to her hair and face.

They made the top of the pass in a single trek. BJ paused barely a moment and said, "That way." The two of them moved forward carefully in the fog. Finally she sighed. "Can we rest here?"

"I can." He dropped easily onto a rock and pulled an apple from his knapsack. He passed her one, and they ate. "Are we out of Crossroads?"

"We left it in that pass."

"I thought the land looked strange." Munching reflectively, he added, "I know what you have in mind."

"What's that?"

"You're going to leave me somewhere out of Crossroads."

BJ tensed, unsure why he looked so relaxed. "Why would I do that?"

"Because I was Morgan's soldier. Because you're afraid I'll kill someone in Crossroads." He grinned at her amiably. "Because it's the only reason you took me with you."

BJ said, "I wanted a chance to look you over." He raised an eyebrow. "Not like that. More like a job interview."

"A what?"

She waved her arms, trying to think of a comparison. "Got it. Have you ever heard of fairy tales?"

"I know a few. Stories of the Fey."

"Right." She looked at him uncertainly, wanting to ask whether fairies were real. He looked back at her innocently, daring her to ask. She gave up and went on. "A lot of the stories have a test. The hero undergoes three trials to see if he's worthy."

"And these are my trials." He stood, swinging his sword wide as he bowed low. "Fear no more. Now you'll know that I'm a handsome prince." He belched and tossed the apple core away.

BJ sighed and stood up. "I'm sorry I betrayed your trust—"

He looked wide-eyed at her. "When did I trust you?"

He chuckled as she turned away and began walking. She noticed thereafter how closely he followed her, less than a sword length behind. It definitely didn't make her feel protected.

Dyvedd stayed close as they descended into a rocky valley with a rose-red canyon below it. They never reached it; instead the trail wound down into a lush, moist valley with orchids hanging from trees. Next, a breeze tore the clouds into streamers as the mist stopped. The air grew dry and hot, and they found themselves on a timeworn cobblestone road, leading into a valley with a vineyard and a building with a red tile roof and a bell tower.

BJ looked around and halted again to do some more sketching.

He squatted, watching her. "Where are we?"

"A new world. The people in that building call it Il Mondo, which just means 'The World.' "

"Why sketch the road?"

"So that I have a map."

"No, I mean, doesn't it just appear in the other books?"

So he knew, or had guessed, all about the *Books of Strangeways.* "Of course it does—after I sketch it in this one."

"Then why can't it just appear in this one?" He took the book away, scanning it. BJ was annoyed in that way people are when someone snatches away a magazine. He held the book up, cover toward her. "Try thinking about the page, and see the map of the road you've walked and the road ahead. Close your eyes, if it helps."

BJ started to reach for the book, then, intrigued, shut her eyes. She saw the bend over the mountains where she had stopped drawing, the side excursion through Rudy and Bambi's world, the veldt with no one else in it, the cobblestones of the world they had come to—

She opened her eyes, startled. Something had moved out of her, stopping as the road ended.

Dyvedd turned the book around, showing the precise, clear sketch, with each world labeled in her handwriting. "And now we know."

BJ reached for the book; Dyvedd slammed it shut, grinning. "And now I have a way home without you."

She was furious and embarrassed; people seldom tricked her so easily. She was also afraid. She stood well back from him, ready to run. "How did you know that would work?"

"It should," he said seriously, tucking the book in his knapsack. "It should work the same every time. It's magic, not luck."

BJ sighed and continued down the road. Dyvedd, whistling, walked a ways behind her.

As they approached the building, Dyvedd eyed the high stone walls and tower narrowly. "Someone's fort?"

"A Franciscan monastery." He looked blank. "Religious retreat. They came to this world from the world I grew up in." By now they were beside the vineyard, close to the monastery gate.

There was a sudden scuffle in the undergrowth and a squeak of terror. A flowerbinder, a massive knee-high white cat, leapt away from something large in the grapevines.

BJ staggered as Dyvedd grabbed her by the knapsack and tugged her behind him, his sword sweeping out front smoothly in his other hand. "And what are you?" he said calmly to the shaking vines.

A dark blur leapt onto the broad stone steps up to the monastery. A wolf stepped warily toward them, teeth bared and growling.

Dyvedd dropped to one knee, sighting down the sword into the wolf's eyes. "Why don't you go for a walk, BJ? Nice day for it. I'll stay here, maybe follow later."

The wolf raised its muzzle, sniffing the air curiously.

BJ, looking over his shoulder, recognized the wolf's muzzle markings. "Gredya?"

The wolf stopped growling. Dyvedd, sword still in place, said, "Can you make it sit?"

BJ said, with more confidence than she felt, "No, but she won't hurt me."

The wolf sat. Suddenly it tilted its muzzle straight up and howled while its teeth crackled and fell out; its beautiful clear eyes misted with blood from ruptured vessels, and its hair fell.

BJ was braced for the moment when the wolf ate its discarded tail; conservation of mass was vital to shape-shifting.

Dyvedd, still holding Dancer at guard, looked sick.

She stood before them, naked without embarrassment. Her dark hair had the fineness and luster of a young child's; her teeth shone new and white, unstained. Her skin glistened with sweat.

Her breasts were full; her belly was enormous.

Daphni padded away from BJ and rubbed against the back of Gredya's leg, bending it and nearly toppling her. "No." She pushed at Daphni, who leaned on her arm. "Go away." She showed her brand new, pearly human teeth in a snarl; Daphni purred. Gredya turned in frustration to BJ. "Make her stop."

"I can't. She knows your scent. She likes you."

"She should stop. I came to hunt."

"Were you going to eat her?" Dyvedd asked.

Gredya looked him over, sword and all, with no fear or interest. "Others, yes. Her, no."

Dyvedd said suddenly, "The people inside—when you growled at us, you were defending them."

Gredya nodded. "I choose to. They feed me."

"So do those fat white cats, but you don't defend them."

Gredya looked at him blankly. The Wyr didn't use sarcasm, and their sense of humor was brutally direct.

BJ searched for words, realizing with regret that vet school had never bothered teaching her to speak to patients. "You're still pregnant. I'd guess you're due in less than a month." Gredya nodded shortly. "Gredya, some species have had . . . difficult births, and some damage when they delivered out of Crossroads."

The Wyr did not bother hiding emotions; Gredya instantly showed fear, but she shook her head. "Not the Wyr. We bear well. All worlds." With a sudden ache she added, "Most times."

Dyvedd said suddenly, "This is the one. The other friend who was—"

BJ said "Yes," mainly to cut him off before Gredya felt humiliated.

When Gredya had been addicted to morphine and enslaved, she was pregnant. Later, not even Crossroads had prevented birth defects in her litter. None were now alive.

Gredya shook herself, a surprisingly canine motion on her body. Her belly wobbled, and she steadied it with both hands. "The Wyr. The others."

It was nice of her to care, when she had been essentially cast out and the Wyr had said her weak litter should be killed. "I'll try to reach them," BJ said. "I'm not sure if I can find them. From what you say, the children should be all right. Maybe not as robust as they'd be in Crossroads—"

"I will come," Gredya said firmly. BJ could not tell what she was thinking.

"Do you want to say good-bye to anyone?"

"No." Gredya strode to the wall. For the first time, BJ noticed a peg, newly mounted, with a tunic, cloak, and breeches hanging on it. "These are mine. A gift." She slipped them on quickly, struggling with the drawstring at her belly. "Now we go." It wasn't quite an order.

"We go," Dyvedd agreed. He stayed between Gredya and BJ. Gredya smiled at him, and the smile wasn't nice at all. He chuckled easily, but didn't put Dancer away.

They walked uphill, moving quickly into another world. BJ stopped at the first fork in the road.

Dyvedd came forward. "Something wrong?"

"You have the book," she said, pointing. "That's the way we came."

"I know. I double-checked."

BJ said, "I'm not going back the same way." She concentrated on her route and tried, now that she knew how it felt, to avoid its printing in *The Book of Strangeways*. Dyvedd's frustrated covert looks in the book told her that she was succeeding.

The road they were on changed to flagstone, then to well-worn limestone, gashed into the hillside like a railway cut. Dyvedd looked from side to side constantly, possibly watching for danger but obviously enjoying the scenery. Once or twice he checked the new page in *The Book of Strangeways*.

At last the trail became hard-packed dirt, with small pockets of grit and sand on it in crescent-shaped drifts. Dust devils swirled on it up ahead, and the grass and brush to either side were powdered with dust.

He knelt, one hand in the dirt. ''Where are the other tracks?''

''What others?''

''I don't know. Deer, rabbit, furfangle, and doodlers—things that eat plants.'' He stood again. Anything that this lot with the big tracks could eat.''

But they saw nothing. They continued walking, Dyvedd looking alertly from side to side, Gredya flaring her nostrils uneasily.

Ahead was what looked like an Irish setter/wolf cross, sitting bolt upright like a prairie dog. Seeing her, it turned and barked sharply.

Thirty reddish-brown heads poked up over the hillside. BJ had the unsettling feeling of someone entering a room where the conversation cuts off and everyone looks; she imagined them all dropping down on all fours the moment before she came, and getting back up on their hind legs the moment she left.

The sentry barked again, staring straight at BJ and Dyvedd. The others came bounding over the hill, long tails wagging. They stopped six feet away from BJ and cocked their heads this way and that, regarding her cautiously.

Dyvedd moved close to BJ again, unwrapping Dancer yet again. Gredya, on BJ's other side, smelled the air and looked deeply unhappy.

''Don't change yet,'' BJ said. Transforming was hard on Gredya. ''We're all right, I think.''

''No,'' Gredya said. ''There are many.''

''Maybe they're friendly.'' BJ took a step forward, then squatted, putting a hand out.

One of the animals, possibly the sentry, inched forward. He sniffed her hand, finally touching it with his nose, which was surprisingly dry.

''It's okay.'' BJ lightly scratched him under the chin, watching carefully for reflexes. He licked her hand once. ''How are you''—she glanced underneath him—''boy? What are you, anyway?''

''Grrm,'' he said, but his tail wagged wildly at being addressed. ''Grrrrim. Grim.''

The other animals sat down, watching the exchange.

"The Grym. A good name for them," Dyvedd muttered. "BJ, what in Dead Snake Hell are you doing?"

BJ had moved forward. "Looking him over, of course."

"Of course. Whenever I meet something with more teeth than brains, I always stick a hand down its throat and up its ass. You paid me to protect you. Don't do this."

"I have to. It's my job."

He turned to Gredya. "You, wolf-woman. Could you find our way back to Crossroads?"

"From here?" Gredya shook her head. "No road."

"I haven't finished it," BJ said apologetically.

"All right," Dyvedd said patiently. "Could you find your way back to the world we just left, and then I could lead us to Crossroads?"

Gredya nodded quickly. For once she looked daunted, not arrogant at all.

"Fine." He turned to BJ. "Go do your medicine."

"Not medicine. Just an exam." She dropped to one knee. "One of you come here." From this angle they seemed to be all teeth; she suddenly felt less sure of herself. "Come here. Come."

The one she had been speaking to came forward. She ruffled his fur, feeling the gaunt ribs underneath. "You're hungry, aren't you, boy? What's your name?"

"Gek!" he called loudly, on cue. "Gek! Gek!"

The others grinned, letting huge tongues loll out of their mouths.

She knelt to do an exam. His fur was well groomed and dry, his body temperature warm but not overly so.

She checked his ears, his belly, and ran her fingers through his fur. There were no ear mites (more a feline problem than a canine), no ticks, no flea dirt. For a wild animal, he was surprisingly free of parasites.

There wasn't a speck of extra fat on his body. She probed carefully, then lifted the tail.

Anal sacs were no pleasure to examine. To her surprise, and relief, his had been expressed recently. She checked the beast's toenails; they were worn to a sensible length. It was as though he had had regular care not long ago.

BJ glanced around. The vegetation, which grew in patches

of single plants, was rich and lush, like a well-fertilized garden. Bees roamed between the blossoms. There was no other life anywhere.

She listened intently; there were no birdcalls either.

Gredya sniffed the air anxiously, her nostrils flared. "Where is game?"

"Gone." She looked at the starving animal lolling below her, then at the landscape which suddenly snapped into focus for her. "There should be more different kinds of animals. There should be more different plants, all mixed in together. This is like a suburb."

"I've got words for it," Dyvedd said, "but not that one." He was circling constantly, checking all the canine's movements around them. Whenever the grass rustled, he spun in that direction.

"It's a place where people lived." The more she looked, the more certain she felt. "You can tell it because it's not wild and full like an uncivilized place—"

"Like Crossroads before you got there."

"No, because Crossroads still has lots of different plants. This is like someone left behind his lawn and his pets." Suddenly she was as nervous as Dyvedd. Who could turn an entire world into a managed, if eccentric, lawn, and why did they abandon it? Were they still around?

"Time to leave," Dyvedd said flatly.

Gredya said more firmly, "Go now."

BJ stared at the hungry, friendly faces around her. "But we can't just leave them."

Dyvedd said, "Of course we can."

The canine faces around them suddenly looked earnest, even frantic. One at the edge of the pack howled.

Gredya stepped forward and snarled. The Grym in front of them fell back.

"Gredya, don't threaten them."

She ignored BJ. "They are like Wyr. Like wolf." She stood staring Gek in the eye. Gek rolled over on his back in submission, still grinning and wagging his tail.

"Like wolf . . ." BJ moved between Gredya and Gek. "You're right; they're perfect. Any money says they're a pack predator." She rubbed Gek's stomach. "And they need saving."

Dyvedd said softly, "Not by me."

BJ in turn ignored him and turned to the pack. "Would you come with me?" They looked happily blank, responding to her tone and not her words. She said in the overly bright voice vets and owners reserve for pets, "You want to come along? Come with me? Want to go for a walk?"

"Gek!" he screamed. "Gek! Gek!"

He rolled back and forth, handlike paws in the air, grinning at her with the amiable stupidity of a golden retriever.

Dyvedd said resignedly, "Can't wait to see you feed them all."

"They'll feed themselves. You'll see."

Dyvedd looked at the trail behind them and at the barely marked path ahead. "How will you get them to follow you?"

"I'm not sure." She clapped her hands loudly; all their ears perked up. "Come on. This way." She made a clucking noise; their ears twitched again. "Come on." Finally she said, "Gek?"

Gek, if that was his name, bounded forward, circling around her like a badly trained puppy on a walk. Dyvedd swung this way and that, watching him.

Soon they were surrounded by the others, sniffing excitedly and waving their tails.

BJ froze as dozens of them at a time leapt out of the grass where they had lain watching. They surrounded BJ, Dyvedd, and Gredya in a wheeling pack that grew larger each minute.

Gredya's nostrils were flared. "I should change."

"Isn't that bad for you? Bad for your children?"

Gredya nodded shortly, biting her lip. When she had tried snarling a second time, none of the Grym seemed to mind. In her human form it wasn't as threatening as she wanted.

By the time they stopped, there were over three hundred of them—all gaunt, all hungry, all playful and easy to please. They followed behind BJ and the others as eagerly as though they were fleeing something horrible.

"I really don't think they'd attack us," BJ said. "They act like they were domesticated once."

"So you're stealing someone's pets." Dyvedd never took his eyes off them. "Do you have other nice habits I should know?"

"Not yet," BJ said.

On the journey back, Dyvedd said, "My calves are tired."

"That's because you walk backward so often."

"I like to watch," he said shortly. The Grym, following them, compressed into a narrow pack behind her whenever she made a path between worlds; gradually they spread and bounded as they walked inside a world. She half expected them to break away from her the moment they found a suitable world. Obligingly, she walked through a land made up of woods, a flowered prairie, and a hillside that smelled of heather and clover and felt perfect for grazing animals.

But none of them stopped to hunt, and the few who strayed dashed back when the one called Gek gave a short, sharp bark. As she went on, she felt their alert eyes at her back, and couldn't help walking faster than she had on the way from Crossroads.

It was nearly sunset when they came into Crossroads, still on the north side but near to the high plains above Laetyen River, which dropped down to the road to Virginia. BJ was tired, but she had intentionally added a final twist to the road to bring it out here.

She looked behind her. The Grym, entering single file, spread into a phalanx and sat like sheepdogs, surveying the valley below. They sniffed the air curiously, and BJ wondered if they could smell the high-walled canyon to the east, where the flowerbinders had lived, or the bowl-shaped valley still farther away, former home of the unicorns.

Gek slunk forward, his eyes watching her cautiously, his tail wagging. Gredya growled hoarsely. Dyvedd raised Dancer menacingly.

But Gek simply thrust his nose into BJ's right hand and licked her palm humbly. Then he sat up and barked, running to the east. A flock of dumboes rose suddenly and the Grym, to BJ's immense satisfaction, fanned out in the grass and pursued them. In a few moments they were gone, vanishing quickly in the high grass and the brushy cover.

BJ sighed and relaxed. She hadn't realized how nervous they had been making her.

"Nice turn at the end," Dyvedd commented, checking *The Book of Strangeways*. "You have a twisted mind." He slammed the book shut and tossed it back to her. "Thanks for the loan."

BJ turned to Gredya. "You should have an exam. You deliver—"

"As wolf."

"Just as well. I can't do much when you're human, but I can check you over when you're a wolf."

"Tomorrow." She trotted into the brush and disappeared.

Dyvedd sighed, at last taking his hand off his sword. "Pay me; I want to go drink."

BJ handed him a sixpiece. "You knew I was carrying your money."

"You didn't say you weren't. Good thing, too; I'll bet you're a bad liar."

"Is that a vice?"

"No," he said, trying to see where Gredya had gone, "but it's the lack of a fine skill."

BJ followed his gaze. "Do you like Gredya?"

He hesitated, then said frankly, "I don't hate her. But I've seen the Wyr kill. They bear watching."

BJ understood completely. She felt much the same way about Dyvedd. "You'll get used to her."

"We get used to so much, don't we?"

Instead of answering, BJ said lightly, "And what about the Grym? Do you think you'll get used to them?"

"No," he said, looking down the hill. "Not ever. I don't like them at all."

He left, whistling.

N·I·N·E

BJ SLEPT IN the next day. The first time she had, she had
felt lazy. Stein, possibly the earliest riser in Crossroads,
chided her: "You're not running by the clock here. If you're
busy, light a lamp and stay up. If you're tired, sleep."

Harriet Winterthur, who had stayed longer than she had
planned, had taken the truck back, along with messages for
Laurie and Stefan and a supply requisition for Sugar. Stein
had been sorry to see her leave; he had been in a remarkably
good mood for the past few days.

BJ had a light lunch, reviewed and organized her records
(a tricky job, since many patients were also the clients and
some of the patients had neither owners nor names). It bothered her that business was so slow; until there were more
species and a greater population in Crossroads, her practice
would hardly be full-time.

In midafternoon, though she had heard no one approaching, someone knocked.

Catchlet hidden, BJ opened the door a crack, then threw
it wide open. "Fiona, what happened?" Fiona was in a
long-sleeved shirt, and in her arms was the bloodiest sweat-
shirt BJ had ever seen.

A dumbo lay trembling in the shirt, ears extended but
unable to fly. The thin membrane over its ears was slashed

in several places, and there was a long narrow gouge the length of its nose.

"How did you find it?"

"Stupid thing." She looked down at it with contempt. "It was easy to catch. I bumped into it in the grass outside Stein's. It leapt up, spread its ears, and thumped down on its belly six feet away. It had a half-grown litter," she said casually. "They hung around squeaking at her until I picked her up, then they flew off."

BJ took its temperature. She checked its light, fluttery heart rate. She lifted its upper lip and checked gum color (interestingly, the gums had black patches), and pinched its skin to check for dehydration (the skin and fur settled back in place quickly, but the dumbo was shedding like a frightened cat). With no reference sources to compare to, the patient's condition told her very little.

BJ remembered how, during her senior year in Small Animal rotation, she had seen a Doberman who had crawled under a barbed wire fence and sliced its nose vertically, exposing the cavity. BJ had still been nervous about Dobes, but the dog had lain quietly, looking up almost shyly, while she stitched its nose. It would be easy to stitch these wounds, but—"Do you want me to sew it up?"

"Of course not," Fiona said sharply. "Last I heard, we were trying to thin the species. I want you to kill it."

"I'll use T-61. It's a standard euthanasia drug." She looked up at Fiona. "You do know that the meat is no good after this?"

Fiona shuddered. "I'm really not that hungry."

BJ prepared an injection. It occurred to her that she didn't have enough supplies to euthanize hundreds of injured dumboes; Fiona would have to get better about dispatching injured wildlife.

But for now Fiona held it, making soft comforting noises, as BJ put her thumb to the inside of a foreleg and turned it out, looking for a vein. The dumbo was breathing rapidly and shallowly; BJ suspected it was in shock.

The limbs were small and thin, but the veins were prominent; it was no problem. Almost as she pressed the plunger, the little body shuddered and the eyes lost focus.

"So fast," Fiona said wonderingly. "Doesn't it want to hold on?"

"Sometimes that's how it happens." BJ struggled to express what she felt. "I know there's no reason to believe it, but sometimes I feel like the animal is on the edge of letting go, waiting for permission. Sometimes I hate putting animals to sleep, but sometimes it feels like I'm giving them permission to go." She stroked the fur on the stiffening body gently.

She added more practically, "Do you want me to dispose of it? I'd love the chance to study it."

"Fine with me. I haven't gotten a kick out of small-animal funerals since my turtle Speedy, when I was eight."

Of course Fiona had named her turtle Speedy.

Fiona reached into a denim pocket. BJ said, "That's okay . . ."

She handed BJ a gold sixpiece. "I'm a paying customer. You need to eat, too."

"All right." BJ broke off and returned one of the wedges from the sixpiece. "Less a courtesy fee." BJ threw the tea-kettle on and fed the stove. In the summer, when she was here, she kept a fire banked in the stove at all times.

Fiona sat at the wooden table in the living-quarters part of the cottage. "How was traveling with Dyvedd?"

"Not bad." BJ hesitated, then admitted, "Annoying. He knew more than I expected about the Strangeways."

Fiona perked up. "How is he with magic?"

"He's not afraid of it," BJ said finally. "I think he knows a little."

Fiona said thoughtfully, "I wonder how much he'd be able to teach me if I offered to sleep with him?"

"What if he turned out not to know much?"

She grinned. "Then at least I'd have slept with him."

BJ said nothing, but decided that Fiona was recovering, if being what she was before was a recovery.

Fiona gestured to the lifeless body on the steel table. "Have you thought about what could have done that?"

"I'm guessing the Grym." BJ sipped her tea, trying to think like Harriet Winterthur. "I think we've seen a predator figure out how to catch dumboes—slash their ears so they can't fly, then chase them down.''

Fiona stared down at the wound and said finally, "It could also be a knife or a sword.''

BJ was inclined to ignore her, but realized that she could be speaking from experience. "Or a fang.''

"If you say so, but they're pretty straight cuts for a fang.'' She shrugged. "You'd know more about that. I guess.''

Fiona, BJ thought annoyedly, found it hard to concede other people's knowledge.

Fiona added, "There's a new species in Crossroads, did you know?''

BJ was tempted to say, "Of course I knew,'' but said only, "They're called the Grym. I brought them here.''

"Oh. Well, I wondered. They've been sniffing around Stein's all morning.'' Fiona pulled a sheaf of notes, and one book, from her knapsack. "I can't identify them, but I think they've been on Earth before.''

"Fiona, I don't think that's possible—'' But Fiona was sorting through her papers impatiently. BJ sighed. "Okay. Let's hear your evidence.''

Fiona said, "There are a number of sightings, on three continents. One was the loup-garou, from France—''

"I thought that was a werewolf.''

"Which would make it more real, right?'' Fiona wouldn't let go. "Some are werewolves, some aren't. For instance, this one, the Beast of the Gevaudan, walked on all fours and killed livestock and children. It had very strange feet—all right, not like the hand-paws; hooflike.'' She showed BJ a woodcut. BJ had to concede that it did look like a clumsy portrayal of a Grym.

But—"That wasn't necessarily drawn by an eyewitness.''

"Oh, it probably wasn't. It just fits in with their accounts.''

"What happened to the Beast of the Gevaudan?''

"It disappeared. One man claims he shot it, but no one found a body.''

"What other animals are there?''

"In central Africa there was a catlike creature called the Mngwa. It was mostly talked about in hero stories, but there were some killings in the twentieth century that people thought might be a Mngwa. Victims were found holding gray fur from some animal—''

''Fiona, the only thing that story has in common with the Grym is that both animals have fur.'' She considered. ''Even then, most of the Grym have reddish-brown fur.''

She looked stubborn. ''I saved this one for last.'' Fiona handed her a description. ''A mongoose, or mongooselike animal, which could talk and which teased and plagued a family in India for some time.'' Fiona was grinning. ''It called itself the Gek.'' She leaned forward. ''Have you heard them bark?''

''That's just the sound they make.'' But BJ was chilled. ''I named one that.''

''What if it's not just your name for him? What if it's his real name, or a title?''

BJ said firmly, ''Fiona, I'd need harder evidence than that to identify a species. Thank you for showing me this, though.''

Fiona frowned and packed up.

After Fiona left, BJ pulled out a leather-bound book and a pen. The title page, in her best writing, read, ''Lao's Guide to the Unbiological Species: an addendum.''

She wrote THE GRYM at the top of a page and left it blank. As far as she was concerned, there was nothing concrete to write yet. On the next page, she wrote DUMBO.

She wasn't sure that the dumboes belonged to unbiological species, but it was as good a place to write them up as any.

She put the book on her lap and turned the chair until she was facing the steel table. She sketched slowly and carefully, then set the book on the tabletop and sketched a dorsal view. Finally she turned the dumbo over to do the belly.

The pouch was prominent, a slit crossing the abdomen laterally. BJ touched it tentatively, then felt the belly. She took up a scalpel and incised the abdomen until she exposed the uterus.

The dumbo had been pregnant again. They definitely had

litters at least twice a year, possibly more. Thank God they had brought in the Grym.

She did a little more dissection, grateful for the first time for all those dogfish and fetal pigs she'd cut up as an undergrad, as well as for the corpses she had dissected in vet school. She was also grateful for all the textbook illustrators she'd taken for granted; she did several more careful sketches and labeled them: Digestive, Nervous System, Reproductive.

Finally she carried the body out and buried it behind the cottage. She always felt guilty back here, as though she were visiting her mistakes. That was patently unfair, she reminded herself; the burial ground should be reminding her that Crossroads was a dangerous place to live.

While she was washing her hands in the stream from the spring, she heard her own truck struggling up the hill. She sighed; she liked seeing Laurie, but Fiona was enough company for a normal day. Still, she was glad the supplies were coming so quickly, and hoped Stefan had managed to slip in some groceries.

She stepped forward when she heard the horn, then stared in delight at the truck.

Stefan slid out, a rose in hand. "Laurie had a surgery at the school." He was dressed in a linen jacket and pants, and in addition to his fedora he had a cane, a gift from Estevan Protera.

The cane had a sword concealed in it, but BJ knew that wasn't why Stefan loved it. He spun it once and leaned on it and gestured at the flat clearing near the stream. "BJ my love, may I take you on a date?"

Stefan insisted on cooking. He was not the expert Melina and others had become; he had brought the dolmades, stuffed grape leaves, in a cooler, and the lamb came pre-spiced from Gyro's Restaurant in Kendrick. He chopped the cucumbers, onion, and tomato himself, and made a sauce for it.

BJ washed her hands at the sink pump, a heavy but treasured import from a Virginia farmhouse. She slipped into a floor-length dress of homespun wool. Later in the summer, even the nights would be too warm to wear it.

"Outside," he said firmly. "If there are no bugs."

BJ thought of the chimerae nest and shuddered. "Not many."

He helped her carry the table out to the level area between the cottage and the stream from the spring. With a flourish he pulled candlesticks and candles from the truck, then a boom box and tapes.

Lastly he set out the long-stemmed rose in a bud vase. "And now, we should eat."

The meal was good, BJ's talk minimal. Stefan talked enough for both of them: bragging about how well his chemistry class was going, doleful about calculus, full of wild gestures and rhapsodies for second-term biology. BJ listened, enjoying his enthusiasm as much as she did the meal.

Once he made her laugh. "Willy, my roommate, is coming back to visit. He wants to have a party."

"Can you take the time?"

Stefan shrugged. "I have to, BJ; he is my friend." But his eyes had mischief in them. "So I said yes, we will have a toga party, and people will wear costumes."

"Sounds like fun," BJ said. "Have you thought about your costume?—Stefan, you wouldn't."

"Why not?" he said seriously. "I think I would make a good faun."

He waited until she stopped and said, "Could you come?" He took her hand. "I think you would make a good nymph, maybe even a good goddess."

"I'll try." But she realized as she said it how busy she would be in the next few weeks.

"You are always so busy. So am I, I know." He stood and put a different cassette in the boom box. We take no time to dance." He looked sorrowful, even ashamed. "That is very wrong."

He held his hands out as the music began playing.

She laughed at the first song, one her mother used to sing while washing dishes:

"Oh, it's a marvelous night for a moondance . . ."

She stepped into his arms. Stefan held her and they two-stepped as she spun back and forth in the moonlight.

After that, they waltzed. They did what Stefan called a gavotte. They did a loose version of a tango, Stefan insisting on putting a flower between his teeth and trading it with BJ. She was always amazed that, the moment he took her hand and led, she felt as though she was the most graceful dancer in the world. Memories of clumsiness, and of fear that she would someday be twitching and uncontrolled, dropped from her.

Shortly, laughing and completely relaxed, she was swaying against him, listening to a country-western song: *"Quarter moon in a ten-cent town . . ."*

He said apologetically, "I am sorry I found no music so very new."

"You could borrow some of Fiona's tapes."

He frowned and shook his head. "That music is good, but not for tonight."

There was a sudden rustle in the grass, and a flicker of light near the cottage. BJ realized belatedly that she had danced away from her catchlet. Stefan looked around and whispered, his eyes wide, "My cane is inside."

"Hide." BJ ducked behind the springhouse, Stefan with her. It felt oddly like the one time, in high school, that she had been caught with a date when her mother came in the front door unexpectedly.

On that occasion her mother was more embarrassed than upset, and no one had needed any weapons.

The shadows, distorted and unidentifiable, were of several beings who walked upright. They held steady across the grass near the cottage door; whoever had the light had paused there. BJ heard an animal cry somewhere in the grass and for one crazy minute thought that the Grym were walking upright, seeking her out.

Then the procession moved forward and she relaxed again. It was a group of the Meat People.

Stefan grunted, impatient but unembarrassed. "I forgot. They came for Midsummer."

BJ checked her watch: June 21. It was Midsummer Night, the summer solstice.

The Meat People stopped in front of them and clasped

hands, singing in piping four-part harmony. Their voices were clear, every pitch pure; BJ hadn't heard choral music since the last time she had been to church.

Than she did a double take. The Meat People were singing as clearly as they could:

"Weee Risssh you-aaa Hafffy Solll-stissss,
Weee Risssh you-aaa Hafffy Solll-stissss—"

BJ put her hand to her own mouth and kept from laughing.

When they were done, she and Stefan applauded. "That was beautiful. Fiona taught you that, didn't she?" They nodded vigorously. "Thank you." She expected them to go on to Stein's, like carolers.

But they didn't leave. One by one they came forward and gave her small presents.

She whispered to Stefan, "I didn't know I was supposed to give gifts at Midsummer. I don't have anything for anyone." His ears twitched with the breathiness of the whisper.

He whispered back, "My BJ, these are not gifts but offerings."

At first she didn't understand. When she did, she was shocked. "But I'm not—"

"Yes, you are. You are our roadmaker, keeper of the Strangeways. Fields, the Stepfather God, chose you himself. You are the Stepmother Goddess."

It disturbed her, but she stepped forward and accepted the gifts: a wooden statue of her in a lab coat chastising a playful flowerbinder, an intricately carved wooden chain necklace, with a bird somehow carved inside a cage pendant, and three smoked hams spiced in a style that made her suddenly miss Virginia. That was probably Fiona's suggestion as well.

She curtseyed. "Thank you. You're very kind."

Still they waited. After a moment she realized, uncomfortably, what they wanted.

She knelt and touched each of their foreheads in turn, blessing them. They bowed and left, singing. She and Stefan watched the lights move down the hill and disappear in the night.

Stefan determinedly turned the music back on. BJ ran to

the house, got his cane and her catchlet, and laid them where they would be useful.

He was shaking his head as she returned to his arms. "We will not need those on Midsummer Night."

"I'm glad." She looked at the table full of offerings. "I can't get used to this. Why are they bringing me things?"

"Because they're grateful for you. Everyone is. I even brought you something."

She laid her head on his shoulder. "I'll just bet you did."

"BJ my love, when you snicker you sound just like Laurie."

By the next to last song ("Stardust"), they were kissing as much as they were dancing. BJ kicked off her sandals. Stefan tossed his hat aside. After that it was a contest: how far could you throw the next item? Shortly they were standing naked; once more Stefan offered his hands, and once more she glided in, feeling the coolness of the grass underfoot.

The first movement of the "Moonlight Sonata" began, softly and clearly. "They were all about night and the moon and stars."

"Yes." He murmured it into her neck, his lips tickling. "Our night. Our moon and stars."

"A fantabulous evening for romance," she murmured back, kissing as she pressed against him. It seemed to her that she could feel every last hair in the fur on his legs.

She was never quite sure how they kept dancing—only that Stefan had an incredible sense of balance, and was very strong.

T·E·N

BJ WOKE TO the sound of immense wings. Once, not long ago, that sound would have given her nightmares. Now she leapt to the window, recognized the Griffin, and ran out to meet him, still fastening her robe.

The figure at his side stunned her. He was already the size of a leopard, his plumage mottling from downy to silver, his fur growing regular. He strode forward alongside his father confidently, but without the arrogant power of his elders.

The Griffin said curtly, "This is Raphael." The young griffin immediately offered a talon.

BJ took it, deeply flattered that the Griffin would share his son's real name. "You look wonderful. How do you feel?"

The young griffin, puzzled, turned to the Griffin, who said, "Doctors always ask that. You may as well get accustomed to answering."

"I feel well." He added hastily, "Thank you. My father says that you hatched me."

"I helped. Actually, your——" She was about to say "your mother," but the look on the Griffin's face, both impassioned and angry, dissuaded her. "Your entire species tended you and the other chicks."

142

The young griffin said, "We prefer to be called fledglings now. I am not a chick anymore."

BJ was charmed. "Of course not. I'm sorry."

The Griffin said brusquely, "Whatever you are called, you are young. You have a very short time to be young and a great deal to learn in it." He turned to BJ. "I wish you to tutor him."

BJ was stunned. The Griffin went on. "I've left a list of light reading, suitable for young adults."

"Young adults?"

"He will soon be a month old. By winter he will be adult."

The list, under a rock beside him, was at least four single-spaced sheets long. BJ, looking at it, quailed. "Are you sure I'm the teacher you want?"

The young griffin had wandered off to the nearby stream, much as a small human would go to play in the water. He was splashing with his wings and grooming them with his beak; BJ noted absently how careful he was not to splash on his lion parts. The Griffin watched as well. "You are the only suitable teacher available."

"But you know so much more than I do." She floundered. "And Stein knows more than I do—"

"Since childhood, Stein has been raised apart from his world." The Griffin stared momentarily over the hill toward Stein's. "Everyone he knew before age twelve was massacred, in Poland. Thereafter he was raised by the kindest and gentlest being I know, but Stein remained angry, and became a warrior."

BJ nodded. The Griffin went on diffidently. "As for myself, I—well, I chose to leave my people, but I retained much of their ways. We are very good at justice, and vengeance, and combat, but there are human ideas I can prize but not impart." He turned back to BJ. "I need you for that. Please. Care for him; he is vulnerable—physically, mentally, morally."

"I'll take very good care of him." She looked fondly at the young griffin, remembering her terrible flight from world to world cradling him. "I'm glad to, and it's kind of a duty.

I don't mean to be rude," she finished carefully, "but you're an endangered species."

The Griffin looked at her gravely. "I prefer to think of us as embattled."

He turned to his son as the young griffin returned. "Obey her in everything she asks." The young griffin nodded vigorously. "I will check on you as often as my work allows." He added, "So far, I am proud of everything you have done."

The Griffin left. The young griffin stood wistfully, rising on his hind legs, and watched his father fly off. BJ watched, too, but with other emotions; it meant so much to see him in the air again.

He settled quickly on a stone, waiting.

"All right," BJ said. "Do you know how to read?"

"A little," he said cautiously.

"That's good." At least she knew where to begin. "And what can you read?"

"Modern, Middle, and Old English; French, Italian, Spanish, and Golden Age Spanish; Homeric Greek, classical and medieval Latin, Mandarin, Farsi, Arabic, and Basque. I'm not very good in Basque," he finished apologetically.

There was a short silence.

"I'm sorry. I know I've had several weeks. Should I know more?"

BJ said with outward calm, "I think you know enough to be my student."

He looked much happier. His feathers perked absurdly, like hundreds of tiny cowlicks.

"Do you know what you are going to read with me?"

"I know that the list is thorough."

It was indeed—four pages, single-spaced, two columns. BJ scanned it quickly to see what order it was in, and how much of it was in English. A few seconds convinced her that it wasn't broken down in any way she could understand.

She tapped the first title. "We'll begin with the heraldry. Do you have the books?" She looked around as though they would be on the grass, and said with relief, "This will have to wait until I can get some of the books."

"Pardon me—" The young griffin was staring down the valley. "I think they are coming now."

BJ's truck, Fiona at the wheel, was winding along the road by the river. The sag of the tires told her that the truck was loaded down. When it began climbing up the hill, slowly as though overloaded, BJ could see that Fiona was grinning wickedly; Fiona enjoyed library runs.

BJ sighed. "First we'll unpack and alphabetize the books"—she caught herself—"in English, and then we'll begin with the heraldry."

Fiona parked the truck and all but ran away, carrying a few prized volumes. The young griffin only helped stack them in columns; he was too frantic for reading to be denied or delayed. Finally BJ nodded to him. "Go ahead." He happily settled down with his first assigned book, and BJ left to get dressed.

She came back outside a few minutes later.

Watching him read was charming and daunting at the same time. He cocked his head like a sparrow eyeing a bug, scanned the page, and flicked it forward deftly with the tip of a single claw. When he was halfway through the book, he switched legs.

The five-hundred-page book took twenty minutes, after which he looked up. "When it says that the bar sinister indicates illegitimacy, what does that mean?"

He turned back quickly to the reference page. BJ looked over his shoulder. "It means the person has a bar across the coat of arms, to show that the person isn't the child of married parents. It's also called bastardy."

He said firmly, "I don't see the point."

BJ was grateful Dyvedd wasn't nearby. "I agree."

He flipped over another page. "Are griffins everything they say here?"

"That will be what griffins signify to people, not what they are." She scanned it. "It says that griffins represent valor, courage, and unshakable justice. I don't know many griffins," she said tactfully, "but I do know that those are the qualities of your father."

"Are those qualities important?"

"Of course they are. They aren't the only important virtues. . . ." She pointed to other traits in the heraldry book. "Vigilance, temperance, honor, truth—" At each word, the young griffin sat straighter. BJ felt as though she were inducting a Boy Scout.

By the end of her list he was standing taller, on his haunches as though he were himself posed on a shield. "I will be all that."

BJ smiled. "You'll try to be all that. Don't be surprised if you aren't always." She gestured at the next rank of books, mostly legends of heroes. "Read those."

His golden eyes shone. "They're about heroes? Do they all have all those virtues?"

BJ hesitated, partly because she was unfamiliar with many of the legends in the volumes before them. "They're about heroes. Some of them don't have all the virtues." She dredged up something she remembered from an undergraduate English course. "Most books about heroes are only interesting because the heroes have failings."

The young griffin said stiffly, "Not to me."

She gestured at the books. "Go ahead and start. I'll carry these in."

She watched him read while she carried the books inside, a stack at a time. They filled the back wall of her home, leaving only room for the pantry door.

She organized them as listed on the sheets of paper; griffins were meticulous, if eccentric. At the end she turned over the sheets to see if there were additional instructions.

On the back of one of the pages were a few lines, with crossing out, written in elegant cursive script in ink. A scratch in the surface, and the feathering of the ink, suggested that the Griffin had dipped a claw in ink to write:

L'aur(ie)

This all too brief expanse of infinite coast
Where we lay touching, all too far apart,
Two countries, lonely worlds, each foreign heart
Beloved, alien, beloved most
For presence now, in fragmentary spite

Of crossed and crossing stars, indifferent
And unimportant after having spent
The long days waiting, and the longer night,

Is Love immeasurable. One small touch
Is everything, and all the world beside,
Love infinite, a speck where worlds collide
In kisses, points made not so much
Of one life as of both; what others call
Fractured and fractal, whole and all in all.

BJ blinked. She remembered the terms from conversation with Harriet Winterthur and Estevan Protera; evidently the Griffin remembered quite a bit more. She looked out the window uncertainly at his son, who had already finished another book and was waiting for her to make everything clear.

The book was *La Chanson de Roland*. BJ was relieved when the young griffin asked nothing about Charlemagne and medieval history, which he seemed to know thoroughly. Instead he wanted to ask about knighthood and how it related to heraldry, and to serving a king, challenging in single combat, and marshaling troops.

After a long and tangled discussion, he said suddenly, "I need to choose a name."

"Why do you need one? You know when I'm addressing you—"

"My father doesn't use his name. It's as though he has a secret identity." He said it firmly and confidently.

BJ floundered, realizing that the Griffin had not yet told his son about the Griffin's being Inspector General. "He may not always acknowledge everything he does—we all do things we don't talk about—"

"Exactly." His eyes shone, rivaling the sun overhead. "Then I'll take a *nom de guerre* as well. My name is—" He hesitated fractionally, scanning the books BJ was stacking, then called out with the joy of recognition: "Roland."

BJ gave up. "All right. You're Roland. You're also wasting time in a number of lessons."

"It's time for me to go home," he said regretfully. "I live with my grandfather."

"With your—oh." BJ said carefully, "Does he know that you're studying with me?"

"He does. He doesn't discuss it." Roland added thoughtfully, "He may discuss it with my father, but I doubt it. Does that mean I shouldn't discuss it with my grandfather?"

BJ almost said no. "Wait until you trust your own judgment; then decide."

"My own judgment..." He stared into the distance. "That's what I really need to learn. How does one learn that?"

BJ was floundering already; teaching a griffin was going to be difficult. "By talking to others. By watching them, comparing your decisions with theirs." She tapped the books. "By reading about other people's decisions, and judging theirs."

He rose. "I need to take some books with me. In what can I carry them?"

He was, BJ thought, a true griffin, careful not to end sentences in prepositions. "There must be something . . . I'll be right back." She ran into the house. Her old knapsack was well worn, but still serviceable; she had been too attached to it to throw it out.

"Did you wear it in combat?"

BJ smiled, then remembered that in fact, by accident, she had a few times. "Yes, but that's not its primary purpose."

He said earnestly, "I'll wear it, then. The way a noble would have a shield with a coat of arms."

On an impulse, she sketched a triskelion on it: hoof, clawed foot, human foot. "This will do for now. That's the only sign I've ever seen for Crossroads."

He frowned and said decidedly, "It should have a griffin on it."

She put it on his back and patted him lightly. "Now it does."

"Thank you." He looked up at her very seriously. "I'm grateful to be born into a world of such goodness and courage."

BJ, who had seen secrecy, addiction, and betrayal in

Crossroads, said only, "I'm glad you were born to come here." She watched him fly off, struggling slightly under the weight of his books. She sighed and went back inside to familiarize herself with the book list.

The next morning, when BJ stumbled outside at sunrise, Roland was already there. He was not alone.

The other griffin, also a fledgling, had brilliant copper plumage.

Both of them already had books out and were reading. When they saw her, they came forward. The second griffin seemed more watchful than Roland, a little more cautious. He also stood near and a little behind Roland, almost as though he were guarding Roland's flank; BJ suspected that his stance was not from fear, but courtesy and duty.

"This is my best friend," Roland said. "We hunt together, we fight together, we talk about everything."

BJ said only, "If he's a friend, then he's welcome." In her mind she could hear the Griffin saying that it was an acute use of the conditional tense.

Roland said with relief, "I'm glad of that, then. I'd like you to meet him. His name is—" He paused in confusion.

BJ smiled, raising a hand as the second griffin tensed and opened his beak. "I'd just like to know a name I may call him."

With relief the second griffin said, "If it please you, I'd like to be called Oliver." The two of them waited expectantly.

BJ, recalling Roland and Oliver in *La Chanson de Roland*, sighed. "Of course you would." For some reason the young griffins, who had been intelligent for barely a month, made her feel remarkably old.

"Then it's all right?"

"I don't name you," she said patiently. "You choose your own names."

"But you are our tutor."

Oh, God. " 'Our'?"

Oliver actually knelt, his front feet bowing. "If you will have me."

BJ thought idiotically, "I don't even have a teaching certificate." Aloud she said, "I'll still have to work in my veterinary practice; that must come first. Otherwise——" She gave in. "I'll do my best."

Oliver said relievedly and a trifle pompously, "Then all is well."

The lesson went well, but breaks in the reading were more frequent; the two of them would want to act out what they had read. She watched Roland and Oliver prancing in the meadow, talons flexed and wings wide (*rampant*, in heraldry). They slashed at the air and peered alertly at the valley below, and they were very happy. "When did I lose the excitement of becoming grown-up," BJ wondered, "and actually become a grown-up?"

But the lessons were livelier as well: argument, counterargument, and an occasional appeal to BJ to settle a dispute.

Probably the most intense debate came when Roland and Oliver got in an argument. Oliver started it, inquisitively and, surprising in a griffin, awkwardly: "Who was the more good, King Arthur or Robin Hood?"

Before BJ could answer, Roland said flatly, "King Arthur, because Robin merely had to be good in a bad world, whereas Arthur had to bring good to a bad world."

Oliver objected, "But Arthur slept with his half sister, attempted to kill his wife by law, and killed the male children of Britain. Surely that makes him the weaker."

Roland, greatly agitated, flapped his wings. "We don't know all of what Robin did. We do know much of what Arthur did." It disturbed BJ that they spoke of both heroes as though they were real, but she couldn't find a way to say so to two mythical animals.

They turned to BJ. "Who was the better man?"

At that moment, she hated the Griffin for putting her in this job.

"I think," she said finally, "that you can't judge between them unless you can picture Robin in Arthur's seat and Arthur in Robin's." She paused, missing the amiable King Brandal, whose only failing as king was loving his queen Morgan to the detriment of Crossroads. "Arthur took the harder task; perhaps Robin would have failed in the same places or made even worse mistakes.'' She hesitated, remembering that she had brought in the dumboes herself, and had brought in the Grym and Gredya. ''I think,'' she finished, ''that when you lead a country your mistakes are no longer small.''

Roland and Oliver were satisfied, but her answer kept BJ up all night.

E·L·E·V·E·N

MIDSUMMER NIGHT WAS long gone, the air rich with the scent of summer flowers. BJ woke with a sore back for the third day in a row. She took Tylenol, did a number of acutely painful stretches, and resolved, not for the first time, to stretch out before doing any lifting.

Her patients the day before had been a lamb who had clearly been attacked by the Grym but had somehow gotten away, and, subsequently, a sheep with long parallel slashes on its abdomen. The first case made BJ wonder dubiously how efficient the Grym actually were, though she was under the impression that the dumbo population was thinning.

The lamb had torn tendons on its left rear leg. Evidently a Grym had leapt at it and hooked into the flesh behind the knee, but the lamb had been able to wrench free. BJ fired up the generator, did an X-ray, and noted with relief that there was no bone damage.

BJ used isoflurane, as little as possible, on the lamb. She had done surgery on sheep but never lambs, and she was monitoring the anesthetic plane carefully. She was quite methodical, but the entire time she missed Laurie; the wrong anesthetic level can easily kill a patient.

Dyvedd had showed up, panting, before the surgery. "Fiona told me." He looked over the lamb.

"It's such a skill, cutting like that."

BJ said lightly, "Have you ever practiced on an animal?"

Dyvedd only said, "Is that how you learned?" He eyed her with mock suspicion. "I'll remember that."

The treatment was brief, and only partly successful. She cleaned the wound and sutured as best she could, but large sections of the tendons were gone forever. In a world with predators, this lamb wouldn't last long. While BJ stitched, she said, "Could you walk outside Crossroads with me again tomorrow?"

"Could you pay me again?" When she nodded, he said, "Where am I taking you, or you me?"

When she didn't say, he grinned. "Meet me at the inn. I'll take breakfast there."

The sheep's injury was more serious: a belly gash extending nearly from the rib cage to the testicles. No major organs had been lacerated. Possibly one of the Meat People had dropped it off and left it as a charity patient or an offering. It was unlike the Meat People, who always paid their way. Kneeling on the grass in front of her house, BJ looked at the wound briefly, then shook her head. "It won't live." She looked at Dyvedd. "If I euthanize it, it's no good for meat. As long as you're here, would you kill him for me?"

He shrugged. "I want to farm. It's part of the trade." Dancer spun forward almost before he stopped speaking, and the headless sheep collapsed. He stared down at it thoughtfully. "I should have caught the blood in a tub, for sausage. Spurted quite a ways, didn't it?"

"Sheep have a lot of blood," BJ said. "Excuse me." She went back inside and very nearly threw up.

This morning she wrote a note to herself: TELL SUGAR TO BRING IN ROTATION. Livestock surgery might not be as exciting as unicorn births, but it was good practice, and BJ had the feeling that they might see some fairly unusual surgery.

As she left her house, Roland flew down, accompanied by Oliver. He bowed, as he had tended to do lately. "Good morning, my BJ. What shall we read today?"

She gestured to the stack of books she had already laid

out. "I'm afraid I can't stay with you. Read as much as you can in these, and we'll discuss them tomorrow." She tried to sound confident; the thought of reviewing materials with Roland and Oliver still daunted her.

"I understand," he said. "Good fortune with your work." He made it sound secretive and important.

BJ left, smiling, but was depressed at how secretive and how important this part of her work was. She was halfway to the inn before her mood lifted; a dozen or so of the Grym left off chasing dumboes (seemingly futilely) to bound alongside her, tails wagging.

This time the way had come to her in a dream: grasslands, deer running and talking, and the stern voice telling Bambi that he would not see his mother again. BJ woke with tears in her eyes, not for the movie but for having seen it with her brother Peter in a rerelease, and she quickly thought out the path to another world.

The walk out of Crossroads was genuinely pleasant, although BJ felt tired. Once again she took them uphill as she tried to follow a road Fields had laid out before she had any gift at following, or making, the Strangeways. But the day was sunny and the wind gentle, and she strode ahead on the twisting path with at least the appearance of confidence while Dyvedd, close behind her, sang and whistled. Once he asked, "Do all worlds open only uphill?"

"Sorry, this one does. We'll be going over mountains."

He looked embarrassed but eager. "Does it make snow in these worlds?"

"Some of them. Yes, it snows."

"What is snow like?"

"It's white—"

"Everyone knows it's white." He said it scornfully, but was immediately curious. "And it just drops from the sky?"

"It's white, and it drops from the sky. It covers the ground, after a while."

Dyvedd said dubiously, "Sounds like pigeon shit."

BJ, startled, said, "You know about pigeons?"

Dyvedd snorted. "That lot flies everywhere. Pigeons, sparrows, and people who sing off-key. Can't get away from them.'' He finished wistfully, ''I'd like to see snow some-day.''

BJ smiled to herself and kept walking.

They turned to the right, rising, and moved through a high pass. BJ pulled her jacket close as their breath made small puffs. Even Dyvedd, accustomed to life out of doors, shivered. ''Can't you make a road through sunlight?''

But as they came through the pass, the clouds cleared and the rocks gave way to sloping meadows; the crags to either side had deep gullies and crevasses which were shadowed even by day. Dyvedd glanced at them, guarding against a potential ambush.

His eyes widened. ''Wait!'' He leapt off the path, staring at a white drift extending from one of the cracks.

He swung Dancer into it, leaving a wide gouge easily. There was a small scraping sound; the surface had hardened and frozen many times. He cut a square hole in it, then asked, ''Snow?''

She nodded.

He plunged his hand into it, then turned and stared at her accusingly. ''You didn't tell me it would be cold.''

''I thought you knew.''

He scooped up a handful and threw it at her. She ducked, edging over to a drift on the other side of the path, and threw a quickly packed snowball at him.

The battle was brief and pleasantly even; he had more experience in war, she with snow. After each of them scored a direct hit, she called a truce. ''We'd better go.''

''I guess.'' He stood, wiping his hands off on his breeches and flexing his cold fingers. He said softly, like a child at a birthday party, ''Thank you for the snow.''

''Everybody ought to see it once.''

''And now I have.'' He looked back at the peaks behind, understanding for the first time the white caps. ''What's the name of this place?''

She shook her head. ''It will be on the map in *The Book of Strangeways;* I don't really know it.''

He frowned. ''I don't understand that.''

''Neither do I.''

He shrugged and fell in behind her as they continued twisting downhill, walking between worlds.

As they walked downhill, Dyvedd sang. He had a pleasant voice, with only a rough sense of pitch; gradually BJ found herself listening.

At the end she said, "What's that called?"

" 'The Frog Who Loved a Cow.' " He added severely, "Someone who works with animals should already be familiar with these things."

"Well, I wasn't. Could you sing the middle part again?"

He sang obligingly,

> " 'And *up* he jumped,
> 'And *up* he jumped,
> 'And *up* he jumped again—' "

At the end of the verse, the frog collapsed in exhaustion and the cow still didn't know he was there. BJ said, "I wish Lee Anne were here. She'd love it."

"What? You know the kind of woman who loves low and vile songs of sex?"

BJ said defensively, "She's a friend." She added, "And, yes, she does."

Dyvedd said courteously, "Then I'm sure she'd be my friend, too."

BJ, imagining a meeting between Dyvedd and the outspoken Lee Anne, was so intrigued that she completely missed the verse about the frog smearing itself with pitch to stick to the back of the cow. She asked him to sing it again, twice.

The final world they arrived in was wide and grassy; unlike the world in which they had found the Grym, it was filled with life. The air was moist from the still-drying dew.

Dyvedd tugged at her sleeve and pointed with his sword. Silhouetted at the top of the hill were three figures, basically human from head to waist. Below the waist were the hindquarters and legs of deer. All three figures were dragging small travois with wrapped bundles.

Two of the standing figures had antlers. The third figure,

BJ noted with fascination, already had a bulging belly. "I should have studied obstetrics," she thought; evidently Crossroads was a very fertile place.

BJ called out, "Rudy? Bambi?"

Two of the figures leapt forward, and one called, "Yo! BJ!" The third figure, clearly older and less agile, watched. BJ stepped to the foot of the hill.

Rudy was still wearing one of his beloved, much faded USF T-shirts. Bambi was in a halter top, her belly sticking out under it; hardly any pregnant woman on Earth would have worn a halter top at that stage of pregnancy.

They bounded forward, their hooved feet digging into the soft turf. At the last minute, Rudy pulled BJ back and tilted his antlers forward, looking hard at Dyvedd. "What gives, man? Is BJ your prisoner?"

He shrugged, lowering the sword fractionally. "I think I'm hers."

BJ said quickly, "Rudy, Bambi, this is Dyvedd. He's guarding me. Dyvedd, this—"

At that point she was nearly knocked down as the two of them leapt forward, hugging her. She blinked as, one at a time, they licked her nose with their large, ruminant's tongues.

The older stag man followed them down. It was Suuuno, the shaman of Rudy and Bambi's people. He smiled at BJ and raised a hand in greeting. As before when they had met, his bare chest was painted—this time with symbols for sun and grass.

BJ nodded to him, cautiously turning it into a bow. "Why did you meet me here?"

He chuckled. "We could ask the same, but we don't need to. I knew you would come."

"But you couldn't know where I—where the new road would be."

"Where someone was about to make a road? I knew that when I woke this morning."

The hairs on her neck prickled. She had only decided on the last turn a few minutes ago.

"Don't be afraid." He moved closer still. "It all comes of walking and watching. I see things." He looked her up and down, awe mixing with his humor. "Since we met last, you have changed. You make roads."

She nodded.

"I see your change." He smiled still more. "All your changes."

BJ felt unnerved, wondering how much he could see about her.

She turned to Bambi. "You look well. How do you feel?"

"Clumsy." She patted her belly. "I don't balance well."

"Of course. Your center of gravity has shifted." BJ had observed before how nimble and surefooted Rudy and Bambi were, seldom stumbling or needing to catch themselves. "How about your appetite?"

Rudy rolled his eyes. "You oughta see her. She eats like a whole herd."

Bambi, with more assurance than BJ had seen in her before, pushed him playfully. "Don't make me sorry we mate for life." She turned back to BJ. "I eat lots of fruit, salad, vegetables, everything." She made a face. "Rudy's even got me eating beans."

"Protein," he said solemnly. "We're herbivores, so we have to sweat getting our proteins." At BJ's stare he added, "I joined a food co-op in San Francisco. Taught me a lot."

Suuuno said, "We have dietary laws; they cover childhood, adulthood, and pregnancy. She is very safe." He was standing back from them, watching carefully.

"Any other balance problems? Dizziness, nausea—" BJ wondered if Bambi's people, The Ones Who Die, could throw up; after all, they were ruminants.

"I'm fine." She frowned, her nostrils flaring as though sniffing for danger. "What's wrong?"

BJ had thought carefully about phrasing the problem of birth defects to Bambi. Vet school hadn't prepared her for talking patients. "Bambi, some of the other species that left Crossroads have had health problems."

She looked blankly at BJ.

"I've helped at a number of births for species who have left Crossroads. There was a higher incidence of birth defects than there would have been if they had stayed inside."

She took a deep breath. "So I'm trying to find and bring back all the species we sent out—"

Bambi, interrupting, turned to Suuuno. "That's why you made us pack." The shaman nodded, his large eyes sympathetic. Bambi's own eyes suddenly went wide, and she clutched her stomach protectively.

BJ said comfortingly, "It's just a precaution. You've already told me everything is fine."

Bambi nodded hesitantly.

"Anyway, you've been missed at Stein's."

Rudy said hungrily, "Books. Man, I've missed them so bad."

BJ was astonished. "What about your college texts?"

He laughed. "They were heavy even to carry across campus. I resold them to the bookstore before coming back."

"But didn't you want to keep them?"

"Keep?" He looked confused. "I did. I read them."

BJ looked at the size of the bundles The Ones Who Die had with them, and recognized the problem: nomads have little room for books.

She said, "There are some new ones. Fiona brought them in, from the university library." She added with disapproval, "She should have returned them."

"Good thing she didn't." Rudy was nearly dancing from hoof to hoof in his excitement. "So, what's the catch?"

"No real catch." She turned to Bambi. "I'll want to examine you."

Bambi's face fell, and she shook her head. "You can't."

"I have to," she said firmly. "A lot could have happened with your leaving—"

"You can't. " She backed against Rudy, who put his arms around her. "I won't let you."

Now Bambi's eyes, even larger than usual, were filled with tears. Rudy turned her away, sheltering her from BJ.

BJ took a deep breath. "Bambi, don't be silly. We need to know that the baby is all right. It'll be a simple exam—"

As she stepped forward, Rudy turned toward her and, to her astonishment, lowered his antlers at her.

Suuuno, stepping forward, moved easily between Rudy and BJ. "I am what you call a midwife."

BJ, annoyed, said, "I'm a doctor. I've trained for this work—"

"As have I." He never stopped smiling. "Both in medicine and in history. May I tell you some history?"

His tone sounded odd, the singsong which went with chants or magic. Dyvedd tensed. Finally BJ nodded.

Suuuno's eyes went unfocused as he said rhythmically, "Long before any of us now were born, The Ones Who Die were taken captive and domesticated."

"Domesticated . . ." BJ looked at them in confusion. "To do field work?"

He said ritually, "For our hands and our horns, for our hides and our hooves, for our fat in lamps and for our meat at meals. Our sinews made the bowstrings which hunted our children. Nothing was wasted, and nothing remained to us but our souls."

Dyvedd said flatly, "Been known to happen." It was the first he'd said in a long while.

BJ stared at Suuuno, horrified. "But you're people!"

Suuuno smiled at her, the smile of a teacher correcting a naive pupil. He had no incisors. "Have none of your people ever taken slaves?"

BJ opened her mouth, caught herself, and said feebly, "Yes, but not to skin. Not to eat . . ." She trailed off, wondering what Stein would have said, as she realized how little history she knew. "I think. All right, people were skinned, and . . . Well, but that was long ago."

Suuuno, no longer smiling, said, "For us it was a short enough time ago that my people sing the songs of it, parent to child, and not a word has been lost. There are still slavers, in many worlds."

Bambi looked pleadingly at BJ, who stared helplessly back.

Suuuno said quietly, "I know what you are now, but you are also a carnivore, and a tamer and taker of animals. In this one thing, you must bow to our wishes."

As BJ framed a reply, he said, "I said 'must.' Or we can't come back with you."

A crowd had gathered, peering over the hill behind Rudy

and Bambi. BJ recognized most of them from Rudy and Bambi's wedding. "All of you?"

"Just your friends and I."

BJ said plaintively, "Can't I at least get you something on prenatal care? Not that I know enough about that."

Suuuno laughed, as though there were no tension at all. "If we have trouble, I will come find you. Then you can tell me what to do."

Dyvedd muttered, "It's tempting to tell him what to do, isn't it?"

BJ shushed him and said reluctantly, "All right." She turned to Bambi. "But in exchange, you have to visit me and talk about your symptoms, and"—she turned back to Suuuno, assuming a more deferential tone—"I would be grateful if you'd tell me what you know about health and medicine for The Ones Who Die."

It was the first time she had said the name in front of Rudy and Bambi; she realized, saying it, what an admission that was. Herbivores by nature, traditional prey, they had as a species committed to sacrificing their lives in the defense of their young.

Bambi leapt forward as though a barrier had broken and hugged BJ. "I want to."

The trip back was brief and, out of deference to Dyvedd's comment about steep roads, mostly downhill. At one point, they paused and looked around, seeing a fairly dry world with what looked like endless wheat fields stretching toward the horizon. The plain was broken by meandering lines of willows and water-loving trees.

Suuuno said, "We've taken a side road."

BJ was pleased with herself. "There's an old friend in this world, someone who was at Rudy and Bambi's wedding. I'm hoping to see her."

Bambi said instantly, "Polyta?" There was enough hero worship in her voice for BJ to feel envious. Polyta was the Carron, a leader of the centaurs called the Hippoi, and BJ had to admit that she was awe-inspiring. Bambi tapped forward eagerly, scanning the horizon and flaring her nostrils as she sniffed the air.

But none of them found any trace of the Hippoi.

"They're nomads," BJ said finally. "I'll find them some other time."

"I'm not sure," Suuuno said, and his voice was flat and disapproving. "This world . . ."

Before he had finished, Bambi and Rudy were practically back to back, looking at the empty plain before them and at the line of trees in the distance marking a river.

Dyvedd said flatly, "Time we left."

Suuuno regarded Dyvedd carefully for the first time. "You are not from Crossroads."

Dyvedd folded his arms, letting them rest on Dancer. "I am now."

Suuuno looked him up and down and said gently and cryptically, "The marks are always there, aren't they?"

Dyvedd turned red and didn't answer.

They returned alone toward Crossroads. On the way, BJ said carefully to Suuuno, "You were right, but why was it important that Dyvedd isn't from Crossroads?"

Suuuno said, "When I studied at USF, the debate was the child of the debate now: what part of behavior comes from teaching, and what from natural selection? The students I knew could argue it all night, either way." He smiled at her again. "Some night when you aren't busy, maybe we could argue it."

"You'd be better off with Stein; he could argue with more background." She added tactlessly, "Or with the Griffin."

Suuuno's smile faded. With an effort he said politely, "We have many songs of his people as well."

BJ walked the rest of the return trip in thoughtful silence.

The arrival into Crossroads was very like Dyvedd's and BJ's first walk together with Gredya and the Grym. Suuuno, Bambi, and Rudy (with a muffled "Later, babe") bounded into the rich valley below, unable to contain themselves. BJ and Dyvedd were once again left alone at the threshold of Crossroads.

They looked down toward the river valley, and toward the smoke that, even in summer, curled up from Stein's.

Dyvedd held a palm out for his pay. BJ, giving it to him,

asked, "What did Suuuno mean about marks being there?"

He said carelessly, "Magicians are always the same, think they can see something you can't. Mostly they do it to themselves." He stepped along lightly and easily, picking up his pace. "Probably he ate a fungus. I'm off to work, then." He stared up at the sun. "Enough time to put in a half day's cutting."

Dyvedd pocketed the coins and jogged off, whistling as though none of the stranger events of the day had ever taken place. BJ walked alone to her home.

BJ didn't ask again, but wondered what Suuuno had seen in him that she had missed.

Below her the young griffins stood reading at their usual breakneck pace. BJ descended toward her cottage, speeding up as she saw that for once the Griffin himself was visiting. Roland looked up from his reading, saw her expression, and tactfully moved on.

The Griffin nodded. "Welcome back. I hope you don't mind my interference; I tutored these potential hellions in your absence."

Oliver stiffened, but politely kept out of the conversation. Shortly he set his book between his wings and strode farther off; Roland tucked his own into BJ's battered knapsack and followed.

The Griffin nodded as they left. "Think of it as a visit from the school superintendent." He jerked his beak toward Roland and Oliver. "They're doing quite well."

"Then I live to teach another day."

"And all the world rejoices." The Griffin came forward, cocking his head as he looked her up and down. "Is something troubling you?"

BJ said, "Did anything unusual happen while I was gone?"

The Griffin arched a feathery eyebrow at her delicacy. "If you mean animal mutilations, none. Throughout Crossroads, a pastoral and singularly boring peace descended. I take it that Conan the Agrarian accompanied you."

"Dyvedd was with me." She added, without expecting to, "He can't help it if he's a little naive."

"It's not his naiveté that concerns me. Nor should it you." He added in a voice carefully devoid of inflection, "It's quite kind of you to defend him."

BJ blushed. "I'm more concerned with establishing his innocence."

He responded, "As I am in establishing his guilt. Your compassion does you credit. Then again," he said thoughtfully, "one would expect compassion of a goddess. Particularly a kind of fertility goddess."

BJ froze.

"Ah. I wondered if you knew." The Griffin cocked his head, staring piercingly at her. "After all, it was barely noticeable even to my senses."

She looked at him, barely seeing him. "I had reason to believe I couldn't be."

"So much for reason," he said smugly. "I imagine it affects your plans."

BJ said unsteadily, "It affects everything." She watched as Roland and Oliver bowed to the Griffin before leaving. She nodded absently to them as they bowed to her.

When they were gone she put on some water, looked confusedly and with some resentment at her birth control pills, and made a cup of Irish breakfast tea. She threw that out and made herbal decaf tea. She spilled some of it trying to sip. Then she pulled a sheet of paper from a notebook and began a list of questions:

Gestation period? Sheep and goats carried only for a few months. She hoped fervently that Stefan or Melina would know the gestation period for fauns.

Nutrition? Her diet was fairly sensible, but she wondered about nutritional problems and unthrifty, weak lambs. She could eat more salad this time of year. She hoped she wouldn't need to eat grass. She realized, with some embarrassment, that this would be a question for Sugar Dobbs.

Which raised another question. She wrote *Field effect?* and underlined it four times, thinking. She had seen a great deal of birth defects and stillbirths recently. She wrote *Ask Protera*, but she wrote beside it in block letters: SPEND MOST OF TERM IN CROSSROADS. DELIVER IN CROSSROADS.

She thought more, wondering how she would manage pregnancy in a world where she couldn't leave her work. She doodled a sketch of Stefan in the margin of the paper, then did another sketch of a faun half-size, with a child's face, then added long eyelashes and a bow to the curly hair. Momentarily distracted, she smiled, trying to make the sketch look like pictures of herself as a little girl.

She gripped the pen tightly and wrote a final question: *Genetics?*

Since she had first discovered that she carried the gene for Huntington's chorea, she had resolved that she would never have a child. Crossroads, coupled with the changes to her own body when she became the maker of the Strangeways, had ensured that she would never develop the disease. So far as she knew, any child of hers still had a fifty percent chance of having the gene for Huntington's chorea.

She could write any number of things: *Ask Protera. Talk to an M.D., maybe Doctor Lucille Boudreau. Amniocentesis and genetic testing? Is genetic testing meaningful for a half-faun child?*

Instead, she left the list on her table and went outdoors. She sat in the sun by the stream and sipped the tea, staring at the countryside and trying not to think at all.

T·W·E·L·V·E

THE NEXT TWO months in Crossroads were wonderful and terrible: wonderful, because every day was clean and beautiful, with something quietly fantastic. Terrible, because something monstrous and inescapable was happening to her body.,

BJ's belly developed a pronounced bulge in the first week; by the second it felt ungainly. She moved quickly into all the problems of pregnancy: pressure on the bladder, more backaches, awkwardness in accustomed physical tasks. If she had mood swings, she wasn't aware of it; however, she noticed that Stein and Fiona, and even Dyvedd, seemed cautious around her. That irritated her.

BJ was accustomed to her body betraying her. After the past few years, she was accustomed to stumbling, to sudden clumsiness, to all the signs of Huntington's chorea and the silent fear that symptoms would inevitably increase. She was by no means ready for this new and strange invasion, and the change in her body, which was remarkably rapid.

Apart from that, each day in Crossroads began the same, and yet it didn't bother her; repetition is tolerable when it repeats something wonderful. Overhead she would hear Roland and Oliver singing, sometimes an obscure drinking song, once a Basque hymn about the Angel Gabriel and Mary in some strange rhythm, once a medieval marching tune, and once a strange melody she couldn't remember when they were done, and which she suspected might not be from Earth at all.

The two of them would plunge straight down as she emerged from the cottage, stoop to within a few feet of her, their talons extended, and turn the stoop into a bow. Then they would say, sometimes apart and sometimes together, "Good morning, lady."

BJ felt the urge to ruffle their feathers, but felt somehow that was wrong. Instead she smiled and nodded back. "I'm glad to see you."

It seemed to please them inordinately.

Thereafter the day would take a simple, easy course. BJ would briefly outline the work for the day. Most of the texts were things she had not read (*Don Quixote*, *The Iliad*), but Laurie had thoughtfully included reference works with the highlights of the books BJ was teaching. Sometimes BJ felt like a fraud; she never said so.

Roland and Oliver would stand side by side, devouring the texts as rapidly as possible, predators' eyes scanning the material nearly a page at a glance. Then, nodding to each other, they would switch texts.

BJ had to fight the temptation to speak while they read; she stared at the upper hills. There was rich yellow on them, these days; the bushes BJ had learned were called gorse were blooming, and the yellow-specked hills and cloud-specked sky were beautiful together. BJ did her own work, but found herself staring outside often.

The motion of the two griffins reminded she forcibly of the fledgling blue jays she had seen, years before, feeding at a dog dish behind a friend's house. They were poised, energetic, and filled with an innocent assurance that nothing could disturb them.

When they were done reading they would argue with each other. In discussion, Roland was the most concerned with nobility, Oliver with loyalty and courage. It had taken BJ a few weeks to realize that each worried most over the qualities he thought he lacked.

BJ would listen, breaking in only once in a while. It was a source of some wonder to her that she was able to break in now and then every day to correct misconceptions. Maybe there really was something to being human that was in itself special.

On one day she couldn't help breaking in. The two griffins had read *Gawain and the Green Knight*, which BJ had struggled through in a sophomore literature course. She listened to the two of them mock Gawain for having made a promise to his host, then promise a woman that he would revere her, then find that the second promise might betray the first.

BJ explained earnestly to them, "The point of the story is, Gawain had two codes, chivalry and courtly love. He had a debt of honor to his host, but he also had a debt of courtesy to his host's wife. When they came in conflict, he made a bad decision."

Roland considered, the membranes floating down partway over his golden eyes. When he finally spoke, he said firmly, "The real point is, he made a bad promise."

BJ could answer that one; her teacher had trapped an entire class. "Of course. Which promise?"

But Roland had an answer for that. "The second one. Whichever promise he made second, the one that could have caused the conflict, would be bad. Avoid too many promises."

Oliver nodded agreement briskly. "So wise, and still so young."

Roland glanced sideways, realized Oliver was being sarcastic, and struck him with the full force of one wing. The pages of the book rippled and buffeted. Oliver staggered, held his ground, and raised both wings, walking forward with feathers ruffled, beak open, lion tail lashing. "Was that a challenge?"

"Of course."

They took to the air, the lesson forgotten. BJ sighed, wondering how to get better discipline at lessons, then lay in the grass to watch them.

Their battle was beautiful but not graceful. They tried to get in position to dive at each other; the one below would snatch at the one above to shove him down and gain the advantage. Most of the time they were simply wrestling in the air, wings flapping furiously to stay aloft and possibly gain altitude. They looked like a fight between Oriental kites.

Finally Roland grabbed one of Oliver's forelegs and did something suspiciously like a hip throw. Oliver, startled, tumbled downward head over heels before regaining his balance, dropping hundreds of feet. Roland, poised above him, stayed almost motionless for a second.

Then he folded his wings and dropped, talons first, forelegs outstretched.

BJ cried out when he hit, then realized that Roland had curled his talons under at the last minute. Oliver grunted with the impact, which carried the two of them to the ground.

Pinned beneath his friend, Oliver finally cried, "I yield me!" but he sounded happy. When Roland moved off, Oliver sprang up and rubbed his beak across his feathers. "You are the better fighter, my lord."

BJ said, "And now, tell him where you learned that move."

"My father. He saw it on something called television, a sport called judo."

"Did Oliver have a chance to learn it?" Roland did not answer. "Did you teach it to him?"

"I never thought to." But Roland wouldn't look her in the eye.

"You wanted to win." BJ wasn't used to being the judge, but she knew that Roland needed this lesson more than any other. "So you were in a conflict between two codes: fairness to a friend, and winning above everything else. Did you think it could happen to you?"

"Never."

"Can it happen to you?"

Roland said huskily, "Never again. I have wronged my best friend." He bowed his head. "Oliver, I'm sorry."

"Forgiven," Oliver said quickly. "Always."

"That doesn't matter." BJ waited until both of them turned to her. "Roland, I wish your father were here to teach you this. Justice matters to him more than anything." She shivered, remembering the bloody occasions on which she had learned that. "Oliver can forgive you every time you wrong him; it won't make you right. Teach that hip throw to your friend, or never use it on him again."

"Gladly."

BJ, looking at the road, said, "We have company arriving."

Roland, looking at the sky, said, "They are friends."

The vet school truck was bumping up the hill, Valerie determinedly gripping the wheel. Frieda, holding the map, looked exhausted.

As they both stepped out, Valerie snapped, "Next time, when I ask if it's a left turn, say yes or no. Not 'Gee, I think so.' "

"Sorry," Frieda said desperately. "I was always pretty sure, but—" She said firmly, "I really hate this."

BJ looked behind her. Over their heads, Sugar grinned unashamedly at BJ; obviously, he had assigned the roles. "Howdy, Doctor Vaughan."

"Hello, Doctor Dobbs. Your patients are coming now."

Cody, sliding out of the truck, gaped upward. Matt watched with concern but no surprise as the rest of the young griffins, in a remarkably disorderly group, flew in and landed awkwardly on her lawn. The sheet which she kept to put over the Healing Sign blew against her cottage, then sagged in the grass.

Laurie came out beside the students; it was a wonder that six people had been able to cram into the cab for a ride that long.

Frieda was staring down the long valley at the river, looking at the mist over distant hills and the gradual fade of grasslands into the horizon. BJ said to her, "Was it a rough ride in?"

She said absently, "It reminded me of high school. In my home county it was illegal to put four people in the front seat of a pickup truck, but we did it some. A couple times I was along, with friends. Usually we spent the whole time fighting about where we wanted to go—" She glanced quickly at Valerie and bit her lip.

Sugar said, "You'd better have an eye to your patients. If they were mine, I'd want to keep an eye on them."

A shadow slid overhead, completely covering the veterinary students. They looked up; Valerie folded her arms over her chest as though she were suddenly cold.

In complete silence and with no unnecessary motion, the Griffin glided in. He nodded to the assembly. "Doctor Vaughan, Doctor Dobbs, Ms. Kleinman." He turned to the group milling on the lawn. "Fledglings." The vet students stared at him; he added as an afterthought, "And of course students, as presumably distinct from fledglings. Welcome to Crossroads, and thanks for your assistance."

Sugar nodded. "Good to see you, too. We're in to give physicals to the new crowd here; BJ thought it might be appropriate."

"Excellent idea." The Griffin glanced casually to the south. "And I'm here to see that none of you is interrupted."

Sugar's eyes narrowed. He said softly, "BJ, is there some kind of local or parental authority you should have cleared with before we set this up?"

BJ said steadily, "I spoke to Stein and to the Griffin. That should be sufficient."

After an uncomfortable silence, Sugar said, "Right. Valerie, take charge."

Valerie swallowed, looking at the Griffin and at the line of silent, politely waiting patients. "Right." She looked around at the assembled audience, took out her notes, and assumed a stance similar to that of a luncheon guest at a Rotary or Kiwanis meeting. She cleared her throat. "When you consider that griffins are presumably mythical, there's an amazing amount of material available on griffin physiology." She stared hard at the Griffin and added, "Much of it is surgical."

In an unusual lapse of dignity, the Griffin scratched at one of the scars on his belly. "Imagine that."

Valerie, unflinching, said, "I'm trying to." She shook herself and returned to the presentation. "The adult griffin's avian parts, the beak and talons, are nearly invulnerable." She added as an aside, "I find that hard to believe."

The Griffin yawned loudly. His right talon raked through a boulder in front of him, with a few sparks which, BJ reflected, were probably for effect. "Sorry. Please go on."

Valerie added, focusing on the paper which she was holding with shaking hands, "However, many features of a griffin are vulnerable. There are no available notes on the reproductive cycle of the griffin—" She paused.

After a stony silence she continued. "Nor is there any information on the physiology of the chick or of the fledgling griffin. There is one note that all species observed are male. *Lao's Guide*, and one observer's note, claim to have seen a female, but both of these appear to be mistakes."

The Griffin said stonily, "Is this a necessary line of inquiry before a physical exam on a cadre of males?"

Valerie said hastily, "Only if there's available information. In the absence of any, veterinarians are best off using data from raptor clinics and from feline physiology, preferably from leonine studies in exotic rotations and from zoo veterinarians." She held out a folder of photocopies. "This is a kind of checklist of health conditions."

Frieda raised a tentative hand. "Valerie? How many copies did you make?"

Valerie frowned at her. "I didn't know how many participating veterinarians there would be"—she glanced at both Sugar and BJ—"so I made a total of ten."

Frieda said, "How many of you can read?"

Every right wing went up.

Valerie took the hint. "Okay, so we don't have enough. You'll have to fill these out in teams. Keep together with your form group, so we know who we're looking at."

Cody began passing out the forms, one to every three of the young griffins. Sugar, leaning against the truck and watching, said, "Matt? You mind helping your classmates?"

Matt said, "I'm not accustomed to chatting with patients."

Roland said politely, "That was obvious, but after all you're only a student. I'm sure you'll get better at it."

The Griffin put a talon over his beak, but Valerie smirked openly, and Laurie smiled with a trace of malice.

Cody dashed to the truck, looking slightly off-balance. "Hang on." He returned with four pens and a blunt but usable pencil. "And I think—" He rummaged in his pocket and pulled out a stubby pencil. "There. Never say playing mini-golf doesn't get you anything."

"Right." Valerie closed her eyes. "If the rest of you can search for something to write with—"

In the end they had ten pens and pencils; the young griffins, in groups, filled out the exam checklist as though it were a questionnaire. Meanwhile, Valerie brought the vet students into a hasty and whispered huddle on avian and leonine birth defects. Before long Oliver, in the first group of griffins, said, "What should we do when we're ready?"

Valerie waved an arm. "One of us will look each of you over. In the meantime, since there's only four of us, the rest of you lie down or sit or do whatever you do when you're not killing stuff."

A Bronze said to her, "We all read. Would it be all right if we read something?"

Valerie swallowed. "Right. Sorry I don't have any magazines; this isn't my waiting room."

BJ stood. "Valerie, if I may interrupt. Roland, why don't you and Oliver get reading materials for your"—she floundered for an appropriate word—"comrades?"

Roland said briskly, "At once." He strode into the cottage. Oliver, in the door, passed books to the eager and impatient fledglings.

Afterward, Roland said politely to Valerie, "If I may say a word." He turned to the others. "These students are here to examine us at my invitation. They are concerned for our health and mean well. Please do not kill or maim them without speaking to me first."

Their silence seemed to indicate assent. Roland turned back to Valerie. "Please continue."

She smiled wanly at him. The waiting young griffins returned to their reading.

Since the young griffins didn't wish to be separated from the books, the vet students did their best to work around them. The students took pulses, heart rates, and even, with muttered apologies, temperatures, then got down to the hands-on exam.

Frieda ended up assigned to Roland, Oliver, and a young

Golden. She knelt to work on them. "I'm Frieda."

One of the fledglings said, "Do you have a title?"

"I'll be Doctor Christoff, if I graduate."

"Then we'll call you Doctor Christoff," Roland said. "And the others shall be called Doctor as well." They regarded each other for a moment, and he added, "Thank you all for coming."

Frieda shook her head and began the exam. "It's a very great pleasure." She smiled to herself, and moved surely and quickly through a thorough check of eyes, ear holes, throat and beak, body, all the way through genitalia, anal sacs, and tail.

Cody, glancing over at her, did the same. Matt, watching, sighed loudly and followed suit.

BJ watched the exams anxiously. The cases she had observed of undescended testicles appeared to have benefited from time in Crossroads; she simply couldn't tell which young griffins they had been. Most of the young griffins were completely normal, with only the variations in size and conformation that the young of any species have.

There were three glaring exceptions. The first was a young Copper griffin with a malformed beak. Cody brought him to Valerie for confirmation. "Malocclusion."

Valerie considered. "In later life, that could cause problems . . . Okay. Matt, have you ever trimmed a parrot beak?"

"You know I have." He seemed detached and irritable, even while he had performed his exams deftly and without problems. "This is one amazingly big parrot, though."

"Then we'll need a good tool. Go to the truck; get the trimmer."

Matt looked at her in disgust, but went. Sugar watched him narrowly as he pulled the trimmer, which looked like an exceptionally long-handled pliers or blunt-nosed wire cutter, and passed it to Cody.

Cody looked up in surprise. "But Valerie asked you—"

Matt said, "I'll watch." Cody shrugged and knelt at the griffin fledgling's beak.

"I don't think this will work," BJ murmured.

But as she watched, Cody carefully trimmed the lower

edge, and small yellow shavings dropped to the ground. "Test that." He pulled his hand back hastily as the Copper snapped his beak shut several times. "Whoa. Okay, that still looks high to me. Frieda, got a penlight?"

Frieda shone a light through from the other side, and Cody went back to work on smoothing down the beak. "Does that hurt at all?" he said without thinking.

"Less than it did," the Copper said, snapping his beak again. "My muscles used to hurt from trying to seal the edges together."

Frieda frowned, looking at him head-on. "It's still not perfect."

"That's my fault," Cody said, "but I'm not sure how much better I can get it with the nippers."

Frieda turned to Sugar. "Can we take the flat bastard from the truck toolbox?"

Sugar laughed, and she flinched, but he nodded vigorously. "Nice thinking."

She dashed to the toolbox and returned. "Hold it like a nail file—well, like this." She demonstrated. "Let the rough part bite into the beak, then stroke it crossways and down to smooth the whole surface. Smooth out the rest of those edges over the next couple days until you feel it's right. Bite a sheet of paper, if you've got some, or a leaf, and check how the marks work. Get it as smooth as you can while your beak is still soft."

The Copper took the file from her. Matt said, "Is that something we're giving away?"

"I promise you'll get it back," Roland said softly. Matt shut up.

Valerie turned up a similar case with an elongated spur on his talons. Shaping a shorter spur was a little like cutting a dog's toenails and a little like whittling on a pencil. Frieda, watching, asked the patient anxiously, "Can you borrow the file later to sharpen it the way you want to? Once you're an adult, I imagine you're stuck with it." She glanced at the Griffin, then at the divot he had left in stone. She seemed more concerned for her patient than she did for her own safety.

"You're very right, Doctor," the fledgling said. "And I, too, promise to return the file."

Frieda glanced at Roland and said lightly, ''Oh, I wasn't really worried.'' Roland puffed his chest out slightly. Oliver cocked his head, staring at his friend.

Matt found the final aberration. ''This one has enlarged inguinal lymph nodes and a nasty ventral pyoderma. See how inflamed the abdominal skin is?''

They looked at each other. Finally Frieda said, ''Is there any risk of this patient having a malignancy?''

Sugar said ''No'' at the same moment that BJ said ''Yes.'' He swung around. ''BJ, if you'd care to explain that, I'd be real glad to listen.''

BJ looked around at the anxious young griffins, careful not to glance at the Griffin. ''Each of these patients has spent a significant time outside Crossroads.'' She didn't explain that the significant time was not a unit of time, but the time of their birth. ''More than likely, that skin rash is the reason the lymph nodes are enlarged in the groin. But there's always a slight chance of lymphoma. It's a good idea to aspirate.''

Matt murmured, ''Oh, good, something by the book.''

Valerie glared at him. Roland said, ''I associate aspiration with breathing. What is it in this instance, Doctor?''

She smiled at him. ''It's pretty simple. First I give him a local anesthetic''—she pantomimed a syringe—''to deaden the pain. Then I use a needle and syringe, withdraw a few cells from the lymph node so that we can look at them under the microscope and be sure he's okay.'' She turned back to the Bronze. ''How's that sound?''

The young Bronze hesitated, then turned to Roland. ''If she injures me, could you kill her?''

Roland glanced at Frieda. Oliver said firmly, ''If she injures you, I'll kill her instead.''

''That's all right, then,'' Roland said with relief. BJ decided that her lessons needed a little more work.

Frieda edged quietly in on Valerie. ''I know it's your case, but I'm willing to do this one if you wish.''

Valerie looked her up and down, saying finally, ''Thanks. We'll do it together.''

''Three-handed?'' Cody was holding a surgical packet from the truck. ''Unless Matt wants in.''

BJ, watching, realized that the three of them wanted very badly for the rotation to be a success. She realized as well that Matt was completely indifferent.

Under Sugar's watchful gaze, Matt came over. "I'll aspirate, if you want. The rest of you restrain the animal."

Every beak swung their way. Frieda said, "Valerie? Can't we skip the restraints? I think their word is good, if they say they won't attack us."

Valerie glanced around. When she answered, her voice was husky, her mouth suddenly dry. "Oh, yeah." As Matt started to object, she said quickly, "Matt, I'll do it. It's my presentation."

The moment she had the syringe in hand, Valerie was steady. Frieda performed a lidocaine ring block over the right inguinal lymph node and said as she finished, "I'm going to touch you, if you don't mind. Please tell me if it hurts or feels numb."

The Bronze said in surprise, "I don't feel anything at all."

"Thanks." Frieda stood and added to the company, "And I must say that it's wonderful to be able to ask intelligent questions of a patient and be answered back." She stepped away.

Valerie moved in and said brightly, "Sir, could you sit back so we could reach the site more easily?"

The Bronze reared back, talons exposed but spread well away from the vet students. He stood stoically while Valerie inserted the needle into the node and pumped vigorously on the plunger. The whole procedure took less than two minutes.

Valerie removed the needle and the Bronze dropped to all fours again. She patted his flank and said automatically, "There you go. You were a brave, good boy."

"Thank you, Doctor," he said firmly. "I always am."

Valerie stood, looking sorry she had said anything at all, and busied herself counting out antibiotic capsules for the skin infection.

As she stepped back, the young griffins moved into a line. Roland, at their head, said to the students, "Thank you for all your help." From his knapsack on the ground he removed a small bag of gold sixpieces. "Doctor Vaughan will help me make change."

Sugar stepped forward to take the money. Matt watched over his right shoulder. The young griffins, satisfied, flew off, the Bronze gliding slightly more than the others. Valerie sagged against the truck.

When his duties were done, Roland strode over to the Griffin. "Thank you for coming, Father." He looked curiously at Laurie.

The Griffin spoke. "It needed doing. Laurie, this is Roland; Roland, Ms. Laurie Kleinman."

Roland knelt before her. "Lady. You are all that I've heard . . ."

She stared, then snickered. "*The Art of Courtly Love*? Oh, I am impressed." She turned back to the Griffin. "Well, aren't you going to fight him to the death?"

The Griffin, annoyed, said, "I would, but he has some silly notion about fealty."

"Thank God you're more disloyal." She stood with her hand behind his head, casually ruffling his feathers. "Not as impressive, but much easier to understand."

Roland, unsure of his reception, swung his head from side to side, his beak opening and shutting.

Finally Oliver, unable to stand this reception, burst out, "Lady, I hope you like my friend. He is the best and bravest, most honorable—"

"Oh, no." But she knelt, offering a hand to Roland. "His father is those things."

"Don't mock them," the Griffin muttered—

—And was clearly startled, his head jerking back in astonishment, when she said quietly, "I wasn't." She took Roland's proffered claws. "I'm very happy to meet you."

Roland, voice trembling, said clearly, "And I'm very happy."

Laurie moved away to confer with Sugar for a moment. The Griffin said, "And what have you learned this week?"

"A great deal."

"I'm quite sure." He glanced at BJ. "Spare me a sample."

Roland quoted, " 'Live pure, speak truth, right the wrong, follow the king; else wherefore born?' "

"My God," the Griffin said bitterly. "From what source did you learn that particular piece of drivel?"

Roland quailed, but only for a moment. "It's from a childhood book of Ms. Kleinman's, called *The Little White Horse*. It was in with the other books by accident. Tell me, Father," he said clearly and surely, "which part do you try not to live by?"

After a long pause, the Griffin said, "I try not to end questions in a preposition." He strode off, leaving Roland triumphant but deserted.

BJ watched as Laurie addressed the Griffin in an angry whisper which stunned the nearby students. Her final reproof, delivered more loudly, carried to BJ: "But he does believe those things. And so do you, deep down. And in case you're blind, he also believes in love at first sight."

A moment later the Griffin returned to Roland. He said quietly, "I apologize. Touché. You struck a nerve. Know this: if I truly had been faithful to Laurie, you would not have been born."

Roland stared at him.

"And species being what they are, I have never asked her to be faithful to me. Nor have I asked if she has been. There are levels of love beyond anything you have dreamed. Please learn that, and be very careful." He leaned forward awkwardly and touched his beak to Roland's. "I'm going now."

BJ came forward and put a hand on Roland, stroking his tawny back as they watched the Griffin fly into the distance and disappear. Finally Roland said in a small voice, "Why doesn't anything I do measure up to what he wants? Why is everything he says a reproof?"

BJ stroked his back continually, and the answer came from her own feelings about her brother Peter. "Because he wants so much of you. Because he loves you, and he's not good at it."

"I love him," Roland said, and the ache in his voice was naked and open. "I want to be with him. Why won't he be with me?"

BJ said carefully, "He has—duties. Perhaps he has spoken of them to you."

Roland turned to stare at her. "He hasn't."

That disturbed BJ a great deal.

Frieda was suddenly at Roland's other side. "Remember that he wants so much of you. That's wonderful. You wouldn't like it at all if he didn't."

He looked at her in surprise. "That's true, of course, but it's not enough to make me happy."

"No," she admitted, "but it might be a comfort. I'm sorry to have eavesdropped. I wouldn't have said anything, but I thought it might be important to you."

He looked at her long and hard, as though trying to see through her. "Doctor Christoff? I suspect you have a lot to say that is important to me. Please feel free to say it, whenever you think I need it."

She put a hand toward his back, pulled it away quickly, and finally knelt in front of him and extended a hand. "Thank you for your help with the exams."

He took her hand. His talon, powerful and sharp, felt surprisingly warm. "Thank you for your help, and for the exams."

He turned. Oliver, on cue, wheeled behind him, and the young griffins flew into the sky. BJ frowned. "They're not terribly graceful yet."

Frieda said thoughtfully, "I'll bet that changes." Laurie, watching, said nothing.

Late that night, when the vet students and Sugar were long gone and Laurie and the Griffin had left as well, there was a whisper of wings outside. BJ woke immediately, feeling futilely for a weapon; she had been expecting this.

BJ's door swung open, and a ruthlessly sharp beak poked in. There was blood on the beak.

BJ said, almost with a tremor, "You've been hunting."

"I haven't even begun to hunt. Don't change the subject." The Silver said coldly, "I can't prevent your involvement with your miserable students—"

"Their names are Roland and Oliver."

"Their names are something entirely separate. Their

names are ours. Remember that.'' He finished, ''But I will certainly intervene, by commission or omission, if you interfere with the rest of our progeny again. Do you understand?''

''More than you'd think. I understand that you can't or won't control them, so you're hoping to control me.'' BJ took a deep, shuddering breath. ''I'll do what they need, if they request it. They are my students.''

''Very well. That is your decision, and a poor one.'' He added, with biting contempt, ''Goddess.''

BJ realized that she was clutching the blankets to herself. Letting go took an effort. ''Tell me,'' she said. ''Your species and your young are predators.''

''There's a leap.''

She shook her head. ''I'm not just talking about hunting for food. You're intelligent, and,'' she said carefully, ''in need of amusement. Do you know if any of your kind assaulted animals recently?''

He said coldly, ''I have assaulted something every day of my life.'' He left. BJ looked at the door with its ripped-off bolt, put a chair against it for now, and went back to bed. Shaken as she was, she fell asleep immediately.

T·H·I·R·T·E·E·N

BJ WALKED AROUND her cottage, picking up small things and putting them in cupboards, washing her teacup, sweeping the crumbs from lunch away. She had been home only a few minutes, and was expecting company.

She realized, as she had in preparing for the funeral, that she was becoming more like her mother: briskly tidying a house before company, hiding, as BJ had said to her once when BJ was an occasionally difficult teenager, "all signs that anyone really lived here." With a sharp ache BJ remembered, on one of her visits home from vet school, her mother dropping a cup and starting to cry as though she had lost a Ming vase. BJ had wondered at her, not realizing how frightened her mother was by a growing clumsiness and lack of muscle control.

For a moment, BJ closed her eyes, thinking of her mother and wishing she was there to talk to. Her life was even more complicated than it had been.

On her last visit to Kendrick for supplies, BJ had gone to see Stefan. Stefan's roommate Willy, back for the second summer session, had sighed loudly and announced that he was going camping. The moment the door closed behind him, BJ said calmly, "Stefan, I'm pregnant."

It had all the flavor of ritual; she would tell him, he would react, and neither would learn anything new about the other. She already knew his possible reactions—worry, panic, denial, even strained support.

Instead, he leapt up and kissed her. "You know I would marry you; I love you. Do you want me to?"

"I don't know," she said, stunned. "I love you, but—I don't know." Part of her was resentful that, when she had handed him a crisis, he had fired one back at her hard and fast. "First I need to know what to do about the baby."

He nodded, watching her. "You look afraid. Please don't be." He held her hands tightly, with the muscles it was easy to forget fauns had when you merely looked at one. "I will do anything, BJ love. What can I do?"

"Quit school," she said on an impulse.

"Then I will," he said, smiling, but wiped his eyes furtively.

"I was joking." He looked puzzled, and BJ knew he should have; it was a test and not a joke. "I have some questions. What is your gestation period?"

"I cannot gestate." He poked her stomach softly. "That is my joke. Three months."

"How much do fauns weigh at birth?" BJ had a sudden, horrid vision of carrying an infant the size of a lamb.

"Very small. We are not large." He added seriously, "Be glad I am not a satyr."

Now she felt better. "I'm always glad of that."

Stefan said hesitantly. "You have not discussed abortion. I am glad, for there are few fauns now. But why did you not?"

BJ quietly resented that he found her questions easy, while all of his to her were complex. "I think—if it weren't your child, I think I could have an abortion. Maybe not, anymore; I'm something different."

Stefan shook his head. "My BJ, you are what Fields made you, but you are still you. What do you want?"

"Look, it's not like an ordinary job, or even like being a veterinarian. People think I'm a goddess, and to some of them I am. My decisions are tougher."

Stefan said stubbornly, "People can always do what they want."

That was a response which BJ found childish, but she let it slide. She listened the rest of the afternoon while he cooked for her (lentil soup), babbling excitedly of what the new lamb might be like; he kissed her constantly. He insisted on going for sparkling cider so that she could have something elegant to drink at dinner. Eventually they made love.

In the morning he kissed her again and said, "Come back as often as you can. Please think about marrying me. Goodbye, my BJ." She kissed him back, thinking absently that Roland and Oliver, having read *El Canción del Mió Cid*, also called her "my BJ," and how different it was when they said it.

The sound of the truck prepared her for the knock on the door. She greeted Sugar, Valerie, Matt, Cody, and Frieda. Sugar took his baseball cap off before coming in. "I wish my house was as tidy as your surgery area, BJ."

"Thank you." This was the first time she had seen them when there was absolutely no connection with work; they were stopping by on the way to Stein's. "Can I get you anything?"

"That's all right. Stein will feed us." He grinned. BJ wondered why he never seemed to put on weight. "If you don't need anything, we'll just head out."

Sugar, BJ reflected, had never been good at small talk.

But in the doorway Cody said suddenly, "You've got a visitor." He stepped aside exaggeratedly. It waddled in, wagging its tail with subdued eagerness, the stiffness of its walk showing pain. Its back was hunched.

Sugar eyed it narrowly. "What in hell is this?"

"It's a Grym." BJ dropped awkwardly to one knee, petting it. It wagged despondently, its tail half-tucked, head lowered. "An extremely depressed Grym." She put a hand under its chin, raising its head to look in its eyes. "Come on, honey, what's wrong?" She leaned forward and, injudiciously, palpated the abdomen. The animal hunched its back.

Sugar said, "This ain't no visitor, it's a drop-in patient. BJ, you planning on taking this on?"

BJ looked at its frantic but unfocused eyes. "I have to."

"I'd bet good money you're gonna have to surgicate. Can you get it on the table by yourself?" He raised an eyebrow, and BJ realized that he knew she was pregnant.

She said nothing. He sighed. "Right. Frieda, you just won yourself a free block of grief. You stay here and assist Doctor Vaughan, *and* write up a record, *and* present before the rest of us when we catch up with you. That will probably be in the truck on the way back home." He turned back to BJ. "BJ, I know I can trust you to keep her out of trouble."

He walked out to the truck before BJ had time to insist that he knew no such thing.

Valerie and Cody walked out together, giving a wide berth to the Grym sprawled on the cottage floor. Valerie thumped Frieda on the shoulder and said, "You take care of yourself, girlfriend." Cody only winked at her, but Frieda suddenly felt relieved and smiled back at both of them.

Matt stayed, leaning in the doorway and looking around the clinic speculatively. He turned to BJ and said, "Who pays you?"

"This is free work."

"Who pays for your materials?"

"There's kind of a trust fund."

Sugar whistled from the truck. Matt ducked out hastily.

BJ turned to find Frieda sitting, head down and lips moving, at the kitchen table. "Are you all right?"

Frieda's head jerked up. "Sorry? I mean, sure." But she added wistfully, "I wonder what the others are doing."

"Stein mentioned something about an injured stag."

She looked at BJ earnestly. "But I could handle that."

"I'm sure you could," BJ said patiently. "But he knew I might want you here."

"That's probably it," Frieda said with no conviction. She smiled tentatively. "Anyway. Where do we start?"

BJ knelt. "You take the front; I'll take the back." She put on a glove and lifted the Grym's drooping tail.

Frieda put a cautious hand under the Grym's chin. It licked it listlessly; Frieda peered quickly in its mouth. "I'll need a better look, but the gums are brick red. Hyperemic. Septic shock?"

"I'll bet on it." BJ added grimly, "And I'd bet it's endotoxemia from a GI foreign body."

"Are there any texts for these animals?"

"Nothing useful." She slid a thermometer into the animal and added, "Fiona found references to something called the Beast of the Gevaudan—a loup-garou, which I thought was a werewolf—then some animal called the Mngwa in Africa—oh, and later she mentioned black dogs in England."

"Black dogs like in Led Zeppelin's 'Black Dog'?" Frieda wasn't sure how classic rock was going to help them just now.

"I guess like that. They appear, nearly always on roads, some of them talk to people, and then they disappear."

"Did Fiona find anything helpful?"

"Not a thing. And since some of the cases she cited talked and half changed into men, I'd say she was off the mark." Automatically she stroked the fur. "All these poor fellas do is bark, play, hunt, and get hurt."

BJ pulled the thermometer out. "Temperature is 103.4. Higher than the others I've taken. That could just be the pain and the fear."

"Pulse 164. Is that high?"

"I'd have to guess it is." BJ nearly blushed, since Sugar insisted on doctors knowing. She felt lightly along the anterior abdomen. The Grym whined but stood still; the abdomen was sensitive. The intestines felt normal.

Frieda said as the Grym shrank away from her, "She's splinting the abdomen." BJ moved her hand forward.

The Grym suddenly shrieked, snapped its jaws once in the air in front of Frieda, and shrank away from BJ's touch.

Frieda bowed her arms out, keeping them away from the Grym but not letting go of the animal. "What was that?"

"Stomach."

Frieda said faintly, "You want to try again?"

"I don't think I'd learn anything." BJ stood. "Time for anesthetic and an X-ray."

Frieda said firmly, "I don't care how well you know these animals; I'd like it muzzled and anesthetized before we do anything more."

BJ was silently impressed. Frieda hadn't been that positive about anything around BJ yet. "Any pre-anesthetic?"

Frieda looked dubiously at the Grym's raccoonlike front paws. "It seems mostly canine. How about Telazol, maybe for a hundred pounds?"

"Sounds good to me. Make it a hundred and twenty; they're mostly muscle." BJ gestured to her cabinets, cupboards, and drawers, all carefully sorted.

They both stepped around the Grym, getting supplies. It watched them unhappily, still well behaved but markedly less friendly since having its abdomen palpated.

Frieda looked back as unhappily. "Shouldn't we muzzle it for the shot?"

BJ sighed. "Of course we should. They just seem so harmless to me . . . the muzzle's in that drawer over there."

Frieda looked around nervously. "Do you have a rabies pole?"

BJ shook her head. "And I don't think it would help us." She patted the trembling Grym reassuringly. "You'd just end up being dragged by a steel cable at the end of a long pole; these guys are strong." She stood. "We muzzle it, then give it the shot and wait. Just keep clear of the mouth."

Frieda returned with the muzzle as BJ prepared the injection. The Grym watched them the entire time.

BJ handed Frieda one side of the muzzle and they slipped it on.

The Grym flipped it off before they could buckle it and spun to snap furiously at BJ, trying to rake across her cheek, and suddenly the friendly, silly-looking animal was neither silly nor friendly.

With a one-handed lunge, Frieda snagged a towel from the counter, spun it around her forearm, and, before BJ could stop her, shoved it at the Grym's snarling mouth.

The Grym snapped forward, teeth sinking into terry cloth. Frieda stuffed the towel sideways in its jaws and held its jaws shut with her other hand.

BJ wrapped an arm around the Grym's body, trying to hold it still. The Grym yelped; wincing, Frieda pulled her arm free, leaving the towel between the jaws, and held its mouth clamped around it.

BJ scrambled across the floor, found the muzzle, and

slipped it over the end of the Grym's nose. Frieda jerked the towel out and helped tug the muzzle in place, buckling it firmly.

The Grym thrashed and sunfished, its body trying to leave the floor. BJ grabbed it behind the neck, trying to subdue it without making matters worse by strangling it. The Grym's snarl was earsplitting in the tiny cottage.

The timing was perfect; while BJ held the Grym nearly in a headlock, Frieda seized the syringe and injected the Telazol in the Grym's thigh. The animal, shaking itself free, dashed away from BJ and turned, its back to the wall, growling.

Within a minute, it began staggering in confusion, still growling. Shortly it lay down and was still, breathing regularly.

BJ and Frieda, by contrast, were panting. BJ looked fondly at the syringe. "I love this stuff."

Frieda said, "I could learn to. Shall we get it on the table?"

BJ moved into place. "One," BJ said carefully. "Two . . ."

On "Three," they heaved the animal onto the table, settling it in place as gently as possible. Afterward, Frieda looked at BJ. "You were definitely right. A hundred and twenty pounds."

"Remember it for the record." BJ paused, collecting her thoughts, then remembered that it wasn't her case. "What do you want to do next?"

"Atropine, if you've got a vial."

"Over there." When Frieda had drawn it up, she injected it under the skin between the shoulder blades. The Grym never moved.

Frieda patted the inert animal. "There you go, baby. No drooling for you." Her mistrust of the Grym was replaced with concern for a patient.

"So, how are you at placing a tube?"

Frieda said frankly, "I've done it. Four hands make it easier."

BJ held the Grym's jaw and pulled the tongue forward. Frieda sprayed the tube with water and inserted it slowly and carefully down the trachea. She tied it to the muzzle with a strip of gauze over the nose, saying, in relief, "I was right. The gums are hyperemic. By the way, the patient's hard and soft palates are crisscrossed with scratches. Something she ate?"

During all of this, the last of Frieda's uncertainty had disappeared. She seemed calm and completely focused on the patient.

Using a syringe of air, Frieda inflated the rubber cuff at the throat end of the tube while BJ applied antibiotic ointment to the Grym's eyes. In school, and possibly in practice, this was called "goobing the eyes."

Frieda attached the tube to the y-adapter and hose on the anesthesia machine. BJ said suddenly, "Is the isoflurane vaporizer full?"

Frieda looked quickly. "Sure. You want halothane? It's cheaper."

"No." BJ turned on the gas and oxygen, setting levels quickly.

"How's the pulse?"

Frieda checked her watch and put a finger on the femoral artery. "Slower . . . wow. it's down to 120. Is that good?"

"Who knows?"

Frieda shot her a worried look. "I always assume you do."

"There's a lot I don't know." They stood, hands on the Grym, feeling it strain against the leashes.

Finally the furry body sagged against the table and was still.

"There," BJ sighed. "That wasn't so risky, was it?"

Frieda stared at her arms. There were a number of red lines, none of which broke the skin. "What should I watch for?" She added, not happily, "My rabies is up to date, of course."

"Not a risk." She saw Frieda's face. "Crossroads," BJ said carefully, "cures a wide range of physical problems just by existing."

Frieda said wistfully, "If I had a physical problem, I'd be very grateful."

They placed an I.V. catheter in the cephalic vein and

started a lactated Ringer's solution. The fluid would support circulation, counteract shock, and keep the kidneys perfused.

BJ said suddenly, "Endotoxins."

"Oh, right, right. Sorry. " Frieda pinched the I.V. line, blocking fluid flow from the bag, and injected Banamine through the catheter. "Injected 1.25 milliliters of Banamine," she said with the slight drone students used when they were presenting or speaking for records.

"Write it down later." BJ added, "Are you getting impatient?"

Frieda looked up, embarrassed. "This part always seems to take forever."

BJ understood completely, but answered, "This is one of those times when the prep won't be half as long as the surgery. Let's start by expressing the bladder."

Frieda gritted her teeth. She had done it a few times in surgeries, but not enough to feel comfortable. BJ held the kidney pan—was making it that shape some kind of joke? With both hands, Frieda felt down the abdomen, then squeezed firmly, slowly, and thoroughly, like someone squeezing a rubber ball. The splatter into the steel pan was gratifying. "How about a stool exam?"

BJ looked up, startled. "Good idea." She inserted a gloved finger in the Grym's rectum. A moment later she said to Frieda, "I'm seeing scant, bloody mucoid stool—"

"You sound just like the textbook. Sorry, I really mean that well. Is anything in the stool?"

BJ poked at it. Several white, sharp chips fell out. "Bingo," she said, realizing that she sounded like Sugar. "Some kind of shell. Clamshell."

"A lot?"

"A little. I'll bet the bulk of it is in her stomach."

"Time for an X-ray." BJ looked at the machine and said helplessly to Frieda, "Would you mind snapping the picture?"

Frieda looked confused. "Sure. I mean, I don't mind. Is this part of my course work?"

"No." BJ still found it hard to say. "I'm pregnant."

Frieda's eyes lit up. "That's why you didn't want halothane. . . . Oh, sure. Okay. Go outside.'' Frieda waved a hand.

BJ didn't wait for Frieda's signal to come back; work space or not, this cottage was her home. She called through the window, ''Are you done?''

''Oh, sure. Just waiting for the radiograph.'' Frieda added shyly, ''Do you want a boy or a girl?''

BJ said automatically, as she'd heard so many friends and relatives say, ''I'll just be happy if it's got ten fingers and ten—'' She bit her lip and shut up.

Frieda opened her mouth for a question, then bit *her* lip and shut up.

Moments later, Frieda walked to the developer, pulled the X-ray, and gasped. ''You've got to see this.''

In the middle of the dark shadow that made up the body wall she could see a huge bright hole, shaped like a huge kidney bean but bumpy at the edges—

What she was seeing snapped into a focus: the animal's stomach was distended until its silhouette was unrecognizable. As she read the shadows and masses of the X-ray, she realized that the stomach was the size of a half-inflated basketball. The irregular whiteness was a huge mass of clamshell fragments, radiopaque and brighter, on the film, than the Grym's own bones.

Frieda traced the stomach wonderingly with her finger. ''Don't they have any restraint?''

BJ said tightly, ''Remember the scratches in the throat? Someone force-fed this animal.''

''Why?''

BJ said, realizing with a sick feeling that it was true, ''For fun. Let's prep.''

They both fell into the controlled impatience of performing all the seemingly endless, annoying, but necessary tasks that seem as though they get in the way of starting surgery.

They finished tying the Grym down with surgical restraints. It wasn't likely that it would wake up, but the consequences could be disastrous if it did.

The Grym's forelegs had ugly half-bare bands where the fur was rubbed off and the skin was chafed. BJ looked at them carefully. "Somebody tied this animal down recently."

Frieda, wide-eyed, said nothing. They both knew it was probably the person who had force-fed clamshells to the Grym.

They shaved its abdomen from the xiphoid down to the pubis; scrubbed it three times, alternating Betadine and alcohol scrub; did a final scrub; sprayed the abdomen with Betadine; and, finally, were ready to scrub, gown, and glove.

While BJ scrubbed, Frieda opened the surgical packs: quarter drapes, towel, gauze, and a pack with lap pads. She opened the packs of gowns, gloves, and a canister of gauze sponges. She set them up quietly and efficiently.

When BJ was gowned and gloved, she lifted the canister lid so Frieda could pour warm sterile saline over the sponges. Frieda prepped herself for surgery while BJ draped the Grym.

BJ started the incision at the xiphoid process, just below the sternum. First she incised the skin and the subcutaneous tissue; then, with a thumb forceps, she pulled the linea alba, the point between planes of hard muscle on the Grym's chest. In her other hand she took the scalpel holder and made a stab incision into the abdomen.

Frieda, watching, remembered her first time cutting into tissue. There is no analogue; she had sliced cardboard, cloth for rags and pizza dough; it was all different.

BJ gestured. "Sorry. It's my clinic; I didn't even think. Why don't you cut?"

"Okay," Frieda said immediately, and picked up the Metzenbaum scissors. Carefully but without hesitation she inserted the lower scissors blade into the incision, lengthening it to the pubis. The Grym, breathing rapidly and regularly, took no notice.

BJ placed Balfour retractors, and Frieda began exploring the abdomen. She gasped. The stomach; usually deep in the cavity, practically bulged from the incision. The stomach was a muddy lavender. The intestines, though not distended, were an ugly purple, blood flow to them almost completely blocked by the distended stomach.

Frieda rapidly placed two stay sutures, one on either side

of the incision site. She passed them to BJ, who held them up to elevate the stomach wall, almost as though she was opening a purse by the handles. Frieda smoothly incised both layers of the organ.

BJ said, "This will take both of us a while."

Eventually they fell into a rhythm, one reaching in while the other elevated the stomach wall. By the end they were reaching into the stomach up to their wrists, feeling for more shell.

Remembering the nervous clumsiness of her own senior year, BJ was envious of Frieda's skills. Frieda probed the stomach carefully, her long, slender fingers moving as deftly as a pianist's.

In all they took out five pounds of clamshells.

After over an hour, Frieda looked up. "I don't find any more. Please check it."

BJ said, "It's your surgery. I'm sure you did fine." But she checked it, and was glad when she didn't find any more shell fragments.

Frieda, turning to the window, give a small cry. BJ spun quickly.

The windowpanes were steamed over on the outside. At the bottom, a row of moist black noses were flattened against the glass; beady eyes stared in intently. The panes were steamed over.

"Did you see them when you went out before?"

BJ shook her head. "One or two, bounding in the distance . . . they look so stupid when they hunt."

Frieda shivered. The faces watching their every move didn't look stupid now.

They closed the stomach, using 2.0 Vicryl on each layer. The final stomach closure, a Cushing-Connell, inverted the tissue to prevent leaking of the gastric contents.

Frieda looked at the mound of removed shells and said wonderingly, "Can this really work?"

BJ said noncommittally, "Once you remove the insult to the tissue, it can spring back if it hasn't been sufficiently devitalized. It has a pretty good chance of coming back if the tissue pinks up. Let's run the bowel."

"The insult . . . I've always liked that term. Do you think

the intestines look better?'' Frieda pointed to where some pinkish color was returning.

''Maybe a little.'' But BJ, relieved, thought so too. If the blood supply hadn't returned, the tissue would die—only slightly before the animal.

Frieda glanced to the window. The other Grym were still pressed against the glass. She waved a bloody glove at them. ''It's okay, guys.'' The ears picked up, and the noses moved; she turned back to her work.

They checked the integrity of the stomach; they didn't close immediately, and had a chance to see normal color returning to the stomach. The blood supply to the stomach could easily have been compromised and necrosis set in.

Once the stomach was closed, they closed the muscles of the body wall, and the fascia, sewing up layer by layer as they had incised. In the habit inspired by surgical rotations, Frieda described each pattern to BJ, who aided and monitored. After a while, Frieda quit looking up for corrections.

At the final layer, BJ frowned. ''You're right; use non-absorbable sutures even though we may never get the chance to remove them. If it were a smaller incision, I'd say use a subcuticular pattern. It annoys the animal less.''

Frieda, not looking up, said, ''Poor beast. Insulted by clams, annoyed by vets.''

BJ said quietly, ''Let's not forget tortured by someone else.''

Frieda said, ''Is anyone looking for the person who did this?''

BJ refrained from saying anything about the Griffin's duties. ''Someone is, yes. He's alone, but very thorough.''

''I'm sure Roland would help, if you asked him.''

BJ, not sure what to say, said only, ''Please don't bring it up with him. I'd like him not to get involved.''

Frieda looked confused, but nodded, still looking at her work. ''I'm nearly done.'' She glanced around the cottage. ''In this place, it feels like a quilting bee. You should offer me tea.''

BJ sighed as they closed; the surgery had been stressful. ''Let's both have some.''

She put on the tea, then took out some paper and passed

it to Frieda. "And now you'd better write the record and surgical report."

Frieda scribbled steadily and thoroughly. Early on she said, "You said the Grym's temperature was 103.4. I know it's obvious, but that's Fahrenheit, right?"

BJ smiled. "Fahrenheit's the standard in Crossroads." She had set it, by keeping records in Fahrenheit.

Frieda went back to writing. "Except for my course work, why do a record?"

"In case the owner shows up."

Frieda smiled, but quit when BJ didn't smile. "Also, I'm keeping records on the animals I've worked on here."

When Frieda didn't say anything, BJ looked up. The expression on Frieda's face said a great deal. "Please. Could I read it some day?"

"I promise."

When Frieda didn't smile back, BJ gave up. Frieda kept scribbling.

BJ signed the record, "BJ Vaughan, D.V.M." On a whim, thinking of the Griffin as professor emeritus, she added at the end of her name, "Adjunct teaching staff."

"There." She passed it back to Frieda. "Show it to Doctor Dobbs and return me a copy by Laurie Kleinman or Doctor Dobbs."

Frieda's hungry expression was impossible to misinterpret. BJ amended, "Or you can come in yourself with it. Be sure to use a map, and you'd be better off coming with someone."

Frieda glanced at the window; the cluster of black noses was still there. BJ stood. "And now, we'd better get this over with." Frieda braced herself as BJ opened the door. The cottage door was surrounded. BJ said clearly, "Gek?"

"Gek," one of them barked solemnly. He came forward.

BJ said, "Your friend is fine. Do you want to see for yourselves?"

BJ let him in; to her relief, he came alone. He sniffed the table, then sat and gave four sharp barks.

The others came in single file, did a circuit into the surgery part of the cottage, stared at the table, and left. Gek sat, watching them. Frieda watched uneasily.

When they had all gone, Gek came forward and humbly set his nose in the palm of BJ's hand, licking it. Then he strode out and screamed authoritatively at the pack outside, "Gek!" followed by a series of short yips.

Most of the pack dispersed. The remainder lay down, guarding the door of the cottage. Gek joined them.

Frieda said as BJ shut the door, "Either they're a whole lot smarter than they look, or they have just got to be domesticated."

"They'd have to be smarter than they look," BJ said, and stopped. Just now, they seemed stupid, vulnerable, and immensely sad.

Frieda said, "I wish they were; then they'd know somebody did this to one of them, and they'd be more careful."

It was more certain sounding than her usual questions, probably because the surgery had upset her. BJ fished momentarily for a response; the ones she found were a lot less certain. "Something to think about later, I guess."

A honking horn announced the return of the others. Sugar entered first, followed closely and nervously by Cody and Valerie. Sugar said deadpan, "Nice audience out there. How'd surgery go?"

"Fine." Frieda handed him the folder. "BJ's going to monitor *her*. She has a kennel out back."

Sugar looked at BJ in surprise; she said, "It's a new addition."

"Lucky you had that ready," he said slowly. "Contingency planning, or a hunch?"

She shrugged. "I was bound to need it for someone sooner or later. By the way," she added as though wanting to change the subject, "what did they serve at Stein's today?"

They glanced at one another.

"Usual stuff," Sugar said slowly. "Stew, mutton steaks, some soup. . . ."

"They had a clam chowder today," Cody volunteered. "River clams, not ocean clams. It was pretty good."

"Where did they get the clams?" BJ said.

Cody grinned. "From the river, like I said. The woman who lives there, Fiona, raked them up with this guy who

helped her, and they let the clams clean out in running water
for a day. Than you steam them open—''

"I've seen it done," BJ said. "With ocean clams."

Matt said, "Actually, it was quite good."

Frieda glanced at the surgical table. "I think I'll pass."

BJ agreed to join them briefly for supper at Stein's. When
they left her cottage, one of the Grym sidled out of the dark
and nudged against BJ, nearly knocking her over. She
looked down, startled; he looked up with earnest brown
eyes. After a moment she gave up and put a hand on his
neck; he sighed and trotted alongside her, wagging his tail.
He insisted on escorting her to Stein's.

Dinner was good, and to BJ and Frieda's relief it wasn't
chowder. Stein announced it, beaming. "Venison kebab.
Onions, carrots, potatoes . . ." He finished tactfully, "other
vegetables."

A voice from the door said courteously, "It sounds quite
good. May we join you?"

Stein swung around and, startled, said, "You boys are
more than welcome."

Roland and Oliver strode in. Oliver looked alertly from
side to side as Roland said politely to Stein, "Thank you
for having us."

Stein said flatly, "You know, we don't get many of your
kind here."

Oliver said back, "And what kind would that be?"

Frieda, passing by, said without hesitation, "Soldiers of
fortune."

Stein nodded immediately. "That's right. Only that Dyvedd boy, and forgive me if I don't think he's exactly like
you."

Roland and Oliver were marvelous company. They asked
pointed questions of Stein and of the vet students; they offered, with slightly awkward social skills, to buy drinks in
thanks for their earlier exams; and they confidently brought
up obscure and tantalizing topics of conversation. By the
end of the meal, Oliver and Cody were arguing heatedly
over who was more important to an army, a cook or a sur-

geon. Sugar excused himself and went to Stein's study to read. BJ said good-night with real regret and went home, where she dutifully checked on the Grym every hour until she fell asleep. Each time she went out, she stumbled through a field of dutiful Grym, crouched watchfully around the kennel.

Shortly after BJ left to check on her and Frieda's patient, "that Dyvedd boy" arrived at the inn. Fiona pulled the boom box off the apparatus at the door. The students pushed some of the tables back and set the boom box facing what was now a dance floor. Fiona was attempting dancing lessons, and Dyvedd was attempting not to laugh.

Frieda bit her lip and looked at Cody, but he was already on the floor, shades on even though he was inside. He gestured to Valerie, who said exasperatedly, "You want me to be an idiot?" but came on out. Frieda glanced at Matt, who studiously glanced away.

Most of Fiona's songs on this tape were dance tracks, mainly up to date. One of the first was a rap remake by Coolio, which in the present surroundings cracked up Cody first and then the other vet students; Cody insisted on a line dance to "Fantastic Voyage."

Late in the evening, Fiona put on a cassette of dance tracks and ballads. Frieda, feeling old simply because she no longer knew all the most recent hits, noticed that not much had changed while she had been in vet school; men danced or talked during love songs by women, and from time to time women sang along wistfully. In one of the last ones, a singer named Des'ree said, "You gotta be bad, you gotta be bold, you gotta be stronger . . ."

On the repeat, Frieda sang along, finishing, "All I know is love will save the day." Stein raised a cynical eyebrow, but the people dancing seemed to take it seriously.

The last song on the tape was an oldie. After the first few notes, Frieda happily threw her head back and said in time with Aretha Franklin, "Rescue me—"

A voice next to her on the dance floor said quite seriously, "Lady, you know I would."

She laughed and, for once, reached out and ruffled his

feathers. Somehow, for Frieda, escape and relaxation would always be associated with affection.

Roland turned and walked out of Stein's. Oliver turned his head, but Frieda, upset and perplexed, followed him first. The last thing she saw was Dyvedd, watching them both thoughtfully.

She found Roland near the outer rock wall, looking earnestly toward the moon. She stood beside him. "What's bothering you?"

"You are human," he said almost coldly, "and weak."

She froze in place.

"You have no natural ability to defend yourself, and you show no interest in learning how. You walk through life unarmed, trusting the world." He glared at her fiercely. "And you sing things like 'Rescue me' and 'Love will save the day.' And with one lunge, I could tear out your still-beating heart. Tell me"—and Frieda could hear the tremble in Roland's voice—"are you not afraid of me?"

In the distance Frieda heard the thump, now rarer, of dumboes soaring and seeking cover. The wind whistled through the scrawny cedars on the ring of rocks around the inn, and, far away, she thought she heard the liquid warble of the birds BJ called firelovers.

She stroked Roland's vicious beak. "For your terrible features, I should be," she said without a stammer or a question. "But I could never be afraid of you."

Roland turned away and fled into the night.

Frieda stared after him. "What happened?"

Oliver looked into the darkness where his friend had disappeared. "It is the one time I have seen him defeated easily in battle. To be fair, it was in battle with himself."

Frieda, who while dancing had felt wonderful, turned her face aside. "I hate this. I wanted to be friends, and all I did was hurt him." She added, knowing how whiny it sounded and hating herself for it, "I feel like I'll never be good, or smart, and I'll always be this stupid, clumsy, nasty little lump. . . ."

She covered her face in her hands. It took a moment to realize that the hard thing bumping her left hand was not a rock.

"Not to him," Oliver murmured in her ear. "Oh, lady, never to him."

Then his sharp beak slid away from her. Frieda stared around wildly as Oliver disappeared into the night, strong wings bearing him away from something which, at his age, terrified him.

That same night, BJ dreamed in detail of a moment when she had been heading back to Virginia. She scratched a turn-off in the dirt, listened to Polyta greeted by her son Sugarly, and could hear the two of them gallop off. The rest of the dream was strange: Stefan waltzing with BJ and pulling an endless stream of dolls from her belly with sleight of hand, tossing them over his shoulder and finally crying when the last one was gone.

When she woke she sat straight up. "I remember." She dressed in seconds and ran most of the way to Stein's, startling a few stray dumboes and two or three happy Grym, who bounded alongside her.

She was barely inside the door as she called out, "Stein, I need to speak to Dyvedd. Is there any way to get word—" She stopped, regarding Stein's raised eyebrow. "Oh, no."

"I'll go knock."

Dyvedd left Fiona's room, tying the waist-string in his breeches and wiping hastily at his hair to brush it back. "Stein said you needed me."

"I have another job, if you'll go with me." She pulled out one of the new *Books of Strangeways* and pointed to the new sketch in the book.

Dyvedd peered at it. "It looks as old as the others."

"The sketch is new. The road is older than some of the others." In her dream, she had been troubled, trying to remember the road she had seen Fields open to let the Hippoi out of Crossroads. BJ had completely forgotten the turnoff she had made for Polyta.

When she woke, she had concentrated, as Dyvedd had suggested on their first trip together, and produced the sketch.

Dyvedd shrugged. "Not a long trip." He grinned. "If you're going to lose me, you'll have to do better than that."

"Neither of us will get lost. Taking you is just a precaution."

"For whom?" He reached out unexpectedly and touched her stomach. "For this little one?"

BJ said much more loudly than was necessary, "I don't like you touching me."

Dyvedd pulled his hand back. "Then I won't do it again."

As BJ passed, Stein raised an eyebrow. She snapped, "I was startled. That's all." Stein's eyebrow did not go down.

BJ left a note with him for Frieda, when she woke up, to check on the Grym. BJ also looked in on Fiona, who was half-awake but still in bed. "Are you all right?"

"I'm fine. Is something important up?"

"Nothing. I'm going to go find Polyta, that's all." She added, because she couldn't help herself, "Well, does he know any magic?"

Fiona simply looked at her with a sleepy smile. BJ blushed. "That is *not* what I meant."

From the door, his pack already on, Dyvedd whistled. BJ sprinted to the door.

As she hesitated in the entryway, Dyvedd looked back at her. "What's wrong?"

"Don't you need to—well, to say any good-byes, or anything?"

His grin broadened. "If I was to wake her all the way up again, well, we'd hardly have time for that."

As they walked south toward the river, he asked, "You're bringing back more friends?"

"The Hippoi. And some of them are good friends."

They took a turn as BJ pointed; behind them, Stein's flickered and disappeared. "What are they like?"

"Very proud. They're kind people, but they have stern laws." BJ added, "They're also half-horse, half-human."

"Depending on the half, that might look foolish." Dyvedd looked at the landscape which had materialized ahead and said suddenly, "How old are you?"

"How old do I look?"

"A snake looks like a rope, till you try to tie a knot in it. How old are you?"

"I'm in my twenties. Is that all right?"

Dyvedd relaxed visibly. "It's good. Sorry. Something about today. . . . I'm just not right inside. That's all."

But he walked slowly from here, his eyes checking the landscape to either side, and his hands never left the hilt of Dancer.

BJ led them unerringly to a dusty road; large circular prints dotted it. Dyvedd knelt, looking at the tracks. "Can you tell which ones are Hippoi and which ones horses?"

"I was hoping you could." But she pointed. "These may be someone's draft horses. The Hippoi don't use carts."

Dyvedd looked strangely at her but said nothing.

Farther on was a low stone wall, designed to keep grazing animals out of a small field. A drag rack for cultivating soil lay tilted against a fence.

Dyvedd looked at the field, then at the drag cultivator, and stopped whistling. It seemed to BJ that his entire body went rigid. "Are you sure this is where you'll meet your friends?"

"I don't know." She was staring at it herself, intrigued. "I've seen them use horses for carrying things; I've never seen them wall animals in before." She considered. "I've never seen them farm at all before; it's not their way."

Dyvedd pointed to dust clouds along an intersecting road. "With luck, that's your friends."

They followed the hoofprints toward the trees by what was obviously a riverbed.

The shrubbery hid the village ahead, as though it were camouflaged. Only things Stein had taught BJ cued her. "Check for distortions and heat shimmers in the air where they cook. Sniff out trash heaps, listen for regular instead of random noise. See if the birdsongs die out the closer you get." Stein had smiled. "It's ugly being civilized, but what can you do?"

BJ saw no weapons so far; she was grateful. At least the Hippoi had come somewhere peaceful. Perhaps she and Dyvedd could get help from the villagers.

A stick-plow lay against a rock. The plow was designed to dig a single furrow, with handles at the back and a metal ring fastened to the front. Long leads made it clear that these people had draft animals.

Dyvedd looked at the plow, suddenly hardened and bitter. "The leads are new." BJ had no idea how he knew.

Dyvedd moved in front of her and pulled Dancer from its sheath on his back. "Not all farmers are friendly."

The fields had regular furrows. After the naturalness of Crossroads, BJ was fascinated to see even primitive plowing. At the end of the field, a trellis held grapevines; the grapes were still green.

BJ stared at it. Dyvedd, turning back to her, said softly, "What's wrong?"

She pointed to the vineyard. "That wasn't the Hippoi. They haven't been here long enough for that."

"Maybe they made friends here." His voice tickled her ear; he was so close as he spoke that she could feel the heat of his breath. "Think they'll be our friends?"

They were quite close now. To their right lay the river; there was drying laundry near it, but no campfires and no tools.

They walked forward, off the road at Dyvedd's insistence, in silence. BJ pictured her meeting with the Hippoi. At first it would be formal: BJ would bow deeply and say, "I greet you, Carron."

Polyta, because she was the Carron, would not bow back. Because she was the Carron, and represented her people's honor as well as choosing their life or death, she would say formally, "I greet you, Doctor."

Then, because she was Polyta, she would pick BJ off the ground and hug her. BJ had been what her mother had called "a huggy child," clinging to legs and running to greet people. Now that her mother was gone, she loved being held by Polyta.

The sound cued her: hooves clopping in irregular rhythm, forward and back. BJ moved out of the underbrush automatically, stopping in place only because Dyvedd put a hand on her shoulder and held her in place with a grip like iron.

The travelers, moving the same direction as BJ and Dyvedd, never faced them. In the end BJ, staring straight ahead, recognized Polyta's horse body first: the beautiful sleek sheen of horse hair, the proud Arab stance, the tail that swayed to match her dark human hair. BJ looked up happily and blinked. The human body she saw wasn't right; it was fat and overmuscled, with brown hair between the shoulder blades and a salt-and-pepper stubble over the scalp.

Then she refocused and understood: someone was riding Polyta. The left hand negligently held something BJ refused to understand for a few moments, but finally realized were reins and a riding crop. The right hand held some sort of small candy, which he was holding in front of Polyta's mouth as he made friendly, clucking noises.

Her back was scarred with the marks of a small whip. As Polyta and the rider passed a bend in the road, BJ saw Polyta's face. Dyvedd clapped a hand over BJ's mouth just in time and dragged her back into the brush.

Polyta never saw them. She was staring straight ahead, slow bitter anger in her eyes. Over her head was a bridle. In her mouth, rubbing open wounds at the points where her lips met, was an iron bit.

F·O·U·R·T·E·E·N

WHEN BJ SHOWED up at Stein's, the birds had not yet quieted down from the dawn chorus that BJ liked when she was awake and thought an ungodly racket when she was trying to sleep. There was no sign of activity outside the inn, but that meant nothing; Stein's—for good reason—was built like a fortress.

She heard galloping hooves and turned around in the faint hope that all the plans for today would be unnecessary.

It was Frieda—but BJ gaped: she was riding Skywalker.

Everyone seems taller in the saddle; Frieda genuinely was. Back straight, shoulders back, she exuded all the confidence of the people BJ had watched riding palominos in the Tournament of Roses parade. She swung off Walker's back; the effect vanished as her feet touched the ground. "Am I late?"

BJ shook her head, staring at Skywalker.

Frieda turned hastily and began unbuckling the saddle. "I need to brush Walker down. I can only take her to the inn, not to—not anywhere else. Doctor Dobbs let me borrow her." She waved the copy of *The Book of Strangeways* self-consciously. "And this, too."

BJ said, "That was nice of him." It was a little like finding out that the President had lent someone Air Force One.

Frieda shifted uncomfortably. "I hope I don't get Doctor

205

Dobbs in trouble. If I get hurt, I mean. I'll be in as soon as I've gotten Walker food and water.''

The boom box at the inn door was silent, pulled away from its starting mechanism. Stein's wouldn't be open for business today.

All the same, on a table in the middle of the room was a fruit bowl and a plate of muffins; a honey jar and a bowl of butter stood nearby. BJ and Frieda looked around for Stein, then each took a muffin. BJ buttered hers slowly, not feeling much like eating; she was queasy in the mornings, but this was more than that.

Stein walked across the inn, waving to them without appearing to look at them. He knelt and removed a floorboard, lifting out several well-sharpened catchlets. He frowned at the door. ''Get that animal out of here.''

One of the Grym, panting and wagging its tail, had followed Frieda in. It barely glanced at Stein and the weapons cache, but sniffed hopefully at the food. BJ grabbed it by the scruff and led it out, patting it. ''Believe me, fella, you don't want any part of today.'' It licked her hand and ran off.

Behind them, Dyvedd said, ''Is there any more breakfast?'' He was dressed in loose-fitting breeches and a tight shirt; both were clean, and he had polished his battered boots. He glanced around the inn. ''Your belly carries your feet, you know. I like a full belly.'' He thumped it; it was all muscle. ''I like my full belly, in fact.''

Frieda said wonderingly, ''How can you be so calm?''

He looked back at her with mild surprise. ''It's only war.''

The conference with Stein, three nights ago, had been brief and decisive. Fiona had listened briefly, then withdrawn. Laurie, who had come in to see the Griffin, sat quietly by him. Frieda, who had ridden in with them, looked from one to the other nervously throughout BJ's story. The Griffin, accompanied by Roland, had listened without comment. Stein had quizzed BJ about the landscape for over an hour, then said simply, "Three days. Tell anyone you think would be interested."

Frieda said shyly, "I'd like to go."

Stein smiled delightedly. "Thank you, young lady. If you can come back here, we'd be glad to have you."

Laurie argued with Frieda for forty minutes and finally drove out with her, scowling furiously.

BJ followed Stein to the kitchen area and said as he threw plates in the sink, "She shouldn't be doing this. She's never trained for it."

He scrubbed the plates automatically, years of practice making him speedy and efficient. "Is that your problem? BJ, sometimes, because of what's happened to them, people need to risk themselves for reasons that have nothing to do with what you think is a sensible risk. Trust me, I know." He threw the last of the plates into the rinse tub. "Besides, you fought for us when you'd barely trained at all." He tossed her a towel and added, with more tact than usual, "For that matter, are you sure you ought to be fighting this time? Considering that you're risking more than just your-self, I mean."

BJ had no reply.

Dyvedd grabbed an apple from the table bowl and munched vigorously. "I'm going out to stretch my legs. Anyone else want to?"

Fiona, coming out of her room, said, "Those muscles need stretching?" Dyvedd grinned and slammed both inner and outer doors as he strode out.

BJ went outside. Dyvedd was twisting his sword through a series of short, powerful moves. He spun it in arcs to either side of his body, spun it one-handed in front, swung two-handed scything curves at full extension, lunged and kicked, lunged and thrust, feinted and kicked, combined a leap and a parry and thrust, and returned to a standing position. BJ was reminded of a friend, a black belt in karate, who had shown her the patterned exercises called *kata*. When he fin-ished, Dyvedd was sweating, but looked as though he had thoroughly enjoyed himself.

BJ sat down resignedly on the ground, tucked a leg, and

began loosening her legs with toe touches. Frieda joined her. Their own stretching seemed remarkably prosaic and harmless.

Stein, watching Dyvedd, was fascinated. "Tell me, young man, what exercises would you design for a short sword like this?" He held the catchlet out, hilt first.

Barely pausing, Dyvedd impaled Dancer in the ground, spun the catchlet, held it in both hands over his head, point in one hand and hilt in the other, and cried in mock terror, "I give up. Don't hurt me."

"There's no need for sarcasm," a dry voice said behind him. "Except for personal enjoyment."

Dyvedd whirled, the catchlet spinning overhead and Dancer in both hands, in guard position. The Griffin was behind him.

"After all," the Griffin said, "I use a short weapon myself." He extended one talon. Whether it was a greeting or a threat was not clear.

Dyvedd nodded, dropping Dancer's point, but not beyond parrying distance. The catchlet landed between them, point first. "Very nice claws. Pity there's only one of you here."

"Oh," the Griffin said bitterly, "that will be corrected soon."

Fiona, who had been silently watching, let out an inarticulate cry. BJ looked up and saw the winged bodies coming from the south. She was reminded, from long ago, of the first time she saw *The Wizard of Oz* and her childhood terror at the sight of the Winged Monkeys.

It became clear, as the winged forms drew closer, that they were a flock of young griffins, flying in a vee, much more practiced than they had been days ago. They landed nearly in formation, Roland first.

Stein murmured, "Now I wonder where they learned that."

The Griffin ignored him. "None of you should be here," he said disapprovingly. "Your beaks and talons haven't hardened yet."

Roland said seriously, "I'm hoping there will be next to no fighting." He gestured at the others. "I brought friends," Roland said, and corrected himself. "Comrades in arms.

They will fight for us.'' He gave a piercing look to his father, who looked stonily back. "Please greet them in return: I am Roland, this is Oliver, and these are known as Siegfried, Beowulf, Rustam, Gilgamesh, Parsival, and''— he hesitated—"Clark Kent.''

"Such a company," the Griffin remarked acidly, "was never assembled under a yellow sun.''

Stein said, "Well, it's very nice to see you boys, but what exactly do you think you are here to do?''

The other griffins turned toward Roland, who said, "The other night, when my BJ spoke to you, Stein suggested finding a way to free Polyta and her people undetected. We can supply a distraction, under the generalship of my father.''

The other griffins stared at him uncertainly. He repeated firmly, "Under the generalship of my father.''

The Griffin said, "I can't imagine your—comrades—telling their fathers later where that led them.''

Roland, seeming to consider, said thoughtfully, "Father, I will accept your advice—and I will take it gladly—but it might be easier to explain to their parents if they received orders from me.''

"Or from Stein," the Griffin said thoughtfully. "No, you're quite right. I suspect, despite your words, that you knew that when you came here. Ask Stein what he wishes to accomplish, and relay it to your troops.''

The other griffins, relieved, nodded assent and turned to Roland. He nodded more slowly. "If that is your wish, Father, that is how it will be, for myself and for my troops.''

The young griffins pushed out their chests and raised their plumage at being called "troops." They were, BJ realized, still very young.

Roland turned to BJ and said courteously, "Is there a map of this land in which we will fight?''

BJ blushed. She could see it, inside, as clearly as if she had been born there; she had not thought to sketch it. "A river runs through it, and we'll enter and leave by the river.''

Dyvedd, who had never let go of Dancer while the young griffins were talking, snorted. "I like duck wrestling too, but this is battle. There are good ways in by land." BJ noticed for the first time that Dyvedd was leaning casually in front of Fiona, who was staring wide-eyed at the young griffins. It made sense, since Fiona was the most terrified, but BJ found herself irked.

BJ said, "There are roads leading in and out—also carts, and wheels, and a sledge with rollers. By the river, there's only a laundry, and a bathing place—"

"And no boats," Stein said. "Such a clever young lady." He beamed at her. "They can't follow us."

"Smart young transport commander," Dyvedd corrected. "If we're in boats, and they're on shore, how are we going to fight them?"

Stein said crisply, "We'll go ashore, in force." He was no longer merely an innkeeper. "Two parties, one for diversion. The other, careful and quiet, runs from the water to the corral, frees the Hippoi and leaves. No killing, lots of noise. Any questions?"

One of the griffins—Gilgamesh, BJ thought—raised a tentative talon. "No killing?" Clark Kent shushed him.

"As you say, then," Roland said. "We kill in self-defense."

"No," the Griffin barked as the others turned to him. "Kill whenever someone deserves it. Do not kill a being defending something it should, family or shrine, but when someone deserves it, kill him."

"You know," Stein said mildly, "in war it gets hard to tell. We're not exactly sitting on the bench on a Monday morning, fining people for drunkenness and brawling on the weekend. For that matter," he added thoughtfully, "even if we wanted to, we have no authority there. It's not exactly like we were in our own country, is it?"

BJ thought it was a nice, circuitous way of reminding the Griffin that the Inspector General was not in charge on this mission.

The Griffin ducked his beak, as close to scowling as his face would let him. "I bow to the superior strategist. Let's concentrate on this mission. Kill as little as possible, concentrating on our objective."

When there was no response, Stein nodded. "All right. Let's go to the river." Clark Kent relaxed.

They descended to the river. The main road south had a

timeworn stone bridge, which looked to BJ like the Roman aqueducts she had seen in travel videos of Europe. Stein turned left and walked below the bridge.

Resting on the gravel in the water's edge were three log canoes, still smelling of fresh-cut pine on the outside and smoke and fire on the inside, which was still rough-cut and charred.

Dyvedd touched one, looking at the trail his fingers left in the pitchy sap. He looked at the inside. "Meat People?"

"In two days." Stein moved to the nearest canoe and began loading equipment. "They planed off the tops, laid coals in, scraped the burned parts out, and did it again, over and over." He shook his head. "Great skills."

Dyvedd said with concern, "Are they going with us?"

"Into battle?" Stein was shocked. "Never again. Shy little things . . . I wonder how they ate until they started raising livestock."

Dyvedd was relieved. "All right, then. I like them well enough, but in a war they'd last as long as cheese in the sun." He glanced around. "Even as we are, we don't look much like an army. No uniforms, no like weapons, no— sameness."

He stooped suddenly in the mud flat beside the canoes, dug his fingers in, then stood suddenly and ran his fingers down BJ's and Fiona's cheeks before they could move. He spun to do Stein's; the older man raised a hand to block him, then lowered the hand and waited. Last of all Dyvedd smeared his own face: three streaks on the left side. He turned to face them. "You see? We do have something alike."

Stein nodded. A kind of uniform. Very good, young man."

Frieda said, "In old movies, it was called war paint. In some real cultures, too, I think."

Dyvedd added seriously, "It will be more effective if we look to be doing the same thing. Training does that."

Stein grimaced. Crossroads had learned that too well earlier. "Let's get going."

BJ poked at the inside. "Why did they wedge rocks in here?"

"Balance?" Frieda said nervously. "Because, if they didn't, it might list or roll?"

"Smart." It was unclear whether Stein was referring to Frieda or to the Meat People. He thumped the side of the canoe. "These will be heavy, but that can't be helped." He grunted, his wiry muscles standing out as he pushed on the canoe.

"Allow me." The Griffin leaned a shoulder against the canoe, digging his feet in until they stood in pools in the gravel, water rushing over his toes. The canoe slid out smoothly, and the Griffin raised a hind leg and looked with distaste at his soaking lion's paw. "Ah, well. First casualty of the day."

Stein gestured to each of them and to the canoes. "Get in."

Everyone but Fiona shuffled forward.

"We need to hurry."

Still Fiona didn't move.

"I'd like to wait here," Fiona said finally.

Stein put a hand on her shoulders and smiled. BJ was thinking how unfair that would be when he said kindly, "No, sweetheart, you can't. You've stayed here for months now, and been cared for, and been helped to get better. Now it's time you know that nothing is free." He handed her a catchlet.

Fiona stared at him, biting her lip. Finally she nodded and tucked the catchlet in her belt.

Stein said with mild exasperation, "Is everyone else ready?"

"Not yet." Dyvedd held his hand out. "I fight for pay."

"I know." Stein looked at him searchingly. "We said we'd pay you."

"Gold only, no scrip, to help with Hippoi. Now it's time you know that nothing is free." He kept his hand out. "Pay before."

BJ was shocked and disgusted. Stein said softly, "To a mercenary who has already deserted once?"

He scowled, his eyebrows lowering and pulling together. "That was scrip. That was—" He turned his head. "Loyalty isn't the only thing that matters . . . all right, pay me later. But I collect debts.''

Stein was unfazed. ''And I pay them. Let's not waste time on this.''

The trip downriver was easy. Frieda, in the second canoe, paddled bow as hard as she could, but they met only what Fiona called class three rapids. Once in a while, at the end of a falls, there was a standing wave three or four feet high; the canoe bobbed over it easily.

The young griffins flew overhead; the Griffin sat, perfectly balanced, in the middle of the second canoe. He seemed to anticipate every dip and ripple, balancing his weight and keeping the rest of the canoe stable. ''Have you ever been in battle, Ms. Christoff?''

''Only family reunions,'' she said, surprising herself. She felt wonderfully free now that they were on the water. She turned to check his reaction.

He nodded solemnly. ''My own family is like that. Please turn forward and watch the rocks.''

As she spun around he added, ''I'm afraid I'll be unable to stay beside you. Please keep close to Commander Stein if you can, and you'll have no trouble.''

''Thank you.''

''No, thank you. It's kind of you to protect our country.'' He added casually, ''My son thinks highly of you.''

Frieda, dazzled, said nothing.

The banks to either side changed several times: basalt, to limestone, to a wide plain with eight-foot grass on either side, and finally to high cliffs of eroded soil, with sparse vegetation. BJ, concentrating on opening a river road, couldn't look back. With each change, Stein called out, ''They're still behind us.''

Frieda craned her neck, anxiously watching the young griffins as they moved from world to world, their wings beating strongly.

''Fiona, watch the banks to either side. See if there's an opening.''

She watched intently after that, only turning face forward

to watch BJ and the lead raft. Finally she called to them, "On the right."

A series of sandstone cliffs, split by a narrow ravine, rose from a strip of sandy beach to the grassy plain above. Stein looked questioningly at BJ, who nodded.

"That's it, then." He waved an arm. The others followed them to the shore.

The boats hissed as they slid onto the sand. Everyone leapt out, and Stein looked at their faces; BJ looked also. Frieda was nervous but resolute. Dyvedd was calm. The Griffin was unreadable; the young griffins looked excited. Only Fiona was frightened.

Frieda said hesitantly, "How did you know the cliffs would be here?"

"I know land. From everything BJ said, they were likely. Besides," Stein finished, smiling, "they were what I wanted."

The others chuckled politely. He went on as though he hadn't heard. "Fiona—"

She tensed.

He went on. "You've paddled canoes a lot?" She nodded. "Tie the canoes together and take them down the rapids below the town. Try to stay on the far side of the river till you get past the bend; the slavers won't bother you that way even if somebody sees you." He turned to BJ. "Will going around the bend clear the village?"

BJ stared at the river, concentrating as she would to see a road clearly. "Yes. There's a gravel beach below the settlement."

"Amazing talent," he murmured, but nodded as though he had known all along. "Fiona, pull the canoes in there and wait for us. If nobody shows, you're on your own."

"If nobody shows," BJ said, correcting him, "wait till night, work your way upstream, and follow the channel we took on the way down. It won't be easy, but you can do it."

She handed Fiona a copy of *The Book of Strangeways*. As Fiona's eyes widened and she grabbed the book, BJ said firmly, "And I'd like this back."

"No problem," she said with obvious relief and set to tying the logs together, end to end.

The rest of them moved across the gravel as quietly as possible, headed for cover. BJ looked back at Fiona, wading ankle-deep as she threaded the bow of the second canoe to the stern of the first. Fiona shoved the canoes out with a paddle and quickly moved into the current.

BJ said, "That was very nice of you."

Stein said, "Practical, that's all."

They watched her. BJ said, "What would you have done if she hadn't been good in canoes?"

"Oh, I'd have thought of something," Stein said vaguely. "Griffin, get your party—" He caught himself and addressed Roland. "Get your party ready to distract the slavers."

Roland said, "We will pretend that we can be captured and domesticated."

Stein finished. "The rest of us will go to the corral and free Polyta's people."

BJ said, "I didn't see a corral."

"There has to be one," Stein said firmly. "Probably two."

Dyvedd looked angry and withdrawn, despite his calm, as they discussed the corral. BJ noted it, but did not understand.

Stein looked at the ravine. "With erosion like that, water has to flow from somewhere. I'm guessing it opens out on the other side—"

"Excuse me for one moment, sir." Roland flew forward alone, Frieda watching him nearly as intently as the Griffin did. He returned shortly. "I can see the opening of a box canyon off to the left, and a larger channel to the right; we'll go to the right. We'll approach on foot, since that will make more noise than flight . . ." He turned. "If that seems sensible to you, Father."

The Griffin eyed him intently. "That's certainly one reason to walk. I assume all of you can walk briskly enough to avoid capture?"

The young griffins stiffened as if insulted.

"Of course. Foolish of me to think you vulnerable in any

way. Nonetheless, I commend that sort of thinking to you in battle today.'' He turned back to Roland. ''Lead on.''

Roland bowed. ''Very well. Forward!'' He added quietly to Frieda, ''Care for yourself today.''

The humans watched as the small party of griffins walked up the low slope to the ravine. They turned right into the rock face and disappeared.

Dyvedd said slyly, ''You'll be a great surgeon some day.''

Frieda looked confused.

''I've heard it said that a great surgeon should have the eyes of an eagle, the heart of a lion, and the hands of a lady. Even if you're no lady, you have two out of three.''

She blushed. Dyvedd looked questioningly at Stein, who said, ''We wait until we hear the noise of their pursuit.''

Almost as he spoke there came a series of shouts and cries, echoing in the rocks. Along with the cries were inarticulate squawks of panic.

BJ looked puzzled, but only until Stein said appreciatively, ''Nice touch.''

There was a sudden commotion, the sound of people moving through the underbrush. The clink of chains was audible. Stein grimaced. ''Let's go.''

He gestured forward along the gravel; he, Dyvedd, Frieda, and BJ sprinted forward, making as little noise as possible.

Dyvedd, in the lead, said quietly, ''Branch—branch—'' each time he swung one out of the way. The others followed suit and, with no trail, they moved quickly toward the slavers' camp. Each of them had weapons at the ready. Frieda, in the rear beside BJ, held a catchlet awkwardly; so far as BJ knew, she had never had practice with catchlets at Stein's.

Shortly they broke through to a trail, overrun with the footprints of soled human feet and unshod and shod hooves. Dyvedd doubled over, staring at it intently. Stein, watching impatiently, waved the others to a halt.

Dyvedd stood up, pointing first to the hoof tracks and then to the right. ''Look at the direction.''

Stein said in surprise, ''Very good. The corral will be that way.'' He pointed toward the confluence of hoofprints.

BJ was irked. In another moment she'd have gotten it herself.

In moments, they were tiptoeing toward a split-rail fence with primitive slant-roof buildings off it. All the buildings on the high-fenced corral opened inward, with slanted roofs on frames for shelter and cover for bins of fruit and other food. A channel at one end, sluiced by a stream from the river, provided waste runoff; a similar channel to a rock-rimmed pool provided water for washing and drinking. The ground was beaten hard by hooves; the Hippoi had spent a great deal of time pacing.

Before the gate to the corral was a board with implements: harvesting flails and scythes, bridles, whips, manacles, and a thin, almost elegant bronze chain with a finger ring at one end; at the other was a tiny clamp. Frieda touched it.

Stein watched her. "Looks like the most harmless thing on the board."

"It's a human version of a twitch."

Stein for once was completely nonplused.

"A twitch," she repeated. "You put the clamp on the animal's lip and twitch it whenever the animal isn't doing what you want. Sooner or later they quit fighting it. A real twitch is for a horse's lip; it would be way too big for—" The implications hit her, and Frieda looked sick. She looked back at Stein. "It's supposedly very humane."

Stein said in disgust, "Yes, I suppose it is." He gestured to Dyvedd to come forward.

Stein strode quickly to the latch; he and Frieda swung the gate open while Dyvedd and BJ kept their weapons ready. As it opened, Stein said quickly, "Dyvedd, in." He ran forward, Dancer swinging this way and that as he checked for slavers.

Polyta emerged from one of the shelters, looking quickly right and left. Her wrists were manacled, the chain wrapping around her human waist. The arrangement left too little slack to reach the gate latch. Abrasions and whip weals on Polyta's and the others' bodies suggested that they had tried anyway.

Polyta nodded to them quickly and kicked one of the food

bins rhythmically: three, then two. The Hippoi lined up quickly, as though this were an ordinary command instead of an emergency. All of them were thinner, and all of their bodies were scarred, though none so much as Polyta's.

BJ looked more intently at Polyta. She was thinner, and her face, unscarred, was marred with anger and self-loathing.

BJ said, "We were afraid you'd be scattered."

"They put us back in here at midday," she said bitterly, "for some food and an hour's rest."

One of the other Hippoi snorted. BJ recognized a few of them: the red-haired Hemera, the older Hippon named Kassandra, and Polyta's consort, Laios.

A cry went up from somewhere beyond the corral. Polyta said hastily, "Don't let us out yet!" She held her chains forward. "Break these."

Stein said, "We'll do it in the field; we should hurry—"

"Now."

Stein hissed, "Why don't we just shout where we are?" But before he was finished, Dyvedd was gesturing for her to lay her wrists to either side of the gatepost. He spun Dancer several times and suddenly grunted, every muscle taut. BJ blinked at the noise and the sparks. The next Hippon was in place before he had the blade free of the post.

Shortly Dyvedd was panting and the Hippoi were free. All still wore their wrist manacles. Stein said to Dyvedd, "I thought you were trained to obey orders."

Dyvedd shrugged. "I never said I was well trained."

Polyta said brusquely to Stein, "All of you hop on, to save time." To her own people she said, "This will be the last time you bear anyone except by your own wish."

Unhesitatingly, they lined up to take riders.

BJ said to Dyvedd, "You hated those chains as much as Polyta did."

"Ugly things." He made to move away.

She grabbed one of his wrists and turned it over. The bracelet-scars were faint, but still visible.

He glared at her, red-faced and humiliated. BJ said, "You knew the plow. You could have said something."

"Mine didn't have leads," he said, not looking at her. "It had a collar."

BJ said wonderingly, "And you still insisted on pay to come free the Hippoi?"

He turned, full-face, and grinned at her. "I don't work for free anymore." He walked over to the nearest Hippon and slapped her flank. "You're my mount." He winked when she turned, furious. "And I wish you had no rider at all. Run free, my love. I'll try to stay light."

He leapt on, with more energy than grace.

The second corral was smaller, but much noisier. Polyta galloped up to it, clapping her hands three times, wrists arched to keep the manacle bracelets from clanking.

The few foals in the corral were suddenly silent. Polyta nodded regally. "That is better. We will open the gate now." She said it quietly, but Frieda saw how her tail was whipping back and forth.

Polyta opened the latch herself. The foals dashed forward immediately: an Appaloosa, an Arab, what appeared to be a roan like Hemera, and, behind them but no less eager, a gangly adolescent human head and chest on a yearling colt's torso: Sugarly, Polyta's own child. He waited for the others to clear the gate, prancing up and down in his excitement.

BJ heard a scuffle. Three slavers had come to the corral.

Stein beat one back, stabbed the other, and shouted to Frieda and Hemera, "Go! Go!" Hemera galloped forward; Dyvedd, trying to balance while holding Dancer one-handed, followed.

The remaining slaver guard ran forward, bolo around her shoulders but completely unready. She looked frantically from side to side and saw the rack of harvest tools. Grabbing a hand scythe, she gave chase, roaring.

Sugarly, barely out of the corral, hesitated. The guard ran up to stop him. Sugarly put up a forearm in defense as the guard swung the scythe into him. He raised an arm automatically to shield himself from the blow.

The scythe dropped as the guard was nearly bowled over.

Sugarly galloped forward in panic, leaving a wide trail of blood in the grass.

Dyvedd, riding as awkwardly as BJ had seen anyone, lurched close with one arm clutching the human torso of the Hippon and spinning Dancer with the other.

With one sweeping blow, he sliced the bolo in half and cut the scythe free of the slaver's belt. It fell, impaling itself on the slaver's leg; she shrieked, clutching herself and falling behind immediately.

BJ, looking back, opened her mouth, but Frieda shouted first, in Hemera's ear. The centaur girl leapt forward, human body straining forward as her horse body pounded and galloped.

BJ had seen griffins fly, and centaurs give birth. She had seen one faun dance to "Singin' in the Rain," and another be a faithful member of a Southern Baptist church.

What she saw now defied expectation: frightened, insecure Frieda leaping from the back of Hemera to Sugarly, her belt off from around her waist before she landed, her weight staggering the small centaur. She gripped his bucking horse-back with both legs and put his bleeding right arm over his head as she whipped the belt around it between cut and shoulder, tying the belt quickly. She grabbed Sugarly around the chest with her free hand and whispered in his ear. He stopped in his tracks, trembling, and applied pressure to the cut with his other hand.

BJ tugged on Polyta's hair. She turned back, startled, and leapt backward toward Sugarly. Frieda kissed the back of Sugarly's neck and said without a trace of uncertainty, "You'll be fine."

Hemera galloped close to her. Frieda planted both hands in the middle of Sugarly's back and swung her body like a gymnast, vaulting onto Hemera's back. Polyta was beside Sugarly the moment they were away, guiding him and holding his arm up.

Within seconds they arrived at the river. Fiona, upstream, whistled and waved; she had not yet cleared the bend with the canoes. The entire fight had taken less than five minutes.

*   *   *

The Hippoi thundered to the edge of the water beside Polyta; they stopped suddenly, staring at the current. All of the adults had black iron manacles on their wrists, heavy enough to strain even their prodigious forearms.

BJ caught the rope Fiona tossed and tied it to a tree; Dyvedd was already pulling it in before she was done. Fiona leapt out, panting. "The current is strong."

BJ looked downstream. The right-hand channel was shallow; the left looked smoother.

Frieda touched her arm and pointed. "That line on the left? It's a waterfall. They could plunge over it and die." She added, "And it's often deep below waterfalls."

Fiona agreed, "The right channel is rough, but at least it's shallow."

Stein arrived, panting. "That wasn't so bad, was it?" He was holding a captured bolo, and his catchlet was red to the hilt.

Dyvedd said expressionlessly, "Slavers behind us. Make a road."

In the distance, back in the village, were cries of anger and grief. Stein added, "Now would be good."

BJ turned helplessly to Polyta, who stood holding Sugarly's arm up, her other arm around his human torso.

She drew herself fully upright. "Make any road you choose. If my people can swim, they will survive; if they die in the water, they die."

BJ burst out, "But they're in manacles!"

"Even so. For me and for them."

Cries and shouts, at first distant, came nearer.

Frieda, trembling, touched Polyta's hand. "Please. Can't they hold on to the canoes, and rest the chains in there? Or maybe we could stay in the shallow water."

Polyta looked down, startled. "You saved my son's life," she said, not sounding like the Carron at all. "Who are you? Why did you care so much?"

Frieda blushed. "It was really just—I thought—well, he looked young, and so nice." She muttered, embarrassed, "I'm a horse person."

Polyta nodded. "I understand." She added, with a ghost of her old mischief, "I am also a horse person." Then she said, "I would like as little swimming as possible, BJ."

BJ turned back to the river, concentrating.

It was at this point that the first of the slavers burst from the brush behind them. Many more followed, sprinting forward haphazardly, in no particular formation. Dyvedd spun around, sword ready; Stein was beside him, catchlet switched to his left hand, the bolo stolen from the slavers whirling expertly in his right..

BJ said quickly, "They're unarmed."

Dyvedd stumbled backward, letting Dancer splash into the sandbar. Stein, more experienced and with lighter weapons, lowered them.

The slavers, confused and weaponless, milled about in the open space between the brush and the water. BJ was reminded, absurdly, of birthday parties in junior high school; there was tension in the air, but no one knew what to do.

The young griffins soared overhead. Landing in front of the slavers, Roland doubled both forelegs over, spreading his wings slightly so that he could kneel without overbalancing. "I am Roland, son of he who is only known as the Griffin. I present these prisoners to you, my lady."

Polyta, nonplused, spoke as to a child. "That is very kind of you, Roland." She reached out to pat his head, pulled back in time. "You mean these people in front of me?"

They parted, frightened, and the Griffin strode through, glaring from side to side, his neck plumage ruffled like a mane. "I greet you, Carron."

"I greet you, Griffin." But her greeting was reserved, and BJ remembered that, according to legend, horses and adult griffins did not get along.

Stein said in almost his normal cadence, "It's good to see you; we were worried." He looked around as the rest of the young griffins settled in one by one. "So, your distraction worked. You escaped?"

Oliver appeared behind them, leading the slaver whom BJ had seen riding Polyta. He stood looking from side to side, his sword (the only one BJ noticed among the slavers) swinging awkwardly, point down.

"On the contrary." The Griffin sounded angry and oddly pleased. "We won."

Roland turned to BJ. "I thought about what you had taught me about not telling everything to an opponent."

It took BJ a second to recall. "But that was when you were fighting Oliver."

"I know. Clearly, though, it applied here, and along with what you taught me about nothing in Crossroads being completely what it seemed—"

"That was a warning."

"Was it? I took it as advice."

"At any rate," the Griffin said, "on Roland's counsel, we landed outside the village and walked through the shrubbery. In addition, we avoided speech. The first humans to come upon us," the Griffin said, clawing through the stone in front of him, "assumed that this party was my litter, and I their mother."

He glared around. "If anyone would like to risk saying something amusing, by all means this is the moment."

Those around him were politely silent.

The Griffin continued. "At any rate, the slavers saw us and coveted what they only perceived as powerful draft animals. As Roland expected, an armed party tried to capture and enslave us."

All the young griffins ruffled, and the knees of the slavers trembled.

"Ignoring but not forgiving that, for the moment. . . . The slavers chased us, we fled on foot upstream, and they followed with ropes and bridles. We fled into the box canyon which we passed earlier. They trapped us against the rear wall—"

"Oh, my." BJ could picture it. "And you flew over their heads—"

"—And trapped them against the rear wall. I took their bolos, and the others rent their shields, tore their ropes and bridles—"

"Whereupon they yielded."

"Whereupon," the Griffin said sharply, "this knight-errant nephew to a manticore began speaking to them in different languages. It turned out some of them speak English badly, and most speak a bastardized version of Ana-valerse—many worlds do; it, Greek, Latin, and English were once the tongues of empire—and they dropped to their knees and begged for their lives."

Oliver nodded toward the Griffin. "And he, with magnificent charity, advised us to accept their suit."

"Piffle." In the presence of a captive barbarian, the word sounded even more foolish than usual. "If we started a massacre, half of them would fight back in panic and overwhelm us by numbers. By winning instead of fleeing, we were left with no choice but to accept. And since one of our prisoners"—he nudged a fat, mustached man with his beak—"was Bondi, the chief of the village, the others surrendered. Evidently they value him." He gestured with a dismissive claw. "Well, here you are, Polyta. If you have a use for a slightly shopworn slaveholder, you're welcome to him."

Before Polyta could respond, Stein said thoughtfully, "We could kill him."

Dyvedd said immediately, "Yes." The others stared at him, and he shut up.

But Roland shook his head. "In taking Bondi, we took his people. They are ours now; he's a person and a symbol." He glanced at BJ. "Much like heraldry."

The slaver, head down, spoke rapidly and earnestly. The crowd behind him wailed. Polyta frowned, arms folded. Bondi was the man BJ had seen on Polyta's back.

Dyvedd said quietly, "He's explaining that Polyta may kill him, torture him, do anything at all, so long as she shows mercy to his people."

BJ said quietly, "What would you like to see them do?"

Dyvedd stared in surprise. "Not my choice, is it? Free him, kill him, pound him to snail snot; does it matter?" He looked down and said with loathing, more loudly than he should have, "Do I care?"

Heads turned. Roland, as if approving the words, nodded. "It is your choice, great Carron. If you wish, you may trample all of them."

A wailing went up from half of the slavers. After some conversation in Anavalerse, the other half wailed as well.

"It isn't wrong," Roland added earnestly. "They've earned it."

Polyta's face hardened. "They have." But she didn't move.

Roland said, "Carron, you seem hesitant."

"You have said I might trample them."

"Or you could forgive them."

Sugarly, his wounded arm still bound tight, huddled against his mother. She put an arm around him and pulled him close, shaking her head. "I must do something. Do I have another choice?"

Roland nodded. "You could make them swear fealty to you."

"Fealty?" The word sounded strange and foreign as she said it, perhaps as strange and foreign as it was to her people.

"Blood oath. An oath binding to death. A promise that, because of the past, they will serve you in the future."

"Do you really think this will be good for my people?"

She looked helplessly at the Griffin, who said testily, "For God's sake, go through with it and quit hesitating. The prisoners all seem as naive as he is."

She turned to Bondi, who stood before her. "I know you understand me," she said coldly in English.

After a long, frozen moment, he nodded.

"Good." She added, in a voice so mechanical it hardly seemed her own: "Kneel."

He knelt. She raised her left hoof and put it on his scalp. Her muscles flexed, and he was thrown to the ground, nose in the sand. She laid her hoof on the back of his head; her leg went taut as she raised her body on that hoof. He cried out, his fear muffled by the sand, and suddenly none of this was merely symbolic at all.

"Do you hear me? Do you understand me?"

"Yes." A tear trickled from his lower eye, and sand crusted in the track on his half-buried face.

"Then understand this." She pressed her hoof down still harder, putting the side of his head in the sand almost to the bridge of his nose. "You live because I let you. You feed your children because I let you. You stand and walk and till your fields and drag plows"—her voice trembled and her arms, unbidden, felt back along her whip-scarred back and sides—"only because I let you."

"Yes." It was no more than a whisper, but his followers around him sighed.

Polyta removed her hoof. "Rise, and serve my people. Never hurt them. Never try to capture them again. Never—" She ran a hand over her bruised lips, where the bridle had been and the twitch had been clamped, and went silent, too angry to speak.

Roland finished for her. "Never take a single slave again."

After a moment Bondi rose, first to his knees and palms and then, shakily, to his feet. He spoke in Anavalerse to his people, stared wonderingly at Polyta, and half bowed.

But he dove suddenly toward Roland. The other griffins raised their claws, but Roland never moved as Bondi grasped one of Roland's front claws, frantically placing it to his lips. "My children are alive," he said, choking. "My people are alive." Tears fell out of his eyes and made small dark balls out of the sand. "Make me do something for you. Please. I will do anything for you."

Roland, deeply embarrassed, lifted him up. "Only serve Polyta, and never take slaves again."

"All my life." He dove, awkwardly because the distance was too far, to Polyta's front hooves. "All my life. I serve." He turned away from clutching the hoof and stared wonderingly at the young griffin. "Who are you?"

"I am Roland." He hesitated, then added quietly to him: "My other name is Raphael."

The Griffin sucked in his breath sharply.

Bondi, watching them both, nodded. "I see. I have a secret, too." He reached inside his shirt, pulling out an age-darkened wooden figure on a thong. "This is Rakhnide. She is for my family. Was for my grandfather, and his grandfather. She watches me, them. So long as all others do not know her."

He stuck the figure straight out to Roland. "Guard her always."

Roland bowed, and let the thong slip over his neck. "Welcome, Rakhnide." He addressed Bondi. "I will hide her and keep her safe.'' He backed away, preparatory to leaving; he glanced around, suddenly aware that the whole village was watching. "And if you can, please teach all of them English," he said awkwardly. "It could be handy. Well, I'll be in touch."

The young griffins flew off, strong wings carrying them north following the river channel. Frieda stood on tiptoe, watching them.

The Griffin, also watching, shook his head. "If this is their beginning, what will their end be?" But he sounded proud.

Dyvedd quickly scooped up water and splashed Frieda's face. She stared at him, wild-eyed. "Time to clean up." He splashed Fiona as well.

BJ ducked, but he was too fast and splashed her, too. He grinned. "You're prettier this way."

He stuck his own head in the water.

Sugarly, unhampered by manacles, leapt in the water laughing, holding his wounded arm high. BJ stared in wonder at his body: though only a few years old, his human torso already had the physical appearance of a teenager.

The Griffin looked back at Bondi, still bowing toward Polyta. "What I have seen is unlikely."

BJ thought of Frieda leaping from one horse-back to another. "Me, too."

Frieda said wonderingly, "Roland was marvelous. He can't be as young as you say."

"I was there when he hatched." BJ said it with fond pride, though she still had bad dreams about the night it happened. "He's only a few months old."

The Griffin arched a feathered eyebrow to BJ. "Scary, isn't it—how fast they grow up?" He added, "Species mature at different rates. Some mature faster than humans, some slower. I fail to see any paradox in that."

BJ nodded. "Look at Sugarly. His human body is teenage, his horse body a yearling."

"But if other species grow up fas—" Frieda shut up.

BJ looked at her curiously. "What?"

"Nothing? Really?" She ducked her head, hiding quickly behind her hair in a way BJ hadn't seen in weeks. BJ had the nagging feeling of missing something important.

F·I·F·T·E·E·N

THE ARRIVAL OF the unicorns was welcome, and as pleasing as it was simple; one day BJ woke up and the air felt somehow different.

It was what Dyvedd would call a "soft" day: light mist and low clouds. A line of white bodies, some large and some small, were making their way single file beside the rough road up to BJ's home. Melina, a very light knapsack on, walked beside the lead animal.

Above them several of the Grym, crouching, sniffed cautiously and dubiously at the air. They were prepared to run.

BJ regarded them sadly; the Grym had learned caution in recent months. She had found another Grym body, slashed purposefully—almost playfully—in a grid pattern across its chest; it had probably died of blood loss.

Now two Grym stared at the arriving unicorns and at Melina, walking beside them. At the sight of Melina, one of the Grym—BJ blinked; from the markings, it was Gek—rose and padded tentatively forward, head submissive and tail wagging.

Melina stopped in her tracks. The unicorn mare beside her stepped forward calmly, and both Grym turned and fled.

BJ looked up, half expecting Roland and Oliver, but the Grym were quite simply afraid of Melina and the unicorns.

BJ hadn't thought the Grym so easily spooked as little as a month ago.

The unicorns touched their horns to Melina one by one and moved up the hill single file. The kidlings, still nearly hornless, nuzzled her as she reached back out and touched their foreheads.

Then she ran to BJ, half bounding on faun's hooves. Fauns, BJ reflected happily, take people as they are and love them.

After hugging Melina, BJ said, "Are you all right?"

Melina was trembling, staring at the retreating Grym. "What were those animals?"

"They're like dogs. They're very friendly, and they don't bite people. Well, mostly. I brought them into Crossroads to be predators, but I'm not sure they're good at feeding themselves." She finished, "I wonder, sometimes, if they aren't abandoned pets."

Melina said firmly, "If that's so, I don't want to meet the master who makes them so afraid. He didn't follow them here, did he?"

"Of course not," BJ said, and stopped. It was a remarkably simple and frightening idea. She wondered what the penalty was, in the world the Grym had come from, for running away from home. For that matter, what was the penalty for stealing pets?

She shook her head. "Come in and have some tea. Was it hard leading the unicorns?"

Melina, following, nodded vigorously, her curly hair waving back and forth. "They do not like roads. All of the time they try to walk on the edge." She added frankly, "It makes me afraid, except that I'm with them."

"You could have asked for help."

"Oh, but you are needed here. And Doctor Dobbs, he had his teaching, and Stefan and that woman Frieda their books." She finished possessively, "Also, I do not need help."

When Sugar, BJ, and the others had driven the unicorns to Virginia for safekeeping, Melina had chosen to stay and care for them. Fauns are natural shepherds; Melina had bonded with the unicorns, whom she tried to tend but who also, quite probably, tended her. As BJ had learned before, unicorns watch over the injured and the innocent.

"Stein will be glad to see you."

"I will go back. Virginia is very pretty—"

BJ nodded absently, staring down the valley at the wide river and rolling hills that she now found the most beautiful of any place in any world.

"Also, I like to be near my church." Melina was a Baptist, and went to a small white church out in the hills. The congregation had accepted her without question, and the preacher, a serious-looking young man with short straight hair and wire-rimmed spectacles, watched over her especially well.

"Are you sure it isn't the preacher you like to be near?"

"No!" But BJ saw to her astonishment that Melina was blushing. It takes quite a bit to make a faun blush. "Well, yes, some. I like Jonathan, but I am too young for him."

"He's only in his twenties. In a few years, that won't seem like such a difference."

Melina looked dubious. "To you, maybe not." She changed the subject. "At least I will still see Stefan."

BJ asked, a little enviously, "Do you see him often?"

"I try to visit him every week. I love him—not like you, of course," she said quickly.

BJ nodded. Since she had become pregnant, she was no longer quite sure how she loved Stefan.

Melina finished seriously, "We were lambs together, you know."

"I know." BJ had always been charmed by the expression. "I'll bet he was a cute lamb."

Melina, relieved, laughed and nodded. "Very full of energy. Full of dancing. Very happy."

It was how BJ pictured Stefan most often, even though he was no longer a child. "Well, try to come back here before the winter. The road in will be terrible in snow."

"Snow!" Melina said in delight. "The first snowfall is so wonderful." She sighed. "I have not seen so many of them, you know."

"One a year."

"Of course. One first snow a year. But the first one I

remember so well, and the others since, there were so few of them . . .''

"So few of them?" *We were lambs together—''* "Melina? How old are you?''

She looked surprised. "I am grown up.''

"I know, but how many years?''

"Years are years." She shrugged. "Five.''

After a moment Melina added, not noticing BJ's expression, "I thought you would know that from Stefan.''

"Yes, well, I guess years are years to him, too.''

Fields, a satyr, had said of Stefan, "He cries easily, like all his kind." BJ had thought "his kind" referred to fauns; it might have meant "children.''

She thought, "I'm pregnant, and the father is five years old." She added to herself as it struck her, "And the baby may grow up as fast as he did." She knew that, when she was a teenager, it was the kind of secret she could never have told her mother—but just now she wanted, more than anything, to talk to her own mother about it.

She said, "Melina, do you want a ride back to Virginia? I have an errand there.''

But first she had to wait for Roland and Oliver. As full as she was of her own problems, that worried her; they had never been late. More than an hour into the morning they flew over the cottage, but they landed beyond it.

They stood on the hillside beyond the stream, discussing something urgently. It looked as though they were arguing, but for once the argument didn't end in friendly combat. Instead they crossed the stream, stepping carefully on stones to avoid wetting their rear lion paws, and came to her.

Roland shifted from leg to leg, troubled. "I must take a leave, my BJ.''

"I need to run an errand today myself," BJ said. "And you don't need my permission to go.''

"I know. But I wished to tell you.''

BJ considered. Roland looked worried, Oliver almost angry. "Have I offended you?''

"Oh, no." He was shocked. "You have been a helpful, clear guide and tutor. And—'' He stumbled and finished shyly, "And I will always remember the great things you taught me." He added in a sudden rush, "You were right. Often there is a conflict between two codes."

BJ looked from him to Oliver, waiting alertly as always beside his friend. "Not between you two."

"Never," Oliver said flatly.

"Between something in your nature—your heritage—and what I taught you."

Roland looked away, evasive and ashamed for the second time since she had known him. "You are perceptive, which I knew. Please ask nothing more."

BJ said quickly, "I'm sorry, but I have to ask. Does this have something to do with all the tortured and mutilated animals we've been finding?"

He bowed in silence and flew off. Oliver, bowing and murmuring politely, followed, and BJ realized with a sudden emptiness that she might never see them again.

Except in battle, as enemies.

When BJ dropped Melina off on a Virginia country road, the faun's face puckered with concern. "Are you angry with Stefan? I'm sure he thought you knew, too—"

"No, I'm not angry." Frightened and disoriented, but not angry. "I just need to talk to him." BJ drove more rapidly than she had intended to Stefan's apartment building in Kendrick.

But when she arrived, Willy was there, and Stefan was gone. Willy said Stefan had gone with friends to Roanoke, to see a Mill Mountain production of *Guys and Dolls*. Willy studiously avoided looking at her body. BJ sighed and drove to the Western Vee vet school, wishing that someone had designed truck steering wheels to fit over pregnant bellies.

At the hospital, BJ looked at the sport shirts and dress shorts on the students passing—those not in coveralls—and she was suddenly, painfully aware of how odd her clothes must look. Her maternity shirt was nothing but a large T-shirt; her jeans an outsize pair Laurie had donated, with an acid comment about her clothes fitting BJ only after BJ was showing. BJ left a list of requested supplies in Sugar's mailbox (too much amoxicillin; she'd been treating large numbers of slashed animals) and dashed out, hoping not to meet anyone she knew.

But Frieda, walking briskly down the hall, nearly ran into her. "Sorry, sorry," she said automatically, and put hands out to steady BJ, then recognized her. "Oh, hi!" she said delightedly, genuinely glad to see BJ. Suddenly meeting someone wasn't so bad after all. "Are you out here to see the doctor? How are you feeling?"

"Tired," BJ admitted. "And I wasn't planning to see Doctor Boudreau, but maybe I'll call her." BJ added, because she remembered senior year, "How about you? Are you getting enough sleep?"

Frieda shrugged. "Nobody does. I'm doing fine, I guess. Nobody's told me any different."

"Do you get any time off?" She added, "Other than the time you spend fighting other people's wars?"

Frieda brightened. "How is Roland?"

"He's still like something out of Camelot," BJ said, not altogether approvingly.

"He is, isn't he?" Frieda added with heartfelt fervor, "I wish I were there."

BJ understood long-term romances. "Do you have time for lunch?"

Frieda looked disconsolate. "My parents are in town. From Wisconsin."

"How nice. Will they be here long?" BJ could not imagine what a family visit would be like; she had always driven home to see her mother and Peter, and in the final months before her mother's suicide, BJ had barely seen her at all.

"Oh, no. I said I was busy, and anyway, they really came to tour Civil War battlefields." That didn't seem to bother Frieda. "They'll start at Appomattox, and move north afterward."

"That seems backward."

"That's the way they wanted to do it," Frieda said firmly. But her voice suddenly changed. "Would you like to have dinner with them? They love to meet my friends and co-workers."

While BJ was framing a polite denial, she saw the urgent look in Frieda's eyes. "I'd love to."

"We'll be at the Marriott," Frieda said happily.

And off she ran, shouting the meal time back over her shoulder. BJ realized she had made the right decision, but went back to her truck and drove at high speed to the mall to pick up a good-looking maternity dress.

BJ opened the glass door of the Kendrick Marriott easily, but waddled through it with difficulty; these days she felt as though it was hard to judge doorways. The past few weeks had changed her astonishingly—the Griffin would have said, wryly, "enormously." She plopped down on one of the houndstooth chairs in the lobby, too grateful for the seat to be graceful. Only afterward did she test with her arms to be sure she could lift herself back out of it.

The maitre'd glanced casually at BJ, then at her belly, then at her bare left hand. He looked away. BJ felt embarrassed and realized that she had become something to which, she realized guiltily, she had always felt superior: a pregnant single woman.

She smoothed her dress down hastily, double-checking to see that she had pulled off all the tags; she stood as Frieda and her parents strode in, her mother first.

"I'm so sorry we're late," Frieda's mother said with almost funereal regret. "Our Frieda was never good at being punctual. Oh, Lord, please don't get up . . . well, all right, to go in to dinner."

Frieda's mother was surprisingly stylish, wearing a skirt-and-blazer combination with an elegantly simple gold necklace. If the silk blouse was a stranger turquoise than BJ expected, and the jacket a brighter blue, they were still matched well enough to matter. Her hair, dyed blonde, still had the shocky look of a recent trim.

Frieda's father wore gray trousers, white shirt, foulard tie, and a blue blazer. There was nothing out of place about his clothes, and nothing eye-catching.

Frieda was wearing a long skirt and a white peasant blouse. The skirt was loose and concealing, the blouse baggy; the effect was as though Frieda was hiding in her clothes. BJ saw to her astonishment that Frieda was wearing a hairband, and her hair still fell over her eyes.

She also had a purse easily the size of a bowling ball; BJ stared at it.

Frieda's mother caught her eye. "We got her that. You can't have a purse large enough when you're going to classes; I remember that well. How about you?"

BJ glanced at the knapsack in the corner, grateful that she had replaced the old one. "These days I have too much even for a purse."

She eyed it dubiously. "Well, Frieda does just fine with that purse; don't you, honey?"

Frieda muttered unintelligibly and slouched into the restaurant.

Introductions were cordial and brief. Frieda's mother was Olla; her father was Paul. BJ stared across the white linen tablecloth at the napkins daintily pleated in the water goblets and realized that she had spent too much time in Crossroads; now this world was alien.

Still, the menu looked tantalizing. BJ glanced up and saw that Frieda, stressed as she was, clearly felt the same way. Graduate school was also an alien world with a limited menu.

A teenage girl came around and filled their water goblets as the waiter behind her said, "May I tell you about today's specials? First, from Chesapeake Bay—"

They all sounded like poetry. BJ, raised within driving distance of the coast, had no idea how much she had missed seafood.

When the waiter finished, Frieda said eagerly, "I'd like the flounder."

"The chicken pot pie would be better for you. You're pinched and thin. Look at you." Olla finished firmly, "She'll have the chicken pot pie."

The waiter looked from Frieda to her mother and back helplessly. When Frieda didn't raise her eyes, he shrugged and wrote something down.

"No fish for me," Frieda's father said vigorously. "I'm a meat and potatoes man." He looked vaguely like meat and potatoes: a beefy face on a rounded body. It was also, BJ realized, the only forceful thing he had said.

BJ said, "I'll have the flounder."

Frieda's mother raised an eyebrow. "The chicken pot pie would be better for you as well. More filling. After all . . ." She gestured at BJ's belly, as though it were something not spoken of but never ignored.

"I would like the flounder," BJ repeated firmly. She added to Frieda, "Would you like to try some of it?"

Frieda raised her eyes. "Yes, I would."

There was plenty of conversation, but BJ found it one of the longest meals of her life.

During the salad, BJ thought how grateful she should be that she had had a parent to whom she had been so close.

During the main course, she thought how glad she should be that she had had even a brief time with a loving parent rather than a long time with someone who was openly disappointed in her.

During the dessert and coffee, she thought earnestly that a single cup of coffee couldn't possibly take as long as this one seemed to. She also thought wistfully of fighting her way out with the catchlet in her knapsack.

Olla watched every bite of Frieda's chicken pot pie, fretting whenever Frieda slowed down. There were few comments; Frieda, BJ reflected, had been a carefully trained eater.

Some of the conversation was intriguing. BJ had asked about their farm, which was mainly given over to raising corn and soybeans. "Blackest dirt you'll ever see," Paul said proudly. "Left by the glaciers. Fifteen feet of topsoil."

"How far from town is it?" BJ asked.

"Ten miles out in the country." Olla adjusted her napkin, which she seemed to do endlessly. "It was hard for poor Frieda, being an only child, you see. Still, she never complained."

BJ, every ounce of her suburban upbringing horrified, said carefully, "But she saw other people, right?"

"Not from the time the school bus let her out to the time we got home. I worked in town, at a realtor's, and Paul was with a tiling outfit to make ends meet. Little Frieda could always take care of herself out there." Olla said it proudly. "Oh, she was in choir for a while, but it got hard for her to make the rehearsals, didn't it, honey? Specially if they got out after I finished work." Frieda smiled thinly. "But she had books, and she had the TV and her own resources, and she did just fine." For a second Olla looked troubled. "Of course, it didn't bring her out much. You know, she's always been so shy."

"Were there other children Frieda's age nearby?" BJ caught herself, irked at how easy it had been to start talking about Frieda in the third person. "Frieda, did you know anyone your own age out there?"

Frieda jerked her head up. "Shirley Johnson, a couple of miles away, she wasn't so much older than I was." In the presence of her parents, Frieda's voice took on a new lilt and a midwestern nasal quality that BJ had never heard in her. "And Leroy Tilkes, he wanted to date me in high school." She said it with some loathing. "I think he only wanted to because I was the closest girl."

"That's just not true," Olla said with artificial enthusiasm. "I truly, really think, you were pretty back then. . . . Well." She sighed loudly.

BJ changed the subject. "Is that when your interest in animals started?"

Paul perked up before Frieda could answer. "Should have seen her. From the time she was six, she was after us to get a cat or a dog, any little thing. 'Course, we didn't have a place for that, with me in construction and Mom working for the realtor, but that didn't stop her." He leaned forward, holding back a surprise. "She put together two scrapbooks, cut out of every magazine in the house. All pictures of kittens and puppies. Must've been fifty pages each. She rubber cemented it into two old photograph albums we'd had, never filled, guess we didn't take as many pictures as we thought we would. One book for cats, one for dogs." He chuckled. "Now I guess they'd call that having a virtual pet."

BJ ventured, "She liked horses, though." Frieda swung to her, astonished.

Olla looked as astonished. "Oh, yes. She did trail riding, and dressage, and even some steeplechase. Had to go near Madison for that. For a time she won ribbons, you know. But mostly she didn't do shows. Paul thought it was the crowds, but I knew better. Frieda loves horses, but I think they scare her." She smiled fondly down at the end of the table. "She's so timid."

Frieda muttered incoherently.

BJ, trying to associate the Frieda in front of her with the woman who leapt off the back of one centaur to tie a tourniquet on another, cleared her throat. "I've worked with Frieda in—field surgery. She's very good. She's been quite confident, actually."

Olla regarded her mournfully. "It's very good of you to say so." She added without warning, "Tell me, are you married?"

BJ flinched.

"Do you have a fiancé?" She added, as though it was forced out of her in sordid shame, "A boyfriend?"

BJ said finally with a smile, "I have a fella." She did not elaborate, and Olla, after a long moment with one raised eyebrow, did not pursue. All the same, it was clear that Olla didn't take kindly to a stranger defending Frieda.

At the end of dinner there was an unsuccessful and remarkably annoying tussle for the check. Paul had snatched at it, but when BJ had objected, it was Olla who said loudly, "It's our pleasure. After all, you have to think of the future." She gestured silently but too broadly at BJ's belly.

BJ thanked her quietly, then excused herself. It had been hard to sit still through dinner, and enough was enough.

After going to the bathroom, BJ slumped in one of the lobby chairs. A waitress roughly ten years BJ's senior, crossing the lobby, looked at her speculatively. "I'll bet it's a girl, honey. You're carrying real low for as early as you are."

The baby felt low, improbably low. Also, BJ felt uncomfortably full, and realized belatedly that she had eaten too much in an effort to dodge conversation.

The Christoffs came out, and Olla said in apparent relief, "There you are, honey. Tired?" She patted BJ's arm mechanically. "Well, it's tiring."

"Thank you for the meal, and it was nice meeting you."

BJ pushed on the arms of the chair, surprised at how tired she felt.

"Don't get up." Olla waved her arms in genuine alarm. "You—well—I—good luck."

Paul, to her surprise, gave her a dry and brisk peck on the cheek. "Nice to meet you. Take care of our little girl."

Olla and Paul strode out of the lobby. Frieda shuffled after them lifelessly.

BJ watched through the front window as Frieda saw her parents into their car. Even though she was the same height as her mother and father, she stood on tiptoe to kiss them good-bye.

As they left the parking lot to head back to their hotel, a runaway dog bounded after the car. Frieda dashed out and grabbed it by the collar, barely checking the traffic around the dog. She muscled the dog back onto the pavement, lectured it, kissed its face, and held it until the panic-stricken owner, an undergraduate male, arrived. BJ watched as Frieda spoke to him, probably about using a leash, and bounded back toward the hotel. The transformation was remarkable.

Striding in energetically, Frieda dropped into a chair beside BJ and let out a long sigh, as though she had been holding her breath through the entire dinner. She turned her head. "So now you've met them."

BJ searched for words. "I'm glad I did."

"I'm sorry if my mother's questions startled you."

"Oh, no." BJ realized that no one would believe that. "I just found them hard to answer."

Frieda said with surprising venom, "She's good at that." BJ had no answer.

The next thing that happened was completely unexpected and left BJ gasping: a sudden, vicious stab of pain that seemed to rip across her abdomen and last forever.

She shut her eyes and opened them, and the pain was gone.

Frieda was looking at her watch. "Have you had a pain like that before?"

BJ said, "I have never had anything like that before."

She was out of breath, her chest still tight with reaction to the pain.

"It looked like it hurt. Can you stand?" She helped BJ up. "Tell me right when there's another one." She looked at her earnestly. "There's also a thing called false labor pains. This is awfully early for anything to be happening—"

Frieda caught BJ under the arms as she collapsed.

BJ found herself back in the chair. Frieda was fumbling in her purse for change, impatiently shoving things aside. "Now I know why I hate this thing . . . BJ, you need a hospital."

"No." BJ pictured going to the hospital, and what it could mean when they delivered the baby. She hadn't planned to give birth outside Crossroads. "I'll drive back—"

But Frieda was shaking her head determinedly, and BJ realized, stunned, that the chair he was sitting in was sopping wet. Her water had broken.

She stood, hastily, and turned to look at the dark, shining spot on the chair; she felt the kind of embarrassment she had at an accident when she was four, in the car and unable to wait for a bathroom.

"BJ!" Frieda said sharply. BJ turned. Frieda was pointing at BJ's leg, where the first trickle of watery blood was visible below her skirt. "Something's wrong—"

BJ took a deep, shuddering breath and pointed to the Western Vee campus telephone directory. "Call Doctor Lucille Boudreau. Now."

S·I·X·T·E·E·N

THE TRIP IN Frieda's car had a dreamlike, disoriented quality; periodically BJ would focus on the intense, stabbing pain in her abdomen so exclusively that she would look up later, astonished at how far they had come. Once she saw that they had pulled up at the vet school and had a quick, terrified vision of having surgery on a dirty steel table off the horse barns—ridiculous, she kept trying to tell herself, since no one would do surgery in unclean surroundings, but she couldn't shake the image.

Sugar Dobbs and Laurie Kleinman burst out of the door on the dead run. Sugar paused only to open the door for Laurie, who half leapt into the car.

They stopped again at the Grass Station in the agricultural testing plot. Doctor Lucille Boudreau, skittering forward but not running, squeezed in beside Laurie and said, "Joshua Cady Memorial Hospital, fast. Eddie owes me a favor."

Sugar frowned. "How's he gonna hide a delivery?"

Her reply, not very reassuring, was, "The way this place keeps records, a missing baby is the least of their problems."

Under protest, Frieda was left in the hall. BJ had the distinct impression that Sugar would be there as well if he had less clout.

BJ clutched her knapsack—books, catchlet, and all—all the way into surgery. First Doctor Boudreau, then Sugar, and finally Laurie had tried to take it away; she had held it tight and said through gritted teeth, "I'll keep it out of the way."

The lights were brilliant, and could be raised and lowered to any height and tilted for angle. Despite her pain, BJ regarded them enviously.

Sugar held a gown for Lucille Boudreau as though he were holding her coat at a concert. She slipped into it without thanking him.

The preparations were remarkably familiar: drapes, trays of scalpels, antiseptic, suture, and needles at the ready. If she hadn't been in pain, BJ would have felt guilty for lying down.

"You've got the whole crew here, BJ," Sugar said. "Surgeon"—he nodded to Lucille Boudreau—"anesthesiologist"—Laurie looked unhappy. He pointed to himself. "Pediatrician."

Doctor Boudreau glared at him. "The patient says you can stay, Doctor Dobbs." She leaned on "Doctor" a little too much. "I'd appreciate your staying out of the way except when I ask for you."

Sugar didn't even look angry, and BJ realized how worried he was.

"Let's take her vitals." Doctor Boudreau stuffed a thermometer in BJ's mouth and took her pulse, focusing completely on her watch. BJ recognized uncomfortably that the doctor was using the moment to collect her thoughts.

Laurie fastened the manometer cuff on BJ. Sugar said, "You know how to use those?"

"I used to work blood drives." She looked at the reading. "One-fifty over ninety-two."

"All things considered, that's not too bad." Doctor Boudreau took the thermometer out of BJ's mouth and asked, "What is it normally?"

"I'm really not sure anymore."

Sugar stared at her. Doctor Boudreau simply nodded irritably. "You should have it taken while you're pregnant. Any recent medical records? Prenatal visits?"

BJ shook her head. A stab of pain distracted her from feeling ashamed.

"She's been out of the country," Sugar rasped. "What happens next?"

"Arrange the curtain over her."

BJ said, "That won't be necessary."

"I'm your doctor."

"I don't want it."

Lucille Boudreau, exasperated, said, "Look, BJ, I know you do surgery. I know you have the hand skills I do. This is not a normal delivery; it's going to be—different. Watching it on yourself is strange." She added, "I know; I've done it. I had a biopsy on a mole and watched some brainless intern suture me badly; that was minor compared to what I'm going to do." She added more kindly, "If you want, we'll pull the curtain away when I take the baby out."

"I'd like that very much." She winced with the sharpness of a sudden pain. "Could we hurry?"

The second the curtain was in place, Doctor Boudreau said, "Laurie, assist."

Laurie unhesitatingly said, "You want her shaved?"

"A couple inches." She leaned toward BJ. "I'm going to do a bikini cut. The scar is smaller, and the entry is easy. There's no real need for the big cut." She added, "You understand that I'm doing a cesarean?"

BJ nodded, hating that she knew so little about this. She hadn't anticipated it at all.

The shaving complete, Laurie determinedly spread the antiseptic scrub on BJ's belly. "How far down?"

Doctor Boudreau gestured. BJ felt the cold of the antiseptic well below her navel.

"Laurie, give me the catheter." She looked at their faces. "Check the tray; it'll be there. Eddie's thorough. He also said he'd come by if I wanted."

Laurie said with a trace of her natural voice, "Eddie takes good care of you."

Sugar's face still showed concern, but there was some smugness in his voice as he said, "Now you know what I go through, Doctor."

Doctor Boudreau shot them both a look which, even to

BJ in her present state, seemed distinctly un-Hippocratic.

Doctor Boudreau muttered, "Let's just focus on the patient, shall we?" Laurie smirked. "Anyway. Here comes the catheter. Um, brace yourself." She blinked. "Let me rephrase that: try to relax."

Sugar stepped to her head. "Hang on for a second while I distract you." He put a hand on her forehead.

BJ realized that he was doing it to step to her side of the curtain for a moment, and she was grateful. Surgery doesn't provide much modesty.

BJ tried to relax, but having a plastic tube inserted is always unpleasant. After a moment Doctor Boudreau said with relief, "It's in."

BJ would have given a great deal not to hear her that relieved at being able to perform a minor procedure.

Doctor Boudreau pointed to the stainless steel I.V. rack in the corner. "Let's set up the drip."

"Of what?"

The doctor looked at BJ as though she were someone who had just entered the room and shouted in a foreign language. "It's saline and Demerol—"

BJ, normally polite, snapped, "Why?"

Doctor Boudreau said gently, "For pain. Also, you're bleeding some."

BJ said in a small voice, "I thought that was just my water."

"It's not life-threatening to you." BJ relaxed until Doctor Boudreau added "Also, in a minute I'll start the anesthetic."

"What kind?"

"An epidural."

"What about the baby?"

"The fetus? What about it?"

" 'The fetus.' By any chance is that my baby?" BJ realized that she sounded like the Griffin.

Doctor Boudreau said, "It will be, if you stop arguing. Laurie, you'll do the anesthetic."

Laurie, who had never been particularly tan, paled further. "Not on a human."

Doctor Boudreau was slipping into the surgical gloves; when she let go over the wrist, a wisp of powder came from the inside of the glove. "It's just anesthetic. I'll supervise."

Sugar said, "You're the only one, unless Doctor Boudreau does everything."

"No," Laurie said flatly.

"No," BJ echoed.

They stared down at her.

"You don't want anesthetic?"

"I don't dare take it."

Doctor Boudreau said brightly, "You know you're not the first patient I've anesthetized."

BJ had done enough office visits to recognize the false cheer in her tone. "Am I the twentieth?"

The silence said more than enough. The doctor said finally, briskly, "I know I'm usually a researcher, but I interned at a women's and infants' hospital; I've delivered babies and given saddle-blocks to mothers. I've also, believe it or not, done cesareans. All the mothers did just fine, and all the babies were perfectly normal . . ."

Doctor Boudreau trailed off, finally having realized the problem.

A racking pain shook BJ. Laurie used gauze to wipe off BJ's suddenly damp forehead. Behind her, Sugar said, "BJ, we've got no choice."

"No," BJ said again.

They looked down. In the operating theater, under the lensed lights, the catchlet in her hand seemed old-fashioned and out of place.

Sugar shook his head. "BJ, if this is just steel-table panic, it ain't right."

That was unkind. Steel-table panic was what sophomores and juniors showed in vet school.

She shook her head. "I'm not—this isn't from fear."

"This isn't a scrape; it's a cesarean."

"No anesthetic," she said firmly. She had given a great deal of thought to getting this far, once she realized it might be necessary.

Doctor Boudreau said, "That's crazy." A moment later she put a gloved hand to her mask; of course it was, but saying so wasn't tactful.

BJ addressed her. "Nobody can guarantee that anesthetic won't hurt the baby."

"Don't be foolish." Doctor Boudreau moved forward. "These same anesthetics have been used on millions of cesareans, and nearly all of them produced a normal, human—"

She stopped, biting at her lip until it showed through the surgical mask.

Sugar sighed. "Okay, Lucille, now you know why I butted in here. Care to consult?"

She said slowly, "What exactly will the baby be?"

"Part faun, part human." Sugar turned to BJ. "You correct me if I'm wrong."

She shook her head feebly, unable to take offense at the moment.

"And there are epidurals that are safe for sheep and for humans. What would the dosage be for a faun baby?"

Laurie said to BJ, completely unexpectedly, "Honey, I always hate guessing, but I can do it."

BJ shook her head. "Not this time."

"Then what do you expect us to do?"

BJ took a deep breath and said as calmly as possible, "How was it done before anesthetic?"

Doctor Boudreau shivered. Sugar Dobbs said slowly, "I can answer that one. Straps, buckles, someone to hold the patient down—"

BJ remembered, from a vacation in her childhood, a diorama at a Civil War battlefield: Stonewall Jackson undergoing surgery to amputate his arm. A burly man worked with the surgeon, ready to grab Jackson and hold him in place. "Laurie could hold me. I have to—"

Doctor Boudreau said quietly, "No. BJ, do you know what the fatality rate was for cesareans back then? Seventy-five percent. A lot of that was infection, but a lot was shock, too. I can't face that," she said honestly, but added, "Neither can you. Normally, if the mother dies, there's a way to raise the baby; in your case that might be tough."

Laurie said, "We'd try, with Stefan's help—but BJ, this just shouldn't happen. Take the epidural."

Another spasm shook BJ. She nodded finally. "But please

be careful.'' She knew it was foolish, but had to say it.

Laurie said, "You got it."

Doctor Boudreau looked at Sugar and said coldly, "Prep the patient."

Without a quiver, Sugar went to work.

"You're on, Doctor." He hesitated, rare for him, and added, "Just cut, like always."

Lucille Boudreau shot him a look over her mask that BJ would have given a great deal not to have seen. The doctor picked up a scalpel.

The incision was smooth, and the feeling in BJ so sharp that she swore the lights in the room changed intensity. Almost immediately the feeling went away, and she felt the scalpel as a disturbing and unnatural tug inside her abdomen.

Sugar leaned forward and wiped her forehead, which had burst into a full sweat. Laurie, pressing down on her shoulders, felt heavy and reassuring.

Doctor Boudreau said, "All right. Since you want to be in on it, I'm about to make two cuts. The first one will be through your abdominal wall. The second one will be through your uterus." She finished tiredly, "Please refrain from stabbing back."

She picked up the scalpel. It flashed under the surgical lights, and BJ, who had never had so much as a tonsillectomy, had never been so terrified in her entire life.

There was a sudden incredible pain, so intense that it barely seemed localized. BJ shut her eyes as though with a headache. As suddenly, the pain cut off and became a strange, foreign feeling, as though her belly was dough and someone was pulling a knife through it.

Once the first cut was made, Doctor Boudreau's entire personality seemed to change. "That was easy enough. Are you all right, BJ?"

BJ, unable to trust her voice and suddenly dry-mouthed, nodded.

"Fine. I'm adding some retractors now, and we're going to pull the incision open. You'll feel the clamps, and you may feel the air in places where you haven't felt it before."

BJ, fascinated, wondered what it looked like as she felt what seemed to be a tug-of-war in her abdomen. Sugar mopped BJ's forehead again.

Doctor Boudreau said with complete confidence, "And now the uterine cut. I'm making a Kerr incision, a low transverse cut. The tissue is thinner down there, and there are fewer blood vessels. It also means that you'll be able to have vaginal births in the future, if you choose to. Here goes."

There was no feeling to that cut. In fact, the intensity of the pain from the baby's impeded downward motion had stopped; the pain from the retraction had stopped. BJ wondered if the surgery was really necessary.

"And more retraction . . . and here we go." BJ felt pressure, a tug as Lucille pulled on the baby's head. BJ felt suddenly nauseated; it was like dropping on an elevator—everything in her abdomen changed places.

BJ was staring at a baby girl. She had a nose that turned up like the one BJ had in childhood photos. She had five pudgy fingers and smooth skin. She had an already slender, graceful torso and hips. She had slim, hairless legs that ended in dainty, light pink hooves.

The baby was wet all over, and a cyanotic blue. Doctor Boudreau said hastily, "Suction bulb," and all but slapped it onto the baby's mouth.

Laurie said bluntly, "That's a hell of a lot of fluid."

"Cesareans always have more," Doctor Boudreau shot back. "What do you think the birth canal's for? Squeezes it out." She was already turning the baby upside down, slapping it, trying to expel the last of the fluid. The baby hung motionless, without breath, for a long empty moment.

Then she gasped and let out a shockingly loud, bleating cry. She bleated again and BJ, for one of the few times in her life, laughed out loud and reached forward one-handed, rising against Laurie's hands.

But Doctor Boudreau held her out of reach. "Hang on. I need to do her Apgar scoring . . ." She trailed off, checking her watch. "In a few seconds, we'll rate her color, muscle tone, and reflexes, and Sugar—Doctor Dobbs will check her heart rate and respiratory system. Scale of one to two." She nodded and they began.

A moment and some muttering later, she looked up. "Five point five."

BJ, still holding out her arm, said, "You gave five categories, one to two in each. That's a total of ten, isn't it?"

Sugar said gently, "Honey, I've always said you were way too smart."

From that moment on, every movement of the baby seemed feeble.

"What's her name?" BJ didn't answer. Doctor Boudreau said, a trace shakily, "I'd like to know a name, fast. It's a tradition where I come from."

Doctor Boudreau, BJ remembered, had grown up in a Louisiana parish, and probably believed baptism was important. That was not reassuring. "Laurel." She swallowed. "Laurel Stefanie."

Frieda had entered the room. "BJ, is everything all right?"

"I think so." She was holding the baby's head tightly to her, feeling alien and wonderful. "Ask them."

Laurie said sharply, "Reply hazy; ask again later."

Frieda said back, just as sharply, "That's not good enough." Sugar's mouth fell open and Laurie's eyebrows shot under her bangs as Frieda turned to Doctor Boudreau. "Doctor? First tell me how the patient's doing, then the baby."

"They're both patients," Doctor Boudreau said. "BJ's doing fine." She was moving her forearms busily, and BJ noticed for the first time that the curtain was back up.

Doctor Boudreau said sharply, "Coming up on five minutes, people, we do the Apgar scoring again."

A long, long, one-minute consultation later, she looked up in wonder. "Ten point oh. BJ, almost all babies do better. That's one hell of a lot better."

BJ, taking her back, said firmly, "She's special." It was the first thing she had ever said where she realized she was talking like her mother.

Doctor Boudreau said, "Oh, my," and added conversationally and a little too brightly, "BJ?"

"Yes?" She was all taken up in two feelings: Laurel Stefanie and an intense, pounding feeling she didn't want to focus on just yet. She also noticed, absently, her white-knuckled grip on the catchlet.

"There's a whole lot of afterbirth in here. Is there anything I should know?"

Sugar said sharply, "It ain't like she's gonna eat it." His eyes flicked sideways at BJ; she caught his eyes and he did something that, at any other time, she would have focused her whole attention on: his ears turned bright red, his cheeks went pink, and he ducked his head and muttered.

But she was too busy to care. Laurel was nursing already, as determinedly and forcefully as any lamb. Her hands groped and pulled, her coordination far above that of any newborn human, and it was immensely satisfying.

Finally Laurel was done. Frieda, her eyes still very wide, lifted her carefully up and held her to BJ's mouth to kiss good-night and hello. "Say good-night," she said cheerfully, as though something in the room was normal and everyday. She added, "I'll just rock her till we figure out what happens next." She sat in the corner, swaying back and forth. Laurel was already asleep.

Sugar muttered, "The kid's got grit," but it was unclear whether he meant Frieda or Laurel.

Or possibly even BJ, who suddenly and irrevocably no longer felt like a kid.

She shifted, and the pain told her immediately what a mistake that was. She said to Doctor Boudreau, "Have you closed?"

"While you were nursing. Everything was fine. Hold still and you'll be fine." She shook her head, perspiration flipping off her forehead. "I can't believe you didn't notice."

"Shock," Laurie said, coming close. "Good job. Listen, the tough part's over. Does it hurt?"

BJ gave a tentative exploratory thought to her own body, and the physical slam hit her. The catchlet dropped and rattled on the floor.

Doctor Boudreau said, "Now that Laurel Stefanie is safely out, would you like a painkiller?"

BJ said carefully and politely, "I would like everything you have."

And passed out.

S·E·V·E·N·T·E·E·N

PRACTICALLY THE MOMENT BJ first woke up, Stefan visited and kissed first Laurel repeatedly, then BJ. ''I came when I heard the message, and then I saw you asleep, and then I saw my Laurel.'' His smile was huge. ''Our Laurel. Oh, BJ, I am so very glad you are all right, and so sorry that it hurt so much.''

He had two shopping bags; one held toys, the other varying sizes of infants' shoes and clothes. ''She will run naked a lot until it's cold, you know.''

''Is there anything else I should know?''

''Just that she will walk very young, and—and she will be a happy child. All of my people are,'' Stefan said firmly. He wouldn't look her in the eye.

BJ fished a plastic flute out of the toy sack. ''She's much too young for that.''

Stefan looked at her guiltily and left the hospital room. He visited again twice, but made only small talk. Both times he brought beautiful flowers.

Two days after the surgery, over Lucille Boudreau's strenuous objections, BJ was back in Crossroads. Part of the objection was that Doctor Boudreau was in love with having her first patient since her internship. She checked BJ every two hours through the night (or so she told BJ, who had been too drugged to care) and the following day.

BJ asked her finally, "How do I look?"

"You look fine. Recovering slightly faster than normal, I'd say." Doctor Boudreau, looking at BJ defensively, did not give the source of her experience; BJ tactfully did not inquire.

"And Laurel?" But BJ, who nursed Laurel every few hours, knew.

"She's fine. Some unusual features"—BJ thought that was awfully tactful to say of a baby with hooves—"but otherwise fine. Recovering from birth trauma much faster than normal." Doctor Boudreau added uncomfortably, "Much, much faster. BJ, I won't lie to you. I've had to check textbooks all through this; I was never a pediatrician. Laurel is way up the scale from a newborn." She stared out the grimy window of the hospital room. BJ was being kept in a side room normally used for broken trays and obsolete bedside apparatus.

Finally she said, "Did you read mythology, BJ?"

"A little," she said cautiously.

"I read a lot, till I got to med school. I loved it. Mercury, and Hercules, and Taliesin in Wales and Cuchulain in Ireland—they were all the children of gods, and they all grew up inordinately fast."

She smiled naturally and easily to BJ. "Relax; I'm not saying that the father's a god, or that you are."

"That's a relief."

"I'm not saying Laurel is either. I'm saying that people who thought that of Hermes and Heracles, years ago, were probably seeing the same kind of birth, with hypermature infants." She smiled to herself, and BJ could tell that Lucille Boudreau was dying to use "hypermature infants" in an article. "They ascribed what they saw to gods, instead of to a different species' growth rate."

"That makes sense." BJ didn't feel like explaining about goddesshood just now. "Doctor Boudreau, you know about some of the"—she floundered—"health-related properties of Crossroads."

She leaned forward. "I would have said disease-related. Is there something you're concerned about?" Lucille Boudreau knew that BJ had Huntington's chorea, but knew very little about what Protera, and now BJ, thought of as the Field Effect.

BJ said carefully, "I would have said symptom-related as well. But healing is faster inside Crossroads as well." She looked Doctor Boudreau in the eye. "It's better for Laurel Stefanie and me to go there. Better for any patient," and she stressed the last word.

The convoy, BJ's truck in front and Sugar and the vet students behind, lurched up the steep hill to her cottage. Frieda, driving BJ's truck, looked at her. "Are you all right?"

"Just tired." Actually, she was exhausted, and she had done little more than double-check Frieda's map reading. Her body was stiff from staying upright in the car seat, and she had the uncomfortable feeling that she needed yet another fresh sanitary napkin. She wasn't sure when she'd have the privacy to change pads. She looked back anxiously at the baby seat—a gift from Sugar and Elaine Dobbs; Elaine, whom she had barely met but to whom she had given a baby gift, had insisted. Laurel Stefanie, wide awake, pounded her hooves on the plastic frame, which was already badly scratched.

"I've got her," Frieda said easily. Other people's problems would always feel easier than her own.

BJ stumbled from the truck toward the house. With Laurel clutched to her shoulder, Frieda ran to assist her and, as an afterthought, pulled down the sheet which hung over the bandaged-animal sign, the Healing Sign over the front door.

BJ glanced up, then at Frieda, who smiled. "Open for business."

BJ nodded tiredly and tottered in.

Just inside her doorway she looked around. Her cottage had been such a homey place; she had plastered the walls herself to make it brighter, as well as easier to clean the clinic side. She had hung wool tapestries on it to break up the monotony; she had organized and reorganized the veterinary supplies to make the storage compact, comfortable, and easy to use.

Now all she could see was danger. The wall hangings, with their wooden top-frames, could be pulled down to strike an infant. For all she knew, the paint and antimildew undercoating she had used were still toxic. And the drawers, with their easy-pull handles, hid all manner of supplies.

"Drawers," she blurted. She pulled one open, revealing a glittering array of scalpels a foot above the floor, including a full supply of replacement blades.

She dropped into one of the kitchen chairs and wept.

Cody came in. "Doctor Vaughan? BJ? What's wrong?"

"Sharp," she choked out. Her shoulders heaved, barely over being sore after the cesarean (air had bubbled up into them, Doctor Boudreau told her). She sobbed brokenheartedly, unable to control herself.

"Postpartum—well, baby blues," Sugar said flatly. "Elaine had it too. She'd cry at the damnedest things, and her tough as nails the rest of the time . . . come on, BJ; take her back." He took Laurel from Frieda and held her out.

BJ shook her head, afraid to touch her. What if she hurt her, or dropped her?

"C'mon, honey. You're her best friend in the world."

Between sobs, BJ blurted, "That's so sad." She grabbed Laurel Stefanie and rocked back and forth, her chest heaving. Laurel, her eyes opening, shut them tight and cried lustily along with BJ.

"Doctor Dobbs, is it always this bad?" Valerie asked, her voice indicating that if it was, she might take some sort of vow.

Sugar shook his head quickly. "Maybe one woman in a thousand. This is pretty extreme. It could be some change in her body now that she's in Crossroads, or—well, other changes."

Frieda looked at him questioningly; he ignored her. "Or it could be from the nature of the baby."

"Are you saying something's wrong with Laurel?"

All the males backed up involuntarily. Sugar said hastily, "She's fine, BJ. Great. Pretty, in fact." He took a deep breath, trying to regain control of the conversation. "But she isn't all human, and, well, I think your hormones might be shifting back faster than normal."

BJ wiped her eyes. "I *know* they are."

Frieda was there suddenly with a handkerchief. BJ took it, blowing her nose and wiping her eyes. "I don't mean to be like this."

"You can't help being a mess," Sugar said, trying to be kind. "You'll straighten out." He turned to the students. "Empty that other stuff out of the truck."

They moved quickly. A crib, two boxes of dubiously appropriate baby clothes, and a seemingly endless parade of cloth diapers came in the cottage door.

Despite how terrible she felt, BJ smiled. "Where am I going to put all this?"

Cody said solemnly, "And you had this place planned so well, too."

Matt had been looking out the door, frowning at the van. Now he stiffened. "Doctor Dobbs."

Sugar was out the door in seconds. BJ, reaching for her knapsack and catchlet, was hardly surprised to see Sugar reaching for his jacket pocket; Frieda, staring wide-eyed, clearly understood the gesture.

Instead of going to the door, BJ stood by Laurel's crib and put her in, shifting Laurel's weight carefully to avoid back strain. "Doctor Dobbs, what is it?"

Sugar said, "A patient."

BJ turned toward the door. "Is there a client?"

"Now there's a hell of a question," he said, followed by a sharp "Frieda! Val! Get back here!"

BJ leaned out the door. Valerie and Frieda were sprinting uphill toward the unicorns, who were approaching unhurriedly in a tight mass. In the center, one of them was draped across the back of another. Both rider and carrier were daubed in red.

BJ hesitated but jogged after Cody to the truck. "Cody, go back and scrub down my steel table. Matt?" she called toward her door. "The surgical drapes are in the cupboard above the window—" As she went on, part of her pictured how awkward all of them would be in the weeks to come, how she should switch the surgical packs and the drapes until Laurel was older. Everything that had been settled about her life wasn't anymore. "I'll set up the anesthetic machine. Sugar, can you help me?"

Sugar hauled the apparatus, with its tanks of oxygen and isoflurane, to the head of the table. He inspected the hose quickly, glanced around, and said quietly, "Matt." Matt stared back at him. "The drapes. Now."

"Is this part of the rotation?"

"Sure is now " Sugar's voice had a quiet edge; BJ half expected him to have his hand in his pocket again.

Matt shrugged and opened the cupboard over the window, removing an entire stack.

Valerie hesitated for a second as they approached the front rank of horns facing them. Frieda all but dove in, and the unicorn horns parted to receive her. Valerie sped up and followed.

Frieda, was already running her hands on one side of the injured unicorn while Valerie checked the other. "I have three lacerations so far, one dorso-ventral and two cranio-caudal; the deep cranio-caudal starts at the shoulder, nearly an inch deep, and runs across the rib cage—"

"I can top that," Valerie said grimly. "Four slashes, an incised section that looks like a pattern of some kind, and a stab. You better check the stab; I don't like the breathing."

Frieda ducked around the back of the unicorn and gasped. Blood dripped down on the carrying unicorn's back, dripping both ways. It seemed to her it was brighter than normal blood. The injured unicorn's side heaved, and Frieda heard a gurgling, slurping sound as bubbles appeared around the stab entry.

"Sucking chest wound," she said flatly.

Valerie said, "Well, I guess."

They were nearly at the cottage door. Frieda and Valerie fell back as the unicorns stopped at the entrance, then turned to look at them.

Valerie and Frieda looked at each other and bawled in unison, "Doctor Dobbs!"

He was there immediately, looking them over swiftly. "Right. Cody, lend a hand. Matt, roll the surgery table to the door."

"That's what a gurney's for," Matt said.

"Well, we're out of gurneys."

BJ found her annoyance with Matt rising, and couldn't tell if it was his stubbornness or her hormones.

Matt rolled the table forward, looking as though his patience, too, was being tried.

Cody staggered in, his head nearly parallel to the unicorn's own. The bloody unicorn body shifted toward Cody as Valerie, on the right side, came in, the veins in her neck standing out with the weight she was carrying.

The body shifted again as Frieda stepped through, then Sugar, every muscle taut as he tried to lift more than his share.

They placed the unicorn on the table, belly up and legs tucked like a sleeping cat. The pose was completely unnatural and stiff. The unicorn stared ahead solemnly, still at peace but breathing rapidly and with an effort.

But Valerie stepped back, putting her hand close to her face. "It smells like spice."

"My hands, too," Cody said immediately.

Frieda rubbed across the unicorn's sides in a space where there was no blood. "He's sweating. I think he's in pain." She looked at Sugar. "We should start with the chest wound."

Matt frowned. Before he could say anything, Sugar said bluntly, "Cody should start. It's his turn for a case."

Cody looked blank. "You want me to present? Now?"

"Nope." Sugar looked grim, even angry. "I want you to start with the sucking chest wound and keep going. Lead the whole team."

Sugar strode to the door. "I've got someone I better tell about this. BJ, watch them, and keep them out of trouble."

Then he was gone, the door slamming behind him as Cody said plaintively, "Can't you tell whoever it is about this later?"

Cody turned around, looked at the faces staring at him, licked his lips and swallowed. "Okay." He scanned quickly. "Two teams, one for support, one to do the surgery. Valerie, Frieda, can you start a jug cath and shock-rate LRS? Matt, you help me. Okay, buddy?"

Matt, not looking like anyone's buddy, set up the anesthetic machine while Cody clipped the area around the unicorn's wounds.

BJ, watching from the chair, suited up for surgery as best she could. Incredibly enough, Laurel had fallen asleep. BJ knelt by the crib, kissed her lightly, then joined the others, keeping her hands sterile and dragging a chair over with her feet.

Cody looked up. "I'm being graded on this, Doctor Vaughan, but the animal's kind of important, too. Give all the advice you want."

She nodded. "You won't need halters or restraints. Unicorns fight them anyway." Matt stared at her, scowling. He had seemed more than a little tense since the unicorn had arrived.

Cody said, "Matt, maybe you could draw up some lidocaine. If we gas this guy before we clear up the breathing problem, I'm afraid we'll lose him."

"Don't you think we should decide that with an X-ray? We could throw him on oxygen and haul him to the vet school."

Cody looked over at BJ, who shook her head. "He'd never make it there. I only have a portable X-ray machine here; it isn't strong enough for a chest rad on a unicorn."

Valerie laid out drapes and sterile packs while Cody clipped all the wounds, scrubbed them with Betadine and alcohol, and reached for the lidocaine Matt had grudgingly drawn up. As Cody injected a ring-block around the chest wound, Frieda said to the unicorn, "Lie still. We'll numb your chest and then make your breathing easier. After that we'll give you something to make you sleep and fix the other wounds."

Matt said witheringly, "When you get back to our world, are you going to lecture your patients?"

"I'll talk to them," Frieda said, reddening, but she thought that she might never talk to anyone else but an animal again. She looked into the still, peaceful eyes of the unicorn and said nothing.

While Cody scrubbed, gowned, and gloved, BJ checked the patient's gum color. It was pale with a bluish tinge.

Motioning Frieda to administer oxygen by mask, she said, "Thank you for all this. You didn't have to help me."

"Sure we did." Matt was double-checking instrument trays, drapes, everything rational and necessary. He was avoiding looking at the patient. "We weren't given a choice."

Valerie muttered, "Grace under pressure."

Cody winked at her, but he also winked at BJ, who smiled back. He said, "Hey, we're a full-service outfit. After this we're washing your truck." He turned to Matt. "We'd better start on the chest wound. I know you've got good ears; check both lungs."

Matt had his stethoscope on before Cody finished. "This one's fine. The respiratory rate's high, but that's just the pain, I'm sure. The other side—" He listened again. "No air moving at all." He glared at Cody. "Why didn't you tell me unicorns had a complete mediastinum?"

Cody shrugged. "This is my first unicorn lung trauma this week—but sure, if there's air in only one side of the chest, the lungs must be walled off from each other."

"Well, the one on the chest wound side is collapsed; we need to place a chest tube."

BJ said, "While Cody's closing the sucking wound"— and he was doing it rapidly—"the rest of you set up to pull the air out of the thorax." She pointed at cabinets and drawers. "Get the sterile three-way stopcock, an eighteen-gauge butterfly, one-inch tape, and the largest sterile syringe—"

"Wait. You've got nothing but a stopcock and syringe?" Matt was openly angry. "How can you practice without any fucking supplies? How can you even think about it?"

"She learned to think on her feet," Valerie snapped, and Frieda all but reeled as she understood the one all-important skill Matt lacked, and how deep the lack went.

Cody said, "Here we go." A few inches below the neatly sutured wound, he prepped a two-inch area, then gently slid an eighteen-gauge butterfly catheter, bevel up, between the ribs. A short, flexible piece of tube connected it to a three-way stopcock and a sixty-cc syringe. Opening the valve to the chest, he easily drew off a syringe full of air; he turned the valve direction away from the body wall, expelled the air, reset the valve, and aspirated more air.

Several liters and what seemed like ages later, Cody moved the plunger, felt resistance and announced, "Negative pressure." He withdrew the makeshift chest tube, grinning as he saw the unicorn's easy respiration and healthy pink gum color.

"Cody?" BJ said as she dropped into the chair by the anesthetic machine.

His head snapped up. "Ma'am?"

She was too exhausted to be appalled at being called "Ma'am." She said gently, "What next?"

"Right. We tap the abdomen to make sure there's no intra-abdominal bleeding—"

"Why don't you just use depth charges?" Matt said. "Come on; you should be doing an ultrasound."

Cody looked around the cottage automatically. BJ said, "Sorry, no ultrasound."

Cody frowned thoughtfully. "Well, if we're lucky, we won't draw off any blood." He clipped and cleansed a two-inch square of the abdomen, then inserted the needle smoothly and quickly, aspirating.

Valerie said, "Cody, how come your lips are moving?"

He said without looking up, "I'm kind of religious just now." He looked at the syringe. "A-men, brothers and sisters. Nothing but air."

BJ was silently glad. She was in no shape to supervise further soft-tissue surgery.

Cody finished, "So now he's stable. We anesthetize him, close the other wounds. Let's put some broad-spectrum antibiotics in the drip—I don't know specifically what works with unicorns—and by golly, we're gonna save the patient." He looked cheerfully around the table. "Go, team."

Frieda smiled at him. BJ, her emotions ravaged today, managed to smile. Even Matt produced a quick grin.

But Valerie, fingers running lightly over the unicorn's legs, stopped. "Whoa."

They turned to look.

"We have another problem." She held up a hoof. It had been chopped or sawed down below the bifurcation, to the raw flesh pad at the beginning of the pastern.

They stared at it wordlessly. Finally Frieda said, "What about the others?"

They checked the other three legs. It was immediately clear why the unicorn had been carried by the serenity of unicorns.

"All right," Cody said heavily. "This isn't the worst injury; it's just on top of a lot of others. Here's what we'll do—"

"We'll put it down," Matt said. Cody turned, open-mouthed. "You know damn well what would have happened to any normal livestock with this much trauma. You've argued that this rotation relates to our other work; prove it."

Cody looked back at the unicorn on the table. The only part unhurt on the animal was its spiral horn, whole and perfect. "This isn't livestock."

"Exactly. And it isn't anything we'll ever practice on again." He came forward. "Kill it, Cody. There's no point."

Cody shook his head and moved back toward the patient. Matt stepped forward calmly and shoved his foot into the back of Cody's good leg, behind the knee.

Cody fell in a heap, astonished. The others stared as though someone had shouted in church.

Matt stared back at them calmly and reasonably; he moved closer to the table. "BJ, what do you have for euthanizing? Otherwise, I'll need to rig some kind of mercy bolt; we need to put this animal out of pain."

BJ tested her legs, wondering how far she could push her body.

Frieda said sadly, "You're wrong, Matt. I'm sorry. But Cody's right, and it's his case anyway."

Matt looked at her blankly. She turned to Valerie. "What about you?"

Valerie had veins showing in her forehead. "I want to kill Matt. If I'm not allowed to do that, I'll just back Cody."

BJ said, "I represent the client, Matt. You'll do what I say." She looked across at Laurel to see that she was asleep before going on. "And yes, in this country I am allowed to kill you, but I'd probably just disable you. " She put out an arm to Cody, bracing herself; she wasn't supposed to lift. "Cody, what will you do from here?"

He ignored her arm, scrambling up to his knees, then to his feet, his gloved hands ahead of him like a fielder; he had kept them sterile. He said as though nothing had happened, "We'll apply Furacin to the hooves to prevent infection. We've got plenty on the truck. We pad and bandage the hooves and hope for regrowth. Does that sound good to you, BJ?"

She nodded, intrigued that she was back to being BJ and not Doctor Vaughan or "Ma'am."

"Great. Frieda, add isoflurane to the oxygen. Val, scrub and help me sew this fella up. Cruciates on the big cuts, continuous on the small stuff. Matt"—he was trying very hard, but had an edge in his voice—"we could use your help to finish this quickly."

Matt shook his head. BJ sighed. "Doctor Dobbs, you can come back in now."

Sugar stepped around the corner of the door as the students stared. "No, I didn't tell her. But what did you think—I'd leave you alone with an emergency case? Cody, good job at bouncing back and holding a team. Matt, step away."

But Matt said, "This whole rotation has been useless." He stepped toward Sugar. "And unethical and illegal."

Sugar said softly, "Are you callin' me out?"

Matt said very loudly, "I'm saying that you misused university funds. I'm saying that you lied to the state about what you were doing with supplies and personnel." He finished, barely acknowledging the other students, "I'm saying that all I have to prove is that you can't acknowledge where all those supplies and services went."

Sugar reached into his jacket pocket. Matt flinched back, then stood still.

He brought out a small folder and grinned crookedly. "Gun's in the other pocket, Matt." He withdrew a packet of typing paper and unfolded it. "Read 'em."

Matt took the papers; BJ saw that they were photocopies of receipts: medical materials, gasoline and mileage logs, even itemized costs for Sugar's and the students' meals at Stein's, and records of reimbursement payment.

At the bottom of each receipt was either "received for" or "disbursed for" and "The Crossroads Veterinary Clinic, the Healing Sign."

All the receipts were signed simply, "Stein."

Sugar took them back. "The originals are on file at Western Vee, Matt. Stein's had a vendor's and a purchaser's I.D. there for a couple years; he buys used equipment from us, secondhand books from the university library, all kinds of things. He even has a credit rating in Dun and Bradstreet, with a Kendrick address."

Matt stared at the photocopies as though they didn't make sense and looking would change them.

Sugar said gently, "Same as your schoolwork, Matt. You can handle assignments, but you need more imagination."

Matt said nothing.

Sugar leaned against the cottage wall, and for a moment he looked remarkably old. "Matt, it only half bothers me that you're not open to strange situations. It God-sure completely bothers me that you're too damn sure of yourself, and you need to be right more than you need a patient to live. Cody was saving its life, and you were ready to kill it, and that doesn't bother you for a minute, does it?" Matt said nothing. "And your mind ain't right, and you don't have any way to deal with the cases you've seen this summer, and you'd destroy me to make it all go away."

Matt looked toward the window, through which BJ could see a unicorn kidling nuzzling its mother, and looked resolutely away, toward the wall.

Frieda put a gloved hand on his shoulder—an easy, relaxed gesture compared to how she might have done it a month ago. "I think the important thing is for you to get out of here."

Matt turned away and walked out. A moment later Frieda said, "He's just sitting in the truck."

"Good." Sugar rubbed his eyes. "Why don't you close that door, scrub back up and help us finish?"

*   *   *

They were removing their gloves and gowns, the surgery done, when they heard a scratching sound, unhurried and persistent, coming from the door. Sugar looked out the window. "BJ, did you plan on monitoring the patient here?"

Cody did a very good job of not reacting. BJ said, "Doctor Dobbs, it isn't my patient."

"Right. Sorry. Cody, I think the serenity wants to take its own back. Do you need Doctor Vaughan to do any kind of follow-up, or is it okay if the patient heals on its own?"

Cody looked at all corners of the room for guidance, took a deep breath, and said finally, "So long as BJ does a follow-up in a week, and so long as unicorns can take medical instructions and follow them, I have no problem."

BJ said, "Of course I'll follow up. You're more than welcome to come in and do the exam," she added particularly to Cody, "even without the rest of the rotation. I could use your expertise."

Frieda and Valerie, behind him, both grinned. Cody said, "Thanks." He added innocently to Sugar, "Shall I issue medical instructions to the client?"

Sugar, with barely a moment's hesitation, said, "Do it. We can't be sure they'll understand the instructions, but they'll do what they want anyway."

While Cody dictated a list of instructions, the unicorn on the table began to come out of anesthesia. At that point, two unicorns nudged Cody gently out of the way and came in the cottage, their hooves chiming lightly even on the wood floor. They levered their horns under the body on the table and moved forward, shrugging the injured unicorn's legs over their backs; they glided side by side, without seeming to be crowded, out the front door.

The last face in the door was from a curious kidling. It looked peacefully at the vet students, then at BJ and Sugar; it struck its forehead against the door, making a soft bell-like noise that startled everyone, and turned to follow the rest of the serenity. In a few minutes they were gone.

The students seemed to follow it out; in moments they were outside, taking the dirty supplies with them. Valerie, looking defensive and challenging, left a stuffed lamb in

Laurel's cradle and fled practically before BJ could thank her.

Sugar returned, carrying a surgical pack and some gowns and gloves. "Here's some replacements." He set them on the counter and carefully wiped off the table. BJ, too tired to help, watched. "We'll take your packs back to be wrapped and autoclaved. You don't need to fuss with all that now. Are you gonna be all right?"

"I'll be fine." BJ glanced out the door at the truck; the students were sitting bolt upright, absolutely silent. "What about you?"

"What? Oh, Matt. Shoot, I've known that was coming for months."

"How did he make it this far?"

"Maybe you don't remember vet school. Some people go to grad school just to keep from facing things. They have assignments, and they're damn good at them, and they never think about the work they're trained for because school is so damn safe. BJ, it's more than his objecting to Crossroads; he can't handle reality, even this reality. He just ain't stable. I had to make him face that."

"Did it have to be in front of the other students?"

Sugar said in surprise, "BJ, I'm teaching them, too."

BJ leaned forward and touched the receipts sticking out of Sugar's pocket. "You never told me."

He tucked them in. "Not your problem. Stein and I handled it. You were busy, and you're not slick enough for this kind of thing yet." He grinned, but the grin looked tired.

BJ said, "He'll still graduate."

"Hell, if he wants he'll still practice. And some day he'll screw up but good, and go down insisting that everything was by the book and he was right. And he'll always believe it." Sugar looked out the window at the truck. "But I had to try to let him know."

He sprayed disinfectant on the table and wiped it again, glancing at the blood on his clothes. "That was fancy cutting on that poor beast. Did you figure out what that five-sided mark was?"

BJ nodded, saying nothing.

"And why didn't you tell the students?" But he obviously knew.

"They really didn't need to know that someone was playing a game like tic-tac-toe in the flesh of an animal."

He nodded. "Somebody good enough to attack a unicorn and win. I couldn't do that." It was one of the rare occasions when BJ heard Sugar admit a shortcoming. "Who could? Who did it?"

"I'm not sure."

"Come on. I've seen you think harder than that. This took intelligence, and there aren't that many around who could have done it—"

BJ ticked them off. "Dyvedd's the obvious choice. Then maybe Gredya; I brought her back to Crossroads so she could have a litter, and she's been hunting for their food. Then Fiona; she's still pretty disturbed. After that, there are the young griffins or their parents. It only started after the young ones arrived."

Sugar nodded. "I guess you know what you're doing."

BJ thought uneasily of the Grym and whoever had trained and domesticated them. "Not completely."

As he left for the truck, Frieda ran in. "Are you sure you'll be okay?"

"I'll be fine." She thought over the past few hours. "Or I'll get help from Fiona or Stein."

Frieda looked dubious. "I'll be back in as soon as I can," she said firmly. "I'll bet Laurie would come; I can ride with her. Or I'll ask to borrow Skywalker again." She looked at the sky wistfully. "Do you think Roland and Oliver will be around?"

BJ, about to confide her suspicions, saw the look in Frieda's eye. "They said they were taking their leave from me. I'm not sure how long they'll be gone."

Frieda nodded silently. At a honk from the truck, she vanished out the door. BJ was left in a cottage that felt for all the world like the scene of the crime.

Laurel, for being tiny and inarticulate, was a surprising comfort.

E·I·G·H·T·E·E·N

BJ RESTED FOR nearly a week. No cases came to her; she wondered if Stein was responsible for that, but didn't much care.

She spent the time resting, nursing, and playing with Laurel. The baby was surprisingly little trouble; she slept through half the night and fell asleep immediately after nursing, then amused herself with her stuffed lamb, and chewed on the rattle and ball Stefan had bought her. BJ was painfully aware that Laurel was already teething, but after a few awkward sessions they'd been able to reach an understanding.

The only real crisis was that in the middle of the first week, Laurel learned to crawl. BJ, completely unprepared, went through the cottage on her hands and knees, removing everything dangerous that came to hand. Then she scrubbed the floor while Laurel bleated anxiously from her crib, desperate to come play in the water.

After that she barred the door, lay on the bed, and dozed fitfully while Laurel contentedly explored the house.

By the end of the week, Laurel was pulling herself upright on table legs and looking speculatively around the room. BJ was keeping a diary, recording as much as possible, afraid to miss a moment.

At the end of the week there was a knock at her door. To

her complete surprise, it was Stein, carrying a body. She took it from him, looking at him questioningly.

He cocked his head at her. "What?"

She shook her own head in response. "I just don't think of you being away from the inn."

"It's an inn where I work, it's a fort if you look close, but it's also where I spend a lot of time. I like it." He sighed. "I still need to get out. BJ, I'm old now; I don't sleep so good. I walk in the mornings. This morning I found this."

They looked down at the dodo, its neck wrung. BJ hadn't seen dodoes since she and the others, exasperated at the helpless stupidity of the birds, had made a dodo preserve of a small island in southern Crossroads.

The bird was also plucked as though for cooking. BJ turned it over, looking for other wounds. "Were the feathers near it?"

"No." He showed her a rumpled cloth. "This was the only thing nearby."

She looked at the homespun cloth, then at the bird. "So someone carried it—"

"And left it on a flat rock near the road, where we could find it. So, what is this? Is it an offering? A threat?" He stared down at the bird as though it could answer. "A joke?"

BJ looked down at it, inert and heavy in her hands. "There's no question, is there? This was done by a sentient being, not by the Wyr."

She wrapped the body in the bloody cloth. "I'll put it in the springhouse till I get back."

"With the butter and the milk and everything?" Stein looked queasy.

"Not right on top of them." BJ smiled. Vets and vet students had a disturbing tendency to keep stool samples in the same fridge. In back of a clinic she had once visited, there was a freezer full of dead dogs awaiting disposal and, in a flagrant OSHA violation, in a corner until one of the technicians went home with it, a wrapped frozen turkey.

She walked to the springhouse, Stein following dubiously. "Well, it's not like you were keeping kosher . . . Listen, young lady, are you planning on going to the island?''

"I have to." She shut the springhouse door and returned to the house quickly; Laurel would wake up any minute, and she wanted to be there. "Laurel has to nurse first, and then I can go."

"Alone?" He spread his hands, ready to argue with her.

BJ hung the diaper bag on his left hand. "Yes, if you'll watch her for me."

The Hippoi were clearly visible from Stein's; they were on the plain below. BJ kissed Laurel and ran down.

Polyta galloped forward as soon as she saw BJ. Polyta looked wonderful; the scars were fading slowly from her back, and freedom clearly agreed with her.

BJ drew herself up quickly and said without panting, "I greet you, Carron."

Polyta nodded back. "I greet you, Doctor." More naturally she said, "BJ, is something wrong?"

"I don't know." BJ looked around at the others; most of them were watching colts run and fight. Few of them, male or female, were unattached. "I need to travel south, and I was hoping . . ."

"For a ride?" Polyta frowned. "BJ, few of us feel like having a rider now."

"I know. I'm sorry." And she was, deeply. "Polyta, it's an emergency."

Polyta said flatly, "Hemera will do." She shouted, "Hemera!" and clapped three times. From the river's edge, Hemera trotted forward, smiling and waving shyly when she saw BJ.

"Hemera," Polyta said firmly, "BJ needs to ride to the south." She added as Hemera's face fell, "You have let her ride you before we were captured, and you will let her ride you now. It's no different."

Hemera nodded, her red hair bouncing with the shortness of the gesture; she reached up to brush it with a hand whose wrist was still callused from manacles.

Polyta said severely, "And this time, do not desert her, no matter what the reason."

Hemera blushed. Once, not so long ago, she had deserted BJ in a trip to this very area.

BJ only said, "Thank you for taking me." She climbed on awkwardly. Hemera took a pole for carrying balanced loads and trotted south.

The journey was steady and pleasant; the road south, one of the few Roman roads still left in Crossroads, was easy to travel. BJ half dozed on Hemera's back until they reached the turnoff over the plains to the southwestern bay.

Hemera tensed as they crossed the dry grasslands near the griffins' home; BJ, holding on to her as they sped up, was tense as well. For the present no griffins appeared. The grass to either side was high enough to hide a standing man, or a crouching lion.

Hemera spoke, for the first time since they had forded Laetyen River hours before. "Would the griffins kill me?"

"The old ones might," BJ said. "I'm not sure the young ones would." With that scant comfort, they rode downward through the tall grass toward a bay sparkling in the sun.

To their right lay a mangrove swamp, roots sticking out into the weedless waters. To their left lay a salt marsh, oat grass giving way to reeds as the sand dropped until it reached a level where the tides piled up decayed weeds and flotsam. Overhead, whooping cranes soared in huge flocks, a painful reminder to BJ, from times past, that one could not predict what Crossroads might nurture next.

Hemera walked hesitantly to the water's edge. The Hippoi seldom if ever came to the seashore; Hemera found it unnerving. A small ripple moved the waters, and she let out a small shriek and half danced backward.

BJ felt patronizingly amused until she noted the carcasses washing back and forth in the gentle surf. The hooves suggested that they were deer; BJ, suddenly afraid, peered intently at the upper bodies and was relieved to find deer hooves on the forelegs as well. The corpses looked strangely like dressed meat; all the fat had been scraped away.

She slid off Hemera's back, catchlet in hand. Apart from the restless, wheeling cranes, there was no other life visible besides her and Hemera. She listened intently; the only sounds were from the birds.

Hemera said faintly, "Did the griffins do this?"

"I don't think so." BJ touched one of the carcasses. Because it had been in the water, it was impossible to tell how long it had lain there. Small beach crabs were grouped around them already, leaving tiny ragged snips in the exposed flesh. "These weren't just killed; they were butchered and left. The griffins would have eaten them if they'd taken the trouble to dress the meat—" She saw Hemera's face and stopped. "Hemera, there's one other thing I need to do. It won't take long."

Feeling faintly self-conscious, BJ stripped. She left her clothes on the pole with Hemera; with some regret, she left her catchlet. It was too heavy to swim with comfortably. She walked to the water, circling around the deer carcasses.

At the last moment, BJ turned. "I'm sorry to leave you alone."

Hemera nodded. "I understand." She added, trying to sound brave, "I will wait here."

BJ looked across at the island, out in the bay. "Wait a while. If I don't come back, or if someone comes that you're afraid of, run off. Don't hesitate." She finished, "Tell the Carron that it was my order."

Hemera nodded, but spread her legs slightly and planted her hooves, like a balky horse refusing to move. "I'll be here."

BJ smiled at her. "Everything will be fine." She turned away, trying to keep the smile on as she waded into the bay.

The water was warm, almost bathlike. She walked out as far as she could, digging her toes in the silt for balance. When the water was chest-high she lifted her feet and swam slowly, reminding herself that it was good therapy to help her heal. After a while, she moved to a sidestroke; even though she wasn't sore, she didn't want to take chances.

She emerged from the water, grateful for the bright sunlight and still air. She looked at the hill above, unsurprised that none of the dodoes peered over the edge of the bluff; they weren't curious birds, and had little reason to be there.

The path up the hillside was still visible, undergrowth creeping in slightly. She climbed it slowly, sorry she hadn't kept her shoes on and wincing at the small rocks.

As she came over the top she saw a group of dodoes, unmoving, all staring at a single bird. That disturbed her; dodoes lacked the concentration these birds showed. She looked past them and saw similar groups all over the island, seemingly in conference in private activities.

The first dodo was impaled on a stake, hidden behind one of his legs; the other leg was bound up tight with bark. His stubby wings were spread rigidly out as if for balance. Three more dodoes, with ribbons in the feathers at the backs of their necks, watched from the side.

Below the dodo was a pattern of rectangles and triangles scratched into the soil, a rock in each pattern—

BJ blinked. It was a hopscotch layout.

She stared at it, refusing to accept what she saw, then looked at the rest of the island. There were dozens of groupings, each different even from a distance.

At one, a series of branches were bent into hoops. A few of the dodoes were staked in position with makeshift mallets, aiming sightlessly at their own sucked-dry eggs for croquet balls.

At another, two lines of dodoes faced each other over an ovoid stone, the center dodo waiting for a "hike" signal which would never come.

It took her longer to identify the games of leapfrog and follow-the-leader.

After that she moved among the groups quickly, identifying the sports almost in shock and looking for signs of life.

Almost all of the groupings were clearly games. Some games she didn't recognize, though the balls, sticks, and goals made the groupings clear.

At one point she paused at a grouping which was unidentifiable yet naggingly familiar. In front of her was a dodo on sticks, some sort of pink dye—possibly from flowers— used to make the body pink.

A few feet over was a second dodo in the same state. Three feet beyond that was another dodo, decapitated, with a bark tube connecting the head to the body to give it an impossibly long neck.

Behind them was a stand of two long upright sticks with a single stick laid across the top of it as a lintel. A clamshell on a short stick jutted out just inside the frame, halfway up.

BJ stared at it for several minutes before she realized it was a cartoonish representation of a door and doorknob.

The whole scene snapped into horrid focus; she was in a mock front yard, populated with a nest of homemade lawn flamingoes. She turned away, sickened, and ran to check the other groups.

BJ looked for evidence to the contrary at every grouping, but by the end she was convinced, from the frequent pools of blood, that the dodoes had been staked up alive.

On the way through the groupings she stumbled, half leapt, and caught herself with that frantic dexterity people use around breakable objects. She looked back and checked the eggs in her way. There were at least a dozen, rolled into a hollow during some sort of scuffle, or possibly by carelessness on the part of the dodoes themselves.

With exquisite tenderness, BJ assembled the cache of eggs and set a stick upright in the middle of them, a bunch of dead leaves fluttering forlornly to mark the mound containing the last possible dodoes on any world at all.

That done, BJ dusted her hands off and surveyed the caricatured sports field around her. It occurred to her, finally, that there had been no insect or predator damage; this had happened in the last few hours.

A wind blew over the island and she jumped, looking around wildly. Whoever had done this might be watching her.

She backed slowly to the edge of the island, glanced behind her in the water, and slid quickly in. When she realized how panicky her strokes were, she took a deep, shuddering breath and swam slowly and carefully.

BJ swam until her kicking toe scraped in the mud. Her flying pulse and gasping breath told her that she had made good time, though she had that slow-motion feeling people get in nightmares. She stood, finding herself in knee-deep water.

She ran to the shore, looking right and left. The carcasses were gone. Hemera was gone.

She heard a splash to her right; she whirled. A brown body, smeared with yellow pulpy streaks, slunk into the underbrush. Water stood out in beads on his fur.

It took BJ a moment to realize what she had seen: a Grym, smeared with something, and trying to hide from her.

She looked around dazedly and noticed a lump bobbing in the weak waves. Facing the shore and backing out, she waded to it.

The body was a whooping crane, the feathers ripped from the abdomen. The bloody, pale muscle tissue looked appallingly like something in a butcher's shop or an agribusiness, a body stripped to its most humanly useful.

BJ blinked and looked again. That was exactly what it looked like; the muscle had been stripped of its fat, just as the deer carcasses had.

She had a sudden vision of a Grym scooping out the fat, smearing it on its body and swimming—swimming—where would they swim?

She stared at the island in the harbor, and shivered. "No."

No one answered. A few whooping cranes from the salt marsh flew overhead, but made no attempt to land.

"Hemera?" she called softly, and again, louder. "Hemera?" There was no answer.

She looked at her tracks, then at the marks in the sand where the carcasses had been dragged away. She felt suddenly dizzy.

She said loudly, "I understand now."

The underbrush was silent.

"That's why you wanted the fat," BJ said loudly. "To repel the water."

She finally said, "Stein had said the dodo you left for us to find might be a joke. We didn't know it was only part of a joke."

The underbrush rustled as hundreds of Grym stood up, Gek in front of them. Dozens of them were smeared with oil; the one she had seen previously had been scrubbing it off. They grinned at her, tongues lolling.

BJ stood trying to cover herself, knowing it was foolish and trying to tell herself that she was no more vulnerable than she would be fully clothed. It was little comfort.

Gek bounded forward on his hind legs. "We barely got done in time," he barked in clear English. "Surprised?"

"Of course," BJ said.

"What fun! We didn't think you'd ever figure it out, especially after the way we cut meat to fool you."

It took BJ a moment to realize that "cut meat" meant "torture animals."

"But now the big joke is over, and we can talk to you," Gek said. "That's good! We've had lots to say. We want to hear you talk." He showed his laughing teeth and lolling tongue. "We want to make you talk."

"Are you going to kill me now?" BJ said steadily.

Gek rolled his eyes. "What fun would that be? Even when we kill you, we won't do it fast. For things who play games, you don't understand a lot about stretching games out. Nice scar." She jumped as he touched it. "Did it hurt?"

She put her hand over the cesarean scar. "A little."

"Not enough," he said disapprovingly. "Should have hurt a lot."

"Where is Hemera?"

He lifted his head and let out several short yips; now BJ recognized them as signals.

Ten Grym came forward, tugging on ropes braided from plant fiber. At the other end, not struggling at all, was Hemera. One of the ropes, tight around her neck, was a strangling noose. Hemera's eyes were as wide as any human's BJ had ever seen, whites showing at the top and bottom over the pupil.

"Didn't want her to run on you."

BJ ran forward and loosened the ropes, taking Hemera's hand. Hemera squeezed it with the strength the Hippoi had, nearly crushing BJ's fingers.

"It's all right," BJ said, stroking her horse-back. "It's fine."

The Grym laughed. Of course it wasn't.

BJ's catchlet was still in the pack on Hemera's back; she

pulled it now, and held it at guard. There was no way to protect the two of them against so many.

"That's what we forgot," Gek said in disgust. "Fencing. We didn't make a fencing joke with the birds."

It was already obvious, but BJ said, "You've been to Earth, to my Earth, before."

"Many times." He turned and shouted to the Grym, "Loup-garou!"

They shouted back happily, "Loup-garou!"

"Mngwa!"

"Mngwa!"

"Gek!"

"Gek!"

"Gek from India," BJ said, marveling. "It wasn't a mongoose after all."

He turned back to BJ. "Of course not."

"And the sword cuts? And the clams?"

"The clams were fun. You know how hard it is to stuff clams down a throat? Big hands won't do it—and you *still* didn't get it."

BJ said with barely a quiver in her voice, "Why did you kill all the dodoes?"

Gek shrugged. "They were stupid, it was fun. It passes the time."

"Some of the—jokes, I didn't get."

"You need to travel more."

"The games you showed weren't from my Earth, then."

"We've been to lots of worlds. Travel is fun. See new things, see new places, meet new people, kill them all." He wagged a paw at her reprovingly. "You cut us off, you naughty meat. Closed all the roads, you and the dead fat man. We killed the food in the world where you found us, and then we couldn't leave." He folded his forelegs over his chest. "We might have starved."

"How did you live?"

He shrugged, an odd gesture on a canine body. "We ate each other. Less fun, but all right."

BJ said simply, "Are you going to kill us all?"

The Grym laughed uproariously. Gek chirped, "Of course we're going to kill you, silly meat. Just not now."

He pointed to Hemera. "Get on her and go tell your friends to get ready. We'll give you all night to plan, and then we'll count to a hundred. Or maybe seven."

He turned his back and covered his eyes.

BJ dressed hastily and leapt onto Hemera, mounting a horse-back easily for the first time in her life. Hemera was galloping forward before BJ was settled.

They had gone fifty feet when BJ heard a noise and looked over her shoulder. The Grym had spun around to face them. Gek let out a bloodcurdling growl and shouted, "Ready or not, here we come!"

They charged, slavering. Hemera screamed and reared, nearly dislodging BJ, then thundered off at double speed. The Grym pursued, growling furiously.

BJ, clinging to Hemera's back, turned her head when the growling stopped. The Grym, no longer pursuing, were rolling back and forth on the ground, tongues hanging out, grinning and laughing. It seemed to BJ she could hear the laughter for a long time.

The trip back took an impossibly short time. BJ longed to open a new road to shorten the trip, realizing in time that she didn't dare. The Gek would track her down the shortcut and would have access to any worlds she crossed. By the end, Hemera was gasping, rocking from side to side with the need to breathe.

She never paused when they reached the ford, simply plunged across the river with an exhausted desperation. BJ, recognizing her strain, slid quickly off Hemera's back and floated clinging to one of her hands, letting the centaur swim unburdened.

The Hippoi were nowhere in sight; they had probably moved to the upper slopes. Hemera galloped up the hill to Stein's; she and BJ were both still dripping wet. They dashed in the road through the ring of stones, Hemera's hooves clattering loudly.

BJ grimaced; her truck was here. Unless Fiona had driven it over, someone had come from the outside and done it; that meant additional people at risk.

The Griffin and Laurie stood beside the truck, talking to

Fiona. BJ felt relief, then a twinge of guilt that she was so happy it hadn't been Stefan.

BJ leapt off; her legs, tired from gripping Hemera, buckled, and she grabbed at Hemera's sweaty back. "Go tell Polyta everything. Make sure the Hippoi are warned."

Hemera nodded, still breathless and sides still heaving; she galloped off almost before BJ hit the ground.

Against all sense or caution, Dyvedd ran out, Dancer in hand. Stein ran behind him, carrying Laurel.

BJ took her away and held her, tightly, eyes shut.

Finally the Griffin said gently, "If you don't have serious news, you're frightening us for no reason."

BJ looked at him, then at all the others. She took a deep breath and said calmly, "I've made a terrible mistake."

N·I·N·E·T·E·E·N

"ALL RIGHT," STEIN said heavily. "We've been invaded again. Successfully."

"I find it hard to believe that no one noticed they were sentient," the Griffin said.

"They did a good job of hiding it," BJ said bitterly. "It was a great game for them."

"Ah, yes. Playful little carnivores." The Griffin regarded her solemnly. "Doctor, do you remember my saying that sentient civilization and brutality were not exclusive?"

BJ didn't at first, but understood too well now.

Fiona said suddenly, "I want to go home."

BJ seized the moment. "Take the truck. Drive back out. I'll make a new road and close it behind you." BJ added, "Take Laurel with you—"

But Laurie was shaking her head.

"What's wrong?" BJ suddenly knew. "Laurel's test—"

"Back yesterday. It's part of why we came." She finished unwillingly, "Positive."

BJ sat very still while Laurie went on, unable to stop herself, "It won't matter for years to come. By then there may be a cure; even Lou Gehrig's disease is responding to drug treatment now, they think, and as long as she stays in Crossroads—"

"Crossroads," the Griffin interrupted quietly, "is unhealthy for reasons of its own just now." He held a talon out to BJ. "I am most sorry."

She took it. The claw felt hard and invulnerable and very real. Laurie's news seemed hard and fantastic and completely unbelievable.

Laurie repeated, "Look, it probably won't matter until she's middle-aged or beyond. She hasn't even grown up yet. Are you all right?"

"Fauns grow up very fast," BJ said.

She felt the talon in her hand twitch suddenly, but the Griffin said steadily, "We will all have the pleasure of monitoring her growth."

Fiona said, "It doesn't matter, BJ. I said I want to go; I didn't say I was going to." She smiled weakly at Stein. "It's time I knew that nothing is free."

Stein, beaming, reached across to her and patted her hand. He turned to the others. "I don't want to push, but we have a battle coming, and we need to face it or get away. Are you all ready to face things?"

"Are there any more bottles of wine?" Fiona asked.

Stein hesitated, then spread his hands. "Why not? They're back by the empties. Don't forget to take a corkscrew."

Fiona tried to smile, doing badly. "I have one on my Swiss Army knife."

She vanished into the pantry.

Laurie said, "Is she all right?"

Stein said, "That's kind of a loose term."

When Fiona returned, they all nodded casually. She poured most of those present a glass (Dyvedd refused, and swigged from the bottle), and sat by herself at the edge of the group, sipping repeatedly and nervously while she watched the others.

The Griffin said, "Fond as I am of table talk, we have something more pressing at hand."

Stein rose. "It's time again."

He moved a table aside, kicked a board with his heel, and stepped back as the board sprang up. He slid a small section of floor aside. "We'll need to see who we can get in touch with, arm them—" He stopped.

The Griffin was beside him in an instant. "Is something wrong?" Then he, too, stopped, staring down.

BJ stepped forward, half-sure what she would see.

The enclosed recess where Stein kept weapons was empty except for ten catchlets. A splintery hole gaped in the far end of the box. Beyond it was a tunnel.

Smeared on the far wall, in rust-brown dripping block letters, were the words "GAME TIME."

Stein knelt quickly and passed up the remaining catchlets. "Out. Now." They went.

On Stein's orders, they threw supplies in the truck and onto their backs. The last thing he did was go back to the inn door. "I want to lock up." He pulled the door to, locking it. BJ watched, wondering why he bothered locking an inn that already had a tunnel under it. With the point of a catchlet, Stein carved three triangles into the door, an arrow under them, and a series of curves and polygons. Finishing, he turned quickly around. "Let's go."

They moved on the road to the west, into the hills near High River. Beyond the ford was a valley, nestled in the foothills. As they climbed, the road faded to a livestock path, then to nothing.

Stein set down the weapons and food he had brought. "Right here." The others shrugged out of their packs; the Griffin leaned to one side and let the rest of the supplies from the inn drop.

BJ turned and stared down the valley; it was a semicircular cut in the hills, dropping down to the river. To her left was a ravine, the stream in it cutting the only easy access over the final lip of the valley. Stein had taken the high ground, establishing a nearly impregnable position.

Fiona followed in the truck, taking a road at first, then driving over the grazed turf uphill. Finally she turned to follow beside the ravine, the engine complained mightily as it overcame the final slope. Before the crumbled edge of the valley rim near the ravine, Fiona floored it and charged ahead. The wheels spun agonizingly.

The truck rocked forward as she gunned the engine, then shot onto the level space where the others were gathered.

The clatter of rolling bottles sounded as she slammed to a stop on the grass.

Stein peered in the passenger window. "Fiona, sweetheart, you grabbed the empties, too."

"Oh, darn," she said vaguely. She shut off the engine and tumbled out, carrying one of the full bottles.

Stein shot her a curious look.

He sat, and the others sat around him. "We need firewood," Stein said. "And guards for the perimeter. And I know this makes no sense, but I would like a set of saplings, six feet high and over an inch thick, cut down and brought to me."

On the last request, Dyvedd shrugged apologetically to the rest of them and disappeared in the woods to their left. Presently they heard the *thwack* of Dancer swinging among the saplings.

Stein turned to the others. "Now we need to plan."

Fiona said again, "We could leave."

Stein said firmly, "I've lived here nearly all my life. I'll die here."

BJ said, "Even if we could leave, think what we'd be leaving behind." She pointed up above them, in the mountains to the north. At their edge, the unicorns were grazing, serene and remote. BJ wondered, if anything happened to her, if the unicorns would come down and care for Laurel. The prospect seemed remote, but so did all other prospects.

Stein, looking up at them as well, said thoughtfully, "Do you think they'll defend us?"

The Griffin tapped on a rock, considering. "I doubt they'll regard our cause as spiritual enough." He added with irritation, "I wish they'd simply feel a nice earthly sense of obligation."

"It's too much like guilt," Fiona said. "They're innocent. No guilt, no obligation."

"How about the Hippoi?"

Laurie grunted. "They'd help if they could find us."

BJ said, "They'll find us. Stein left a message." The others turned to her. "The carving on the door. You worked out a code with Polyta, long ago."

Stein chuckled, sounding normal for a moment. "Such a smart one."

Dyvedd returned with kindling. "There are some logs, too." Laurie went back with him. The Griffin watched her.

Frieda said tentatively to him, "I think he can be trusted. She'll be all right."

He turned to her. "I appreciate your assessment of Dyvedd, and concur. On the other hand, any definition of 'all right' which involves being here is useless."

Stein said, "He's right. We can do a few things, but that's about all." Dyvedd returned, bearing a bundle of freshly cut poles; Stein took them and began whittling with a catchlet.

Without being asked, Frieda made the fire. The Griffin, surprisingly silent, helped her assemble logs and build it.

An hour before sunset they heard musical instruments. Dyvedd looked up, confused. "Who can that be? The Meat People don't play that kind of tune." The style sounded familiar to BJ, a little like country-western two-steps, a little like rock and roll, with something else thrown in.

Fiona said suddenly, "Cajun. It sounds Cajun. My God, it's zydeco."

BJ, her chest tight, said, "They've found us."

Stein looked down in the valley, and his face got a curious expression, equal parts surprise and nausea.

The Grym were moving up the valley in a snake dance. Some of them were wrapped in wool cloth from the Meat People. Some of them were wrapped in clothing which looked like saris and djellabas from Earth; BJ blinked, watching them. All of them carried catchlets, or spears, or musical instruments. They danced enthusiastically and easily on their hind legs.

Looking at them, BJ wondered bitterly how she could ever have thought they weren't sentient.

They came to within forty feet below them and danced past, singing something in a mix of French and English. Once in a while they would throw their heads back and shout in unison, "Loup-garou!"

The Grym leading the dance line was playing a bagpipe. He led the line forward, to just within sight, and then held the bag forward. BJ squinted; it appeared to be made of skin—

Frieda gasped, pointing. "There's a face."

The bag was made from one of the Meat People, the eyes, nostrils and mouth stitched shut. They watched, horrified, as the face expanded and contracted as the Grym squeezed the bagpipe. For one frozen second it was the size of a normal face, and BJ recognized Dyvedd's friend Mohnrr.

Dyvedd roared, spinning Dancer; he charged forward.

Without seeming to think about it, Stein thrust forward the stick he was whittling on until it stuck between Dyvedd's ankles. Dyvedd flopped down chest first, then bounded up and glared wildly at Stein, Dancer poised before Stein's throat.

Stein knocked it aside with the stick. "In the morning." Frieda's eyes widened at the command in Stein's voice.

Something gave inside Dyvedd and he nodded, dropping his eyes. He sat apart, his arms locked around his chest, shivering. Fiona put an arm around him and offered him the wine bottle. He drank.

Toward sunset the Grym danced down the hill again. Later, in the bowl at the bottom of the valley, they could see bonfires.

From time to time they watched the Grym partying; the music never stopped. Fiona paused, in the middle of a sip of wine. "BJ? Could we still leave?"

She looked at the fires in the valley. "They tracked us here, didn't they? They're carnivores; they could smell their way to follow us, too quickly for me to close a road. If we left, they could follow us. After that they could take others, to other worlds." She added, because someone needed to know, "And I'm not sure, if we all left here and all the roads were closed, that I could open a road back again."

Fiona nodded. "And it's not a good time for experimenting." She passed the bottle to BJ, who barely sipped; she needed to be able to nurse.

BJ found herself thinking of all the species and friends she had brought back to Crossroads: the Hippoi, the unicorns, Gredya, Rudy, and Bambi. What had she done? And all those roads were open.

As darkness came, they opened a third bottle of wine, and a fourth. There wasn't much talk.

Stein looked sadly at the final bottle. "I was saving this for something." He shrugged. "Some years you can't win."

Fiona held out a hand and he passed the bottle back, watching as she emptied it. "Everyone sleep. We'll need energy in the morning."

Fiona frowned. "You can't order people to sleep."

"Of course I can. I just can't make them obey." He himself sat up, whittling on the pile of cut sticks.

Fiona moved away from Dyvedd and lay down, muttering. A moment later she was snoring.

Dyvedd smiled faintly, watching her. "Faster than goose shi—" He stopped, looking at BJ. "She falls asleep faster than horses run." He came over to BJ. "What about Laurel?"

"Faster even than Fiona." BJ remarked annoyedly without thinking, "And that's pretty fast."

Frieda, head still on one elbow nearby, looked at her with interest. Dyvedd chuckled, unembarrassed. "When you live at an inn, these things happen." He took off his breeches, spinning the legs around into a circle on the ground. "Put her down between us."

BJ bundled up part of a tablecloth as a pillow, leaving the rest to drape over her.

Stein, sleepless, sat up and whittled on the long sticks which Dyvedd had cut. His face, as he cut at the stick ends, was expressionless.

After a while, she was aware that Dyvedd was sitting up, facing down toward the valley. A little after that, she fell asleep.

T·W·E·N·T·Y

BJ woke to find Dyvedd, sword lying over him, on his side
with his body wrapped around Laurel. As he breathed, her
hair moved, tickling in his nostrils; he showed no sign of
waking up.

BJ rolled over to see Polyta looking down, smiling. "Do
you pay him to watch her?"

"I paid him to watch me." She got up on one elbow.
"Maybe I didn't pay him enough."

BJ stood, dressing quickly; the fire had nearly died and
the morning was cold. She saw the Hippoi moving across
the landscape, barely speaking, each with an assigned task.
Some gathered belongings, some poured water on the fires
of the night before, others watched the colts.

Frieda, in an oversize Western Vee sweat shirt, joined
them. She stared with BJ at the Hippoi. "They don't look
like warriors."

"My people will fight," Polyta said flatly. She said it
with neither joy nor mourning.

Frieda looked down the valley, where smoke rose from
the Grym's fires. "How many of them volunteered?"

Polyta was astonished. "I told them to."

Frieda framed a question and then gave up.

BJ, watching as Laurel nursed, said absently, "Stein will
tell you where you have to go."

Polyta looked appalled. Stein, in earshot, said, "Carron, if I may—"

Polyta turned toward him. He pointed at the ravine on the left. "Your people could move down that, next to the water, and hold it against an army. Double-file, you'd fill it at the top, then three abreast further down, up to six at the bottom." He looked up respectfully. "If you will."

She straightened, towering over him. "We shall hold it until we die, Stein."

He bowed, winking at BJ while his face was hidden from Polyta. BJ was too preoccupied to smile.

"Can you tell yet how many of them there are?" Frieda bit her lip. She'd asked too many times.

BJ didn't get upset. "No new estimate. Maybe three hundred, maybe more."

Frieda stood with her catchlet clasped in front of her. She looked like she was asking her high school drama coach how to say her lines. "Where do you want me?"

Stein patted her hair. "Anywhere but here, pretty head. You stand by me, unless you think of something better."

Dyvedd said sadly, "Comes of my sleeping late. Now he'll have all the pretty smart ones, and I'll be put between two wild boars."

Frieda laughed. "Oh, you."

He swaggered over to BJ and whispered, "Keep me from dropping this sword; I need some sleep."

BJ murmured, "Don't drop it," but she felt better. She felt better still as she watched him tickle Laurel Stefanie behind her knees, making her giggle and kick.

"You should wait till they're older," Stein said disapprovingly. He was going to say something more, but stopped and cocked an ear. "What's that?"

Laurel's ears twitched. The rest of them listened: from the valley came muffled clanging, some thudding drumbeats, stray notes from something that might have been horns or trumpets, and a strange, tuneless chiming.

Frieda peered into the valley. "That sounds like metal. How are they doing that?"

"The catchlets," Stein said suddenly. "They hang one up and hit it with another. Plus, they're banging them to-

gether." He shook his head. "All that sharpening and pol-
ishing, and they do that. Disgusting animals."

BJ heard a thin, reedy squeak from the homemade bagpipe. She shut her eyes.

Fiona appeared, flanked by Laurie and the Griffin. Fiona's
eyes were red-rimmed with lack of sleep, but she looked
furiously angry. Laurie's face was grim. The Griffin's eagle
eyes, as he stepped forward to survey the valley, were unreadable.

Finally he backed away from the rim. "So, Commander.
How long until they find a way to flank us or climb up
behind us?"

Stein shrugged. "Hard to say. When they get bored fighting us, they'll think of something. The one advantage we
have is they don't want to kill us. Not in battle, anyway."

"They'll have to kill me," Fiona said. She was holding
a freshly empty wine bottle, a Côtes du Rhone, so tightly
her knuckles were white. She didn't look the least bit drunk.

Stein had moved to a small pyramid of canvas, draped
over something. "Carron?" Polyta ambled over; Stein
bowed to her. "I offer my gratitude for your willingness to
fight here."

She nodded regally. "Of course we would."

Stein smiled. "I also offer these." He pulled back the
canvas over a bundle of poles.

Polyta, uncertain, said, "They are very nice, but the poles
we use for carrying goods have notches at either end—"

"And they probably don't have sharp points at one end;
am I right?" The skin around his eyes crinkled as his smile
widened. "Don't show the ends at first, then stab them forward when the first Grym climb up." He finished, "I just
hated to think of them biting at your nice feet."

"Hooves, Stein." But she was smiling, and she clapped
her hands together. The Hippoi turned as one, a startled
herd. "Kassandra! Hemera! Give one of these to each of
the adults."

Laurel, waking, struggled in Dyvedd's arms and punched
him. He sat upright, sword already in hand, then caught
himself and stuck his finger over Laurel's stomach, poised

to tickle. She grabbed it, pulling frantically. He puffed his lips at her, and she laughed. "Where are you going to put her for the fight?" he asked quietly.

BJ pointed to a tree, well back from the slope. "Her carrier will hang there."

He looked at BJ as though she were a murderer. "God's own banging balls, BJ! During a war?"

BJ snapped, "I wanted her somewhere else." Generally good at hiding her emotions, BJ had already found that where Laurel Stefanie was concerned they rushed into the open. "I thought about it all night."

"Could you send her to another land with someone—anyone? If you asked, they'd take her."

"I thought of that." BJ admitted, "I wanted that." It had been the worst temptation of her life, before speaking to Laurie, to give Laurel to any of them and say, *I'm a goddess; do this for me.* "But she can't live outside Crossroads."

She added suddenly, "Would you take her, hide her somewhere in Crossroads?" She saw Dyvedd waver. "She'd make a wonderful farmer." Laurel smiled up at him sleepily.

Dyvedd looked down, troubled. "Wouldn't one of Polyta's people be better? They can run faster, and some of the women could nurse her, I think . . ." He trailed off, and finished finally, "I'm needed here. I wanted to farm, but I'm needed here. I wanted—" He stared down at the valley, which was noisier by the moment. "I did want one thing out of all this to live—" He handed Laurel back, turned away abruptly, and began stretching, practicing with Dancer.

The drumming below grew louder, the smoke denser. Periodically, idiot snatches of song in no recognizable language floated up to them. It was often followed by raucous laughter.

Laurie scowled. "How long do we have to listen to this?"

Stein said without turning his head, "As long as they want us to."

Laurie stormed back toward the truck. "Terrific. This whole world is about to fall, again, and we're about to be captured and tortured to death by a low class of werewolf with a sick sense of humor, and the only one I ever loved is going to die in battle. I,'' she announced with an eerie calm, ''am gonna have a cigarette.''

She fumbled in the glove compartment and retrieved a pack, opening it one-handed with the effortlessness of long habit.

Fiona stood. ''Don't shut the door.'' She dragged her duffel toward the truck; BJ heard a clank coming from it.

A few minutes later, Fiona came back with an armload of wine bottles, each two-thirds full. BJ could smell gasoline. ''Could I get some help tearing up rags?''

''Back away from the fire,'' Stein said flatly. She backed off, setting the bottles down. ''Still, you have a good idea there.''

''They're called Molotov cocktails—''

''Imagine that.'' He took two and decanted the gas from one until it filled the other. ''Fill them to the brim, young lady. Otherwise when you light the wick, the air in the bottle can light the gas before it leaves your hand.'' He smiled, oddly wistful. ''If we had time, I could show you how to make a wick out of matches and tape. Strange, the things that remind you of your childhood . . . Is there any more gas?''

Fiona, deflated, said, ''I left a little in the gas tank.'' She looked around for BJ. ''In case you need it again.''

''Thanks.'' BJ was touched. Fiona seldom thought of other people's needs.

''Next time,'' Stein said, ''ask before taking things, won't you?''

Fiona frowned. ''That's foolish. You might say no.''

Stein rubbed his eyes. ''Let me show you how to stuff the rags. Tight is better, and you twist them . . .'' He stepped to one side with her, his duties as commander forgotten.

Hemera had finished handing out the sticks; she was standing near Frieda, who turned to her. ''Can I ask something special of you?''

Hemera hesitated, then nodded. They walked off and spoke.

The Griffin had not moved since they had arrived. He

glanced their way and nodded satisfiedly. "If they talk long enough, they may miss the first wave of the charge." He stared back down the valley.

A moment later he looked around piercingly. "Would you all mind listening for a moment? It's not likely to remain quiet here forever."

They came around, standing uncertainly on the valley rim.

"Ladies. Gentlemen." He cleared his throat. "We are met above a battlefield where the fate of Crossroads will probably be decided. I wish I could tell you that we are going to live."

BJ realized that it was a version of his address to the online RAF.

"I'm not glad to die, of course. No one should be. The world"—he moved slightly toward Laurie—"is rich and full, often sweet beyond measure.

"But if I must die, and we all must, then I have always wanted to die among friends, and to die for something in which I believe. If my death is today, I will do that. Thank you for joining with me. I could not ask for better comrades."

They were all silent. Suddenly Fiona cried out, pointing to the sky; this time her cry was hopeful.

A blurry dot in the south was growing larger every second.

The dot split into a circle of bodies, wings beating in rhythm. They turned, tracing the rim of the valley, and it was clear that the circle was a cone.

The Griffin said approvingly, "Excellent formation. It's hard to establish their numbers; the parade below will be confused."

The Grym, forgetting to play their instruments and wave their weapons and banners, looked this way and that. For a moment they seemed no more than frightened prey looking for cover.

The cone continued along the rim. As it passed overhead, BJ saw Roland, in the lead, nod. The Griffin raised a wing in acknowledgment and, after they had passed, sagged. "No more than thirty of them. For a moment, I had hoped—well, never mind."

He squinted at the young griffins and muttered, "They're looking for something. What is there left to find?"

Apparently satisfied, the young griffins flew back over the Grym, who had regrouped. Suddenly the nose of the cone—Roland, with Oliver on his left wing—dropped down.

The Griffin said, "No," and more sharply, as though they could hear, "No!" It was the first time BJ had heard him sound afraid.

The young griffins followed their leaders, diving straight down into the waiting Grym.

Mere feet above their heads, the cone blossomed in all directions, like fighter jets at an air show. Griffin fledglings swooped low across the Grym in strafing runs, claws extended.

Fiona cheered. The Griffin said, in a cry that sounded torn from his throat, "You young fools, you'll be killed!"

Stein raised a warning finger. "Don't do anything rash—"

He was drowned out by the opening of the Griffin's wings, snapping out full. A single leap took him over the valley rim as he glided noiselessly toward the battle below.

Stein shrugged and said tiredly, almost conversationally, "That's that, then." He lifted the ram's horn and blew the charge, suddenly tall and stern, and he strode forward into the valley.

BJ was nearly knocked down as Laurie, cigarette in mouth, squint-eyed in her own smoke, bounded downhill swinging a catchlet. Fiona leapt behind her, struggling with the bottles. BJ took a last, despairing glance back at Laurel Stefanie, ran back and kissed her, and careened downhill, hurrying to catch up with the others. She looked around for Frieda and tried not to think what lay ahead of them.

The charge downhill seemed to take forever, though it was less than a quarter mile. She looked down on the Grym as they reorganized to fight back against the young griffins, slashing at taloned forelegs and improvising weapons. A banner, thrown high, hung in the air until a griffin flew into it. Tangled, he fell to earth; four brown bodies leapt on him, and BJ half shut her eyes at their shrieks of joy.

One of the nearest Grym, seeing them, cried out; a front

line formed and charged to face them. There were less than fifty in the charge. BJ looked at their own pitifully small band and wondered again where Frieda was.

A drumming steadier and louder than the Grym's sounded to her left. Polyta was galloping down the slope at the head of her people. She raised her sharpened stick in both hands and gave a throat-tearing, ululating cry that the rest of the Hippoi echoed.

BJ was nearly knocked down a second time, this time by Dyvedd, who dragged her sideways, looking up the slope in sudden panic.

He needn't have bothered. Hemera sailed high over their heads, putting them both in shadow with her front legs straight forward and her hind legs straight back. Her hair, mane and tail flew out like banners of war. On her back, knees and thighs gripping tightly, was Frieda, a lance pointed straight ahead as she called out directions to Hemera.

Dyvedd steadied himself, then offered an arm to BJ. "For a goddess, you fall down a lot."

"I get pushed a lot," she panted, and they ran again.

The Griffin's silent flight ended twenty yards in front of them. Dropping behind the first rank of Grym, spinning as he landed, he smashed back through them in a fury of flashing talons and ripping beak. The Grym bolted in panic, then turned. Behind the Griffin, a Grym leapt on his flank, digging its claws in—

Only to be speared by Frieda as Hemera galloped past the Griffin, then whirled, kicking out with her hind hooves at the battle line. It fell back still farther.

Incredibly, the lance had stayed in Frieda's hands. She stabbed a second Grym, holding tight at the impact, which nearly stood her upright on Hemera's back. The wounded Grym chattered angrily at her—

And, as BJ watched in horror, pulled itself up the pole arm over arm, the lance passing through its body, until it was within striking range of Hemera. Frieda glanced helplessly down at her catchlet; she would have to release the pole to pick it up.

The attacking Grym suddenly sagged backward. Laurie,

who seemed to be everywhere, pulled her bloody catchlet back, spun to smash it broadside across a second Grym, and charged back to the Griffin's flank, whirling the catchlet over her head like a war club and shouting with raw fury.

Stein caught up with them. He thrust a catchlet forward, disarmed and stabbed a leaping Grym, and pulled free quickly. "Back the Griffin. Circle up!" He was barely winded. Aside he said to Laurie, "Where did you learn to fight like that?"

With a forehand smash she clouted a Grym sneaking up on its belly. "Girls' field hockey. Is that a problem for you?"

Stein shook his head dazedly. For the first time in a long while, BJ grinned.

At the ravine on the left, Hemera and Frieda had joined the rest of the Hippoi. Frieda was stabbing forward and pulling the lance free with a quick twist; she wounded many more than she killed. Several other Hippoi, watching her, had adopted the same tactics.

One of the Grym darted between the lances, chattering, and slunk into the herd. The Hippoi reared and whirled, unable to strike while it was underneath each of them.

The Grym, crawling beneath Kassandra, rolled on his belly, tongue hanging out like a golden retriever begging to have its stomach scratched. With his front claws, he ripped Kassandra's abdomen in parallel six-inch gashes. Even in her horror, Frieda noted an odd reflex: the older Hippoi, eyes wide with the pain, clasped her forearms for a moment across her human stomach.

Polyta leapt and, with her horse-body, knocked Kassandra sideways. With a single furious thrust, Polyta pinned the snarling Grym on its back to the ground. Her face terrible to look at, she reared and brought down her full weight on the carnivore.

But the Grym had seen what their cohort had done. Tucking their weapons into their belts, they slunk forward, pressing to dive under the bellies of the Hippoi.

The Hippoi, startled by the new tactic, reared and shifted. Hemera was jostled out of formation, suddenly vulnerable. Frieda stabbed, slashed, and battered with her lance, trying to drive off what seemed like a sudden sea of Grym.

One of them suddenly grabbed the lance and tugged. Frieda nearly fell off before she let go. The Grym stood upright and spun the pole, aiming the point at Frieda's throat. "Some fun, huh?" he screamed. He drew the lance back for the final blow—

And fell, choking, as a thin black bolo spun around his neck, tightening as the weights at either end passed each other.

Two more Grym dropped, strangling, in a tangle of bolos. Bondi charged forward with his men and women, retrieving bolos as they dispatched the Grym and spun and threw again. Bondi had pulled his sword of office, using it more as a shield to ward off attacks while he aimed a throw; he also used it to salute Polyta, then hastily charged again with his men and women to retrieve bolos and throw repeatedly.

BJ caught only glimpses of the Hippoi. She and Dyvedd fought side by side, almost under the Griffin's wing. BJ was moving as quickly as she had in her life. Sometimes her blade caught steel, sometimes it struck fur. Once, one of the Grym bit down on it, shaking the end like a playful dog while blood streamed over its lips. It even wagged its long, ropelike tail. She wrenched the sword free; the Grym yelped, putting its paws to its mouth almost comically.

She spun free to see Dyvedd fighting three of them, twisting Dancer this way and that to parry blows without a chance to strike one. The three were enjoying it hugely.

To counter a lunge, Dyvedd swung right, exposing his back. One of the Grym leapt forward; BJ moving automatically, slashed down on its arm.

The blade passed easily through the thin forearm. The Grym dropped its sword and turned on her.

Dyvedd, using the distraction, stabbed one of his opponents, beat another back, and swung Dancer over his head as he spun toward BJ. Dancer passed through the Grym from top to bottom before the carnivore had time to yelp. Dyvedd said quietly and earnestly to BJ, "Don't get hurt." It would have been funny if he hadn't sounded so urgent.

Bondi's people leapt between the Hippoi and the Grym.

Their weapons—nets and bolos—were made for capture, not killing; soon the Grym were freeing each other and stopping in to middle of battle to play with and test the new weapons.

One of them threw a net in the air and snagged Oliver as he dove overhead; the young griffin dragged the net past the Griffin before falling to earth in a tangle.

Swiping across two of the Grym, the Griffin leapt easily over the rest of them, slashing the net with one stroke.

Oliver rose, shaken. "Thank you, sir."

"Rejoin the others," he answered crisply. "How goes the fight?"

"Still losing, sir." He tested his wings before flying; one of them had lost the outer pennon feathers. "We knew we would, you know."

The Griffin muttered, "Did you know we'd all die with you?"

BJ, catching up with Laurie and beside him, parried the Grym, but from that moment on she felt no hope.

They fought well, but there had been nearly three hundred Grym when they began. Shortly there were two hundred and fifty, pressing in on three sides in mock charges and feints while they waited for exhaustion and mistakes. Gradually Bondi's people, the Hippoi, and Stein's troops were driven toward each other.

The Grym quickly evolved new tactics to deal with the young griffins; one Grym would ward off aerial attacks while another pressed the ground assault. Darting to the other side of the Hippoi, a cadre of the Grym nipped legs and waved catchlets threateningly. Gradually, the Hippoi and Stein's troops were forced toward each other. Roland's troops still flew overhead, baffled and unable to press their attack.

Finally the Griffin and Stein were side by side, effortlessly avoiding each other's thrusts but with barely room for any offense. "You see what they're doing?" the Griffin said.

Stein nodded. "Crush us in till we can't fight, then disarm us." He called to Fiona, "Bring the bottles out."

Fiona, exhausted but too angry to admit it, tucked her bloody catchlet in her belt and pulled a bottle from her knapsack.

"Hold it still." Stein lit the rag and said, as calmly as if he were coaching softball, "Now throw it against a rock near them, hard enough to break the bottle. Throw it, now, *quick—*"

Fiona, mesmerized by the flame, shook herself and threw the bottle at a rock fifteen feet away, in the middle of the Grym second line. Before it hit, Stein shouted, "Forward, now!" They charged, stopping only when the Grym returned to fighting. By then, eight feet had opened up between Stein's forces and the Hippoi.

Stein lit a match and turned to Fiona. "Another. Placement counts a lot."

This time she threw it quickly—too quickly. A bloodstained brown forearm shot up and caught the bottle by the neck, waving it triumphantly. "Mine now!" The Grym screamed. "Mine, mine, mine—"

The exploding bottle drenched the animal in gasoline, creating a shrieking, thrashing, flame-covered body that danced along the battle line before dropping. BJ coughed as a wave of smoke, smelling of burned fur, blew through the company.

The rest of the Grym pounded each other on the back, wiping tears from their eyes; they thought it was the funniest thing they'd ever seen. Stein's forces, not laughing, gained another ten feet.

The Grym were fast learners; the remaining three bottles bought very little space. Fiona took her catchlet back out and the painful, inevitable retreat began again.

To Frieda it seemed like hours of lunging, thrusting, and parrying. It was probably less than half an hour before she found herself nearly backed against BJ. She gripped the lance with both hands like a batter, swung it against the forearms of a Grym and knocked his catchlet free; she stabbed him, pulling the pole free quickly with the wrist-twist that had become habit. She shouted to BJ, "Is there something I should be doing?"

BJ wiped her brow. How had she come here, and how had she managed to survive the events of the past few weeks? "You've done fine," she panted. "We all have." She raised her catchlet in time to hook and deflect a lunge that nearly reached her.

Roland swept low overhead, his claws bloody for the first half foot. "Never give up. Never tire. All may yet be well." He added softly, nearly hovering over Frieda, "Care for yourself, lady, as I care for you."

Frieda raised her lance in a weary salute and tapped Hemera on the left shoulder. They whirled and plunged back into the front line of battle.

Exhaustion finally took its toll; BJ's catchlet was slapped out of her hands by a stinging broadside blow. Dyvedd leapt in front of her, shoving her back against the Griffin's flank. Fiona, the least practiced of any of them, was disarmed by a quick twist of her opponent's blade; she stood open-mouthed and offended while the Grym simply ignored her until Stein grabbed her shoulder and pulled her to safety.

Surprisingly, Stein fell before Laurie; one of the Grym hooked Stein's catchlet in the crosspiece of its own while another leapfrogged over the first to beat Stein's arm down. His forearm suddenly dripping, Stein fell back.

That left Laurie, Dyvedd, and the Griffin. Laurie glanced sideways and snorted, "Well, hell." Bondi's people were nearly all bound with their own bolos; the Hippoi had been herded into a tight knot, and the Grym were setting up an enclosure rimmed with the Hippoi's own lances.

Seven griffin fledglings, bound in banners, nets, and bolos, thrashed helplessly on the field.

Half of the Grym were dead. That left a hundred and fifty of them to fight fewer than forty defenders.

Dyvedd looked back at Stein; BJ thought that Dyvedd looked like a young boy, afraid and alone. "What do we do now?"

"Die here." Stein spread his empty hands. "If you can."

"We will," the Griffin said sharply. "Die angry, die happy, die feeling alive." He sailed forward, nearly cutting a Grym in half with his beak and grabbing the fallen catchlet in his talons. He tossed it sideways; it landed, quivering, beside BJ. "Die well."

BJ grabbed it, but her fighting was more desperate than happy. She stole a last look at the valley rim behind her, where Laurel Stefanie hung in her carrier. Soon Laurel Stefanie would be hungry.

Dyvedd was knocked unconscious with a broadside blow. Laurie was lassoed and bound.

The Griffin, charging to rescue her, was all but covered in Grym as he was borne to the ground, still struggling.

BJ swung and parried, knowing she would only last a few minutes longer, when Frieda sat bold upright on Hemera's back and pointed, screaming loud enough to be heard in both defending forces. A thin, furious cry echoed faintly across the valley.

The Griffin's head snapped straight up, tossing a pinwheeling Grym into the center of the Hippoi. "It can't be."

BJ stared. On the horizon, with no attempt at all at disguising numbers or power, hung a line of adult griffins, moving steadily forward.

"My God," the Griffin said dazedly, "he did it." He freed the rest of his body, rising through the pile of Grym as though they were stuffed toys, and bellowed, "Roland!"

"Yes, Father." Roland hung in the air above him. The young Griffin's body was scraped and torn, and the wing with missing feathers was still more battered, its underside dappled in blood.

"Pull your troops to the north side. Free the Hippoi to take the left flank—"

"Of course, Father." He cried loudly, three times—a prearranged signal, clearly; the young griffins, Oliver included, dove down from all points of the battlefield and attacked the Grym holding the Hippoi.

The Grym, startled, fell back. Polyta reared, lashing out with her front hooves; Frieda hung on as Hemera dashed forward and did the same. As the surviving Hippoi rallied, Frieda used her lance as a pole and vaulted off Hemera's back. She ran to the slavers, loosening the bonds around them and gesturing toward the Grym.

The line of griffins was closer. The single cry had been joined by others, raw and angry.

The Grym milled about in sudden panic. Frieda, lance in hand, stabbed forward and killed one before it realized there was an attack on the ground. By then the freed Griffin was charging, BJ and Laurie at his right, and Stein, swinging a reclaimed catchlet, at his left. Dyvedd had stumbled to his feet and was swinging Dancer as he moved forward unsteadily.

Fiona, her lips set in a thin, tight line, picked up a bloody catchlet and followed.

The Grym turned to defend themselves, glancing at the sky behind them when they could. The griffins' colors were visible now: silver, bronze, gold, copper plumage on tawny bodies. Their features came into focus, harsh and implacable. Their razor-sharp bills shone in the midday sun.

The Silver dove, screaming angrily. The others cried out and plummeted after him, a single line of talons and beaks.

The Grym scattered, but it was too late; the older griffins scythed across them, mowing down dozens at each pass. Moments later, Gek himself, in the ruins of a patchwork costume which included a feathered hat, threw down his sword. "This isn't fun anymore."

Stein said sharply, "Is that a surrender?"

"Call it what you want," Gek said irritably. "We quit." He gave a short series of yips; the remaining Grym threw down their weapons. BJ blinked; there were only sixty of them left.

The Silver settled on the bloody grass before the Griffin. He glanced around at the wounded, at the young griffins, and at the defeated Grym, and said levelly to the Griffin, "I expect to hear a perfectly marvelous explanation for all this."

T·W·E·N·T·Y·O·N·E

"THE EXPLANATION," ROLAND said clearly and calmly, "is mine."

He settled in beside the Griffin, confronting the Silver. His front legs were awash in red blood from bites and claw furrows. His talons, in contrast, were brown with dried blood.

Frieda moved toward him. Laurie, shaking her head, held Frieda's arm.

Roland bowed. "Thank you for saving our lives."

The Silver was unimpressed. "It shouldn't have been necessary."

Roland's troops, battered and weary, settled in behind him, completing a circle around the remaining Grym. "It shouldn't," he agreed. "But we were unable to win alone." He added thoughtfully, "You could have let us die—"

"Don't be foolish," he snapped. "You are our only progeny. Of course we'd come—"

His raptor's eyes snapped wide open, round as an owl's. "And you knew that."

"Oh," the Griffin said amusedly, "he was counting on it."

"He's your son," the Silver said in annoyance. "Couldn't you control him?"

"Could you control yours?" the Griffin said softly. The

301

Silver looked away. "It is good to speak to you, though I don't expect the experience to last."

"Nor shall it." He turned aside. "As for you, you young fool—"

"Call me Roland, if that makes conversation easier."

The Silver flexed his talons in annoyance, grinding through a boulder.

Oliver, watchful as always in the presence of danger to Roland, edged up. "And I'm called Oliver."

"And this," a voice behind them said, "is barely Clark Kent."

Oliver turned his back on the Silver, moving to where two young griffins bore a third between them, his body slung across two lances borrowed from the Hippoi. The middle griffin's head hung unnaturally low, and his broken wings would have drooped in the dust if they had not taken care to hold him above it.

Roland knelt, cupping Clark Kent's head in his talons. The wounded griffin's eyes opened partway. "I'm sorry. I was so little help."

"Never say that." He stroked Clark Kent's bloody plumage as smooth as it would come; much of it was gone. "You fought well, and saved many of us."

One of the eyes opened completely. "You won?"

"You won," Roland corrected firmly. "And because of that, we won."

"Ahhh." Although only his head could move, his entire body seemed to relax, sagging against the poles. "That's all right, then."

A faint cry made them all look up. Perhaps attracted by the bodies on the field below, a kite wheeled effortlessly on the breeze. "I will miss flying," Clark Kent said wistfully. And died.

Frieda and BJ leapt forward, ignoring the elder griffins. The sagging head told them all they needed to know; the spinal cord had been severed.

Frieda looked up angrily, tears in her eyes, saying nothing. She moved to Roland's side and ripped cloth from the bottom of her shirt to clean his wounds.

The Silver snapped, "I don't expect you to touch him."

Frieda snapped back, "Then kill me." She never stopped brushing the blood away, and she hadn't bothered to look at the Silver.

Dyvedd, appearing out of nowhere, elbowed BJ. He was panting from running, holding Laurel, who was staring at him sleepily, untroubled. He brushed the blood out of his scalp one-handed and made faces down at her as BJ took her.

It was still bothering BJ: how had the young griffins known to come to their defense? She looked questioningly at Roland, who looked away quickly as though he knew her thoughts.

BJ turned to the Silver and said suddenly and simply, "You knew."

Frieda said, "About what?" and put a hand to her mouth. "The Grym."

The Silver nodded. "And, as you've guessed, we told our young. Foolish of us." He looked coldly at Roland. "We warned them to be wary of the Grym, and I made them swear an oath not to warn you about them."

BJ looked at Roland. "A conflict of promises—"

"An idiot child's game," the Silver interrupted. "Instead of staying sensibly, they flew out of Crossroads for aid"— Bondi bowed uncertainly; the Silver ignored him— "brought them in by some godforsaken river route which you, madam, had carelessly left in place, and risked all we care about."

"You should do that more often," Roland said. "Risk all you care about, and you discover why it's precious."

Frieda, by his side, addressed the Silver for the second time. "It would make you happy."

Roland added quietly, "It would make you worthwhile."

That clearly stung. The Silver retorted, "You have been listening to fragile, sentimental, thoroughly negligible beings. They die easily, and they die in droves. You shouldn't waste your time caring for them."

"My mother used to grow orchids," Frieda said. The Silver turned to her, momentarily confused; she was bent over Roland's wounds, not looking up as she spoke. "She had a greenhouse, and a misting system, and she spent hours on it. When I was growing up, she still had the potting bench, out in the back yard; I used to have peanut butter sandwiches and fruit punch at it. She'd tell me what the flowers looked like, and how hard it was to keep some of the varieties alive. That was why she quit, before I was born; she said she got tired of wasting her life on something fragile."

Now, finally, she turned to the Silver. "I think if she hadn't given up, my life would have been better. So would her own."

Roland, turning his head, caressed her bare arm with his bloody, deadly beak. The Silver blinked.

Laurel muttered interestedly, poking at BJ's chest. BJ distracted her by putting a little finger in her mouth to suck, and addressed the Silver. "You've let me risk people I care about, after I saved your children."

The young griffins stared at her, fascinated. The Silver said brusquely, "You were well repaid. I didn't kill you for your insolence that night."

BJ said levelly, "You kidnapped me and threatened me with death and torture even though you needed my help. You know I'll help the griffins again." She was aware of Frieda and Laurie behind her. "Or someone else will. I expect you to warn us the next time Crossroads is in danger."

The Silver, flexing one of his talons in the dirt and rock, glared at her. "You're reckless, requesting favors rudely of a raptor."

BJ said, "It wasn't a request."

The Silver, furious, turned to fly off. The Griffin said loudly and clearly, "Ramaiel."

The Silver froze, stunned. Several of the older Griffins gasped.

The Griffin continued. "There was a war here, not long ago. I sided with you, against those I love most, to save the chimerae. Need I remind you why?"

He said, his voice trembling, "You have said more than enough."

"I have barely begun. You had already cast me out, but I was loyal then. Do not fight against Crossroads again, either with talons or with negligence."

The Silver opened his mouth to reply, and the Griffin added, "Or I will challenge you for leadership. And I will win. I have fought in three wars and trained on two worlds. Consider that, and go away now."

The Silver thought for barely a moment, then spread his wings and wordlessly went south. The other griffins, except for the younger ones and the Griffin, followed in silence.

Roland said, "I'll visit him. He will learn."

The Griffin shook his head. "Your grandfather will not change. I can never be you, and he will never be what either of us have become."

There was a struggle among their prisoners, and Gek came forward suddenly. "You talk too much. You don't fight, you don't bite. What fun is that?"

The Griffin nodded. "Excellent point." He turned toward the surrendered party of Grym. "Roland, is it time for some fun?"

The Grym bunched up even tighter, watching Roland with wide eyes.

"War is not play, and justice not fun." Roland looked them over. "Gek. Come forward."

The Grym leader moved slightly forward. Bondi, holding his sword instead of the bolo he had used most in battle, moved to guard him.

"Gek," Roland said, "you should be punished for what you have done, for what your people have done. If you can think and speak, you can know right from wrong, yet you chose wrong. For that, I will ask the leaders here if I may name your punishment—"

"No." The Griffin came forward, with measured paces.

Roland, stunned, said, "Father, you plead for him?"

"I plead something else entirely." He looked at the assembled crowd. "We've heard a great deal of nonsense about chivalry today. By all means, let us hear some more. I have been the Inspector General of this country for many years. Some of you knew that. Many more of you have known it after recent events. This thing"—he gestured at Gek, who chattered viciously—"has committed many injustices here. I claim his life as my right."

After a short while, Roland nodded. "To do with as he

deserves. You have it.'' He collected himself. ''Commander Stein? My BJ?''

BJ said to the Griffin, "Do what you have to."

Stein added tiredly, "The boy is right; you have his life. You always had it."

"All right." The Griffin sat back on his haunches and spread his wings wide, wider than BJ had ever seen them except when he was flying. Bondi gaped, his sword slack in his hand.

The Griffin stood tall. "You may all look, or you may go away, but this must be done." His talons shone in the sunlight, and he spoke to Gek, echoing Roland. "Come forward."

Gek pounced, but sideways, onto the negligent slaver, and seemed to wrap around his neck like a stole. "Arterial," BJ thought automatically as she leapt forward, but it was too late; Bondi collapsed, astonished, one hand pressing on his carotid artery.

He looked quickly and apologetically at Polyta, but he knelt to Roland. "Yours," he said huskily, swaying but staying on his knees, staring up the short distance into the golden eyes. "Lord," he said, suddenly smiling, happy. Roland caught the body, lowering it to the ground.

"Please," the Griffin said to Gek, and BJ realized with a chill that his voice was shaking. "Do not make this pleasant."

Gek pulled the sword from Bondi and swung it triumphantly at the Griffin.

The Griffin swung his right foreleg up, parrying with open talons and not quite parrying the blade with full force. Sparks flew from his talons as it struck and slowed.

Gek snarled incoherently, jerking the blade back and stabbing it forward in a blur.

The Griffin clapped his talons together; they clanged as they hit the blade and slowed it, inches from his breast.

Gek screamed, spittle flying from his fangs as he swung the blade upward to bring it crashing down on the Griffin's exposed head.

The Griffin sliced upward sideways precisely. The sword clattered against the stones, a piece at a time.

Gek curled his lip back and stabbed forward with the hilt. The Griffin, with a single forehand slash, spun the hilt into the sky. Gek leaped forward to attack, rolling on his back to rip at the Griffin's already scarred belly—

And was striking at nothing. The Griffin, rising into the air, stretched down with his talons and pinned Gek to the ground, arching his body out of reach of Gek's slavering jaws.

"And now," he said deliberately, "you will enjoy the fun you have promised others so very often."

His talons tightened on Gek's body, but it was his rear feet which walked slowly and deliberately up the animal. Part of BJ's mind marveled that, because of the Griffin's fearsome front talons, she had seldom paid attention to his leonine rear feet and their curved claws.

Gek, pinned in place, snarled and struggled. Presently he began screaming.

Frieda put her hands over her ears, then, to BJ's astonishment, took them down and stared forward resolutely.

The next few minutes were as long as any in BJ's life. Bondi's people, Polyta and her people, the young griffins, and Stein and the other humans watched. Even the amused giggling of Gek's own people died away, and nothing made a sound but Gek, who could no longer help himself.

"These aren't my rules," BJ thought, and waited as long as she could possibly stand. Finally she said, "Griffin."

"Yes."

"Please finish."

"As he did with Bondi, or something more creative?"

Roland said pleadingly, "Father, a little mercy would lighten the sorrow we've seen today."

After a long moment, the Griffin nodded. "Yes, I suppose it would." He stared at his son, straight on and not like a predator at all. "If only for the novelty."

Gek was dead almost before the sentence was complete.

The Griffin looked up from the corpse. "BJ."

"Yes." She was startled. Perhaps because the Griffin rarely offered his personal name, he seldom used first names. Even Sugar, to the Griffin, tended to be "Doctor Dobbs."

"You've done quite well, so far. You've marshaled troops, arbitrated treaties, and offered judgments. Still, I don't think it's what you wanted for your life."

She shook her head violently, holding back tears. Laurel, sensing something wrong, murmured and tugged at her hair.

"Still, we need a king. If not you, who can there be?"

"There's only one candidate; you know that. In fact, you've planned on it for a long time." She realized, saying it, that it was true.

The Griffin knelt to Roland. "Pardon this bloody beak, my liege."

"Father!" Roland knelt, trying to nudge his father into rising. Eventually Roland glanced at the others, watching around him. Slowly, unwillingly, he rose.

BJ knelt, simply and deliberately. Those around her, even Polyta, followed.

He stared around at all those kneeling, their bruises and wounds from battle still fresh. Slowly he nodded. "I will rule you, then. And I will serve you. Rise now."

The young griffins bounded up, wings quivering. Roland beckoned to Oliver, who was already by his side, alert. "When I can't lead our comrades, you will do so."

Oliver bowed his head. "As you wish, my liege," and it was clear from the pride in his voice how long he had wished to call Roland that.

"For now, we must tend to each other—heal wounds, comfort grief, bury the dead. We have few dead"—the muscles in his neck tightened all the way down to his leonine chest—"because they wished us captured alive. Even one dead would be too many."

The remaining slavers, standing near the Hippoi, wept unashamedly. Roland stepped forward and touched the cheek of Bondi, as tenderly as he might have picked a flower. He turned suddenly to Polyta. "Lady—" He shook his head. "Carron, I know this man did you and yours as much wrong as one kind can do another. All I may ask is—" He blinked, and continued. "In the end, he risked and lost his life for us all, and I would be very, very grateful if you would be there when I lay him to rest."

Polyta took a deep breath, her eyes shut and her human body tensing, muscles rippling under her still-scarred back as she gathered strength. She opened her eyes and said calmly, "You will not lay him to rest, Roland. He said he would serve the Carron, and he died after fighting for the Hippoi. We will burn his body, after the manner of our kind, unless his own people wish otherwise." She added, speaking to the slavers, "You are welcome at his funeral."

Roland turned to them. BJ, following his gaze, saw for the first time how lost and disoriented they were. "Well done," Roland said to them. "You fought in a strange land, against an unknown opponent, and you saved a world. I grieve that you lost your leader . . ." He finished, at a loss, "What can I do for you?"

"Bondi is gone," an older woman said in halting English, unsure of herself. "We have no ruler . . . what will we do?"

"Choose a new leader." But Roland added, "How do you choose new leaders under ordinary circumstances?"

"The ruler dies." An older man stroked his graying mustache. "If we know one who is ready . . . we have no one." He looked back at the other slavers, who nodded vigorously.

"I see." Roland said tentatively, "Is there anyone here whom you would choose to rule?"

Polyta put her hand to her mouth as several of the slavers pointed to her wordlessly.

Polyta shook her head violently. "Roland, please, no."

"I didn't want to ask you." He raised a talon, gesturing helplessly at the Bondi. "They—you're the only one they know here. Please, can you lead them until they choose a leader of their own?"

The silence was long. Finally Polyta said bitterly, "They won't have to wear bridles. They should be grateful."

Roland said in relief, "Surely no one is as great as you." He bowed to her. "Take these people in hand." Before she could reply, he was gone, moving among the wounded and shouting orders.

Polyta moved off among the slavers. Fiona, looking after Roland, said, "He's the new king? I don't see how he can wear a crown."

BJ watched Roland as he moved from person to person, calling for first aid, offering thanks or praise, his eyes always flickering ahead to the next place he might be needed. "I don't see why he needs one."

T·W·E·N·T·Y-T·W·O

THE ROAD OPENED easily, as though it had never really closed. The first part only was moist. Gradually the dust colored the plants on the side of the road, the clothing of the walkers, even the fur of the Grym.

They padded along, tongues hanging out, a few whimpering from their wounds. Frieda had insisted, under Roland's watchful eye, on suturing the worst of the Grym's wounds. BJ had joined her. At the Griffin's insistence, they had used no anesthetic.

Their new leader nipped at the heels of the wounded like a Border collie, enjoying their discomfort as they squeaked and struggled up the road. BJ said to her, "Are you the new Gek?"

"Gek? No," she chattered. "Only one Gek. He's dead now. Pretty good job, too. It was fun, at least at first. I'm Gehl."

"Gehl." BJ kept her eyes on the road ahead, making it more convoluted than any path she had ever made. "You'll need to be a leader soon."

"I am now." She tripped a limping straggler and, when he stumbled, bit through his throat and let him drop. "What could be better?"

BJ glanced back at the red-brown body sprawled in the

dust. The Grym only looked back to laugh. "Not all worlds are as easy as this one."

"So? We get by." She smiled, showing her teeth. "We make our own fun."

"I know." The plants were sparser now, and the dust kicked up around their feet in clouds. To either side of the road, yucca grew, and lizards, frightened at the sight of the Grym, dashed on fringed feet across the dust, splashing as though it were water.

A bird overhead screamed. Gehl looked up at it longingly. "We came from this way. Not much food here."

BJ said, "We're nearly there."

She turned to the left. The Grym followed, flanked by griffins. Dyvedd, in the rear, readied his sword.

They stood at the crest of the hill and looked around.

The flowers from earlier in the year had died. The trees were losing limbs. The stream in front of them, barely a muddy trickle now, had cut a gorge in the land and exposed the dead roots of the grass. The first layer of soil was dotted with white chunks of bone.

Gehl peered from side to side in disbelief, her nostrils quivering. "How did this happen?"

"You killed whatever eats the grass," Fiona, behind BJ, said. She gestured at the bones exposed by erosion. "The grass grew and choked the flowers, the bees and butterflies died off, the birds that ate insects died off—it's called catastrophic change."

BJ gestured at the stream. "But there's water still." In the mud across from them were small paw tracks. "There are a few animals here still. You may have to live on short rations till their population grows." BJ struggled for words and finished, "You'll learn how to take care of things."

A carrion crow flew by. All of the Grym tracked it hungrily. It roosted in a dying tree and regarded them with interest, content to wait.

"We'll get you back," Gehl said. Her tongue was lolling out from thirst now. "We're real smart, and clever too, and we'll find a way."

BJ backed up, keeping an eye on the Grym. Dyvedd stood

next to her, Dancer circling in front of them. Behind him, Fiona and the Griffin waited.

As BJ moved backward, the road in front of them shimmered. The Grym rushed forward, pausing in the face of weapons.

Gehl leapt for BJ's throat; Dancer, flickering in Dyvedd's hands, swung across the Grym's jaws with a broadside smack.

She held her muzzle in her paws and screamed, "Don't leave us. It's dry and barren. We'll die here. How will we have any fun?"

"You'll find a way," BJ said. "You're real smart, remember?"

With a stick, BJ scratched a line across the road. It was like closing a glass door; the hot air wavered in front of them where a moment before the road had continued.

The Griffin peered at it mistrustfully, claws up. "Can it be reopened?"

BJ said, "I don't know who else could besides me." She realized it was not a sufficient answer; the griffins could fly from world to world, as could several other flying species. "It's all I can do."

"Almost." Dyvedd stepped past her, carrying a rock the size of a watermelon easily in his left hand. He set it in the hill above a huge boulder, then stabbed Dancer into the earth between the boulder and the stone and tugged furiously on the sword. The stone dug into the earth, and the boulder pulled free of the hillside an inch, then stopped.

Dyvedd gasped, "Can I get some help? This is heavier than dead men's tears."

With the Griffin's help, they set the rock upright. At BJ's direction, they put a picture on the rock: an herbivore skull and a wilted flower. "Will that signify anything to anyone but us?" Dyvedd asked.

"It should," BJ said. "You don't make roads unless you're intelligent."

"In that case," the Griffin said, "I'm going to contribute."

Pushing into the rock with a single claw, he inscribed

carefully: LASCIATE OGNI SPERANZA, VOI CH'EN-
TRATE.

He stepped back to admire his work. Stein said thoughtfully, " 'Abandon all hope . . . ' Travelers who don't know
Italian will still get into trouble."

The Griffin said, "It will encourage them to read Dante."

Fiona had left next to no gas in the truck; the warning
light on the gas gauge was flashing on long before BJ made
it into Kendrick. All the way, she was crawling up switchbacks and upgrades, waiting for the engine to cough and
stall. For the final ten miles, inside Virginia, the light was
on steadily and all the passengers were watching it.

It meant remarkably little to Dyvedd. He sat beside Laurel
Stefanie's car seat and clutched Dancer, trying to pretend
that he was relaxed. BJ prayed they wouldn't be stopped by
park rangers, state troopers, or anybody else.

Laurie got out first, at the edge of the Jefferson National
Forest. The Griffin slid off the top of the truck gracefully
and came around to the front cabin. "May I have the map?"

BJ handed him a sketch. "Check the one in the university
library as well. I don't plan on changing the road, but there's
no sense in your taking chances."

"None of us ever wishes to." He nodded to Frieda. "It
was excellent meeting you, Doctor. I am sure I shall have
the pleasure again, if Ms. Kleinman can arrange a dinner."

He offered a talon through the window; Frieda grasped it
firmly, unafraid of its sharpness.

He pulled it back and saluted Dyvedd with it. "I trust I'll
see you in Crossroads."

Dyvedd raised the hilt of Dancer in response. "You'll be
welcome on my farm."

"I will look forward to visiting your farm," the Griffin
replied, and BJ detected no sarcasm at all.

He raised a single claw in admonition to Laurel Stefanie.
"And you, young lady—if that is really what you are, which
I doubt—when next I see you, I want no running, no gur-
gling, no disobedient and undisciplined dancing, and NO
BLEATING." He shook a claw in her face.

Laurel Stefanie, with a bleating laugh, reached for the

claw and pounded her hooves in a drumbeat on the already battered car seat. The Griffin sighed in mock exasperation and withdrew.

He faced BJ. "My son may need advice. Give him as much as you can."

"As much as I have. He's largely self-taught."

"I'm afraid not." The Griffin, very gently, laid a talon on her left arm. "He is self-read, at very best. Someone taught him to become a hero, and I am extremely grateful."

He turned, Laurie at his side. Together they disappeared into the underbrush, up a well-hidden trail to the house.

BJ stopped at a convenience store outside Kendrick for gas. She taught Dyvedd to pump, mainly to stop him from fidgeting. Their next stop was a nondescript, quiet brown apartment building. Half the cars were gone from the lot; it was a weekday, and students were at classes.

BJ walked Frieda to her door. "I want to thank you for all you did. I'll talk to Sugar about your having missed classes; he'll find an excuse—"

"I only missed four days, two on a weekend. I'll get by." Frieda looked dazedly around at how ordinary, how non-traumatic and easy, everything in her life looked. One or two battles, she concluded, gave you a remarkable sense of perspective about crises.

Except for one crisis. "Roland."

"Yes." BJ felt a stab of pity. She had been through this farewell, had seen it in Laurie's face and a shadow of it in Harriet Winterthur's, often enough to recognize it.

"Tell him I—he ought to know that I—" She straightened and said carefully and clearly, "Tell him I love him for his noble heart, and will always miss him."

"I'll tell him." BJ looked around carefully, noticing that in the paintings, posters, and photography on the walls was a great deal of animal life and no family photos. That helped her with her final decision. "And you'll tell him again, when you see him."

Frieda stared at her, stunned. "He can't visit," she whispered finally.

"He can't," BJ admitted. "He's a king; he'll be too busy. You know he's busy now."

Frieda smiled involuntarily; Roland had dispatched Oliver and the rest of the young griffins with instructions to find and hatch the remaining dodo eggs, nurturing the young as best they could. To their credit, not one fledgling griffin had objected.

BJ went on, "And I'll be busy, too. We'll have new species, new predators and prey, probably a lot of damaged livestock until things settle down. Plus, I'll need to spend time with Laurel, and someone to watch the practice at the Healing Sign when I'm not there, and I'll need someone to drive back and forth from town with supplies—"

"You can't mean it." Frieda was shaking her head back and forth, suddenly breathless. "You can't."

"If you'll take the job." BJ tried to remember Sugar's words to her. "You won't have telephones, or television, or VCR's. Maybe my generator can run your laptop, but we don't have much fuel. And you won't be able to tell your friends or family where you're working, and pay is in gold—"

Frieda leapt forward and hugged BJ so tightly she could barely breathe. Frieda was laughing out loud, beautiful again. "I can do all of that." She jumped back and shook her head, trying to imagine the offer. "I can do anything, for that."

BJ nodded, daunted; Frieda's enthusiasm would take getting used to. "All right. I'll send a message to you just before graduation."

The stop at the school was brief. Sugar was absent; she left a note in his mailbox and a message with the secretary for when he called; the secretary pointed out that Doctor Dobbs was on vacation in the west, and BJ said patiently, "I know. Believe me, he'll want this message." She glanced around the corridors, not surprised to feel that they were still bleak and unfriendly but astonished to find that they no longer felt confining.

Harriet Winterthur stood when BJ returned to the lobby. "I'm ready." She was carrying a stuffed book bag that clearly contained clothes, books, and, to BJ's amusement, a badly wrapped bottle of white wine.

On their way out of the vet school, Matt, his hands in his pockets and walking fast and hard, brushed past them without speaking.

Valerie, in his wake again, looked BJ full in the face. "Thanks for the crazy experiences."

"You're welcome. I hope it was worth it."

She grinned, full and happy. "Wouldn't have missed it. Wish I could tell somebody."

"Where are you going from here?"

"Ambulatory rotation. Large animal. Wait, you mean after I graduate?" BJ nodded. "No idea. We'll see what comes up."

"Romance," a voice intoned. "Adventure." Cody stepped up beside Valerie and, to BJ's astonishment, slid an arm around her.

Valerie kissed him and said to BJ, "Something wrong?"

BJ realized how her face must have looked; attitudes toward mixed-race couples weren't always good in this end of Virginia. She said hastily, "Oh, no. It's just that I worked with both of you, and never realized you were a couple."

"We weren't," Cody admitted cheerfully. "But we got thrown together and, well, what the heck."

Valerie frowned. "What the hell," she corrected, and kissed him again. "I must be crazy."

"Yup. Plus I don't see how we're finding the time." He glanced at his watch. "In fact, we're not."

Valerie left. Cody hesitated in the door. "It was true, what you and Sugar told us? Crossroads can heal viral problems, maybe even heal genetic problems?"

BJ nodded. "Some genetic problems. Plus it's a field effect; it doesn't always work outside Crossroads. It's hard to explain."

Cody looked down briefly at his right leg, then grinned at her. "Oh, well. You're right; it would have been to hard to explain." He waved and left, an arm around Valerie before he had limped three feet.

BJ regarded them thoughtfully.

BJ felt as though she could have closed her eyes for the drive to the final stop. She cut off the engine and coasted slowly to the curb, slowing her arrival.

Dyvedd said, "Do you want me to wait here with Laurel again?" His voice made it clear he wanted to go in this time. Harriet looked up from her book.

"I'll take her in with me. Come on, sweetheart." BJ lifted her out of the seat, startled as always by how fast Laurel put on weight. BJ put leather shoes on her, with booties stuck in the toes, and tugged her forward as she half hopped, half danced into the apartment building.

Willy was gone, thank God. Stefan, ears twitching as he listened to the student radio station blaring Broadway hits, was engrossed in an organic chemistry textbook. He bounded up when BJ entered and kissed her passionately.

She kissed back for only a moment. "Stefan, we have to talk."

"Not yet. Let me see the girl my baby." He held his hands out. Laurel, suddenly shy, clung to her mother's leg and turned her eyes into the cloth.

"Laurel Stefanie, that's not nice." BJ realized with wonder that she had already begun sounding like her mother. "Turn and wave to him." In a flash of insight she added, "See his feet?"

Stefan had been studying barefoot. Laurel's eyes widened as she saw his hooves; she pattered over quickly, talking nonsensical sounds in rapid-fire. Stefan snatched her up and kissed her, crooning.

When he looked at BJ she said, "How soon will she be talking?"

"Very soon. A few weeks."

"And reading?"

"As soon after that as you can teach her."

"And how long until she's fully grown?" She hadn't known she would feel cheated. Stefan avoided her eyes. "You could have told me."

"I tried." He looked down. "At first. I said you thought I might be too young. And you were a veterinarian, and I thought you knew, and oh, BJ, I wanted you so much."

"I wanted you," she said. "If I'd known you were five . . . Stefan, how long will she be a child? How long till she grows up and goes away?"

"In two years she will be grown. In three she will be

ready to find a mate of her own. BJ love, I didn't know that
would hurt you.''

"I didn't know either.'' She added, less steadily, ''And
I'd like you to stop calling me that, even though I love
you.''

He looked at her in complete confusion. Laurel, annoyed
at his distraction, punched at his shoulder; he let her grab
his fingers but otherwise ignored her.

BJ put an arm around him, feeling strange even as she
did so. ''You and Laurel look like older brother and younger
sister together. I love you that way. I'm sorry. I know it
seems unfair to you—''

"It is unfair.'' But he wasn't crying; in the short time she
had known him, he had grown up remarkably. ''BJ, would
you want me to wait for you for twelve, fourteen more years
until you thought I was old enough? I can't.'' He searched
for words and burst out, ''I am not a griffin.''

"In hard situations, most of us aren't,'' BJ said. ''I'm
saying if you want to see someone else, go ahead. But you
should tell them your age.''

"But I don't want anyone else!'' He hugged Laurel a
little too hard; she kicked and complained. He set her down
and watched, bereft, as she trotted back to BJ. ''You'll still
see me?''

"I promise. We'll have dinner, we'll talk, we'll even
dance together.'' She added, because it needed saying, ''We
just won't make love again.''

He stared at her, dark-eyed and brokenhearted. ''You
brought so many wonderful things to my life . . .'' He gestured at his textbooks, at the videos and compact discs, at
the framed posters of Astaire and Kelly and Nureyev on his
walls. ''I would trade them all for you alone.''

"You're growing up very fast.'' She kissed him, on the
cheek this time. ''I'll keep an eye on that.'' She ruffled his
horns. ''Remember that time when I said you were my fella?
You were a good fella.''

He nodded, the tears finally coming even though he was
smiling. ''And you were a wonderful love.''

He kissed Laurel twice before they left. BJ let out a long,
slow sigh as he closed his apartment door; she had not been

able to predict what it would be like breaking off a romance with a five-year-old.

She passed Laurel to Dyvedd. "Buckle her in." She turned around and started the engine.

When he was done, he leaned forward, and his fingers touched her cheek. "You're crying, Doctor."

BJ wiped her cheek carefully. "Sometimes I do." Harriet Winterthur, discreet or unaware, said nothing. None of them said another word on the drive back to Crossroads.

It was several days later. Stein, Harriet, and Dyvedd followed BJ into the hills above the cottage. For the first part they were following a cattle trail, a foot wide and rock-hard, pounded into the landscape.

The cattle trail became a stone path, rising out of foothills into the mountains. Harriet looked back nervously, but the mist hid Crossroads as well as the road ahead. BJ turned to the right.

They heard the sound of a four-wheel drive. BJ called, "Is that you?"

"Better be," Sugar said. "Can't even tell, in this fog."

"You'll have to walk." BJ added, barely apologetic, "I'm not opening this as a full road. Come toward me, on the goat trail."

She heard a truck door slam, and heard muttering: "Hope you like jail, hon." "Sug, I like not getting caught." There was the sound of sliding bodies.

Elaine Dobbs stepped out of the mist, her six-foot frame towering over BJ's. She was dressed in a scarred leather jacket, jeans, and hiking boots; a sheath knife hung at her waist. Her long dark hair draped across two things: the tranquilizer rifle slung across her shoulders, and the sleeping timber wolf slung over that.

BJ stared open-mouthed, remembering only belatedly that she herself was supposed to be a goddess.

Sugar, carrying the second wolf, followed. For once in his life he seemed like an anticlimax.

The moment the wolves were on the ground, BJ knelt and checked their gums. Sugar chuckled. "Don't you trust me?"

"Would you trust me if I handed you a loaded gun?"

Elaine laughed at that. BJ looked at her. "It's good to see you again. Will they be missed?"

She nodded. "They're yearlings, but they've been tagged. It'll be blamed on the local ranchers."

BJ felt the heaving sides of the wolves; the breathing was rapid but strong. "Will they adjust here?"

"Wolves adjust anywhere they can feed and have territory." She looked down the hill, into the mist. "They'll be just fine. They'll be the male and female alpha wolves here."

BJ, remembering Gredya and her impending litter, said thoughtfully, "For now." Sugar swung toward her, but said nothing.

The mist was burning off the hills, the valley clearing out foot by foot and the blinding white giving way to brown-and-green landscape. BJ stood apart from the others intentionally. When Sugar joined her, she said, "We should talk about the rotation."

"Right. My teaching evaluation." He grinned at her, but eyed her cautiously.

BJ shook her head. "You're a good teacher. I just think you had other motives for picking the students. Matt you wanted to shake up."

Sugar said flatly, "I wanted to show him there's more to diagnostics and surgicating than he could get out of books. I wanted him to find his own imagination, and I wanted him to go get help if he needed it. Tell me I was wrong, if you think I was."

After a moment, BJ went on, "And Cody. You thought he needed Crossroads the way I did: to heal his body."

"You ever meet somebody who deserved even more than everything he got in life? I wanted Crossroads for him that way. I was wrong. Laugh at me, if you've a mind to."

She shook her head. "You were dead wrong choosing Valerie, though. She's angry a lot, but she has a lot to be angry about. Crossroads can't heal that."

Sugar snorted. "I wasn't healing a damn thing. I just wanted to get her the hell out of Western Virginia for a while."

"And you thought Cody and she might fall in love."

Instead of being startled or upset, Sugar grinned at her. "So it worked."

BJ, angry at his cockiness, burst out, "You've got to quit playing with people's lives."

"No, ma'am." His quiet firmness startled her as much as being called "ma'am." "You've got to start."

She looked at the tranquilized wolves, at Harriet Winterthur standing unobtrusively close to Stein, at Roland and Oliver circling watchfully overhead. She stared at the new road she had made, seeing in her mind all the side destinations it could open.

"I already have," BJ said.